I0729757

ONE MORNING SUN

ALSO BY AVI SILVER

Two Dark Moons (Sãoni Cycle #1)
Three Seeking Stars (Sãoni Cycle #2)

Pluralities

PRAISE FOR THE SÃONI CYCLE:

"From start to finish, Silver explores belonging, sustainability, family and empire with epic heart and masterful poise. The Saoni Cycle is essential fantasy reading."

—Brandon Crilly, award-winning author
and games writer

"Deep and sweet and thrilling by turns."

—Every Book a Doorway on Two Dark Moons

"...A well-written story with a hefty, engaging plot, current issues and relevant chãracters that will arouse your curiosity and pull you into their worlds. All I can say is enjoy the journey."

—ReaderViews on Two Dark Moons

"There's hope, there's thoughtfulness…so much to love here."

—SFF Yeah! (Book Riot) on Two Dark Moons

ONE MORNING SUN

AVI SILVER

MOLEWHALE PRESS

One Morning Sun is a work of fiction. The characters, places, events, and dialogue portrayed in this book are drawn from the author's imagination. Any resemblance to actual events or persons, living or dead, is purely coincidental.

Text Copyright © 2025 by Avi Silver

All rights reserved. No part of this book may be reproduced in any form or by any electronic or mechanical means, including information storage and retrieval systems, without the prior written consent of the publisher, except in the case of a reviewer, who may quote brief passages in a review.

Published by Molewhale Press
www.molewhalepress.com

First Edition

Print edition ISBN: 978-1-7752427-9-6

Cover art by Haley Rose Szereszewski
haleyroseportfolio.com

Map, interior illustrations, and book design by Sienna Tristen

The author gratefully acknowledges the creators of the following type-faces, which were used in designing the text of the book: 'Gentium Basic', 'Garamond Pro', 'Sqwoze', 'Century Gothic'

For those who must be themselves in shadow.
I'm here in the sunlight, whenever you're ready.

(And for you especially, old friend. I love you.)

(and others)
the hmun of gãepongwei
qiao sidh
Sc ~ sorwei chapal
Kp ~ kongkempei
Hz ~ hosaisi
nF ~ nona fahang
At ~ ateng
Ø ~ qiao sidhur
base camp
ãotul
gãepongwei
—each to itself, but
all in harmony

Prologue

"AM I A HUMAN, Grandmother Nor?"

"Yes, my darling," the old woman said. "Why do you ask?"

Heipua frowned, leaning their cheek against the cool cave wall, watching a trickle of water shimmer down the ridges of stone. They had found a spring deep in the tunnel system, and learned that it was the core component of *mountain marrow*, a drink that was reserved for the wise elders of Ateng. Heipua was only seven, but they were allowed to drink the water. Grandmother Nor said the gods wouldn't mind. They couldn't see Hei in here, anyway.

"Human people all live together," Hei said. They couldn't see humans very clearly up close, but they knew this much. "They say hello to each other and cook each other food and have babies, which are very loud."

"They *are* very loud, aren't they?" Grandmother Nor said with a wry smile. She petted Hei's hair, and their eyes fluttered shut. It was their favourite feeling. "The grown ones are, too."

"I'm not loud," Heipua said, "now that I'm not little anymore. And I try to say hello to everything, but you're the only one who says it back with your words. And I'm no good at cooking, and I don't want any babies at all."

"You don't need to be worrying about cooking or babies at your age."

"Will I have to when I'm older?"

"Cooking, yes, if only so you have more meals that you like. Babies, not so much. Not if you don't want to."

"I don't want to," Hei said vehemently. "I do not want to be stuck in here with a baby."

Grandmother Nor hummed in acknowledgment, peeling a piece of fruit she had brought for them. Heipua felt like they'd swallowed a salamander as they realized that that was what had happened to Grandmother Nor: she'd got trapped in the caves with a baby, because Hei had been born bad. She said that wasn't true, and the problem was other people. But there were many, many other people, and only one Heipua. Could all of those other people be wrong?

They returned to their question, running their fingertips through the water. "Are you *sure* I'm human? Other humans don't have to hide like me."

"You're a different kind of human," Grandmother Nor said. She handed them a segment of soft fruit, and Heipua took it carefully between their fingers so their hands wouldn't get sticky. "A very special kind. Do you feel like a human?"

Hei considered this as they ate. They had all the right parts that humans had, the same number of eyes and arms and legs and fingers and toes. They spoke like a human, sometimes. But they didn't know if that was the same as feeling like one. "I feel like a cave. Like there are many parts of me, and many things hidden inside, but no one can see them except for me. And you, because you come and visit me, and you look."

Their grandmother didn't respond for a long time. Hei looked at her, and saw even in the dim light that her hair had gone more grey, as though a vein of wovenstone had begun to spread.

"Do you want other people to look?" Grandmother Nor asked.

This was a scary question. Heipua wanted to say yes, because they were curious about what it would feel like. But they also wanted to say no, because they were afraid that it would hurt. Like the time when they tried to climb up a rocky wall and cut their hand on a sharp edge. It had stung and their blood had felt very hot, and they'd had to wait until the next day to show Grandmother Nor.

Hei decided not to answer. "I found a bird skeleton yesterday. I think it flew inside through one of the exits and got lost."

"That happens sometimes."

"It makes me sad."

"It is sad, yes," Grandmother Nor agreed. "But it gave the armour bugs something to eat, which will make them plump and nutritious when it's our turn to eat them. It's a part of the life cycle. All species work together to make this world into what it is. We're all connected."

This made sense to Heipua, even if they didn't like the idea of the bird getting lost. Even though they weren't part of the hmun, they were connected to all sorts of things in the mountains, the mushrooms and the bugs and the moss, the wind and the water and the stone. They could make tapping sounds with their fingernails like insects, and whistle in time with the slots in the cave walls. Sometimes they thought this was better than words.

When they sat at the exits—which they supposed were also entrances—they would look out over Eiji and wonder what sounds were down there. What colours to see and what things to touch. They were friends with the mountains; could they be friends with the rainforest floor? The tops of the trees? The misty waterfall, far in the distance?

There were lots of humans, but they were all the same kind of animal. The way Heipua saw it, there were many other kinds of living things. So maybe it didn't matter if Ateng didn't like them.

They wished it would, though. Even though that wish made them cry sometimes, they couldn't stop wishing it anyway. They didn't know how to make the feeling go away.

Hei tried to change the subject again, to escape the hard question they had asked. "I found a new spot where I can visit the sun. You have to crawl, but then you can look through the gap and watch the sunrise. It's very orange, and it makes the other mountains look purple and the trees look gold. Will you come with me to see it tomorrow?"

The old woman smiled apologetically, and Hei knew that her answer would be no. They looked away, trying not to show that they were disappointed. "It sounds like a beautiful discovery," said Grandmother Nor. "But I don't think my knees would do a very good job. How about you take an extra close look next time and paint me a picture with your words?"

"I can try," Hei said, but they already knew that words weren't enough. *Warm* wasn't enough. *Bright* wasn't enough. *I like this* wasn't enough. *I love you* wasn't enough.

They had human words in their mouth, but only one person to share them with. How would they ever get better if they couldn't practice with anyone else? Hei liked being quiet and speaking with their hands, but they wanted as many ways possible to say hello to everything.

"Grandmother Nor?" Heipua held their palm to the wall, catching the water in pools between their fingers.

"Yes, Heipua?"

"If I'm very good, can I try to be a human with everyone else? Just for a day? If they don't like me, I can come right back, and everyone can pretend it was a dream. I'll never talk to anyone again after that, I promise."

"Oh, Hei." Grandmother Nor took them into her strong arms, cradling them against her chest. They curled up like a baby fern, trying to make themself the perfect shape to hold. "It's not about if *you're* good. It's about if everyone else is willing to be. And my darling, I think they will. Not yet, but someday soon. When they are, you can make human friends, and share all the sunrises that you want. How does that sound?"

The idea felt big inside of them; they let out a big breath to match, to make sure there was room to hold it. As they imagined the possibility, they hid their face against their grandmother. "There's a sunrise every morning. Do I have to make a new friend for every single day? That sounds like too many."

Grandmother Nor laughed, kissing them on the head. "That would be too many for me. I like my quiet time, just like you."

"Then how many friends should I make?" Hei asked worriedly, trying to figure out the rules. "Do I need to do it all at once?"

"You take your time," Grandmother Nor said. Her certainty was soothing. "As much as you need. It's not about the number of friends you have, but how they make you feel." She reached out, picking up a small chip of wovenstone, and placed it into Heipua's hand. They held it protectively. "You said you feel like a cave. When you meet someone who treats you as well as you treat the mountains, *that's* how you know they're a good friend. That's when you invite them to visit."

"Do you really think people will like me?"

"I think they'll love you, Heipua Minhal. All they need is the chance."

Part One:
Eiji

ONE

EVERY KID DREAMS OF BEING a hero, don't they? Sohmeng always had, at least.

When she was little, young enough that people were still calling her precocious instead of obnoxious, she'd roped everyone she could into playing pretend with her. Her brother, her parents, her damdão, her grandmother, her neighbours—even some of her teachers joined in, and Sohmeng's imagination grew bigger than the whole sky.

She told fibs so spectacular that adults had to stifle laughter as they scolded her. She put on elaborate and incomprehensible performances, changing the plot as it suited her, twirling around in a towel that she insisted was a gown. Multiple times, she'd had to be stopped from feeding her playmates flowers that she declared would give them special powers. In Sohmeng's mind, she shone bright enough for the moons to take notice, and so she behaved like it was true.

It was different, as she got older. Somewhere along the way, people stopped laughing. Parents started encouraging their kids to play with someone else. It didn't matter if no one knew she was Minhal—there was something else bad about her. Something she didn't understand.

So her imaginary world became a private one. Whatever stories Sohmeng told were mostly for Grandmother Mi. The shape of her daydreams changed; they took on a new storyline, one where she was making her grand return from some impossibly big adventure. She would climb the mountains of Ateng with a new discovery in hand, so useful that the Grand Ones would all commend her. She would say *watch this!* and everyone would look, and no one would even roll their eyes. She would be loved and celebrated, held up by her community.

Now that it was actually happening, she had no idea what to do with all the attention.

When Sohmeng's team finally made it across the barest bones of the reconstructed Sky Bridge, they were welcomed into Fochão Dangde in a burst of frantic excitement. After more than three years, Ateng was no longer cut off from the rest of the world. A group of travelers from another hmun had crossed their threshold—along with Sohmeng and her father, freshly back from the dead.

But before any Grand Ones or nosy neighbours could get a hold of her, Sohmeng pushed through the crowd, searching for the only people that really mattered.

She didn't have to look far to find them. Lit up by a sunbeam through the mouth of the cave, Grandmother Mi was being held steady by Viunwei, who looked close to collapsing himself.

"*Sohmeng!*" Her brother grabbed her by the shoulders,

looking her over as though she'd only fallen that morning. For a moment, she thought he might scold her, but before he could find the words, he yanked her into a hug. "It's you, it's really—burning godseye, you're *here*."

After moons and moons of absence, well over an entire lunar cycle, Sohmeng felt like a different person entirely. But the sound of her brother's voice and the smell of her grandmother's hair rooted her past to her present, and brought her exactly back to the feeling of being a child. Maybe that was just the force of how much she had missed them. Or maybe it was because her father was right there with them—a little older and a little more chewed up, but still the same gentle presence of her childhood. Home at last.

"My son," Grandmother Mi said, holding Tonão's face in her wrinkled hands as she wept. "My son, my *son*, my boy, my Tonão."

Sohmeng choked up; she had never seen her grandmother cry before. Viunwei was different—he'd always been a big baby—but for once, she couldn't find it in herself to tease him. She was alive. Against all odds, she was *alive*. Down in Eiji, she had long moved past the tragedy and terror of that day on the mountain, but her family had been living in a reality where she was long gone. Where they'd had to learn to live without her.

Being faced with their grief set off waves of her own, made her feel sorry and protective and confused all at once. She hadn't realized how badly she would be missed, and that was its own sort of sorrow.

If Hei were here, they would have led her somewhere quiet, taken her hands in theirs, and let her talk out her feelings until she ran out of words. But Hei was down in Eiji with the sãoni, and there were things Sohmeng needed to do before she could return to them.

First, introductions. It had been a long time since Ateng had received any visitors, but the members of the hmun hadn't forgotten their hospitality. People practically lined up to meet the team from Nona Fahang, and Ateng's remaining Dulpongpa speakers put their skills to the test. A magnificent meal was put together in the communal kitchen, and the sound of everyone talking echoed off the cave walls long into the night. The novelty of the moment was overwhelming, but the welcome was undeniable.

The ongoing Dulpongpa translation was useful for Ahn, who was doing his best to stay in the loop without getting under Sohmeng's feet. Before they'd crossed the Sky Bridge, he'd been insistent that she spend most of this time with her family.

"Don't worry about me," he had insisted, braiding her hair in a Qiao Sidhur style. "We will see more of each other. They're the ones who need you right now."

But much as he was trying to stay out of the way, Grandmother Mi would not allow it. Being a woman of excellent taste, she adored Ahn immediately. Which meant a lot of pinching his cheeks and teasing him. She kept sending him on small but convoluted errands, pleased by the way he tripped over himself to fulfill them.

"He's a good one, isn't he?" she said to Sohmeng, watching Ahn search valiantly for her slippers. "Very helpful."

"Yeah." Sohmeng rested her head on Grandmother Mi's shoulder. "He tries really hard."

When it came to Ahn, everything was different from the last time they had entered a hmun. Where the people of Nona Fahang had recognized him as Qiao Sidhur, as a potential enemy, no one in Ateng had context yet about the Empire's invasion. Until all of the details were laid out, Ahn was allowed to simply be a person like any other. Sohmeng wondered if he'd ever been able to do that before.

She was almost sorry to break the illusion, but it had to be done. Repairing the Sky Bridge was only one reason they had returned to Ateng; now, Sohmeng had the opportunity to explain why the bridge had been destroyed in the first place, and how they were working to make sure nothing like it ever happened again. So the next day, she went to Chehangma's Gate.

"It was a disruption to the ecosystem," Sohmeng said. "When the Qiao Sidhur army first landed three years ago, even further north near Hosaisi, they got right into the path of the sãoni migration route. Rather than move *out* of it when the sãoni attacked, they fought back. It threw everything off, which is why it looked like they swarmed the mountain out of nowhere."

Grand One Hiun frowned, their kind face unable to hide its doubt. "So you're saying a problem on the other side of the continent is what caused this?"

"It does sound strange, but it is the truth," said Tonão Sol. Sohmeng was beyond grateful that he and Polha Hiwei were there to back her up. After all, despite everything she had done over the past few months, she was still technically a child in the eyes of Ateng. If she hadn't been living with the sãoni herself, she might have had trouble believing her own story, too. "The sãoni have always been a part of Eiji. It's why sãoni warriors have always accompanied trading parties, why we stuck so carefully to known paths. But this swarm was unprecedented. Our best assumption is that when individual colonies were pushed too close together, they got more territorial. The attack on the bridge was a tragedy, but it was also a freak accident."

"But they still haven't moved from the base of Fochão Dangde," replied Grand One Hiun. "How do we know they won't attack again?"

"Especially once the bridge starts getting rebuilt," said Grandmother Ker uncertainly.

Sohmeng could sense the anxiety rising in the room. While she'd spent months living with the sãoni, even coming to think of them as family, they remained one of the things the people of Ateng feared most. Not just predators, but monsters.

"I don't know if that's something we actually need to worry very much about," Sohmeng said. She reached for her father's hand, squeezing it. "The sãoni warriors are good at their jobs, and we're not … we're not sending people directly into their path anymore. They're curious, and super food-motivated. Honestly, the fact that we've been overharvesting eggs from the yellowbills might also be helping—it makes the territory less ideal for hunting. Eventually the colony's going to eat through this area and have to move on. And I've heard their alpha is getting older anyway, and not really that aggressive as far as sãoni go."

"And where," Grand One Chisong asked, looking closely at Sohmeng, "are you getting this information?"

Sohmeng knew she would have to talk about Hei eventually, and she chose to tread very carefully around the topic. Her dad and Polha didn't offer any information beyond what she shared, and she did what she could to stick to the truth without breaching Hei's privacy.

"They're an exile from one of the hmun, who was adopted by a colony of sãoni. They saved my life when I fell, and I've been traveling with them since. They probably get the sãoni better than anyone in the entire rainforest."

"An exile?" Grandfather Se said with a snort. Sohmeng hadn't missed that frog face.

"We also wouldn't have been able to fix the Sky Bridge without them," she said, allowing herself the pleasure of glaring at him. "Lots to think about."

From there, Tonão took up the task of explaining the loss of the batengmun and holding space for the council's grief. Polha Hiwei spoke of Nona Fahang, the influx of refugees and the danger coming down from the north. She introduced the Fahangpa word *Gãepongwei* to the Grand Ones, the word for all the hmun as one. Together, each member of the traveling party painted a rich picture of the world below the mountains, all of its trials and triumphs. And Ahn spoke of the Empire.

"My home is a place that believes in growth," he said, standing calmly before the Grand Ones. Sohmeng was impressed by his composure; these were the people who'd made her feel about three inches tall her whole life. "Growth, I'm truly sorry to say, that comes at the expense of others. The land we call Qiao Sidh—it was many lands, once. And then it became one, through conquest. And my sister would like this to happen here, as well. For Gãepongwei to also become Qiao Sidh."

"Each to itself, but all in harmony," Grandmother Ginhãe said, a gentle chastisement.

Ahn clearly had no idea what that meant. Sohmeng stepped in. "We all agree that we can't let Qiao Sidh take over our homes, but it's what they're trying to do. If all the hmun can band together, it'll be easier to negotiate with the Empire. Show that our home is our own, and if they want to visit, they need to be guests about it."

"And if we must stand against my people," Ahn carefully interjected, "we can have a unified front."

Ahn had brought this possibility up multiple times, that his sister might not listen. But Sohmeng wasn't willing to jump to violent conclusions yet. It felt defeatist. After all, if Ahn could learn and change, why couldn't everyone else? It was just a matter of talking things through.

"We have a plan," Sohmeng said, trying to keep control of the conversation. She wanted her news for the Grand Ones to mostly be positive, to put the attention on her solutions rather than the problems. "Once we leave, we're going north to talk to Ahn's sister. She'll hear us out."

"It seems you remain Par as ever," Grandfather Li said with a smile. And even though it was a compliment, an honest to gods *compliment*, Sohmeng's stomach sank.

For all her big talk about being herself, Sohmeng had immediately choked when she came back into Fochão Dangde. Everyone had addressed her as Sohmeng Par, same as they always had, and she went along with it.

It wasn't that she didn't want to be Sohmeng Minhal— but there was so much else happening, wasn't there? So much to explain, and all of it bigger than her. She couldn't afford to have people arguing about if she was bad luck when she needed them to listen. But it felt awful to betray herself so quickly. Then Eakang had followed her lead and introduced themself as Eakang Chisong, which felt even worse. She had promised they'd be in it together as Minhals, and then her own fear had backed them into a corner. They hadn't deserved that.

It complicated her return home, to remember why some small part of her had secretly been relieved when she went plummeting off that mountainside. She wished Hei were here, and she was glad they weren't.

Sohmeng took a deep breath, trying not to stare at the empty Minhal chair in front of her. "Between bridge repair and honouring the batengmun, I know that Ateng has a lot on its plate right now. And because we're so far south and so high in the mountains, I'm not too concerned about the Empire making contact. But we thought it was important for you to know what's going on in Gãepongwei."

"After these years of isolation, I think we're overdue to connect with our neighbours," said Grand One Hiun. "And what an auspicious time it is for new relationships. You've come home at the perfect time, haven't you?"

"I . . . have?"

"He didn't tell you?" Grand One Hiun asked, surprised.

Then Grandmother Mi started cackling in her chair, and *that* was how Sohmeng found out that Viunwei was getting married.

"You didn't *tell* me?!" Sohmeng exclaimed later in a much shriekier echo of Grand One Hiun. "Viunwei, *what*?"

"I was trying to make the day about you!" Viunwei groaned, rubbing his face. "A thing you always want!"

Grandmother Mi had laughed all the way back to their house, and was still laughing now in the other room. She would have to bring the old lady some water before she hurt herself. Sohmeng paced around the house, waving her arms around. "You're marrying Jinho. Jinho! You're doing it, you're actually doing it?"

Viunwei stood stiffly before her. "Yes. Is that a problem?"

"No! No, what? Do you hear yourself? Viunwei, I think it's *amazing*. It's only ..." Sohmeng hesitated, working her way around the words. This was a sensitive subject—Jinho had barely been able to look at her after they'd first hugged upon reuniting. "Well, last time I saw you—"

"Things change," Viunwei said. He sounded firm, certain of himself. "Losing you ... it put some things into perspective."

"Like that you totally like each other and I knew it?"

"*Sohmeng.*"

Being right came at a pretty heavy cost, but Sohmeng decided she'd find a way to bear it. She knew it would be a pain for Hei to wait an extra week or so, but they'd already included buffer time in their plans. Things were undeniably urgent, but her brother didn't get married every day. Plus, up until now, Viunwei had been planning a wedding without his sister there—now, he had both her *and* his father back.

Tonão had jumped at the chance to play an active role in the wedding preparations, from consulting on the food to making decorations by hand. It was bittersweet in some ways; Sohmeng knew they were all feeling the Lahni-shaped absence in the room. But it made her smile to see her father reconnecting with the family he had made in Ateng.

"I can't believe this was mine," Tonão said, not for the

first time, as he made the final adjustments to Viunwei's wedding shirt the night before the ceremony. He stepped back to examine his handiwork.

"Does it look alright?" Viunwei asked nervously.

"More than alright!"

There was meticulous embroidery all along the arms, depicting the lunar phases of every married couple who had used it in their wedding. The loose garment had been passed down the family for six generations. Sohmeng was amazed that, despite having no shared biological material, Viunwei and her father were close enough in size that it didn't need much adjusting. If she'd been the one getting married, it would've squashed her boobs and hung down to her knees.

"I think you're all ready," Tonão said, resting his hands on Viunwei's shoulders proudly. Viunwei stared back at him, and Sohmeng watched the corner of his mouth twitch, which was the first sign that the crying was about to start again.

That was her cue to slip out the door. Besides, she needed to talk to Jinho.

Sohmeng found him in his family's house, flanked by his two very energetic younger sisters, each attached to one of his legs. He was laughing, trying not to fall as he walked around while they dangled from him. Jinho was so easygoing, the opposite of Viunwei. But when he saw Sohmeng, he froze.

"Sohmeng!" one of the girls hollered, breaking the quiet. "You're going to be our sister! Does that mean we have to give you our toys?"

"Nope. And I won't be giving you any of mine, so don't

get any ideas." The girls seemed reassured by this. Smart kids. She glanced at Jinho, who hadn't moved. "Mind if I borrow your brother, though? You can go chase Ahn if you want, he's pretty fast but I bet you can take him."

They took the bait faster than hatchlings, and then it was just Sohmeng and Jinho, and the memory of when they'd last seen each other.

"So." Jinho tried to smile again, but she could see how awkward it was. He tucked his hands in his pockets. "What can I do for you Sohmeng? Is your brother bothering you already?"

"It wasn't your fault," she blurted out. She couldn't do this small talk thing, this pretending that everything was alright. "I need you to know that."

Jinho froze. He was looking at her with the faint panic of someone who's been confronted with a topic they thought they could avoid. Sohmeng couldn't blame him. It had taken a whole bunch of courage on her part to approach him at all. The fall was terrifying, the fall had *hurt*. But the way Jinho had screamed as the rope snapped? That lingered. She'd put him through something horrible.

She took a deep breath. "This is an important night for you. I mean, you're getting *married*. And I'm going to be there, and you'll have to see me, so I need you to really, really hear me when I say that what happened was not your fault, Jinho."

"Sohmeng, you don't have to—"

Before she could stop herself, Sohmeng marched up to Jinho, wrapping her arms around him tightly. After a beat, he accepted the hug, holding her as though she might break.

"Please listen," she said. Her voice softened. "Please?"

When he finally nodded, Sohmeng said what she needed to say. "It wasn't your fault that I fell. You told me to be careful, and I didn't listen. I fell, and that was on me. It wasn't you, and I'm sorry for how scary it must have been."

Jinho was shaking. He held her tighter, his voice wavering. "You were the one who fell, you shouldn't be apologizing to me."

"I am, though. I'm sorry. I'm sorry I scared you."

Sohmeng wasn't always the best at saying sorry, but it was easy this time. She meant it. She was sixteen, still only at the beginning of her journey into adulthood. But she had grown since touching down in Eiji, and looking back, she could see the ways in which her bullheadedness had hurt people. Sometimes staying true to herself meant making other people unhappy, or uncomfortable—but she never wanted to be so careless.

Sohmeng had returned from Eiji a hero, with plans to fix the big problems that troubled her world. But she couldn't do that without first fixing the problems she'd left at home.

Jinho sniffled, bonking his head against hers. "I almost said no. When he asked me to marry him."

"*What?*" Sohmeng's eyes went wide. "Why? Why would you do that?"

"I didn't think I could ever speak to him again, after— after you fell. After I couldn't save you. But he said the same thing as you, that it wasn't my fault. And he said you were right. That he'd been a jerk, and he loved me, and he wanted to marry me. He proposed because of you." Viunwei had told her this, how her fall had *put things into perspective,* and for all Sohmeng wanted to get smug about that, the distress on Jinho's face sobered her right up. "I've felt so selfish for saying yes, Sohmeng. How could I say yes, after how I failed you?"

"Um, I just *told* you that you didn't fail anyone. If you're feeling weird about anything, it should be your taste in my brother." This startled a squawk out of Jinho, a hand coming up to cover his mouth, and Sohmeng broke into a grin. "And so what if it was selfish, anyway? Be selfish. It's your wedding day. That's what it's for!"

"I don't know if that—"

"Well it's what *my* wedding day will be for, and I'm the person who fixed the Sky Bridge. So, I dunno, maybe I have a lot of good ideas."

Jinho laughed shakily, and Sohmeng watched him, chewing her cheek. He was still the boy she recognized from childhood, but he was different now too, same as her. She hoped he still went outside and collected those yellowbill eggs. She hoped the sight of Eiji still took the breath from him in all the good ways, too.

"I'm glad you're back, Sohmeng," Jinho said. "It hasn't been the same without you. It's been . . ."

"Quiet?" Sohmeng teased.

"Yeah," Jinho said warmly. "It's been quiet. Make some noise tonight, will you?"

Sohmeng lifted her chin proudly, grinning her perfect gap-toothed grin. "You can count on me."

Two

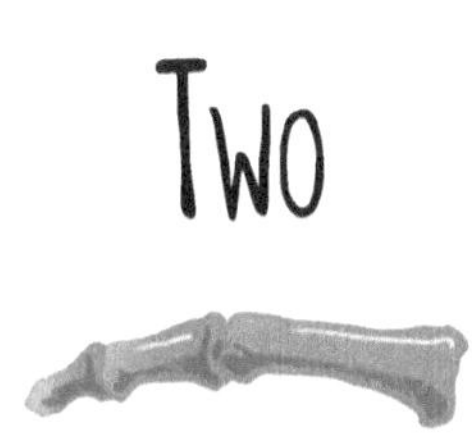

THE LAST WEDDING AHN HAD ATTENDED had been with Schenn by his side. It was a full Imperial affair, held for a cousin of Ahn's in the sweeping halls of one of the country palaces. He didn't know her terribly well, but she was close enough in relation that it would have been a slight not to attend. When the invitation arrived at Kørno Wan's training school, the Masters agreed that it would only make sense for Schenn to come along.

Ahn was thrilled. Schenn, on the other hand, was uncharacteristically nervous. He dug through his modest wardrobe, panicking about having nothing acceptable to wear. It was obvious to Ahn that the royal family would pay for an outfit. He couldn't understand why that seemed to make Schenn uncomfortable.

"We'll take care of you," Ahn insisted. "*I'll* take care of you. Besides, your family was generous with me when we visited for Haojost's solstice festival. Why shouldn't mine return the favor?"

"Your family rules the *Empire*."

"Then we have the money to throw around. Let us do this for you. If it makes you feel better, I'll take it out of my own allowance. Please?"

Ahn must have gotten through to him somehow, because Schenn perked up at the tailor's later, cheeks pink as Ahn assessed his best colours with the consultants: poppy red, cassis, deep olive green. When Schenn cautiously said he liked the gold lining on his jacket, Ahn could have cheered. Their rapport opened right back up on the carriage ride back to their hotel. Ahn quizzed Schenn on relatives' names, laughed as Schenn imitated his Imperial accent.

The day belonged to Ahn's cousin, but it felt like theirs, too. Schenn was getting a deeper look at the life that could be his. That *would* be his, one way or another.

The ceremony had about four hundred people in attendance, and, as with all Imperial weddings, it went long. The vows themselves were a combination of poetry and legal documentation—to be to one another as a candle, and also to strive for a minimum of three children if possible, and also to transition their estates to one another in the event of death. Ahn's favorite part was the binding that came at the end of this ceremony: two complicated knots were cut through to release old vows, and a fresh one was tied.

After that, hours were spent on the dedication of gifts for the couple and their families, with extra respect paid to the Éongrir line. Bards performed long ballads; young warriors presented entertaining and occasionally absurd feats of strength; spiritualists made predictions for the happy couple's marital future. During this time, the guests lounged in settees and murmured quietly as they picked at the endless buffet. Eventually, a bell signaled that the rituals of the evening were over and the party had begun.

Some guests gathered outside under sweeping tents of silver and blue to admire the gardens. Others moved to the adjacent ballroom where the dancing was starting. This is where Ahn led Schenn, hushing his complaints and promising that the frog pond wasn't going anywhere.

"Dance with me, won't you?" Ahn asked, his fingers intertwined with Schenn's. "It's a wedding."

"Don't use that sparkling *I'm a prince* face on me," Schenn chided.

"Why, because it'll work?"

Schenn rolled his eyes, but he was smiling as they stepped onto the floor. Together, they glided across the tiles, and Ahn discovered that the dances he could do in his sleep tripped Schenn up. It was relentlessly endearing, how clumsy Schenn got the moment the sword was removed from his hand.

When the time came to switch partners, Schenn gracefully excused himself for a snack to avoid stepping on any literal toes. Ahn took the hand of a noble and went through the motions, making polite conversation. All the while, his gaze kept returning to Schenn, who stood by the wall with his hands behind his back and a crease in his brow, dressed up in the finest fashion of Qiao Sidh.

He was handsome, and out of place, and perfect.

Do you think they'd let us get married instead? We could ask, Schenn.

If Ahn had been braver, maybe he would've said it. If Ahn had been more naïve, he would have even believed it were possible.

"Did you follow the ceremony, dear?"

Ahn was pulled from his reverie by an unfamiliar voice. He turned to see someone he didn't know, with Sohmeng's grandmother standing beside them. Ah—a translator.

He nodded to them gratefully before looking at Grandmother Mi. "Most of it, yes. Thank you for your accommodations—your hmun has been very generous with me."

"We don't get a lot of newcomers. Who could say why? I've always thought that scaling mountains is downright leisurely." The old woman winked, making one of the moon tattoos on her cheek jump. "Come, sit with me."

As the youngest of a large family, Ahn hadn't had a very strong relationship with any of his grandparents. His mother was well into her forties when she'd given birth to him, and his father was a few years older; the only grandparent Ahn really remembered was his maternal grandmother. She had been over six feet tall, with a sharp tongue and an unsmiling face. She had scared him.

Ahn took Grandmother Mi's hand as she sat down, helping her keep balance. The skin on the back of her hand was thin and delicate compared to her rough fingers, and she held on with unexpected strength.

"Oh, I love a wedding," the old woman began with a happy sigh. "Such fun, such a blessing. We can get grim up in this big rock, we really can."

"It's been a hard few years, from what I've heard," Ahn replied.

"You've heard right," she said. "But take a look at the timing of all this—a bridge rebuilt, a union formed. The gods get funny about these arrangements. They like to stick their noses in, I think. As far as gods have noses."

Ahn didn't know much about the opinions or noses of Ateng's gods, but he hummed softly in agreement anyway. He wanted to be polite. Grandmother Mi caught on and chuckled, patting his arm.

"Sohmeng said your people don't share our gods. Do we seem strange to you?"

"I—" Ahn stumbled over a response. This felt like dangerous territory. "No! I mean, different people have different beliefs—"

"*You're* quite strange to me," Grandmother Mi interrupted matter-of-factly while her translator blanched. She shifted in her seat, looking over to where her grandson and his new spouse were gathered by the wall of candles, talking with their friends. "Very strange. A prince. I didn't know they still made princes. It's a story-word here, you know."

"Sohmeng mentioned it's not a part of your culture."

"Certainly not since Polhmun Ão."

"Polhmun Ão?"

"Polhmun Ão," Grandmother Mi repeated, like it was obvious. At Ahn's apologetic expression, she stared at him in horror. "What, my granddaughter hasn't told you any of the good stories? All these years of me entertaining her and she hasn't passed a thing on? Who did I raise! *Sohmeng!*"

Sohmeng's head popped up from a cluster of people she was eating with. She'd been chattering with Ahn excitedly the night before about how her cohort was finally *talking* to her, treating her like more than a burden. Ahn had said he was happy for her, but it also troubled him. He couldn't fathom why her apparent friends would withhold their company, or why the adults in charge would allow this.

She walked over, her long dress swishing. Ahn swallowed.

"What is it, Grandmother Mi? Ahn causing trouble?" She gave him a mischievous look, and Ahn let out a breath of helpless laughter.

"Ahnschen is perfectly fine, wicked girl." The old woman pinched Sohmeng's cheek, gesturing emphatically for her to sit down. "But you—a stranger arrives, and you don't share any of our stories? That's what strangers are for!"

Sohmeng groaned, but she did look abashed. "We were busy trying not to get him executed, there wasn't exactly time!"

"Well, there's time now."

"*Now?*"

Ahn watched words fly between the two of them like a throwing disc. Grandmother Mi was energetic, playful like Sohmeng without being as coarse. If anything, Viunwei Soon, with his more serious nature, was the one who stood out most in the family. Ahn felt for him.

"Fine," Sohmeng relented. "Which story am I doing?"

"Polhmun Ão." Grandmother Mi's eyes twinkled. "*It begins again.*"

"Really?" Sohmeng looked confused for a moment, but it faded quickly in some silent exchange between her and her grandmother. "Huh. You know what, yeah—that's a good spot to start. But I'm doing it in Dulpongpa. I want Ahn to hear it my way, and straight from me." Sohmeng probably didn't mean for the words to feel so intimate, but Ahn's neck warmed anyway. After calling over a translator, she adjusted her dress and settled into a comfortable position. "Lead me in?"

"It would be my pleasure," said Grandmother Mi, and she began to hum. Her voice had the raspy, shimmering quality of the elderly, and it vibrated pleasantly deep in his ears.

Sohmeng began clapping in a steady rhythm: *One-two, one. One-two, one.*

Taking the cue Ahn didn't yet follow, a few people nearby joined at the table, creating a private bubble in the midst of the wedding, bearing witness to a story. Ahn realized that he had never heard Sohmeng sing before, and his stomach flipped in anticipation—

"Listen up," Sohmeng announced, and a snort interrupted Grandmother Mi's tune. "Do you know what happens when the world breaks?"

She stopped her clapping, and the gathered people took over, drumming their hands in a new rhythm on the table, on their thighs. Ahn's fingers twitched, wishing he could join in.

"It begins," they said, "it begins again."

"We don't remember *why* it all began," Sohmeng said over the sound of her grandmother's humming. Doing their best to follow Sohmeng's intonation, the translator followed her in Atengpa, "but we know why it ended—and why it began again. I'm speaking, obviously, of Polhmun Ão."

She clapped—*one-two, one. One-two, one.*

"It begins, it begins again."

"A *city*, we call it. Bigger than any one hmun, bigger than any *five* hmun combined. It rises higher than the treetops, big and walled and impossible, but not back then. People gather to it like bees to pollen, and its walls are lined with gold, and its inhabitants know all the secrets we don't know anymore. We dream them sometimes, beneath the moons. We dream of the home that came before home."

One-two, one. One-two, one.

"It begins, it begins again."

"We can't go back," Sohmeng said, a note of regret in her voice, "but we remember what we share. Two moons in the sky, same as right now. Ama and Chehang, Chehangma by day. The eyes of the heavens, watching over us in all things, covering us in their moods. And they are *moody*." The translator sounded mildly scandalized, but it got another guffaw out of Grandmother Mi. "Once every cycle they go dark. They look away, leaving us to the unknown."

Minhal, Ahn recognized. This was Minhal. In Nona Fahang, Sohmeng had been Minhal. Par, then Minhal— and back to Par again, up in Ateng.

"Polhmun Ão grows and grows until it's nearly overflowing. People packed together like honey in the comb, ruled over by a single queen, a luminary tethered to the ground. But when the world bursts open, not even the moons can cut through the darkness. What made the gods so angry, none of them could say, and so none of us can either. A Minhal for the ages, night and night and night."

One-two, one. One-two, one.

"It begins, it begins again."

"Birds fall out of the sky, the water goes sour, the earth shakes out its own trees. And the people of Polhmun Ão, clustered so closely together, they watch the food they can trust dwindle. They burn in the rain. All the honey turns to sickness, and down goes the city of everyone."

Empathy ached in Ahn's chest; he had never envied an emperor's position. Millenia past, a volcanic eruption destroyed an entire civilization in the caldera that would eventually become Qiao Sidh. Ahn had always heard it described as a *tear in the realms*, where smoke blanketed the sky from one side to another.

Had there been a ruler then? Had they even had the chance to try and save their people?

"A single person is not enough to relight the sky, and the queen knows it. So she gives away her power." At first, Ahn wondered if he had misheard. Abdication was unheard of in Qiao Sidh. But Sohmeng didn't make it sound shameful in the slightest. "She gathers the brightest and wisest and eldest minds in all of Polhmun Ão, and they use their years beneath Chehangma's watchful eye to interpret their will in the dark."

Ahn's gaze landed on the tattoos on Grandmother Mi's face, marking her as a speaker for the Mi phase. Catching his eye, she gave him a wink.

"Who knows how long they talk for?" Sohmeng asked, holding out her hands. "The night never stops, after all. But eventually, the truth finds them: the time has come to leave Polhmun Ão."

One-two, one. One-two, one.

"It begins," the city's descendants say; "it begins again."

"And the sky opens—"

One-two, one. One-two, one.

"It begins, it begins again."

"And the gods look back upon their people with two eyes, bright and full. And these people, grateful and grieving, say goodbye to their hivemates. They spread far across the land—across *Gãepongwei*," Sohmeng said, giving Ahn a meaningful look as she used the Fahangpa word. It was coming together, the connective tissue of this land. A history he never could have known just by looking. "They make their homes in the healing wounds of the world, each hmun led by a circle of luminaries old enough to remember what came before. They live each to themselves, but all in harmony. When the world breaks—"

One-two, one. One-two, one.

"It begins, it begins again."

"It begins," Sohmeng repeated, "it begins again."

She breathed out slowly, her storyteller performance coming to a close. The drumming ended soon after, until all that was left was Grandmother Mi's humming, and then that stopped too. A moment of quiet held before energy burst from the small crowd that surrounded them—the mark of a story well-told.

"Not so bad at all!" Grandmother Mi exclaimed, giving Sohmeng a kiss on the cheek.

She chuckled a little as others echoed the sentiment, looking more nervous than Ahn had expected. "Yeah?"

"It was wonderful," Ahn insisted. A tray full of stone tea bowls was passed around, and he handed once each to Grandmother Mi and Sohmeng before taking one for himself. "You told the story well. It was very vivid."

"Everyone tells the legends differently," Grandmother Mi explained to Ahn, patting Sohmeng's leg. "It's why we have the call-and-response, and the tune. It keeps the story true to itself, but lets the narrators tell it from their hearts. I think we all heard your heart in that one, mm?"

"Thanks," Sohmeng said, blowing on her tea. "It was actually my first time doing it for like, a group? Of adults, I mean. I told stories to the kids all the time, but this was different. It was kind of cool."

Despite the bustle of attention, something felt off to Ahn. For all that Sohmeng boasted about how great she was, she didn't seem to know what to do with this positive attention from her community. It wasn't modesty that Ahn was seeing—it was uncertainty. Caution, even.

A child leaned on the table, getting right up in Sohmeng's face. "Sohmeng Par, it was *more* than cool! You've gotten way better since last time."

She poked them in the forehead. "You're a real punk, you know that?"

Sohmeng Par.

It had never been unusual to Ahn that Sohmeng had several names. In Qiao Sidh, he could be Eløndham, Ahnschen, or Ahn at any time, and that was without his rank names being brought into it. But it was different here; aside from Sohmeng, everyone seemed to have a single phase attached to their name.

Ahn sipped his tea, reaching for a memory. Before the Chisong festival in Nona Fahang, Sohmeng had said something, something short and sharp about Minhals being undesirable whereas Chisongs were exceptionally celebrated in Ateng. After hearing the story, he saw why, and it unsettled him.

There was something else, something about being removed, Sohmeng had mentioned that Minhals were removed from Ateng. Removed how? He hadn't thought much about it, so caught up he was in his own terror of execution, or exile—

Realization landed like a blow. Sohmeng wasn't a Par in Ateng by choice. That was why she hadn't corrected anyone. That was why Eakang had been going by Chisong.

Being a Minhal wasn't just undesirable here—it was catastrophic.

Despite the joyful gathering, despite every visual indicator that the people around her weren't about to become aggressive, Ahn was overwhelmed by the desire to take her hand and leave this place. He wanted to bring her back down the mountain to Hei, so they could do whatever it was that made Sohmeng cackle so freely. He had countless questions for her, and none of them were safe to ask in front of her neighbours.

In an act of good timing, the newlyweds made their way over to the table; Viunwei Soon had an arm around Jinho Tang, smiling with pink-cheeked pride. With the group's attention turned back to the pair, it wasn't so intrusive when Ahn asked Sohmeng if they could speak privately.

After a quick hug for Viunwei, Sohmeng followed Ahn through the crowd as he looked for a space away from the party. The sounds of the celebration were muffled, but the echo chased them everywhere. It created the illusion of being followed, and with the light so dim compared to what he had grown up under, he found himself on edge.

"Um, Ahn?" Sohmeng eventually asked. "Where are we going?"

He paused abruptly, realizing that he had no idea beyond *away*. He'd walked them nearly to the wall of the mountain, tucked between rows and rows of houses. "I'm . . . not sure. I just wanted a moment alone with you. To talk."

Sohmeng's eyebrows raised. "Well, you've got me. What's up?"

"I wanted to ask more about your story," he began, but he faltered. An uncomfortable beat passed as he searched for where to begin. "The description of the darkness, it was very . . ."

"It's intense, yeah," Sohmeng quickly filled in, her arms crossing. "End of the world and all that. But it's a classic and Grandmother Mi asked, and after leaving her thinking I died, she can pretty much ask for any story she wants for the rest of her life. Grand Ones usually like stories about why they get to be Grand Ones. I get it, I'd also be going in for the ego boost."

It was a deflection. Ahn wasn't even sure if she was trying to parry him, or if it had become instinct to shift away from talk that landed on a dark sky. "Sohmeng, is there . . . anything you'd like to tell me?"

"You're being kind of weird, if that counts."

For all that Sohmeng was trying to look calm, Ahn could see that she was bracing. There was something heavy in the air now, some invisible tension stretching between them. It reminded Ahn of how things were with Schenn toward the end, both of them pinned by the weight of a conversation that needed to be had, but couldn't find its way into words. It needed to be different, this time. The question he had was far too important to be left unsaid.

"Are you safe here?" he asked abruptly.

This seemed to catch her off-guard. "Sorry?"

"Are you—" He faltered, hearing a vehemence in his

own voice that was unusual to him. "Are you *safe* here, in Ateng?"

Sohmeng hesitated, then spoke slowly. "I mean … it's my home."

Carefully, Ahn brought his hands to her arms. Maybe he was overthinking, overreacting. But he would rather look like a fool than ignore a loved one in danger.

"Sohmeng Minhal," he said, soft as he could, as though the walls might be listening. "Will they exile you, if they know?"

Sohmeng's eyes widened, and he could see then that this was something she had asked herself many times over. Guilt hit him in the gut. It was a terrible thing to do, to speak a fear aloud to its holder, but how else could he be sure?

After a moment, Sohmeng shrugged beneath his touch. "I don't know. No one knows about it, besides my family. That I was born under Minhal." She looked away from him, down the winding path between the houses. He could imagine her running through them as a child, loud and laughing. Right now, her voice was very quiet. "I used to be sure they would, if they found out. I worried maybe it was the right thing to do actually, because I was so unlucky."

"You're not unlucky," Ahn said.

Sohmeng shoved him playfully. "I know—"

He caught her hand. Pressed it to his heart. "You are *not* unlucky."

She had told him before about how difficult she was. Overstepping boundaries and being too much, needing to be heard at the expense of her own listening. Ahn thought that was an ungenerous interpretation of her character. He liked that Sohmeng was direct, and unafraid to stand her ground. Like most people, she wanted to be loved for who she was. That didn't seem like a crime to him. If anything, it made isolating her seem all the more cruel.

And whether or not they knew she was Sohmeng Minhal, that *was* what the people of Ateng had done to her. Ahn tried to be mindful before he started bristling; he'd been judgmental of the cultures in Gãepongwei before, and he didn't want to fall into that trap again. But he still thought Sohmeng deserved better. He wanted to give her better.

A voice came to him—not Schenn's, but Hei's, transporting him to their frank discussion huddled high in the clouds: *You talk to her. No more hiding.*

"I think you're wonderful," Ahn said quietly, his voice very certain despite the nerves rattling inside of him. "And beautiful, and worthy of a good life where you do not need to be afraid. I spoke to Hei, and they told me I need to be honest with you."

"Ahn, now is so *not* the time to reveal some big stressful secret about Qiao Sidh."

He squeezed her hand in his. "It's nothing like that, Sohmeng. It's—" Bigger? Smaller? Easier to bear, or else infinitely more complicated? "I care for you. Very much."

Sohmeng's lips parted in a soft *oh* as she realized what this conversation was about. For once, she didn't seem to know what to say.

"I know you've told me you don't experience romantic interest the same way I do." Sohmeng's expression got even more owlish, and Ahn cheeks went warm. This was always such a vulnerable thing in courting, taking that first step. And this was on top of the added complication of how they had met. It would make sense for her to reject him for a number of reasons, many of which had nothing to do with his personality. "But that *is* the way I feel about you. And I suppose I wanted to know if that's alright with you. And if it is—well, first, is that alright?"

"I mean ..." Sohmeng tucked a stray piece of hair behind her ear. "I mean, yeah? I can't tell you how to feel. And I like you too, Ahn, I'm just not mushy about it. And Hei likes you, even if they show it funny."

"I know," Ahn said, and he realized it was true. Alone together, up on that slim mountain, he and Hei had begun to understand more of each other than he could have expected. "I'm very fortunate."

"Pretty much, yeah. That little lizard is slow to warm up to people." Sohmeng's fingers tapped against his sternum, and Ahn realized he was still holding her hand there. He released her gently, but she kept hold of his palm, playing with his fingers. "So ... there's another question hiding in there?"

Ahn smiled. "I find myself seeking the honour of being in partnership with you. Would that be acceptable?"

"What kind of partnership?"

Ahn paused for a moment, wanting to make sure he got the language as close to what he meant as possible. "Intimate partnership. It feels romantic on my end, but that doesn't mean I'd need you to feel the same way. I'd like to be closer to you, and put a name to that closeness. When I hold your hand, I want my meaning to be clear. I would kiss you, if you'd allow it."

Sohmeng broke into a toothy grin and tugged on

his arm, pulling him down closer to her level. "Éongrir Ahnschen, do you *like* me?"

"I do!" he laughed. "I just told you I do."

"Oh he *likes* me!"

"He does," Ahn said, and a slow warmth radiated from his earpiece. *Both of us do.* "I know things are unpredictable right now. We still have work to do with my sister, and I cannot promise what the future holds once we've completed our task. But for now, for as long as it makes sense, what do you say? Would you have me in this way?"

"I say yes, obviously," Sohmeng said, like it had ever been obvious. "We'll have to talk more with Hei first, of course. I want to make sure we're all happy with how we do this thing. But yeah. For as long as it makes sense—sure Ahn, I'll be your partner."

"You will?" Ahn felt his heart swell.

"No, I'm lying. *Yes* really, you big beautiful doofus."

Ahn looked down at Sohmeng, her face the perfect picture of smug satisfaction. He would enjoy this time for as long as he had it, no matter what may come. The unknown didn't have to be catastrophic; darkness didn't have to be dangerous. Sohmeng could be out of place and completely perfect, the same as his first love had been.

"Would you look at that," she said, "I went ahead and landed myself a *prince*, even if he is eleventh-born."

"*Prince* is just a story-word, isn't it?" he countered. "I'm just a man, really. Just lucky." He brought a hand to her cheek, leaning in carefully. "May I . . . ?"

Sohmeng rolled her eyes and grabbed him by the shirt. He made a noise of surprise as their lips abruptly met, grateful and laughing and lucky indeed.

Three

IT WAS QUIET WITHOUT Sohmeng around. This was expected—Sohmeng had always been very loud. Not loud in the unbearable way, the way that grates like when your elbow catches a rock, but loud like thunder. Or rushing water, the insistent push of rapids when they're building momentum, or soup on the edge of boiling. Sohmeng was loud in a way that resonated in the parts of Hei that liked to be filled, and so they loved her.

They were considering this as they held their hand still in one of the tributaries of the Ãotul River, waiting for minnows to come nibble their fingers. The sun was leaning into the later part of the afternoon, shifting the shadows on the ground.

During their time in the northwestern parts of Eiji, Hei had not found it hard to wait while Sohmeng and Ahnschen were stuck inside Nona Fahang. They enjoyed Sohmeng's company, but it was restful to have time with the family, and with themself. To not be expected to speak.

Hei had not spoken a single human word in four days,

and their shoulders were soft beneath their ears.

This is what they liked to do instead of speak hmunpa: lie against Mama and hum, chase around the hatchlings to teach them to be fast, climb things, stack stones in interesting locations, think. They were thinking about a lot these days, lots of uncomfortable things. Everyone had finally left Nona Fahang, but then they'd had to come back to Ateng. And soon, north.

North to what? To Ahnschen's Ólawen, for a polite conversation? Hei had their doubts that that would work out.

And if they were right, Sohmeng and Ahn would be onto a new strategy—one that most likely involved finding more human allies. That idea made Hei's head ache. If not for Sohmeng, they never would have considered engaging with any hmun ever again.

They were still working out how to even manage traveling with the Fahangpa who had joined their expedition. Polha Hiwei, Eakang Minhal, Mochaka Tang, Pangãe Ãofe. Hei had approved them all as sãoni riders, and they were showing themselves to be respectful and competent enough, but they were still humans. Still new. It helped, at least, that Hei didn't know what they were saying half the time. This was likely something that would have made Sohmeng crazy, but for Hei, the ability to tune out the party's Dulpongpa made their near-constant talking bearable. They did not mind being left out in this way; if anything important was happening, Sohmeng would tell them.

And Ahnschen, he would tell them too, wouldn't he?

Hei frowned. They needed to adjust to that, to the idea

that Ahnschen might have things to say that they wanted to hear. They spread their fingers in the river water, let the coolness brush the spaces between them. A lone, brave minnow investigated the edge of their fingernail, then darted away.

Hei wanted to hear more than they would like to admit.

Where Sohmeng was direct in a way that was comfortable, a way like the sãoni were direct, Ahnschen was confusing. He made Hei feel like they didn't know where to put themself. It frightened them even now, watching the way he stumbled through Eiji. Clueless, helpless, like a hatchling fresh out of the egg. He had his sword, yes, but without the sword? Just a boy, soft and smiling.

Eiji didn't need you to smile. Eiji needed respect, and understanding. Hei could see that Ahn was trying to understand Eiji, but he didn't know its beating heart. He was not from here, and was only beginning to know the effort it would take to cultivate a relationship with this new ecosystem.

The minnow returned, nipping at Hei's knuckle. They watched it closely, and they thought some more.

How could someone be so dangerous, and so much the opposite at the same time? What were they supposed to do when the threat that Ahnschen posed seemed to shift depending on the light?

They trusted him with Sohmeng; they had told him as much. Ahnschen struck Hei as someone who knew how to be very good to other human people. The right words, the right movements, a nice voice for laughing. Warm hands. If he had not been aligned with the Empire, the people of Nona Fahang might very well have liked him from the start.

The Empire. Qiao Sidh.

Hei had spent a long time running their thoughts around the word *empire*. Was it more like a mound of fire ants, pungent and stacked high and proud? Or more like a system of fungus, a mycelial underworld that could go unnoticed even as it set its intent miles and miles across the land? Sometimes Hei wanted to ask. Other times they thought it best not to, felt a quaver in their chest when they began to imagine so many new people in the rainforest, clueless as Ahnschen and without his right words.

Behind them, Green Bites called for Singing Violet, who answered with the friendly annoyance of established mates. There would probably be eggs soon, and hopefully more healthy hatchlings out of them. With things as they were, every member added to the colony was a good thing. This was true of many creatures right now: not just the sãoni, but the yellowbills that roosted in Ateng, and the mossy oaks in the north, the ones the invasion had razed. Those trees had probably been rooted there for centuries, and now they were gone. It took such a long time to grow a creature, and no time at all to cut it down.

Hei huffed an exhale through their nose, gently shooed the minnows from their fingers, and stood, shaking out the parts of their body that had gone stiff from a long time crouching. No more thinking of Qiao Sidh today.

They wandered through the copse the sãoni had settled in, saying their greetings as they went. The sãoni Ahnschen had named Qøngem was pleased to receive a round of chin scratches, but the other, Sølshend, warned Hei off with an irritated thump of her tail. Hei did not take this personally. There had been some little dramas since they arrived: arguments between would-be mates, territorial spats. The sãoni were perplexed and discomfited by being led around, being asked to stay still for no reason they could see. A few had tried to wander off, and when it looked like nothing Hei did was going to make them listen, they'd tried one of Ahnschen's gestures alongside their snarl. It worked, and Hei was left unsettled for the rest of the day.

The way Mama's colony communicated had transformed. It was different from any other sãoni in the rainforest. It likely wasn't something that could be undone.

But for all it troubled Hei, Mama didn't seem to mind. She had always been strong-willed, as any alpha should be, but she was taking this change in stride. Far better than Hei had expected, given how many changes had been asked of her already.

Shortly after the humans ascended the mountains, Mama had settled down under a pair of silkflower trees and stayed there. Chin rested on her fore-legs, she watched the days pass with a quiet huff or two. When Hei asked things of her, she mostly conceded.

Now, they sat beside her, frowning, and stroked along her cheeks.

Okay?

Okay.

Mama, okay?

Food.

Hei brought food. They had caught some wild birds and set them high in a tree so they'd have a chance at preparing them later. That was one of many inconveniences of the human body—it didn't do so well swallowing things raw and whole.

They passed one of the carcasses to Mama, who chewed briefly before gulping it down. Hei tucked in beside her, listening to her breathe, trying to match their own breathing to the rhythm. Despite the sãoni having a higher lung capacity, it wasn't very hard. They had done it many times before. Over the years Mama's breathing had begun to rattle more, her scales growing dull like clouds veiling a sunny day. But she was still Mama.

A face came to Hei's mind. Grandmother Nor.

They squinted through the canopy at the outline of the mountains, looming like the crest of some ancient, patient predator. *Ateng.* Did everyone feel safe there, high above? Hei never had. The cave systems had been home, but they hadn't been safe. No one feels safe when they're a secret, Hei thought. But they also didn't know that many other secret people. They would have to ask Sohmeng to confirm.

Sohmeng. They missed Sohmeng.

The breath of the sun caught behind their ears. It was the mid-afternoon wind, the one that came when Chehangma's heat finally broke through the canopy, pushing the cool air up and away. Today, the wind carried the smell of overripe fruit, preparing to fall from the vine.

Stay, Mama.

Mama did not seem disinclined to oblige. Hei nudged her forehead one more time with theirs, then stood to prepare a shelter. This was a new habit; in the three years they had travelled with the sãoni, Eiji had always provided plenty of cover, a cavern angled away from the rain or a burrow Hei could snuggle into after their brother had eaten its former occupants. It had always seemed silly, pointless, to spend an evening dragging sticks and leaves into a lean-to, just to leave it behind in the morning. The colony did not build things, and Hei was part of the colony.

But this had changed with Sohmeng and Ahnschen around. The first time had been during a tremendous thunderstorm heavy enough to soak through the canopy; the second had been when they passed through an area swarmed with stinging caterpillars, and one dropped off a leaf onto Sohmeng. Hei could not quite remember when it became an everyday occurrence, but it had, a ritual they performed to give Ahnschen and Sohmeng their own small human space. It was an illusion, of course. The sãoni could investigate any time they wanted—anything could, if it were brave enough. But it made them feel safer, and that made Hei feel calm in turn.

Sohmeng and Ahnschen were not here, but Hei built the shelter anyway. They told themself this was in case they returned this evening; they had no way of knowing how long the humans would stay in Ateng before making the descent. It was good to be prepared.

And if the humans didn't return tonight...perhaps Hei could use the shelter themself. Maybe. The only caves nearby were the ones leading to Ateng, and they never wished to set foot in them again. Not for a typhoon, not for anything. It would be nice to feel protected. They might even take off their sãoni leathers and let the delicate air touch their skin.

Hei spent the afternoon doing this human thing, without a human in sight. Their family did not mind, and so they tried not to mind either.

Four

"COULD I ASK YOU something, Sohmeng?"

Sohmeng was fixing one of Grandmother Mi's dresses; the woman's fingers had gotten shakier since they were last together. She looked up from her sewing to see a frowning Viunwei. "What's up?"

Tentatively, her brother took a seat beside her. Despite his wedding having only been a few days ago, he was spending most of his time with Tonão and Sohmeng. Jinho said he didn't mind—they had the rest of their lives together, and his family's return was nothing short of a miracle. Still, Viunwei didn't seem to know what to do with Sohmeng. His awkward, frantic bursts of affection were sincere, but they also felt unnatural.

No matter how grateful they were to see each other, their relationship had been strained before the fall. Even if the two of them wanted to get closer, neither was sure where to start.

"I was wondering about. You know—" Viunwei gestured in a general down-facing direction. It took him a moment to gather the word, to gather himself. "Eiji."

"What were you wondering?"

"Is it . . . " Viunwei hesitated. "Was it alright?"

"Um." Sohmeng didn't know what *alright* meant in this context. She wasn't sure if Viunwei did either. "Yes? I mean, it's the rainforest. It's different from up here."

"I—I figured. There are all sorts of insects, and poisonous plants. And the rain, it can come down fast, you could break an ankle and then the climb up would be awful." Viunwei was speaking quickly, using words that Sohmeng remembered from their childhood. Their mother's words, getting them scared and riled up before bed. When their eyes were wide as a pair of Chisong moons, she would grin and say: *I know you'll love it as much as I do!*

Lahni Par had dreamed of bringing her children into Eiji when they were old enough to safely make the journey. Sohmeng had pleaded to go more often than Viunwei, but Viunwei had asked for detailed reports of each and every journey. That was how he showed his wonder. Sometimes, they would play rainforest together, drawing giant leaves on the walls in chalk and running from imaginary animals.

"All of that's true, yeah." Sohmeng put down the sewing, looking at her brother properly. He was a married man and a dedicated member of their community, newly inducted into leadership even, but he had never set foot on the forest floor. It wasn't a given that he ever would. "Eiji will eat you up and spit you out if it wants to. That's why you need a good guide."

"Like Mom and Dad." Before Sohmeng could agree, Viunwei's face suddenly scrunched in a pained expression that he tried to cover with his hand.

"Hey—" Sohmeng scootched closer, wrapping an arm around him.

She was getting a lot of practice being present with people who were hurting. The people of Ateng were heartened to see the Sky Bridge on its way to repair, and relieved to have answers about the tumultuous change in the ecosystem, but they were grieving, too. Grieving the batengmun, the finality of it all. It had been a hard few years. Maybe they were only feeling things fully now that some closure had emerged. Maybe that was always how it was going to happen.

It didn't look like the danger of the Empire had really landed for them yet. Maybe it didn't feel so pressing, since Qiao Sidh was currently on the opposite side of Gãepongwei from Ateng. Maybe it was that one of the two generals of this apparently threatening presence had shot the arrow that began the reconstruction of the Sky Bridge. Maybe it was just that they could only process so much at once.

Part of her wanted to shake them, to get people worried so they wouldn't be caught unawares. But that wasn't fair, that was her own fear talking, and good choices were hard to make when people were all wound up.

Sohmeng rubbed Viunwei's back, thinking of how calmly Hei would hold her hands when she panicked. She'd picked up that skill from them. "I have a really good guide."

"Do you?" he asked, his voice strained.

"I do. They were the one who found me, after I fell off the mountain like an inconsiderate jerk." She rested her cheek against his bony shoulder as he made a predictably

Viunwei sound of horror. They were opposites in so many ways; her body was soft where his was sharp, short where he was tall. She was warm where he was cold, and brusque where he was sensitive. But strangely, the more she got to know herself, the more her brother began to make sense. "Their name is Hei. I wish you could meet them, but they're more comfortable on the ground. Dad likes them though. And so do I. We're sort of a thing."

Viunwei let out a hoarse laugh. "Does that Ahnschen know about this?"

Sohmeng groaned. Viunwei, being Viunwei, had taken it upon himself to approach Ahn a couple days after the wedding and demand to know his intentions with Sohmeng. Ahn had taken it incredibly gracefully, but Sohmeng could have died. "Yeah, he does. It's fine."

Viunwei shook his head, mumbling to himself. "You're unbelievable."

"What's *that* supposed to mean?"

He turned to look at her properly, disbelief all over his face. "You demand your way into a new role, nearly *die* for it, meet a sãoni-riding stranger in the woods who you take as a partner, reveal a plot for the hmun network to be overtaken by a foreign empire, take *another* partner who is the prince of that empire, and repair the Sky Bridge, all in what, a matter of months?" He laughed again, and for a moment Sohmeng bristled, but she realized soon that he wasn't making fun of her. "I should have listened to you a long time ago."

Now that was unexpected.

"...say more on that?" Sohmeng asked, trying not to sound too hopeful.

Viunwei sighed, looking up at a skylight in the mountain, where a wispy beam of sun caught the glittering minerals in the stone around them. The early morning mist of the cave's microclimate had settled into the moss so that it twinkled. Sohmeng had nearly forgotten what days like this felt like.

"My Tengmunji was frightening," Viunwei said, and he sounded tired. "Me and the other batengmun kar—there was tension between us, on how our new community should be managed. We all went in so sure of ourselves, so close to one another. But things went wrong. Normal adult things, in retrospect. Relationship problems, people getting sick. But no adults were there to help, and no matter how big the mountain was, it was like we couldn't get away from each other. It was suffocating."

Sohmeng frowned. This had always been the part of Tengmunji that she had looked forward to: the chance to work things out in their own way.

"It was a long two years. We found a way to manage it, but by the end—we weren't friends anymore, Sohmeng. We had our small groups, but the community we began with? It was fractured. It still is."

Sohmeng shook her head. "This doesn't make sense. You all came back and it was a success, I never saw any of you fight—"

"We made an agreement. All of us. We kept our Tengmunji in the mountain we'd had it in, and went home to Sodão Dangde, and we behaved like adults." He paused for a moment. "It was difficult, but we were glad to be out of there. I always worried that it would be harder when we came back to this mountain, to where it all happened.

But then I figured it would only be another two years, and then we'd return again. We could bear that much."

"...it must have been scary when the bridge fell, then. For a lot of reasons."

Viunwei nodded, his mouth a grim line. "Watching you here, so eager to go through what I did—it made me angry, Sohmeng. It made me scared. You're a pain, you know? A real pain, you've always been."

"Thanks, Viunwei."

"But you're my sister, and you've got spirit. I didn't want to see that broken down. I didn't want you to be disappointed any more than you already were, seeing how different I'd become."

Sohmeng couldn't deny that that had been true. She missed the person her brother had been before; she hadn't understood where his transformation had come from. Truthfully, if it hadn't been for Hei's story of their own Tengmunji, she still might not understand. It was easy to long for something when you didn't have to face its ugly realities.

"So...what does this have to do with how you need to listen to me more? I seem to remember you saying something about that."

"Not my exact words, but—sure." Viunwei rolled his eyes, but he was smiling. Sohmeng had accused him of brooding and sulking a thousand times over the years. It twisted her belly with guilt; he could be sulky, sure, but also maybe he was just sad sometimes. "You were right to want to be an adult. To not want to be stuck in the same place, having the same arguments. I was trying to protect you, but I was hurting you." He was getting choked up again, and this time Sohmeng's own throat tightened. "I'm sorry, Sohmeng."

"Me too," she said, and meant it. "We're okay, yeah?"

Viunwei exhaled heavily. "Yeah. We're okay."

They sat together for a while, feeling the heavy cloak of old hurt trying to slip off their backs. It was a little uncomfortable, but a relief too. A new thing that didn't have to be scary.

"When you go back down to Eiji," Viunwei said, "you'll be careful, right? I know you said you'd come back to visit while you work on this whole . . . plan. But—"

He made a face, and Sohmeng could see everything he didn't want to say aloud. She didn't really *want* him to say it. It was painful to imagine. Not because she was super scared of dying, not more than anyone else was, but because she didn't want to imagine him dealing with it a second time. Her family had been through enough.

"I will," she said with a firm nod. "As long as you take care of Dad."

The decision had been made shortly after the wedding— under the Ãofe phase, which lended strength to difficult decisions. After three years away, Tonão Sol would be staying with his mother, son, and new son-in-law in Ateng.

"What about your family in Nona Fahang?" Sohmeng had asked despite herself. Seeing her father back in the mountains was a comfort, but she also knew that home had become more than one place for him.

"Jaea and Pim know. We'd discussed the possibility before I left, what it would mean for us as a family." Tonão had sighed. "It's only a goodbye for now. I intend on traveling between Ateng and Nona Fahang—once the bridge is built, we'll be able to use a safer route. It's hard, especially with Kuei being so young. But . . . I have family here, too. I can't choose."

With her lives above and below, Sohmeng knew how that felt. In Eiji, Sohmeng got to be the fullest version of herself: to be fearless and silly, to speak Sãonipa and run amok with Hei. But Ateng was her first home. She had been born in these mountains, raised on the mineral taste of the water, her voice echoing from her very first words. It was the origin of all of her shame and her pride. It housed the people who would do anything for her *and* the people who rejected her. Who would have cast her out.

The cruel parts of Ateng's culture had been enough for Hei to turn their back on it for good, and Sohmeng didn't think there was anything wrong with that choice. But she wanted to make room for the complicated parts of loving a place that didn't know what to do with her. She wanted to try, even if it meant continuing to hide being Minhal.

That got a lot more difficult when she had to watch Eakang doing the same thing.

Eakang Minhal moved through Ateng under the guise of being Chisong, curious as ever but quieter too. They did a lot of watching and listening, but were reluctant to speak even with translators available. It gave everyone a subdued impression of Eakang that felt wrong to Sohmeng.

When she found a moment for them both to slip away, she took Eakang on a walk deeper into the cave system, where the mushrooms used to grow thickest before they were overharvested. Where Hei hid when they were a kid.

"Hey," she said, lowering her voice to avoid catching any echoes. "I just wanted to say sorry."

"Sorry? How come?"

Sohmeng's stomach twisted. She braced herself, trying to explain the obvious. "I said we'd both be Minhals together, and then I fumbled it. That wasn't cool of me, and now you have to do this whole Chisong thing, and . . . yeah, I'm sorry."

Eakang slowed their pace, frowning. "That's really not something you need to apologize for."

Sohmeng didn't know what to make of that. Growing up, these conversations had typically gone in the opposite direction, with people explaining that she wasn't sorry *enough.*

"I'm serious," Eakang continued, running their fingers along one of the veins of wovenstone. "I don't need that apology. Sure, it's strange going by Chisong, but it's not hurting me."

"But phase-mates stick together," Sohmeng said uncomfortably. "Or whatever."

"But it's different." Eakang wasn't deterred in the slightest. It was like they had absorbed all of the confidence that Sohmeng had lost over the past few days. "I'm not Chisong, but I might as well be with how different our lives have been. Being Minhal was always easy for me—it *is* easy, even now. So it's not a big deal for me to pretend, especially when I'm leaving in a couple days anyway. They can't make me hãokar about it."

"It's not like I'm sticking around either."

"But you want to come *back,* right?" Eakang asked, though they seemed to know the answer before Sohmeng nodded. "Claiming Minhal here would change everything for you. That's a *big* choice, and it has nothing to do with me.

When you introduce yourself as Sohmeng Minhal in Ateng, you should do it for you."

When. Sohmeng wanted very badly for it to be a *when*, not an *if.* But it was true—that reclamation would transform the shape of her entire life. Was she ready for the consequences that might follow? She wasn't sure. Maybe not yet.

"I guess I thought I was braver," Sohmeng admitted, and wished she didn't sound so vulnerable.

"You're one of the bravest people I've ever met," Eakang Minhal insisted. "And you're smart. If it feels like telling the Grand Ones the truth would be a bad decision right now, don't do it. The gods won't mind, and neither will anyone else who cares about you. You can always be Minhal with me in Nona Fahang."

When Sohmeng had first met Eakang, that very sentiment had grated on her. It was earnest and kind, and she couldn't tolerate it. After being told over and over again that she was a bad influence in Ateng, after she had lost her right to be with her age-mates, Sohmeng hadn't known what to do with someone who was so enthusiastic about being her friend. Especially *because* she was Minhal.

Her heroics with the Sky Bridge had earned her back the privilege of speaking to her age-mates (that or the Grand Ones' rules didn't apply to someone who'd come back from the dead) and the rest of Ateng was welcoming her back into the community at large, which was a thing she had yearned for literally for years. And yet, if the hmun found out she was Minhal, she knew it would all be taken away again.

But there were people who had been on her side since the beginning, and Eakang was one of them. Sohmeng didn't need to prove anything to them. She didn't have any secrets that could make them cast her out.

"Thank you, Eakang." As Sohmeng spoke, some unknown tension left her body. She wondered how long she had been carrying it for. "I really, really appreciate it."

After ten days in Ateng, Sohmeng knew that it was time to leave. She could only expect Hei to keep Mama and the colony in one place for so long, and General Ólawen was waiting for them up north. Her time with Viunwei and Grandmother Mi had been special, especially with her father having returned home, but Ateng was still Ateng, and Sohmeng knew deep down that she would only ever return to it as a visitor. She was closing the door to a future that wouldn't be hers.

It was bittersweet when she was summoned to Chehangma's Gate with the rest of the traveling party for a farewell from the Grand Ones. Even though Tonão would be staying in Ateng, he joined them, his hand in Sohmeng's. Beneath the holy skylight, Ama and Chehang were respectively waxing and waning gibbous under the Hiun phase.

"Please give all of our gratitude to the people of Nona Fahang," Grand One Hiun said emphatically to Polha, Mochaka, Pangãe, and Eakang. "We have gifts to send, but no thanks is truly adequate for what your hmun has done for Ateng."

"*All in harmony.*" Polha bowed her head as she quoted the second half of the saying. "It's good to be neighbours, Grand One."

"We wish all of you a fruitful journey north," added Grand One Chisong. "Thank you for all you have done for Gãepongwei so far, and for what you continue to do now. If there's any way we can be of service, you know where to find us."

"In Sodão Dangde," Grandmother Mi said happily, "not too long from now at all!"

Grand One Chisong smiled brightly, their moon tattoos rising on the apples of their cheeks. They were the youngest Grand One in Ateng, the person who had heard out Sohmeng's plea to be allowed a transitional job. They had called for the vote that gave her the opportunity to make the mistake that would reshape her life for the better. If they had been alone together, Sohmeng might have thanked them for it.

"Well," Grand One Hiun said, "if there isn't anything else—"

Tonão cleared his throat as footsteps began echoing from the walkway down to the Gate. Trying to figure out who in their right mind would come barreling into a meeting with the Grand Ones, Sohmeng looked over her shoulder and saw—

"Viunwei?" Sohmeng blinked a few times, doubting her own eyes. For all the nostalgic *oh how things change and yet remain ever the same!* thoughts she'd been having, she didn't expect to summon her brother again. As far as she knew, he didn't have any plans to thwart or complaints to lodge.

"Ah!" said Grandmother Mi. "Just in time."

"I'm so sorry for running late," Viunwei said, bowing furiously as he tried to catch his breath. "My sincerest apologies—have I missed it?"

"We were about to get started," said Tonão.

Sohmeng looked at her family members, bewildered. "Missed *what?*"

Slowly, Grandmother Mi rose to standing, steadying herself on the edge of her chair. She looked around the circle of her fellow Grand Ones, and though she was grinning same as ever, Sohmeng saw that she was quite serious.

"Mi, what is this?" asked Grand One Hiun.

"Don't tell us you're going with them," cackled Grandmother Dongi.

Grandmother Mi waved off the joke with a chuckle of her own. "My family has come today to make a request of the Grand Ones. I speak to you now as Euna Mi, mother to Tonão and grandmother to Sohmeng and Viunwei."

Tonão stepped forward, his son beside him. Sohmeng looked at the rest of the party, who were as confused as she was. It was only her family who seemed to be in on whatever this was about. Tonão took a deep breath, lifting his chin as he spoke. His quiet voice resonated in the open space, commanding attention. Requesting respect.

"I would like to discuss the matter of my daughter's Tengmunji," said Tonão Sol, and Sohmeng's heart stopped. "I know I have been gone for some time now, and I am biased, but I believe she is overdue to be recognized as an adult."

Sohmeng waited for him to be interrupted, to be shot down the same way she had been time and time again, but no protest came. Instead, Grand One Hiun gestured for him to continue.

"Through circumstances outside of her control," Tonão said, "Sohmeng was denied the opportunity to complete this rite of passage. But since entering Eiji, she has worked closely in community, displayed immense bravery and creativity in the face of challenges, and crossed from one side of the mountain to the other. I would say that she has more than earned the position of an adult."

"It wasn't traditional," Viunwei added, "but these aren't traditional times, Grand Ones. Sohmeng has made the most of what the gods have given her, and done more in one cycle than I did in the full two years of my Tengmunji. More than I can honestly say I've done in my whole life."

Sohmeng didn't know what to do, what to say. Part of her wondered if she should be making her case alongside them, but she couldn't find the words. She looked anxiously at her grandmother, but the woman was completely calm. Euna Mi had protected and advocated for Sohmeng for her entire life, and she was doing it again now.

"Frankly," said Grandmother Mi, cocking an eyebrow, "she's achieved more than some of *you* old farts ever have."

"Mom, *please!*" Tonão hissed, sounding very much like Viunwei.

"Oh come on," the woman exclaimed, "she fixed the Sky Bridge!"

Sohmeng's face burned as she turned her gaze to the rest of the people who had helped her. She didn't want them to think she was getting sole credit for the work they had done together. But no one looked upset. Ahn and Eakang were holding hands and watching intently; they both seemed to be struggling to hold back their own commentary.

"What do you think, Sohmeng Par?" asked Grand One

Hiun. Above them all, the light shifted. "Do you feel as though you have done the work required to enter adulthood?"

Sohmeng remembered every moment she had fought for herself in this very spot. Every plea, every demand, every argument against the unfairness of what was outside of her control. She had craved her adulthood from the moment it had first been denied her, even when she *hadn't* yet earned it. She wanted her life to be her own.

And now, it was. Whether or not the Grand Ones validated her, Sohmeng had seen herself as an adult for some time now. Their approval wouldn't change what she knew to be true.

But they were asking, and so she told them.

"Yes," Sohmeng said, "I do."

"How about we put it to a vote?" suggested Grand One Chisong. They were already lifting their cup of mountain marrow in a *yes*, and they weren't the only one. It didn't take long to realize what the outcome would be.

Beside her, Viunwei let out an exhale. Sohmeng looked up at him, searching his expression for the embarrassment she was so used to, that wincing look whenever she was too much. He had always insisted she not draw so much attention to herself. But there was no shame here. Only care, and relief.

"You did it, Soh," he said softly. He held out his hand.

She took it.

FIVE

HEI WAS RUBBING MAMA'S LEGS when they heard the travelling party coming down through the cave system of Sodão Dangde. They closed their eyes, identifying one voice at a time: Sohmeng, Ahnschen, Polha Hiwei, Pangãe Ãofe, Eakang Minhal, Mochaka Tang. It wasn't so different, distinguishing human voices from tracking the calls of animals. Hei did not hear Tonão, but that was as they had expected. They hoped his leg hadn't pained him too much during the climb.

Mama rumbled quietly, but stayed where she was. She hadn't moved from her spot in the past few days, and Hei had taken to bringing her food, trying to convince her to at least nibble at it. She hadn't so much as sniffed it today.

Stay, Mama.

Hei nuzzled against her forehead before approaching the mountain's trade entrance. They poked at their teeth with their tongue, swallowed a few times as they readied themself to be with others. Luckily, Sohmeng was typically happy to lead the talking.

"Oh thank the *gods!*" she exclaimed, throwing her arms around Hei. She released them and spun around, looking at the sãoni. "They actually stayed put?"

Hei nodded. "They did."

"All of them?"

"All."

Sohmeng hooted and ran over to Mama, rubbing her belly and cooing. "What would we do without you Mama? You're a role model to the lizard community, you really are."

The sãoni let out another low sound, raising one leg slightly to give Sohmeng a better angle. Hei's head felt fuzzy. They stood quietly, watching Sohmeng, holding onto the image, trying to make it as familiar as sunrise. To keep it.

The others came wandering over, and the muscles of Hei's back tensed in preparation. They were still getting their voice back on, which was harder when they were being observed by other people. Thankfully, everyone behaved as Sohmeng had instructed, greeting them without lingering. Hei addressed them with a nod.

If it was easier, if they weren't feeling heartsore and full of still water, they would have said something like: *I am grateful you returned from your excursion unharmed. I hope the people of Ateng were hospitable. Please do not speak to me right now unless you are Sohmeng. Or maybe—*

"Are you well, Hei?"

Ahnschen stood beside them, that careful smile on his face. He looked healthy, comfortable. Different from back in Nona Fahang, where his movements were shame-heavy. The hatchlings bounded over, climbing his legs, and he gathered the littlest into his arms with a grunt.

"Getting bigger," Hei eventually said, and when Ahn tilted his head in question, they nodded to the small sãoni. "Hatchlings."

"Ah!" Ahn laughed. One of the sãoni gnawed at his shirt, and he redirected it with a quick snap of his fingers. "Yes, the hatchlings. It's funny, for a moment I thought you were talking about yourself."

Hei's brow furrowed. "I am the same."

Hei knew that nothing was ever the same, really. Every day every living thing changed, shedding skin or scale or hair. Blood pumping, blood dying. Ingesting and expelling, absorbing what they needed and leaving the rest behind. But that wasn't what Ahn meant, and they weren't in the mood to try to explain themself in Dulpongpa.

They looked back at Sohmeng, who was kissing Mama on the head. That fuzziness rose in them again, and when Atengpa finally came out of their mouth, it felt clumsy.

They began with her name: "Sohmeng?"

She looked over at them, bright-eyed. "Mhm?"

"I need—" Hei hesitated, feeling very much like a child hiding in the caves. Listening, but not sure how to enter the space. "I need to talk to you please. Just us."

Sohmeng brushed herself off and headed over to them. Behind her, the party was organizing supplies donated by Ateng. That would be useful. They took her hand and began to walk away when an instinct struck them. It was uncomfortable, stumbling. But Hei always followed the compass in their core. It had never pointed them wrong before.

They touched Ahn's forearm, not quite looking at him. "You too, Ahnschen."

The three of them gathered a short distance away from camp, settling down in the same place they had spent the night before splitting up. Hei had counted ten days since then. They were on track to reach Ahn's sister by the next turn of Minhal, as promised.

Except perhaps they weren't.

"Mama is dying."

The words came out with clarity, and they hoped it would not be mistaken for coldness. Each day, the grief had found its way somewhere new. Hours of groaning with their face hidden, trying to shake out the feeling. Pressing their forehead into Mama's skin, pressing and pressing, struggling against all that they could not fix.

"*What?*" Sohmeng stepped forward. "But, no, that's not—"

Her words stumbled to a halt, her face twisting with dismay. Hei nodded, waiting for her to find what else she wanted to say.

Ahn spoke first, slow and careful. "How can you tell?"

Hei spoke in Atengpa, and Sohmeng quietly translated beneath them. "When we arrived, I thought she was tired. Learning new instructions, going off course. It's confusing for a sãoni, especially an older one." They looked up at the mountain, tracing the patterns of greenery as they played back the experience. "But then she lay down in her nice spot, and she stayed there. Her breathing is heavier. She isn't eating."

"Could she just be sick?" Sohmeng asked insistently. "Could we do something?"

"I don't know."

"Are you *sure* she's dying?"

"I don't know," Hei repeated, their jaw going tense

around the words. They watched a bird spread its wings, riding along the wind. "But *she* does. She's showing me."

Sohmeng's translation cut off, and she cursed. When Hei looked back at her, she had her palms over her eyes, and Ahn had placed his hand on her back, rubbing in circles. But he was watching Hei, a furrow in his brow, waiting for something.

"We will likely be late to your sister," Hei attempted, unsure if that was what he was looking for.

"That's fine," Ahn replied, and it sounded like his honest voice. The one that was rough like sand, but very soft as well. It was the voice of Ahn's that Hei preferred, so they listened. "Ólawen can wait."

Sohmeng nodded. After a moment, she wiped her tears, attempting to compose herself. "Yeah. Yeah, that doesn't matter, Hei. Are you—Hei, are you okay?"

They had worried she would ask that. It was such a *human* thing to ask. To search for information that they already knew the answer to. It was meant to be a kindness, Hei understood. Sohmeng had done it with them many times before, and sometimes it felt good to respond. To say it outloud, and show that they would like to be held, and spoken to gently.

It had not always been safe to do this. When they were small, they had needed to cry somewhere far away in the caves, so they would not be overheard. But they had asked Sohmeng and Ahnschen to come with them somewhere private, and both of them had seen Hei cry before.

"No," they said, their breath tumbling over itself. They wished it were storming again. "I am sad about my mother, and I am not okay."

"I'm sad too, Hei," Sohmeng said, and Ahn nodded. With one arm around Sohmeng, he opened the other for Hei, and they stepped into the embrace.

For a while they stood there in silence, and soon Hei noticed they were breathing all together. They listened to the breaths, felt the rise and fall of each of their chests. It swayed them, soothed them.

And so they prepared to say goodbye.

The rest of the party were equally shocked by the news, and saddened by it too. Despite the fact that their original plans had been so urgent, everyone slowed down. Together, they worked to do the only thing they could: make Mama comfortable.

The great sãoni did not move from her place beneath the tree, so that was where she remained as she was attended to. People took turns bringing her water to drink, which she accepted even though she was not eating. Sohmeng squeezed some fruit and mixed it in, which Mama lapped at contently. Inspired, Pangãe and Mochaka worked together to make juice for everyone, and they sat around the sãoni and enjoyed it together.

Hei rubbed Mama's legs, and soon Ahn joined in, and then the others, too. There were seven of them, one for each leg and one for her chin, and they all massaged together while she rumbled so loudly that the other sãoni came over to investigate. At one point, Green Bites got so jealous that Sohmeng had to give him a massage too so he'd stop storming around.

"I think she likes the company," Sohmeng said one night, holding Hei close. "Isn't that something? There she goes adopting us again."

On the third day, Eakang came to Hei and asked if it would be alright to sing some goodbye songs. When Hei agreed, Eakang sat by the sãoni's side, stroking her head spines and singing in Fahangpa with their bright young voice.

Goodbye to my friend, safe journeys ahead!
Run fast, fly well, remember us—
We'll sing for you again.

The others who knew the song joined in, and offered more after that. Some of the melodies were upbeat, others very sorrowful. Mama seemed to like them all, and so Hei let the singing continue. It was like nothing they had ever experienced before.

"Ahnschen's got a few musical gifts of his own," Polha suggested as she built a campfire. "Do they sing goodbye songs in Qiao Sidh?"

"We do," Ahn said, and so he sang a few of them too, his fingers moving strangely against his leg in the absence of an instrument. Polha had been right about his voice. It was clean like cold water and sturdy as the soul of a tree. Hei had to put their head on their knees to listen.

In Ateng, Sohmeng said, they mostly told stories. "Stories about everything we like about the person, good memories. We want to share everything that we loved about them, ideally before they go. But we do it after, too. They can hear us in the stars either way, right?"

"Is that where your people go when they die?" Ahnschen asked.

"Yup. They get right up close to the gods." Sohmeng looked up at the sky. Both moons were out tonight, and they looked right back down at her. "It's probably a pretty good view."

Hei had never heard of this before, but they liked the idea of seeing the rainforest from above. One by one, the humans in the colony shared their funeral rites, and Mama received them.

The other sãoni seemed to know what was going on. For the most part, the colony had gone quiet, watching and waiting, keeping vigil. Occasionally, they would come over to sniff at Mama, who growled at them and thumped her tail. The hatchlings' presence didn't bother her as much; she allowed them to scuttle around her until they got bored.

"How do you think they know?" Sohmeng asked, sitting by Singing Violet.

It was Ahnschen who responded. "Many animals do. They behave differently before they die. If they live in community, they can sense it in others, I believe."

"Death makes itself known," Hei agreed, thinking once more of Grandmother Nor. For all they had their doubts about the godseye, they wished privately that Sohmeng was right about her becoming a star. Maybe she and Mama could meet, when it was done.

Between goodbyes, the party was doing what they could to plan around their new circumstances. At first, they had been very perplexing about the whole thing, insisting that Hei didn't have to be a part of the conversation. This was ridiculous, since Hei knew the most about the sãoni. Plus, the idea of having "time to grieve" didn't make sense either. They would be grieving no matter what, but no one could sit around being sad all day.

Feelings changed. They went up and down, moving throughout Hei's body. Sometimes they were so heavy that Hei couldn't stand. Other times they were fast and light. It was all grief, but it was other things, too.

So they ignored the nervous looks people gave them, and they sat down to address the issues.

The first was Qiao Sidh, because it was always Qiao Sidh, because Qiao Sidh had gotten them into this in the first place. With the timing as it was, their Minhal deadline was getting tighter by the minute.

"I believe Ólawen would wait for a few days," Ahnschen said, tucking his silvertongue hair behind his ear. Hei's eyes flashed to the knucklebone there. "But not long."

"Nona Fahang has plans in place should we not arrive in time," said Polha Hiwei. "And the letter you left should help—no one could imitate your hand."

It had been good thinking on Ahnschen's part to leave something behind in Nona Fahang. Proof he had been there, and was alive, and requesting not to have the hmun burned down. Still, Hei had doubts that Ólawen would read the letter at all before attacking. Ahn did not say as much directly, but Hei suspected he felt the same.

Hei was sympathetic. It was difficult to have your family act in unexpected ways.

This was the second problem. With Mama gone, Hei had no idea who was going to assume the role of alpha.

"Fights happen," they had said during one of the group meetings, scratching their sãoni claw in the dirt while Sohmeng translated. "Colonies fracture and split off. When Mama won against Blacktooth, several of Blacktooth's sãoni joined our colony. Others answered the call of the new alpha and went to her. But with a natural death? I don't know. I've never seen it."

"Could there be a fight?" asked Mochaka warily.

"Maybe." The thought made Hei's stomach turn.

"It could also go to whoever is the next most dominant," Ahn suggested. "I've seen that with other animals. Could that be possible, Hei?"

"Maybe," they repeated, tense. "I don't *know*."

Sohmeng groaned, rubbing at her face. "If it's Green Bites, we're seriously *screwed*. I have no idea how we'll get him to listen to us."

From there, everything devolved into worries and speculation. Hei was exhausted. Everyone already knew there wasn't enough information to make a decision. Why were they continuing to spin in circles?

Compared to the human worrying, Hei found that the goodbye with Mama was not so complicated. Death was sad; death was a deep hurt. But it was also the way of things, and all around them. A part of the system, essential and inescapable.

And Mama was not trying to escape. She slowed and slowed, eventually refusing water as well as food.

Hei, she said one evening. *My baby.*

Yes, Mama?

My baby.

There was nothing more to be said after that. Hei cleaned up her claws until they shone and stroked her beautiful scales. Eakang and Sohmeng led everyone in gathering flowers and stones, which they arranged thoughtfully around the sãoni. She looked like a living piece of art, dignified and content, throat stripes glowing purple in the final hours before dawn.

Her breathing became heavier, interspersed with long

pauses. Hei lay down against her, listening to each deep fill of her lungs, each rattling release.

Stay, Mama, they thought, scrunching their eyes shut.

Go, Mama, they said instead in their sãoni voice. *Okay. Okay.*

When everything finally stopped, Hei was curled up against her in a bed of foliage, the glimmer of morning sun breaking through the mist. They sucked in the breath she would not, and let out a sob. It was heavy in their chest, and so they let it shake out. Big deep sobs, like the ones Mama had found them with.

They cried and they cried, and the humans with them cried too. One last goodbye song.

It did not take long before the rest of the colony realized what had happened. They broke their quietude, rising up to sniff at the circle of humans, blue tongues flicking out as they chirped and clicked and questioned.

Alpha? Alpha?

Alpha.

Hei sat up slowly, lifting their hood over their head. A few of the sãoni were interacting now, growling at one another with an emerging aggression. One of them, a larger and older male, stalked towards Green Bites, who was postured for a fight.

He snapped at the other male once, twice. After a moment, the sãoni ducked its head in concession. Green Bites bit down gently, walking past the others, who ducked their heads in submission as well. A claim was being made.

"Oh no," Sohmeng groaned. "Oh no, oh *no.*"

There were a few more challengers. One even had a brief wrestle with Green Bites, but it was quickly resolved, and without even much bloodshed.

Hei did what must be done. With a final press of their cheek to Mama's, they stepped forward. It was their brother who would be the alpha, and so they would accept him.

They met his eye, he who had been a hatchling alongside them. They dropped to their knees, lowered their head to the soft earth, and waited.

"Burning godseye," came Sohmeng's voice.

Nothing happened. Hei waited for a beat, and then another. When they finally raised their head, what they saw was Green Bites, chin low to the ground. His eyes were narrowed, his body still and patient. Waiting.

Alpha.

The colony was stretched out before Hei, ducked in submission.

Alpha, the sãoni said, one after another. Hei would have wondered if it was a mistake, but sãoni only ever said what they meant. Sãoni were honest, and earnest. They knew what they were asking for, and so Hei knew what they had to do.

They rested a palm on Green Bites' head and leaned down, biting his neck with their blunt human teeth. The bone did not so much as scratch his scales, but he accepted it nonetheless. The colony bowed lower, their voices overlapping, filling the silence of the copse with agreement and intention.

Hei. Alpha. Hei.

Behind them, the same name, attempted in the limited range of a human voice box. Hei turned to see Sohmeng, grinning with a pride that made Hei's ears go hot.

Ahnschen was the first to kneel, lowering himself the way Hei had to Green Bites. The other humans followed one by one, until Hei was the last person left upright in the party—in the whole *colony*. They delivered a bite first to each and every sãoni, and then to the humans, too. Each of them accepted the ritual with grace.

And then Hei turned to Mama, perfect and quiet on the forest floor. They knelt before her, pressing their forehead to hers, savouring this last moment as her child before they stepped into the role of her successor.

When Hei stood once more, their eyes were clear, their heart steady and true. The grief remained, but had changed yet again, evolving into something fresh. A lodestar in their chest.

"We leave at midday," Hei said, and the colony listened to their alpha.

Six

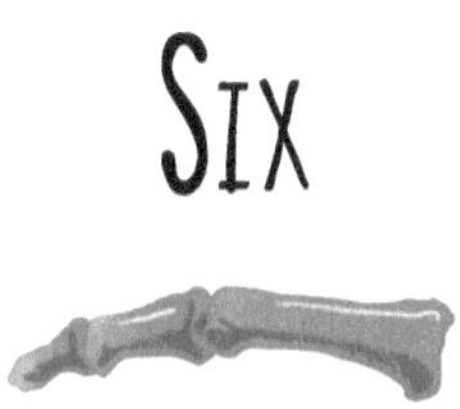

AHN HAD FELT IT BEFORE, the way loss could cleave open a new path. With the world so fundamentally changed, possibilities opened wide, whether you wanted them to or not.

When Mama was the alpha of the sãoni, the plan had been for the colony and its riders to travel as one up to the Qiao Sidhur camp on the northwestern coast. They would be following the rough direction of the migration route, with Hei trying to direct Mama and create urgency as best they could. Success wasn't impossible, but it certainly wasn't without its challenges; human or no, leaders didn't typically appreciate being ordered around.

But now, with Hei leading the colony, the situation was different. Hei was in control of where the sãoni went—how far could that control be stretched?

Ahn thought about this as they mounted their sãoni to leave Mama behind, and he was still thinking about it by the time they made camp that night.

"Are you the only rider that the sãoni would listen to?"

Ahn asked Hei as they foraged together for dinner.

"Sãoni follow the alpha. You know this."

"But if the alpha isn't around? Would they still follow your instructions without you there to enforce them?"

Hei gave him a long and doubtful look, but they didn't push back against some experimenting. If the sãoni would accept Hei's authority *and* let themselves be directed by human riders, it would be far easier to set up communication between the hmun. Better yet, it would make traveling much more efficient—and with Qiao Sidh at their door, time was of the essence.

For the next few days, the party attempted to combine Hei's new authority as the alpha with the training techniques that Ahn had been working on since Nona Fahang. They workshopped new calls that were meant to display rank among the humans, and tested how far the sãoni would be willing to roam before returning back to Hei for further instruction.

Despite the fact that Ahn had proposed it, he was nervous. Animals were not the same as humans—they did not follow a clear chain of command, especially when they split up. For that matter, even humans weren't always inclined to follow directions. Rebellions happened all the time.

But it didn't make sense to pass up the chance to try something new. So when Polha and Mochaka each went for a test run with their sãoni over a couple miles and returned unharmed, the new plan was made.

Eakang and Polha would travel up to Sorwei Chapal, a hmun in the western confluence of the Ãotul River. It was the next closest hmun to the Qiao Sidhur basecamp, after Kongkempei and Hosaisi; If the village did not yet know about the oncoming threat of the Empire, this was the opportunity to inform them and potentially brace for invasion. And if all went well after Ahn's meeting with Óla, they had a convenient rendezvous point.

Meanwhile, Pangãe Ãofe and Mochaka Tang would return to Nona Fahang with news of their excursion to Ateng. Slowly but surely, connections would open up between each of the hmun, uniting Gãepongwei once more.

"*No,*" Sohmeng said again, flicking Ahn on the arm. "Not reuniting us. Just opening up a conversation."

"Right," he said, "you're right, my mistake."

It was difficult, managing this culture clash. Every time he thought he'd wrapped his head around the concepts he was learning from his friends, he'd say something that betrayed a worldview aligned with the empire he'd grown up in.

Sohmeng was patient with him about it, insisting that that kind of relearning would take more than a couple months. But Ahn was frustrated. It was like his old thoughts couldn't keep up with his new intentions.

He tugged at his earpiece, wanting to ask Schenn for advice. But that was complicated, too. The more he sat with it, the more he was confronted with the uncomfortable reality that he had probably behaved with similar carelessness towards Schenn. The awkward questions about his home, the insistence that the Empire could offer him a good life. Schenn had had a good life before Ahn. Gurinn had had a good life before the Empire.

Ahn wanted badly to correct his wrongs, and the

wrongs of his family. But it was a big problem to solve, and he was only one person. He was grateful to have the traveling companions he did, who pushed him to be better while giving him grace when he made mistakes. It made it even more important to him to do right by them.

It had been a long time now since Ahn had traveled with only Hei and Sohmeng as companions. How cautious they had been back then, working their way towards discovering shared language, offering tentative reassurances that they would let the other live. The three of them had all come so far, working their way into a careful dynamic which was evolving even now.

One afternoon, Ahn and Sohmeng went to Hei about their potential partnership. Despite the fact that it had been Hei who demanded that he be honest with Sohmeng about his feelings, he couldn't help his nerves.

"So is that okay with you?" Sohmeng asked, nudging her foot against Hei's. "I know you guys talked about it, and you and I have talked about all the goofy looks he was giving me—Ahn, don't make that face, it's true—but I want to check that you're sure."

Hei looked between the two of them, considering. After a moment, they said, "Room for everyone. But also…" They glanced to Sohmeng, switching over to Atengpa. Now that they were no longer with everyone from Nona Fahang, Hei was much more inclined to speak their mind and allow Sohmeng to translate when necessary. "But I do not want it to be all three of us all the time. I still want time with Sohmeng on my own."

"Yeah, I'd like that too," Sohmeng said, then clarified to Ahn, "I'm not trying to leave you out or anything!

I just, y'know, lizard time is important to me. I don't want everything to suddenly change."

Hei chirped judiciously in agreement.

"I wouldn't want to get in the way of your time together," Ahn said. One of the hatchlings crawled over, plonking its chubby head in his lap. "It's actually uncommon for people to have multiple committed partners where I'm from—which seems a bit restrictive, the more I think about it? But, yes, your relationship to each other is important to me. It deserves space."

"I want my space too," Hei said. "By myself."

"Take the whole jungle if you want," Sohmeng said with a grin. "You make the rules around these parts." Ahn couldn't help but smile as Hei puffed up their chest. "What about you two? Do you want any time alone together?"

Hei frowned and chirped at the same time Ahn asked, "Us?"

"I mean, yeah?" Her grin turned sly. "Unless you're both here to take turns spoiling *me*. No arguments about that."

Ahn wasn't sure what to say. While those weren't the exact words he would have used, he'd assumed that he and Hei would both be separate partners to Sohmeng, and friends with one another. Because they were friends now, weren't they? At least, that was how Ahn felt.

Hei looked equally stumped. Their cheeks took on a pink tone as they eventually muttered, "Ahnschen is Ahnschen."

"Hei is ... Hei," Ahn replied. Simple though it was, the sentiment did feel right to him. Hei was Hei, an ongoing presence that he had grown fond of. Without Nona Fahang's wall between them, they were finally getting a chance to learn how it felt to be in each other's company. In many ways, it was still new.

In Ateng's mountain range, Ahn had promised Hei that he would be good to them. All they had asked for was the warmth of his body, and so he kept close. If he could be a campfire that Hei was content to snooze nearby, that would be more than enough for him.

"Your eloquence," Sohmeng said, looking between them both in wonder, "is *astonishing.*"

That night, curled up together under the stars, Ahn was the last one awake in the colony. The sãoni quietly rumbled and snored, throats dimly illuminating the space like giant fireflies. Sohmeng was happily squished between Ahn and Hei, spoiled exactly as she had asked. They held her together, and Ahn watched the rise and fall of Hei's ribs as they slept.

He marveled in his good fortune. After fleeing Kongkempei, when he realized that he was well and truly lost in the rainforest, terror had struck him in all directions. What would he eat? Would he be able to protect himself from predators? What would he do without any other *people* around?

These fears made perfect sense; humans were social creatures. Moving in numbers made things safer. But if Ahn was being honest with himself, it wasn't just about physical safety. Embarrassing as it was to face, unlike Hei and Sohmeng, Ahn dreaded the idea of being by himself. Of being trapped in his own head.

Ahn had grown up surrounded by people. Family,

yes, but more than that he had attendants and servants and tutors and guards, a whole retinue designed to keep him occupied and cared for and catered to. During his time in the palace, he began most mornings with his attendants bringing him to the baths, and then to a massage. Even if he was not speaking, there were always people around. And when there were people, he was often inclined to speak, if only of light topics. The newer servants of the palace always seemed taken aback when he addressed them, or asked after their families and interests. He sent gifts for their children's birthdays, even attended a wedding or two. It broke some of the formality between the royalty and the common people, but Ahn was eleventh born. It didn't matter so much.

University gave him even more opportunities to keep himself busy with classes and clubs and parties. When he couldn't sleep, he didn't have to—there was always something happening late at night in Asgørindad. Sometimes he felt a frantic buzzing inside, a deep over-stimulation. But then he would go somewhere peaceful, and he would think of Schenn, and it would get worse.

Both then and now, being alone ached most when Ahn thought about Schenn. From the time that he claimed the Path of Conquest, he'd been told that he would never be alone again. To complete your Six-ing was to be bound in all things, even after death. Ahn still had obligations to Schenn's family, and attended events and holidays in his place, treating Schenn's parents with all the respect he showed to his own. When Ahn married, his spouse would marry Schenn too, with a whole portion of their wedding rituals dedicated to that part of the relationship. It was not a pact that ever ended.

Ahn wasn't thinking about wedding rituals with Sohmeng and Hei, but he knew that he needed to tell them about Schenn. They had entered into a partnership without the full picture, and that was wrong. It was disrespectful to everyone, perhaps Schenn most of all. He owed it to the three of them to find the courage to make introductions.

He spent most nights practicing in his head, trying to figure out how to broach the topic. A large part of him even looked forward to it, with the nervous anticipation of hoping friends would like each other. But whenever he tried to speak, his throat locked up and refused to let the words out. It was almost funny: all that training as a swordsman, and still his body wouldn't listen to him. If only he could bypass its defenses.

It happened, eventually. Though not how he would have liked.

It was while they were packing up from an afternoon rest with the sãoni. The colony had needed almost no time at all to adjust to Hei's leadership, and even though the wedding and Mama's passing had slowed them down, they were looking on track to arrive for Minhal. Sohmeng had been using this as an excuse to take her time whenever possible, which could be problematic when sundown was approaching. There was only so much time they had before the sãoni cooled down and got sleepy.

"We are being late," Hei said insistently, trying to nudge

Sohmeng along. This, of course, made her go slower.

"Hei come *on*," Sohmeng whined, literally digging her heels in. "I'm still getting the feeling back in my butt, this route has been so bumpy!"

"Cannot be late."

"Since when have you ever cared about being late? So much for the sacred pace of the natural world!"

Hei growled in exasperation, waving their arms in Ahn's general direction. Sohmeng turned to him with an exaggerated pout, crossing her arms.

"Aaaahn, tell Hei that an extra twenty minutes won't make your sister do *war*."

Ahn choked on his own spit.

Hei pressed their palms to their browbone. "Sohmeng."

"Tell Hei that rest is a necessary part of every war strategy." She looked pointedly at Hei. "He said that, he literally did."

"*Sohmeng.*"

Sohmeng put her hands on her hips, raising her voice with a grin. "Tell Hei that—"

Her drama was cut off by a sharp bite on the neck, and they both descended into their uniquely scrabbling sort of play. Biting and wrestling, yelling, laughing themselves hoarse. It made Ahn laugh too, made him watch them with helpless affection. He was doing what he could to learn how to play along, to see if he had a place in this particular dynamic.

Presently, Hei was on their back, hands and teeth clamped around Sohmeng's forearm while Sohmeng tried to smoosh their face into the ground. The sãoni were beginning to pay closer attention, a couple coming over to investigate what was going on between the alpha and their mate.

"Alright, alright," Ahn said, gently extricating them from one another. "Let's break it up."

Hei conceded with a sniff, rubbing where their cheek had been grabbed, but Sohmeng gave Ahn a dramatic look.

"You're just going to let them boss me around?" she demanded, shaking his arm. "You won't defend what's good and right?"

Ahn let himself be shaken, grinning. "And what would *good and right* be, Sohmeng?"

"The *right* to do whatever I want at all times!"

Hei snorted, but Ahn could see the way their mouth pressed into a smile, highlighting the distinct freckle on their upper lip. They were mostly a serious person, but Sohmeng relaxed them in a way that he could only aspire to.

"That is a very important thing," Ahn agreed, fixing her hair. "But I don't think I have a say in what you and Hei get up to."

Sohmeng threw her hands into the air, pacing around in a circle. "Unbelievable! I'm lucky enough to get two hunks by my side and they won't even fight for me!"

Hei squinted. "You told me to be nice."

"Like—like for fun I mean! Like *sports!* Feats of strength!"

"Do you do that in Ateng?" Ahn asked, surprised.

"I mean not me, but yeah," Sohmeng said, exasperated. "I'm talking about like in the stories. There's a whole chunk of the Polhmun Ão epic that's literally just a census of warriors, which is so freaking boring, but then they all beat each other up and it's basically one long poem and it's beautiful! I don't know, fighting's not stupid when it's pretend. Could I not have a *little* poem?"

Ahn hadn't expected this cultural overlap. Performative (and not-so-performative) duels were common in Qiao Sidh; with so many people on martial paths, combat was as much an art form as dancing. The idea of sparring was honestly something of a comfort. He glanced at Hei, expecting them to shoot down the idea, but they didn't appear to be averse to it.

"Do you want to . . . ?" Ahn asked slowly.

Hei shrugged, glancing from Ahn to an empty area amid the trees. Sohmeng let out a whoop and rushed over to find the best seat among the sãoni.

They lay down the rules together: no weapons, no true intent to harm, either stop at the first sight of blood or when someone concedes. Ahn was the one who proposed most of these, having fought multiple public duels in his life. For all that Sohmeng had demanded this duel for her honour, she looked a bit wide-eyed at how easy it was for him to build this game. It sat strangely with Ahn, how much of him she did not know.

"I fight like I have claws," Hei said matter-of-factly. "Even with no claws."

"I'll avoid them then, to be true to your form."

"No fighting like you have a fake sword," Hei clarified, looking at him seriously. "Looks ridiculous."

Ahn huffed a laugh of agreement, getting into position. Considering that their first meeting had been a genuine altercation, it spoke to their blossoming trust, that they were now doing this for sport.

"Okay," Sohmeng said, holding Singing Violet's tail across her lap. "Ready ... go!"

Ahn waited. Breath even, body poised. Hei did not immediately go on the offensive; they stalked around him, sãoni hood up. Ahn kept his expression neutral, counting back from three in his head.

Asá, hvøs, sammi—

He lunged.

He was choosing to go at a performer's pace, to spar with beauty instead of efficiency. That was the point of a public duel: to make it interesting. This also gave Hei, who had no martial education, room to respond.

Their fighting style was like nothing he had ever seen. Ahn had expected the clumsiness of someone who had not been trained in any discipline, but while Hei was not exactly polished, they knew how to be in their body. When Ahn swung at them, they didn't hesitate to duck, to sidestep. It appeared more instinct than choice, which nonetheless revealed a certain level of skill.

It was not a difficult match, but it brought Ahn's mind to an even, quiet space. He assessed his opponent as a near strike to their side earned him a hiss. They could dodge with minimal effort, but they struggled to land anything on him. Whereas Ahn settled the longer they went, Hei got more worked up—a common problem for passionate warriors. But it also made for a healthy competitiveness, which was admirable.

The conscious effort to hold back slipped from his mind, and still his body did as he asked it to. Perform, adjust, move like the gears of a clock, like the bent back of a dancer, like the whine of strings in an orchestra.

Sohmeng cheered from the sidelines and Ahn smiled.

When he swept Hei's legs with a kick, they yelped with surprise and tumbled to the ground. He supposed they hadn't fought many, or perhaps any, human people besides him. It was impressive, then, that they were holding their own like this.

"Sãoni have many legs, don't they?" he asked calmly, offering them a hand.

"And *teeth*," Hei replied, panting, and that was all of Ahn's warning before they grabbed his arm and yanked him to the ground.

Their bodies crashed into each other, and the sudden closeness set off alarms in Ahn's head. No one had fought with him this way, messy and reckless, since the academy. He tried to wrestle them down, but a bite to his shoulder distracted him long enough to get flipped.

So much of combat was about grace, tradition. Here was a partner who improvised, who fought dirty in the way of someone with a bunch of siblings and no other way to pass the time once the farm work was done. It was refreshing—it was *baffling*, left him breathless with joy.

He found himself pinned on his back. His partner, sweaty and smeared with dirt, leaning in close with a wicked grin. Ahn, dizzy and delighted.

Hei swiped their hand across his chest, an arc which followed the curve of his scar, the flash of terror and pain and instinct as his body split open—

Ha. Got you.

—and Ahn felt everything.

The way it stopped being a game, the way none of the

Masters cheered. This wasn't a seaside tussle, wasn't a practice session with wooden swords. This was wrong, it was all wrong, it was everything they had trained for.

Ahn had held back at first, but that only made his partner angry. It was a disrespect, and he reacted as though it was. Their bodies were locked in a flurry of frantic inevitability, and Ahn wanted to shout, wanted to speak, but they were not allowed to. And his throat was stuck anyway, stuck the whole time, they were both *trapped* here.

Schenn hit first blood, and some brief agony crossed his face before it hardened into resolve. He went in for the next strike, the blade poised to fall hard into the side of Ahn's neck and Ahn could do nothing but react. He reacted, he ducked and took his sword and drove it up until it pierced through something soft—

What if we didn't do it what if we didn't do it we don't have to do this please don't do this

—Sohmeng screamed.

The sound slammed Ahn back into himself. Hei was on the ground, Ahn with a knee pressed into their belly, a stick held high in his hand. He didn't even remember grabbing it.

Air flooded his lungs and he stumbled off of Hei. He couldn't breathe, couldn't think. He needed to get away from them, from all of them. He needed to flee, he needed to *die*—

His hands were tacky with blood, his chest was burning, the resinous incense was so thick in his nostrils that he felt sick. The sweet smell, how it mingled with the iron. The sound of Schenn beneath him, his breathing all wet and wrong.

His face, his face. That crooked smile, a shaky hand coming up to Ahn's earlobe.

Ahnschen it is then, huh?

The world went black.

Seven

SOHMENG WAS STILL SHAKING. This had been going for a while now, her body unable to let go of the panic even as her rational side assured her that there wasn't any danger. The image of Ahn with the stick in his hand, the look of despair on his face even as he went to hurt Hei, to *kill* them—

It was a lot.

The moment Ahn had realized what he was doing, he'd jerked back like Hei had burned him. He was inconsolable, clutching his chest and gasping for air until something broke and he fell into loud, hysterical sobs. If Mama had been there, she would have been curled around him in a heartbeat, chirping and rumbling her concern.

Sohmeng didn't make it that far. She was frozen, unable to process what her stupid idea had almost done. She had promised Hei that Ahn wasn't dangerous, and things were going so *well*, and now she had no idea what to do. No idea what to even think.

By the time her limbs unlocked, Hei was already by

Ahn's side. They moved slowly, cautiously, speaking soothing words in Sãonipa while he struggled to breathe. When Ahn could finally speak, the words came tumbling out in a stream of Qiao Sidhur, the same sounds over and over.

Sohmeng followed their meaning even before they transformed into Dulpongpa. No one could have mistaken that for anything but an apology.

She crouched beside them and tried to tell Ahn that everything was okay, but the words didn't seem to reach him. To be fair, they barely reached her either, frightened as she was. Then Hei took Ahn's face in their hands. They stroked his cheekbones, inhaled deeply and intentionally, tapping against his jaw to get his attention. Eventually his ragged breathing began to match Hei's steady pace. They sat there for a long while, patiently waiting it out.

Sohmeng found her own breath eventually, but she couldn't sit still. She went to the sãoni instead, stroking between their head spines and shushing troubled chirps; the scene had made the colony nervous. It didn't seem like it had been the sparring itself that unnerved them—Sohmeng could only assume that was because they were used to tussles, and Hei hadn't made any distress calls. No, it was Ahn's fear that was spooking the sãoni. The pained sounds he was still making, on the other end of the clearing.

"Sohmeng, will you put on a fire please?"

Sohmeng was pulled from her thoughts by Hei's voice. With a jerky nod, she set about getting the tinder bed ready, gathering kindling. Usually physical work settled her down when she was stressed, but this time it was no good. When the fire had to be left to smoulder down, she started looking for something they could eat. She doubted they'd be traveling any further today.

By the time her foraged yams were cooking, Hei had coaxed Ahn to the fireside. He lay with his head in their lap while they rubbed his back. A couple of hatchlings curled up by his legs.

Silence stretched. Hei didn't look bothered, but Sohmeng felt more rattled with every moment. She wanted to say something, but she didn't know where to start. She had never been afraid like this before, not when it came to Hei's safety. That first fight with Blacktooth, most of her fear had come from the sheer intensity of the situation. It hadn't been personal; she and Hei had barely known each other. Now they were her partner—and so was Ahn. The idea of losing either of them, or losing one of them to the other, made her panic in every part of her body.

"Hei," she said, switching to Atengpa. "Are you—are you okay?"

A soft chirp; they held out a hand for her. She gripped it tightly and sat by their side. "I am okay, Sohmeng Minhal."

"You're not hurt?" It felt so silly to ask. She had seen every part of the match, after all. But she needed to hear it anyway.

"I am not hurt." Hei took her hand, holding it to their cheek. She could feel the makeup beneath her fingers, freshly applied this morning after a scrub. They hardly even complained when she did it anymore. "Are you afraid?"

"Yeah. I think I am."

Hei nodded, nuzzling into her palm. "That's alright."

"Okay."

It helped to hear, to know there was no rush to fix her feelings no matter how they conflicted with what she believed. Because, not even that deep down, Sohmeng knew Ahn hadn't tried to hurt Hei on purpose. That much had been obvious based on his reaction. Frankly, she was worried about him; she had seen Ahn anxious before, but never anything like this.

Sohmeng had been told plenty of times in Ateng not to be nosy with people's private business, but this was something she had to push on. She felt weird and confused, and she needed an explanation.

The yams finished cooking, and Hei and Sohmeng ate quietly while Ahn lay still, breathing slowly. After a while, he spoke.

"I am sorry," he said in Dulpongpa, so quietly Sohmeng almost didn't hear. "I am so sorry."

"You have said this," Hei replied. They offered him a chunk of yam, but he did not take it. After stealing a bite, they placed it back down on its banana leaf.

"Ahn..." Sohmeng asked. "What happened?"

Ahn winced, and she reached down to fix his hair. It had been frightening to watch him lose himself, but she wasn't actually angry at him.

"There is something I should tell you," Ahn said. "Something I have needed to tell you, that I have been thinking about and unable to manage." He pushed himself slowly up to sitting, and Sohmeng brushed some stray leaf litter from his shirt.

"We're listening," she said.

"It's difficult." The slow movement of the words over his tongue highlighted the point. His voice was pained, his expression determined and exhausted. "But you must know, it's only right. We're all in a partnership and I owe it to you both. And him." He touched his earlobe, fingers shaking. "I owe it to him."

Sohmeng glanced at the piercing there. It had been a gift, Ahn had said, from someone he loved.

Following her gaze, Ahn reached for Sohmeng's hand, bringing her fingers to the piercing. "Would you ... ?"

She touched it, feeling out the ridges. "It's bone, right?"

"A fingerbone. The—" He said a word in Qiao Sidhur, then gestured to his own hand. The metacarpal of the pointer finger of the left hand. Sohmeng wondered how specific the translation was, if it covered all of those details. "It belonged to him. To Schenn."

Sohmeng froze, her mouth partially open. Hei spoke before she had a chance to.

"He is dead?" they asked. "Your Schenn?"

"Not mine," he replied, his voice hoarse.

"But he is dead."

"He is."

Sohmeng still didn't know much about Qiao Sidhur customs, and she did what she could not to be judgmental. After all, after Mama died, Hei had taken a private moment to remove some of her claws and teeth. They repurposed them for themself, a way to keep her close and to carry her legacy as the new alpha. Death was weird, and it made people do weird things, but this was a lot for her to take in.

"Do ... " Sohmeng released the bone carefully. "Do you want to talk about it?"

"Not particularly," Ahn said with a strained laugh. "Or I—maybe I do? I don't know. But I have to."

"No," Hei said, looking at him intently. "You do not have to anything."

"I *do* though. For—for him. I have to do it for him."

Sohmeng took his hand, bouncing it lightly in her grasp. She wasn't sure how to manage this topic without making things worse. "Okay. So ... what happened? How did Schenn die, Ahn?"

"I ... killed him?" Ahn said, and it sounded almost like a question. "I killed him."

Some foolish part of Sohmeng had thought of Ahn only as a warrior in name. A story-word like *prince*. It wasn't until the moment when he'd had Hei's life in his hands that Sohmeng had really seen that he was capable of killing people. It left her without words.

"In Qiao Sidh," he said, "there is a ritual. We call it your *Qøngzhir Asten*. Your Six-ing. If you are walking the Path of Conquest and wish to advance to the sixth rank, this is the final step. Schenn and I took it together. We trained together for years, learning martial arts at a school called Kørno Wan. We both specialized in bladecraft, though our classmates had some different specialties. Mounted combat, hand-to-hand."

"How many of you were there?" Sohmeng asked.

"Eighteen students. Nine pairs. We were selected out of a larger pool of warriors and then matched based on our compatibility. We entered Kørno Wan at age eleven and graduated at sixteen after training with our other halves. Living together, learning together, sleeping side-by-side. When our Six-ing was done, the nine of us qualified for a military ranking lesser soldiers would have spent much of their lives working for. It was an honour."

The nine of us.

"They made you kill each other," Sohmeng said, and she couldn't hide the horror in her voice.

"It was an honour," Ahn repeated softly.

"Wait, so they—" Sohmeng cut herself off, feeling nauseous. Beside her, Hei was saying nothing, watching Ahn with an inscrutable expression. "Is this like your Tengmunji? Kids on the Conquest Path just *do* this?"

"Not often. Adults who walk the Path more slowly will do it later in life. But eligible students, ones who are identified as remarkable in some way, are nominated by Masters and then invited to the training schools. Spiritualists make the matches. Schenn was—he was part of a group that was selected especially for me, as the eleventh prince. We sparred and had a . . . magnetism. We liked each other."

"And so you had to kill each other."

The words came out hot, angry, and Hei clicked at her sharply. Sohmeng clenched her jaw. She had sworn she'd try not to be judgmental, but *this*. This was shocking. This was upsetting, upsetting as a circle of lost childhood friends. Worse.

"It was a choice," Ahn said.

"You chose this fight?" Hei asked.

"It's an honour," Ahn repeated once more. The scary thing was, he almost sounded like he meant it. "A Six-ing is not meant to end a life. It begins a relationship. The half who survives remains in this realm, and the other goes—the other way." Seeing Sohmeng's confusion, Ahn took a moment to figure out a translation. "In Qiao Sidh, we believe there are two realms—two worlds, side by side. Close to one another, but not the same." He gestured up where the moons would be in the night. Sohmeng's stomach hit the ground. Minhal. Of course it was Minhal. For all that she tried to claim it and make it a positive thing, in this moment, she felt like a child again, ashamed and terrified of the dark. "In the bilateral realm, Ama is white and Chehang is red. Dawn is dusk, and dusk is dawn. Schenn is alive, and Ahn is dead."

Understanding settled like a weight in her gut. Ahn and Schenn.

"*Ahnschen*," Sohmeng said quietly.

Ahn nodded, and the way he smiled at her then looked almost shy. "It's why I touch my ear, like this—" He did the motion, one Sohmeng had seen a million times and never thought too hard about. "I touch the finger of his left hand with my right. It lets us make contact with each other through the realms."

Hei hummed thoughtfully, and again Sohmeng marveled at their composure. She couldn't imitate it in the slightest. Her head was swimming with questions, with anger, with protectiveness. The idea of losing him or Hei was devastating, and she had known them both for less than a year. What must it have been like, to be forced to kill his friend after so much time together? How were the both of them talking like this was *normal*?

"In Qiao Sidh, we believe that Schenn can speak to me through this earpiece. Guide me."

"Do you hear him?" Hei asked.

Ahn hesitated. Whatever fondness had been on his face faltered, replaced with a flash of grief. Doubt. "Sometimes."

His hand came to his heart, and Sohmeng remembered it: the great big scar across his chest. She had first seen it in Nona Fahang, and several times since when they swam or washed their clothes. She hadn't thought much of it; even if she'd never considered him a killer, she knew Ahn was a warrior, and in the stories, warriors usually had scars. But she understood now: that was the injury which had led him to seek a weapon, to force Hei to the ground for a killing blow. Schenn had put it there.

"I need to tell you this," Ahn said carefully, "because he is with me. With us, in this relationship. Where I go, he follows. He's my family and my shadow and my guardian, too. He will be a father to my children. If I ever ascended the throne, he would be a twin emperor in the other realm." He hesitated, then looked between the both of them, scanning their faces, searching for a reaction. Sohmeng tried to control her expression. For all she felt complicated, she didn't want Ahn to think this was his fault. "It is important to me that you know him. I should have told you sooner. I'm sorry."

Hei offered him some food again, more forcefully this time. Ahn tentatively accepted it, taking a small bite.

"Happy to know Schenn, Ahn," Hei said.

Ahn's shoulders lowered visibly, a sigh of relief escaping him. When he looked at Sohmeng, so nervous and hopeful, she had no idea what to do. She cared about Ahn, and was willing to meet any friend of his, even if the circumstances were unconventional. But this was *atrocious*, and she was upset. Furious, even.

This wasn't just a bad breakup. It wasn't even just a death. It was a horrible thing that had happened to him, and worst of all, he didn't even seem to know it was horrible.

Was there any way to become an adult that didn't hurt?

That didn't break kids down and take something from them, leaving them strangers to themselves?

Ahn took her hand, careful as if it were a baby animal. His hands were bigger than hers, calloused without being rough, with long fingers suited for the harp. He had killed the person he loved more than anyone with those hands, and he hadn't even wanted to. Honour or not, it was all over his face, his body. He hadn't wanted that at all.

"Sohmeng?" he asked softly, looking at her with worry. "Is that . . . is that alright?"

It wasn't alright. It wasn't fair.

"That I've got three partners now?" she asked, and she had no idea where the levity in her voice came from. "As long as he's handsome, why not?"

It made Ahn smile, and Sohmeng tried not to feel like a complete liar. Because it was true, she *could* accept all parts of Ahn, and that included Schenn. But she couldn't pretend what had happened was okay.

He pulled her into an embrace, and she held him tight. Over his shoulder, she looked at Hei helplessly. They met her eyes, steady and unfaltering. They inhaled, slow and intentional. Exhaled again.

Sohmeng breathed with them, her heart pressed to Ahn's heart, her cheek against his ear and the bone that pierced through it. She imagined Schenn touching her face the way Ahn did, warm and familiar. And she couldn't hear his voice, but she did her best to think hard in his direction, to send her intentions his way.

We'll figure this out, Schenn. We'll help him.

EIGHT

HEI WAS STILL GETTING USED TO being addressed by Mama's name. The first time they received that full-throated call in such confident unison, they were startled like a bird from a branch. Startled, and humbled, and proud too. Who wouldn't be proud to follow such a legacy?

It was something they had imagined for themself, in the way everyone imagines something special when they're alone in their mind. But it had been a fantasy, nothing more. Hei knew their family saw them as a sãoni—even with their smooth skin, their five-fingered hands—but they'd never guessed that they were also recognized as a leader.

And yet.

Alpha, the colony called. *Alpha?* the colony asked.

Hei did their best to answer, and to lead them well. After all, a displeased colony was known to split in a crisis, and they couldn't afford to lose anyone, especially not now.

It made them sick some days, the way their family had become a resource.

"It's like that with people too," Sohmeng had attempted when Hei voiced this. "We work together, and we get what we need from one another in order to keep everyone alive. It can be clunky, but it's how we look out for each other."

Hei thought this unfair. Though they were human and sãoni both, that did not mean human and sãoni societies had equal needs. "Before the Empire came, the sãoni did not need to look out for anyone besides their own colony."

"I know. It's annoying, but it's where we are, right?" Sohmeng squeezed their hands. "You said so yourself."

Hei had said so. And it remained true. But they didn't *like* it.

When they focused simply on the facts and the need for strategy, Hei could manage being a part of this ever-shifting plan. But when they thought about it too much, the unfairness felt like it could topple them.

The sãoni were not meant to be commanded by humans, or to be controlled. There was an order to things, predators and prey and the great dance of being alive together through the endless compelling hunger. The sãoni had always been predators, in Hei's mind. It was sheer and unexpected luck that had brought Hei into the colony when they were meant to be prey.

However, there were other interspecies relationships besides predator and prey. Parasites, like the tick on the monkey's back. Symbiotes, like the cleaner shrimp on the fish's belly.

The predator-prey line had become blurred between humans and sãoni. Their relationship was no longer so simple. Which opened up the question: was this new way of being parasitic or symbiotic?

The humans used the sãoni to get from one place to another, regardless of the will of the colony. But the will of the colony was controlled by the will of the alpha. Hei was the alpha now, and so it was their will. But Hei was also human.

Parasitic or symbiotic?

The humans altered the migration of the sãoni, but they also fed the sãoni. But the sãoni could feed themselves. But the humans could help prevent overfeeding in any one area, which brought a level of balance to the system. But it kept the sãoni complacent.

Parasitic or symbiotic?

They spent an afternoon practicing riding with Green Bites, using both their Sãonipa and the calls they had developed with Ahnschen. Compared to the well-conditioned hatchlings, Green Bites had been far more resistant to this new form of communication. But now, with Hei in command, he listened more, and they had to admit that it was nice to not get snapped as frequently. They could simply say *stop* and have him stop.

But this also made them lonely. Frustrated. Some of these changes were undeniably good, but they were still *changes*, and Hei had not had room to prepare for them emotionally. They found themself wishing that Mama was here, wishing she could tell them what to do.

But Mama would not have been able to guide Hei. Sãoni did not train their successors. This was a human wish they were having, and it made them squirm. How it stretched them to need to be both.

"I think I will tell Ahnschen," Hei said to Sohmeng one day.

Sohmeng paused, mouth open to take a bite of fruit. Hei realized they had not given any context for their idea.

"About me," they clarified. "In Ateng."

"Oh!" Sohmeng put down her food, eyes wide with surprise which soon transformed into concern. "Hei, that's . . . I mean, are you sure?"

"I think so." They didn't understand why she was looking at them like that. Did she not want them to tell Ahnschen? It didn't seem so outlandish to Hei; the two of them had had plenty of personal talks recently. "Is that a problem?"

"No! Not at all! I'm just . . . I didn't expect it." She glanced over in the direction where Ahn had gone to wash his hair in a nearby river. Hei had explained that the Ãotul would be spilling into a wide lake tomorrow afternoon, but he was meticulous with his hair sometimes, and washed it whenever there was a chance. "I know it was a really difficult experience for you. Even telling me was hard, that night in the mountains. I'm glad you trust Ahn—but I don't want you to feel like you *have* to tell him or anything."

This was only more confusing. "Why would I have to?"

"I—" Sohmeng broke off into a laugh. She shook her head and rubbed her cheek against theirs. "Nevermind, I'm being silly."

They clicked in agreement, pressing back into the contact.

Hei decided to wait until the colony arrived at the lake before broaching the conversation. It would only be the second time telling the story, and they wanted to make sure they knew what parts they wanted to share, especially because they would be telling it in Dulpongpa.

When they made it to that sparkling basin of water, Ahnschen let out a long whistle of appreciation. Sohmeng, on the other hand, outright shouted about it, sending bewildered squawks through the colony. It warmed Hei, showing her things she had not seen before. Her reactions made them tingle, made them proud, as though they had filled the lake themself. They wondered how she would feel when she stepped barefoot into the sand by the Great River. They hoped she could still enjoy it rather than simply be distracted by Ólawen.

Soon, Sohmeng went off to circle the perimeter on Singing Violet's back, and that left Ahnschen and Hei alone.

Hei was coming to enjoy their time one-on-one with Ahnschen. He did not do as much nervous talking as he used to, and sometimes when he sang to himself they would just listen for a while. They were learning the rules of being in each other's company, of making contact. Hei did not always want to respond, even if they were glad to listen to Ahnschen talk; Ahnschen did not like it when they snuck up behind him. After a few incidents of wanting to bathe in the best spots of the river at the same time, they agreed to give up waiting to take turns so they could get back on the road more quickly.

This lake was large enough that they could find separate spots to bathe, but they had fallen into a habit. Ahnschen had also said something about it being safer not to swim alone, which Hei supposed was true.

The water was cool and refreshing without sending uncomfortable prickles up their body, and the direct sunlight shone down to warm their back. Reluctantly, they were scrubbing at their face again. Their skin *did* feel better with the regular washing, but it also made them feel bare. Strange. Human.

"Ahnschen?" they called, giving their face one last rinse and turning around.

"Over here," he replied. He was cleaning his hair again, standing nearby with water up to his ribs. They could see the scar across his chest, the scar Schenn had left him with.

Hei rubbed at the side of their arm, touching the raised mark where his blade had cut through, searing hot from fire-sand. The memory no longer stung them. When Ahnschen went back to Qiao Sidh, they thought, it would be a nice way to know he had been here.

They waded over to him. "I want to talk."

Ahnschen smiled softly, his brows lifting. "I am always glad to speak with you."

Gentle words, gentle smile. Sohmeng often said that Ahnschen was very nice to look at. Hei personally thought Sohmeng was prettier, and much better to hold. But they could not deny Ahnschen was pretty too, in a different way. His shoulders were broad, his chest firm and flat in a way that Hei would have liked their own to be, if they'd had any say in the matter.

"...Hei?" he asked after a moment, and Hei realized they had forgotten to respond.

They ran their fingers through the water, watching it ripple. "There is a story," they said. "A story of—me."

"Alright. I'm listening."

It was easier, Hei discovered, to tell the story of their exile a second time. The first attempt had been so frightening—it was a new thing to speak into the world, a shame they had known for as long as they had known how to be ashamed. Back then, sharing the truth of their past had made their present world feel tenuous, made their very existence feel threatened.

They saw the same thing happen to Ahnschen, when he told the story of his Six-ing those nights ago. The terrible pain of a secret revealed, and the paralyzing fear of being abandoned for having revealed it.

This time, Hei knew they would not be left alone when their story reached its end. This knowledge did not remove the pain, but it quieted the fear, and that in turn made more space for the pain to be where it needed to be. It gave them room to properly grieve Grandmother Nor—and to grieve Mama, too, so recently gone. It allowed them to ache for Maio Chisong's approval even now, and to miss the whimsical stories Dimanhli Ker told as she wove them matching bracelets. Their sorrow remained, but it was lighter to hold when shared with another.

"My name in Ateng is Heipua Minhal," Hei said, when it was done. "But I am Hei."

They had been watching the gentle bob of a lilypad while they told the story, tracking a dragonfly whirling through the air. After a moment, they decided that they would look at Ahnschen's face. It was serious, and a little sad. A look like when Mama had died. A look from his heart, his tender heart.

It was a good quality to have, a heart like this. Kinder

than Hei's and Sohmeng's both, guarded in a strong and capable body. He was compassionate in a way that Hei had always hoped people could be when they were young. On the nights where they ended up tucked against his chest and he wrapped his arms around them, they would close their eyes and think that this is how they always wanted to be held.

A capable body, a tender heart. But his mind—hurting, fractured. They wondered what kind of a place could create a warrior like this, what stone could hone his blade even as it dulled his claws.

"Of course, Hei," Ahnschen said in his soft voice. He made a strange face then, clearing his throat. And then—

Hei burst out laughing. "Is this—my *name*, Ahnschen?"

"I—" He looked at them sheepishly, running his fingers through his hair. "Well, I mean—"

"You think this is my name!"

Hei was delighted. It was wrong, very wrong. Close in the way a human could get close, but also not very close at all. They dunked underwater, blowing out bubbles, and then came back up.

Ahnschen was grinning, rubbing his hand against his neck. Hei hesitated, then lifted onto their toes, grabbing Ahnschen's shoulder to pull him closer. They pressed their cheek into his, feeling the drag of skin on skin without the oil of their makeup. There was the faintest hint of stubble on his jaw; Sohmeng would have to help him shave again, useless as he was without a reflecting glass.

When Hei pulled back, Ahnschen was looking at them with big owl eyes. Hei released his shoulder, but he caught their forearm in his hand.

Sometimes words got stuck in Ahnschen the same way they did in Hei. It was not so hard to be patient while he searched for a way to free them. There were other things to look at and listen to, to smell and touch and sense. The ripples in the water, the birds arguing above, the smooth stones pressing into the arches of their feet.

"Thank you for telling me," he eventually said. "That must have been—"

"No talking about this," Hei responded, wiggling their arm from his grasp. They cupped water in their palms instead, pouring it over their neck. "Just telling you."

"Just telling me," he repeated. He nodded to himself, and leaned back into the water until he was floating. His palms were up, facing the sun, and Hei thought it would be nice to place a hibiscus flower there, if they had one. But they didn't, and so his hand was just a hand.

Content, Hei walked to the shore, sitting on a large rock to dry off. Sohmeng had brought them down some extra clothing to wear from Ateng, soft things so they weren't in their sãoni skin all the time. Sãoni leather dried quickly after a wash, but Hei couldn't deny that the soft clothing was better to sleep in.

However, rest didn't come easily that night.

Hei was used to Ahnschen and Sohmeng's talks in the evening, the way they would pick up their pace of speaking until Hei nearly felt dizzy. They both got loud when they were enthusiastic about something, and Sohmeng's cackle echoed through the whole rainforest when she pinched Ahnschen's cheeks.

This evening, mirth was hard to come by. The tension in their voices had wound tighter and tighter the closer they got to the basecamp; proximity to Qiao Sidh seemed to steal their easy rhythm. Sitting close to the fire, Hei passed a smooth stone between their hands and watched the two of them in silence.

"Ahn, all I'm saying is that it feels pretty premature to start making battle plans," Sohmeng said, not hiding her exasperation. "We don't even *have* armies here."

"I hear that, but it's not a given that negotiations will be successful. We need to think ahead in case things don't go our way. It's a possibility, even if it's unpleasant."

"Yeah, but going in acting like it's already doomed to fail, it—I don't know, it feels inauspicious to me! I don't want to invite that in. This whole idea sounds aggressive, like we're showing up in bad faith. What's the point of trying to talk if we're already thinking about violence?"

"Preparation," Ahnschen said, doing a poor impression of someone who was calm, "is what helps *prevent* unnecessary violence."

"All violence is unnecessary."

"Sohmeng, you can't honestly—"

Sensing that this was going nowhere productive, Hei abruptly tossed the stone into the fire, making the embers pop. Ahnschen and Sohmeng jumped in unison.

"*Too much*," Hei said, waving at them like a pair of irritable hatchlings. These tight-wound tempers were making their skin itch like a sunburn. "This stops or I go walking. Okay? No more of this biting."

The scolding seemed to bring the two of them back to themselves. Ahnschen tugged at his earpiece with a murmured apology, which Sohmeng echoed. All the bluster melted out of her, leaving her looking as tired as Hei felt listening to them.

The fire crackled, and Hei stretched out their legs. After a few minutes, Sohmeng spoke again. This time, she didn't sound ready to argue, so Hei did not find it necessary to click at her.

"Are you really that worried about your sister, Ahn?" she asked uncomfortably. "Do you think a fight could actually be on the table?"

"I wish I didn't, but I do," Ahnschen said. "She's strong-willed, and older than I am."

"Viunwei's older than me, that doesn't mean I listen to him." This provoked a chuckle out of Ahnschen, which turned Sohmeng's somber expression into a grin. "But he's also a weenie."

"He's a perfectly nice—"

"—*weenie*, yeah, I know."

The mood was lighter than before, but Hei saw the way Ahnschen fidgeted, as though all his anxiety had moved to his fingers. Ahnschen was worried about as often as the sãoni were hungry; it made it difficult to gauge how much of that worry should be acted upon. He had a tendency to show his throat and defer to the nearest alpha in difficult situations. But he wasn't foolish, and Hei didn't tend to ignore warnings about danger.

"I know that Ólawen loves me," Ahnschen said. "From the bottom of my heart, I believe that. She's always been there for me, and that isn't a given in my family. But if I wasn't *me*, I'm not sure she'd entertain this conversation at all."

"Well . . . lucky enough, you *are* you," Sohmeng said,

giving him a nudge with her elbow. "But you don't have to do this alone. Don't underestimate us."

"Okay," Ahnschen said. He took Sohmeng's hand and pressed a kiss to it, which seemed to satisfy her. But Hei wasn't convinced.

When it came to the matter of Ólawen, neither Sohmeng nor Ahnschen's opinions were reliable. It had less to do with Sohmeng's stubborn optimism or Ahnschen's nervous disposition, and more to do with the fact that they simply did not have enough information to plan several steps ahead.

Until they were all face-to-face with the general, everything was a matter of speculation. And as far as Hei was concerned, the moment speculation led away from curiosity and towards fear, it stopped being a useful way to pass the time. It was like when Mama was dying and all the humans were fretting about who would be alpha: none of them, Hei included, ever would have guessed that Hei was an option, and so all of their worrying had been pointless. And noisy.

Hei took a heavy breath as they watched Ahnschen and Sohmeng cuddle closer. As green and purple sãoni throats sleepily glowed around them, Hei considered which parts of this situation were actually within their power:

They could not control Ólawen. They could not control the weather. They could not control Sohmeng or Ahnschen. They could not completely control the sãoni, only lead them as best they could.

That was something. Hei couldn't control most things, but they *could* control their choices as a leader. The day they said goodbye to Mama and accepted authority over the colony was the most meaningful of their life so far. Every single creature that submitted to Hei's bite that day was under their protection. They took the responsibility seriously.

On the other side of the fire, Sohmeng and Ahnschen were talking about the future again. They weren't squabbling anymore; instead, Sohmeng was practicing Qiao Sidhur with Ahnschen, which made her focus and him blush. Hei imagined that was good for both of them.

Hei thought of the taste of sweat on Sohmeng's skin, the soft bump of Ahnschen's spine between their teeth. This responsibility extended to their entire family, human and sãoni alike.

They inhaled, listening to the crackle of the flame. Whatever trial or triumph came next would depend on Éongrir Ólawen. No matter the outcome, Hei would be there, watching, with sharp claws and a keen eye. It's what their mother would have done.

Part Two:
Qiao Sidh

Nine

WHEN AHN STOPPED HIS SOLDIERS from attacking Nona Fahang, he'd set a timeline for his return. *When the moons go dark*, he had said. In the moment, it felt like the most efficient way to plan; Lita Soon was injured, along with several others, and he didn't have time to work out a precise date on the calendar. Part of it had been with Sohmeng on his mind; she spoke often about the daily and weekly astrology, and he thought invoking her phase name might bring some luck.

Romantic as the gesture had been, the timing was tight. They'd had a full fifty days, but he hadn't factored in any possible delays, and while he couldn't have prepared for a wedding and a funeral, still he felt every passing hour more intensely than the last.

It was the final day of Minhal. That evening, the first sliver of the red moon would appear, welcoming in First Par—an invitation for his sister to begin her march south to Nona Fahang.

Ahn tried hard not to catastrophize, but no matter how

much distance they covered on sãoni-back, fear always caught up to him. What if Ólawen had lost patience and left early? What if she had interpreted his timeline as the *first* night the moons went dark? What if the traveling hours they had lost to his meltdown had ruined everything?

By the time the forest around them began to change, he could have fallen off of Sølshend in exhaustion and relief. But he kept himself steady; when they hit the basecamp, he would need to be Éongrir Ahnschen-Eløndham.

Soon, the smell of saltwater grew thicker in the air, and the texture of the soil began shifting closer to that of sand. They saw more and more trees that had been cut down, the wood presumably repurposed for fire or shelter. The sãoni lumbered past a tree stump that was nearly four feet wide, and Hei clicked unhappily, the colony echoing all around them. Shortly after, tracks started to appear along the earth, packed down from many feet, and the green foliage around them abruptly yielded to shimmering white sand.

And then, Qiao Sidh.

Compared to Nona Fahang's banyan fortress, the camp sprawled out in the open without a concern in the world. Tents were raised on wooden beams, laundry hung from lines; Ahn recalled how efficiently his soldiers had built this settlement from nothing. Architects were brought along on campaigns for this very purpose, to innovate with whatever materials they found that allowed them to subdue the wilderness into home.

Madøng steeds, like Lilin, were tromping around in their pens, trilling to one another and pecking at the ground. Large communal cooking pits were crackling, the soldiers' lunch sizzling on the grates above the flames, and the familiar smells of home floated in overtop the earthy aroma of the rainforest. Beyond all this, the ships, gleaming long and lithe in the shallows. Unguarded.

The Qiao Sidhur army didn't feel the need to shelter itself. They were confident that none could overtake them, even in a foreign land.

So Ahn felt bad, a little bit, watching his fellow soldiers scramble in panic as a full colony of sãoni emerged from the woods.

The army had encountered a few sãoni early in the campaign, of course. But this many, and with people *riding* them? That was enough to make even the more seasoned soldiers trip over themselves trying to get to their weapons.

"Ahn, I think they're freaking out," Sohmeng assessed, accurately. Ahn couldn't tell if she sounded more smug or concerned.

With a carrying sãoni call, Hei directed the majority of the colony to stay back—and fortunately for everyone, they listened. Ahn was seated on Sølshend, the sãoni that had accepted him most warmly. Its hatchmate, Qøngem, stayed close by, clicking menacingly at a group of soldiers who had drawn their swords. Ahn used a sãoni command of his own to direct his mount further into the clearing; Hei and Sohmeng followed closely behind on Green Bites and Singing Violet.

"I am your prince—" he called out in Qiao Sidhur, his throat relaxing around the language of his homeland. "Éongrir Ahnschen-Eløndham, Qøngemzhir, Sølshendasá, Siengunghvøs."

The eleventh beloved son of the royal family, Ahn, twinned to Schenn in the bilateral realm; ranked sixth in Conquest, third in the Arts, and second in Philosophy.

It poured out of him like a song, this title of his. It stopped his people in their tracks, same as it had last time. Despite the initial shock of seeing the sãoni, they didn't seem surprised that he had returned. They had waited for him. Óla had waited for him.

"I have returned to you," he said. "Bring me my sister."

"Yes, sir!" someone called. A cluster of foot soldiers took off to the other side of camp, and he nearly fell from the sãoni with gratitude. The worst of his fears was behind him.

"How's it looking, Ahn?" Sohmeng called, her voice as curious as Hei's clicks were cautious.

"She's still here," Ahn said, looking back at his companions with relief. "And the camp hasn't mobilized, so maybe—"

A woman approached him then, dropping to one knee before him and the sãoni. Her silver braid fell over her shoulder, exposing the shaved side of her head. On her scalp was a stark tattoo of the sun.

"General Ahnschen," she said. Ahn's mount leaned forward with a menacing sound, but she did not move, simply holding tight to the sword at her hip. "We are grateful to see you alive."

Ahn recognized her immediately—Hidhrolo Noula Qøngemtsou, Idhrenqang. A long time friend of Óla's, and the person who had practiced Dulpongpa alongside him in Kongkempei. Capable, well-mannered, inclined to say nothing unless asked, and only then to say something brilliant. The sight of her face knocked the wind from him.

He was here. At the camp, with his army. He could smell sage and thyme in the air, could find the madøng tracks in the dirt, the outline of their three sharp toes. He understood every word of the snippets of conversation that reached his ears.

It wasn't home, but it was close. And despite his feelings about the invasion, it was a comfort to return to the familiar.

Ahn leapt off Sølshend to go to Noula, immediately pulling the officer to her feet. "Noula! Noula, my friend. Are you well, are you safe?"

Noula stared at him, bafflement plain on her face. "Am I—? Eløndham, *you're* the one who has been missing."

"You *are* well then." Ahn released her, trying to get his bearings when Qøngem bumped his nose into Ahn's side. He stroked the sãoni's face, forgetting to switch back to Dulpongpa as he spoke. "What, you can't share the attention for even a moment?"

The sãoni rumbled, pleased, and Noula cleared her throat.

"Eløndham," she said slowly, rolling each syllable over her tongue. "Forgive me, but I would suggest you have the beasts step back. They are upsetting the madøng."

Irritable squawking proved her right, and a quick look told Ahn that a few soldiers were on the verge of doing some squawking of their own. He walked over to Hei, switching back to Dulpongpa. "I think we should give the camp some space."

"Fine with me," Hei said, barking Sãonipa orders to the colony. They receded several more paces back into the forest, inky shadows among the twisted trunks, rumbling all the while.

Sohmeng tugged gently on Singing Violet's head spines, keeping her in place while the sãoni grumbled at the mixed messages. "Are you okay, though? I don't feel good leaving you alone here."

Ahn took her hand, pressing the back of it to his cheek. She flushed, glancing at the soldiers, but Ahn didn't pull back. It wasn't so different from biting someone, he thought.

"These are my people," he said. "Keep at a distance, and I'll make sure no one causes you any trouble. I'll be back soon, and we'll know what to do from—"

A loud whistle broke across the beach. Sharp and resonant. Commanding. In an instant, the whole camp was at attention, and that's how Ahn knew it was her.

"That you, baby brother?" Ólawen called as soldiers parted to make way. And like a child, Ahn ran. Ran right to her, and threw his arms around her as tightly as he could.

Ólawen had always been Ahn's favorite sibling. She had taught him everything he knew to begin on the Conquest Path, and she always seemed glad to see him. She'd mess up his hair and call him *baby brother*, and bragged about him to all of her friends, even when he was a kid. She said he was going to be the second greatest warrior in the whole of the family history—after her, of course. She said he could do anything he put his mind to.

The rest of Ahn's siblings were older than him by more than a decade, and regarded him with something between indifference and disdain. They were on the path to win the Emperor's approval and be granted the throne, with no time for the distraction of a child sibling. Ahn and Óla were different; they were young, born too late to prove their prowess and ascend. They were spares, and they were friends.

"Óla," he said into her shoulder, grateful she didn't have her armour on. It felt like being a toddler again, being carried around by her and thrown into the air. "Óla, I—"

"You little nightmare, you perfect boy," she said, giving him a shake. Her voice wavered in a way he had never heard before, and it made him choke up. "You *never* get lost again, do you hear me? Never do that to me again. I'll strip you of your rank and send you back to art school with the rest of the fools." She grabbed his cheeks, kissed him firmly on the forehead. "No, don't do that *either*, don't get soft on me before you've even said hello."

Ahn laughed helplessly, swallowing down the tears that threatened to rise up. "I'm sorry I'm late."

"You should be," Ólawen said with a playful scoff. She tapped her earpiece, shaking her head. "Now I'm going to have to deal with the better half telling me she was right, and she knew you were alive all along. You're keeping her smug, baby brother. It isn't fair."

Wen's face flashed before his eyes. He had only met her once or twice, but she had made an impression, even on a child of six. Her round cheeks, her tentative smile, her soft voice. Delicate, deadly.

He forgot his own voice for a moment, and Óla used the silence to turn her gaze on the sãoni. One of the smaller ones let out a growl, practicing its menace, and Óla unsheathed her sword. "And what's all this, then?"

"Ahn—" Sohmeng began, but he was already stepping in front of her and Singing Violet. At the sound of a weapon unsheathed, Hei was back with Green Bites in an instant.

"Óla, put down the sword," Ahn said.

"Are these the ones who captured you?" she asked, and her tone could've been mistaken for curiosity by someone who didn't know her.

"No one captured me," he insisted, speaking quickly. Óla was looking Hei up and down; Hei didn't even flinch. Tension seemed to rise all around them, ringing at a quiet but grating pitch. "This is Sohmeng and Hei, the people who rescued me when I was lost. They have looked after me, and they brought me here to you. They ride with the sãoni, who they have tamed, and they are my friends."

For a moment, Ólawen was quiet, assessing the humans and their colony of sãoni. And then the sword was back in its sheath, quick as anything. With a magnanimous smile, she looked from Hei and Sohmeng to Ahn.

"Well why didn't you say so?" she asked, clapping Ahn on the back. "Tell them they're welcome for lunch. Do they have tethers for the beasts?"

"Not quite—"

"Ah, pity. Well." Óla spared Ahn's partners one brief, diplomatic nod before looking back to him. "Tell them I'm grateful to have you home, and I wish them a safe journey."

"Óla," Ahn said, mustering up firmness in his voice. It could be hard to get his sister's full attention sometimes. She was used to talking, leading, being listened to without question. Sometimes, he thought, she forgot they were meant to share equal rank in this campaign. "They will be staying a short distance from the camp and returning after you and I have spoken. There is much we have to discuss."

Óla raised her eyebrows, looking faintly bemused. "Is there?"

"*Óla.*" His voice was soft now, on the edge of desperate. It wasn't a way he was particularly proud to sound. "Please."

Ólawen gave him a funny look, elbowing him playfully in the side. "Alright, alright! No need to get melodramatic. Grab your stuff and get to our tent. If you can't spot it, then you've been away too long."

She was halfway to leaving when Sohmeng's voice called out—

"Éongrir Ólawen-Eløndhol, Qøngemding."

It was pronounced perfectly. Months of Ahn running through Qiao Sidhur at Sohmeng's bidding, of watching her persist through every fight with a tricky consonant cluster or an unfamiliar vowel, and now here she was, confidently addressing by name the foremost general of the army invading her land.

One look from Sohmeng, and Ahn didn't miss a beat translating for her.

"My name is Sohmeng Minhal," Sohmeng said, patting the side of Singing Violet's neck as the sãoni released a huff of air. She did not look afraid, and *that* scared Ahn. "I know you and your brother have a lot to talk about. But before he leaves, I need to know—has your army moved any further south?"

Ólawen did not answer right away. She was looking at Sohmeng with a peculiar expression, something that could have been close to respect. "No, we haven't. We were waiting for General Ahnschen's safe return."

Sohmeng visibly relaxed. Behind her, Hei watched Óla, as still and silent as a mountain lion. "Thank you for telling me. I look forward to meeting you properly once you and Ahn have had a chance to catch up. Hei and I won't be far, so if you need us, just ask."

"Huh. Nice girl." Ólawen whistled. "Idhrenqang?"

"Yes, General?" Noula stepped forward; based on the use of her Discernment title, Ahn already knew what Óla would ask of her.

"Tell Sohmeng that her offer is very kind."

"Óla," Ahn said, glancing up at Sohmeng apologetically as Noula obediently took over the interpreting. "I really don't mind—"

"Ahnschen, you graduated from Kørno Wan—I don't think you need an extracurricular in translation. Give Noula the chance to use her degree, would you?" Ahn didn't know what to say to that, but Ólawen didn't give him time to respond. She wrapped an arm around him and guided him into the camp, and he felt his legs move to keep pace with her. "Join me, brother. Tell me what you've found in the Untilled."

Soldiers paused what they were doing as he and Óla walked by, bowing their heads in respect of their generals. This ritual had followed Ahn his whole life, and he had never thought much of it before. This was what it was to be a part of the Éongrir family. The world would stop for him, no matter the circumstances.

The back of his neck itched, but he didn't scratch. *Unbecoming,* his governess would have said.

When they entered the tent, everything was exactly as he had seen it last: a draping nest of fabric in Imperial silver and cornflower blue, with embroidered embellishments and a tasteful hint of beading. A practical woven mat was laid over the sandy ground, with a less practical rug on top of that. There were engraved stools, and a couple of blanketed pallets for when discussion—or drinking—went long into the night. Most importantly, at the center sat their war table, upon which was laid their map of the Untilled, littered with ornate silver tokens to mark *us* and *them*.

Neither Ahn nor Óla had stepped onto the Path of Aesthetic, but they both recognized the importance of good design on a campaign. There was elegance in Conquest, when performed admirably. It could, and should, be beautiful.

Enshrouded in that myth, Ahn told Óla where he had been for the past four months—nearly equal to the amount of time he'd been in Gãepongwei before he'd lost his way.

He began with the fire in Kongkempei. He'd become disoriented, he explained; he lost control of Lilin, and before he knew what to do, she had bolted into the forest. Despite the fact that Óla had her own other half advising from the bilateral realm, he omitted Schenn's part in directing him away from the battle. It felt oddly private, and Ahn found himself protective of Schenn's choices.

Hei and Sohmeng were sketched with similar vagueness: two members of southern hmun, one of whom took up life in Eiji from a young age and rode with sãoni. He left out the nature of their relationship. Depending on how everything went, that could come later.

"They were searching for aid for Ateng and found Nona Fahang—that's the hmun your soldiers were targeting when they found me."

"Yeah, I got your hair." Ólawen snorted, ruffling what he hadn't cut off. "What reason would they have had to lie?"

Ahn's face flushed. "I don't know. It felt...like I had to show you I was alive. I had to be sure you knew, and that you'd wait for me."

"I'd wait for you anywhere, kid. And for a good long time, obviously," Óla teased. She tugged at her earpiece with a fond smile. "Besides, like I said, my better half cooled me down. She loves you, you know? We both do. You're easy to love."

When his sister said those words, Ahn believed them. Óla had always been honest, honest to the point of cruelty sometimes, and that meant her affection was a powerful thing. It wasn't something he wanted to lose.

"Alright," Ólawen said, "time to fill me in. What happened in, ah, Nona whatever? I would've thought you'd come straight home once you had your people with you."

"In Nona Fahang..." He hesitated, unsure of how to explain. "I was—imprisoned, I suppose?"

"*What?*" Ólawen's smile vanished. He watched her grip tighten on the edge of the table.

"No! No, *no.*" Suddenly struck by visions of the fortress hmun burning, he scrambled to rephrase. He couldn't be careless with his words like that. "It's different there, so different, Óla. Imprisonment isn't even the right word, it's nothing like back home. Mostly I just—sat in a pygmy hog pen."

"They put the eleventh prince of Qiao Sidh in a cage full of animals." Ólawen's eyes narrowed, and Ahn tried not to flinch. "How did this happen? Did they hurt you?"

Ahn thought of Lita Soon, the scrapes and shoves and small humiliations he'd sustained at the man's hands. He shook his head no.

His time in Nona Fahang had not been easy. He had been scared and lonely and profoundly uncomfortable. He had spent many nights wondering if he would ever see his home again, longing to gaze up at the mountains of Hvallánzhou, to tighten his cloak and blow clouds with his breath. He ached for the sands of the southern coast. He missed the food of his childhood.

Those thirty days *had* been painful, but not for the reasons Ólawen was imagining. Fear wasn't what had kept Ahn in Nona Fahang—it was shame. He was not threatened with hurt, simply made to sit with the hurt he had caused. It was agonizing, and it had been necessary.

Most importantly, it was *not* a reason to go to war. In fact, it was the very opposite.

"I agreed to it, Óla," Ahn explained slowly. "They put me on trial."

"What *for*?"

"Because . . ." Ahn looked at his sister, feeling his words dry up as it struck him how difficult this was about to be.

Ólawen was nine years older than him, twenty-eight now, and she shone in every way a warrior ought to. Accomplished, boisterous, unyielding. She had spent most of her youth winning tournaments and breaking noble ladies' hearts, and transitioned smoothly into adulthood by putting down a series of small rebellions. As far as Ahn knew, she had never failed at anything in her life. She commanded a crowd with the unselfconscious ease of someone who took their bright future as a given.

And yet, in reality, Ahn's future had more options than Ólawen's. Outside of Conquest, he had his studies. He was cultivating his talents on the harp with Master Hvu; he had connected with friends outside of the aristocracy. Óla, on the other hand, had never bothered to take even a second Path. She'd never had any interest. Half of her relationships had ended because she was unable to invest in anyone as much as her military career.

Did he even have a chance of getting through to her about this? How was he supposed to explain his perspective without seeming foolish, or downright insulting?

"Well?" Óla asked, breaking him out of his reverie. She took his arm, worry on her face. "Ahn, what did they think you had done?"

As he struggled to find his words, the memory of Nona Fahang found its way into his body. Blindfolded, knocked against the winding branches of the banyan maze, Lita Soon's grip firm enough to transfer his grief into Ahn's body. A tangle of confusion and sorrow.

And contact, too. Schenn's voice had been so clear in his ear: *Listen to my words. Trust me.*

No voice came now, but the sensation did. A rich warmth from ear to collarbone, pushing from skin deep into muscle, the same as it had back then. There was a tingling in his jaw, as if words wanted to emerge, though he couldn't say if they were Schenn's or his own.

He took a shaky breath. If bullheaded Óla could listen to her better half, then he could try to do the same. "It was about Kongkempei."

"What about it?" Óla asked.

"They said the hmun had been destroyed. And that—

I mean, that's a crime, isn't it? So they were judging me for it, and determining if it was safe to keep me in Nona Fahang."

"Well I hope you didn't claim any guilt, because the village is fine."

Ahn froze. "What?"

"It's *fine*," Óla repeated. "The parts that were destroyed in the fire are already being rebuilt, I left one of our best in charge."

"What about the, the people who—"

"The dissidents were executed, and we've negotiated with the rest. This is Conquest, Ahn. We pick up swords for a reason, but after that? Everything's simple. We already got a name set—*Køngkanna*. Nice, right? Even the locals picked up on it fast."

She said it so comfortably, so confidently. Ahn felt sick.

"But, but we ..." Ahn attempted to speak, but he was stumbling. He'd never been naturally persuasive, and while his Philosophy lessons had helped, all his confidence went right out the window when his family was involved.

Óla, on the other hand, was charismatic, and more than happy to take charge of a conversation before any silence could stretch. She gave his shoulder another firm squeeze. "You've always been gentle, baby brother. It's sweet. But blood feeds the soil."

Ahn closed his eyes. Schenn, having ranked in both the Fertility and Conquest Paths, had taught him that adage in Kørno Wan.

Look, it doesn't just sound cool. It's also true! In Haojost, we fertilize with bloodmeal. The plants eat up the nitrogen. You really don't know this? What do they teach you in the capital?

"Óla," he said, and hated himself for how soft his voice was, how uncertain. His hands were shaking. "The way we're doing things … I don't think it's right."

There was a pause. After what felt like forever, Óla sighed heavily. She began to walk away, and for a terrified and unreasonable moment, Ahn thought she was simply going to leave, unwilling to entertain the topic any further. Instead, she opened a trunk at the back of the tent.

"Look," she said. "I know I've been heavy-handed on this campaign so far. I promised we'd be equals, two generals side by side, and I've been overshadowing you. I apologize for that." Ahn hadn't heard a lot of apologies from Óla in his life. He fidgeted, trying not to hope. "Old habits die hard, I guess. I'm used to running the show. And I know it's not right, but I still see you as a baby sometimes. Even with that sixth rank of yours. And that's not just disrespectful to you, that's disrespectful to Schenn." Hearing his name made Ahn's stomach jolt. He had no idea how she talked about the Six-ing ritual so easily. Even Wen's name still unsettled him. "But now that you're back, I can work on that. Here, let me show you something."

She reached down into the trunk, pulling out another box with a grunt. "I hadn't wanted to give this to you until we made it further south, but … well, why not? You've had a rough go. And enough time's passed already, right?"

Ólawen opened the box. In her hands was the last thing he could have expected: a harp.

Ahn pulled himself to standing, rushing over like she'd revealed one of his childhood puppies. It was beautiful, constructed from spruce and strung with eighteen strings, twin to the miniature harp he'd first learned on. The carvings were different, with patterned knots rather than ferns, but he didn't mind that it wasn't his instrument from home—in fact, he was already unsure of how to successfully care for it in this climate.

But oh, to have it in his hands. To know he could play again at all.

"Óla," he said, fingers hovering over the harp. "Óla, this is . . . "

She grinned, pushing it into his hands. "It's yours is what it is. Do you like it?"

"It's *beautiful*." Ahn looked at her in amazement. "How did you get this?"

"I brought it with us from the capital, silly boy." She crossed her arms, looking pleased with herself. "You surprised?"

Ahn held the harp tighter, thinking of the early days of the campaign. His anxious nights, his quiet confessions to Óla that he wasn't sleeping well, that he wished he could play some music to settle down. She'd hugged him and called him a softie, told him to keep his attention on what mattered.

"I'm—yes, I'm surprised." He swallowed, tracing the carved wood with his thumb.

"My plan was to give it to you once we started making some real progress. Didn't want you to lose focus before then, you know? You're a smart kid, way smarter than me, but you get so *scattered*. Your tutors used to go nuts about that. But there I go, treating you like a baby again." Óla bonked her head with the heel of her hand, that grin still on her face. She strutted back to the war table, looking over the map. "But hey, you're in charge too. So as long as you get your job done, you play your little instrument all you want. Boost morale, whatever. And between your recitals, we'll take the continent. Bring them some music."

Even in his hands, the harp suddenly felt far away. Everything did. His earpiece was throbbing now; he swore he could hear the blood moving through his body.

They built a road. They brought music, beautiful music.

"They already have music," Ahn said, so quietly he doubted Óla even heard. The words weren't just for her, they were for him. Him, and Schenn, and everyone else who had been implicated in the past two centuries of Imperial expansion. The illusion of cultural exchange, intended to mask the violence beneath.

Ahn put the harp back in the box. The inside was plush velvet, with an imprint sized perfectly for the instrument. He closed it over, delicately as he would a coffin. "Óla, this isn't right. What we're doing here, this campaign—it's wrong."

"Ahn," Óla said, giving him an odd look. "Really?"

"Really." The certainty in Ahn's body was finally coming through to his voice. "People live here, Óla. I love Qiao Sidh as much as you do, but we can't just . . . *impose* it on other people. We have no right to barge into their homes and ask them to be grateful for it."

"You're sure oversimplifying things here, Ahn."

"But it *is* simple, isn't it?" Ahn asked, looking at her beseechingly. Now that he understood what the Empire was doing, now that he could see it from outside of the framework he had been raised in, he couldn't unknow it. "We're coming into their homes, and we're killing them."

Óla's nonchalance faltered. She sucked in a breath

through her teeth, tapping her knuckles against the table with irritation. "Fine. You want less blood? There's less blood. You can manage negotiations like they taught you in school. We'll take the continent, but we'll take it *nicely*. Deal?"

There was no taking a continent nicely. Ahn had already heard the myth of a gentle empire.

There are cracks in the road, Ahn. It wasn't put down even, not even at the start. Maybe you don't see them, but I thought you ought to know.

Better late than never, right?

Better late than never. He steeled himself.

"I'm willing to listen to your ideas, Ahn," Óla said, more insistently this time. She pushed off the table, unhappiness radiating from her frame. "Alright? So whatever this is, drop it."

"My idea is that we need to go *home*," Ahn replied. He approached her, palms open beseechingly. "We need to go home and talk to Mother and Father. I want to tell them what I've learned here. I think we need to start rethinking what Conquest means in Qiao Sidhur society, it could—"

Óla cut him off with a scoff, rubbing her face with one hand. Her easy-going posture had transformed into nothing but sharp edges, and Ahn wanted very badly to make it better.

"Ólawen," he attempted once more. "I . . . I know you brought me here. I know this was a gift from you, and I wanted to prove myself to you. To make you proud. I *still* want that. You're my sister. But I can't do it like this. This is so much bigger than us, and I—"

Óla's hand came down against the table, sending the silver tokens clattering off the map and onto the floor. "They're going to *kill you.*"

Ahn leapt back, heart pounding. His hand had unconsciously gone for his sword. "I...what?" His mind scrambled to right itself. "Do you mean the people of Gãepongwei? Because they wouldn't, that's not how they do things here."

"Not *them,*" Óla snapped. She sounded angry and exhausted, and he couldn't tell which direction the feelings were being pointed. "Eløndhvos. Eløndtsou, maybe. I don't know how many of our other siblings are involved."

Ahn went cold. "What are you talking about?"

"You heard me, Ahnschen."

"How do you know?" he asked weakly.

"Three assassinations were stopped in the year before we left." Óla couldn't look at him as she said this. Agitated, she grabbed a cup, filling it with elderflower wine. "Your guards were trailing you at school, but after the first attempt, I sent my own as well. It's clear where those attempts are coming from."

Ahn was at a loss. Fratricide was not unheard of in the Éongrir family history; with a lineage that was determined based on merit and preference, jealousy ran rampant, and with a family this large, competition was inevitable. But it didn't add up.

"I don't understand." Ahn looked at her helplessly. "What have I done to cross them? I'm not any threat to the throne, Óla, they all *know* that."

"That's where you're wrong," Ólawen said tightly. "Father's considering naming you his heir, Ahnschen."

Silence tore through Ahn's throat like a blade. He could barely swallow, nevermind form words. It felt like a bad joke. It didn't make sense.

Ólawen let out a humorless laugh. "Are you kidding? You can't be that foolish." When he said nothing, she stepped towards him. Ahn resisted the urge to back away. "You survive your Six-ing at Kørno Wan, only to go off to *public school* at Asgørindad. You live with all the common students, ingratiate yourself with the Masters, the staff, the local restaurant owners. You put on harp performances, attend little harvest festivals, use your allowance to fund your, what, social clubs? Community centers? All of this while maintaining your responsibilities as a member of the royal family." Óla rested her hands on his shoulders, pressing them firmly in place. "You have a fanbase, baby brother. They're calling you *The People's Emperor.*"

"I never wanted that," Ahn choked out. "I just wanted to try something new. I just needed a break."

"I know." Óla's voice was grim.

"It wasn't supposed to matter. Óla, *I'm not supposed to matter.*"

"Well, now you do." Óla sounded harsh, but he could hear the pain in her voice. He realized that she wasn't angry with him. She was scared. "People are talking and Father is listening. And our siblings know."

The room felt as though it was getting smaller, bearing down on him. He imagined Óla's touch was meant to be grounding, but it only made him feel more locked in place.

"You know things are tense back home," she said. The corner of her mouth twitched. "Father's not getting any younger, and questions are rising about succession.

Our spiritualists are talking about a *new age* coming in. And if you come back with all these ideas about how the world should work—ideas, you should know, that have been mumbled about by farmland philosophers before—you're going to have even more attention on you. And if people start *listening*? You know what'll happen."

Of course Ahn knew. This happened every time a new ascension was coming. It was possible for leaders to name an heir to the throne either in life or posthumously; Ahn's father had already said he would do it while he still walked this realm and could counsel the incoming Emperor. Whether that was invaluable aid or a slight against the new leader's autonomy was a matter of opinion.

Knowing his father's stance, Ahn had always expected that there would be feuding in his lifetime. Either political or physical battles between his siblings, or else distant relatives. His mother's brother had been vying for the throne longer than Ólawen had been alive. It was inevitable that people would break into factions, and until a new emperor was crowned, some degree of violence would become a reality.

But Ahn never thought he would be thrown into the mix. It was yet another instance where, foolishly, he had disregarded his own power.

"I don't want this," Ahn repeated shakily. "To be killed, or to be emperor."

"I know," Ólawen repeated in turn. She gave him a shake, jolting him to look at her. Her face was determined, focused, and all he wanted was to trust her. Who else could he trust? "So stay with me. Make something of yourself that isn't the People's Emperor. Leave the trouble back home, and take the continent."

What haunted Ahn was this: if he did not know Hei and Sohmeng, if he had not spent these months with them in Eiji, saying yes wouldn't be all that hard. He could hide behind the fact that *this is just the way things are*, as though he had no say in the outcome. He could play his harp and call it artistic exchange, as though he didn't also have a blade at the ready. He could protect his own hide and pretend it was for the good of others.

It was dishonourable. It was tempting. It was more complicated than he knew what to do with. He did not want to make this choice.

"Ahn." Óla's voice was sharp again. "Think about it."

He *was* thinking. He was thinking, he was thinking, he was trying to think—

"This is what you've always wanted. Why give it up?"

What he always wanted. That—was that right?

"Think about what Schenn would want."

Ha.

Ahn stumbled back from Óla, his lower back banging against the war table, and everything suddenly became very clear. There was an abrupt pop below his ear, and all of the pressure in his head recalibrated as his lungs remembered how to take in air.

Óla was still talking, still trying to convince him, but it was no longer her voice that he was hearing.

Yeah. Me again. Look—no matter what happens, this will still only be the second hardest thing you've ever had to do.

Deep breath, Ahn. Here we go.

Ten

SOHMENG WAS A NOSY PERSON by nature. She had always been this way, asking questions that were none of her business and, on occasion, snooping places that she didn't belong. Out of respect for Hei, it was a quality that she had been working on reining in. She didn't need to know everything that was going on all the time.

But she *did* need to know what was happening in the Qiao Sidhur camp, and being restricted to the treeline was making her nuts—especially when the Great River was *right* there.

The sound of the waves was something between a thunderstorm and a hush, and she could smell the water high in her cheekbones. It looked like it went on forever, and even though she knew she couldn't see Qiao Sidh on the other side, she still wanted to run right up to the shoreline and check anyway. Instead, she had to content herself with squishing her toes in the soft white sand—which was pretty cool, but hardly enough to satisfy her.

She could appreciate why Hei wanted to create distance

between the soldiers and the sãoni. Everyone was on edge, and without Ahn there as a barrier, the situation was unpredictable. But that didn't do anything to make Sohmeng less curious. These were the people who had attempted to claim Gãepongwei without a second thought, the ones who had thrown the sãoni off their migration pattern without even realizing. They were completely out of touch with the land, along with all of the creatures and cultures that inhabited it. And yet they didn't seem to notice.

What kind of people could live like that? If Sohmeng could connect with them, could she explain to them why this behaviour was wrong?

"Sohmeng, *no*," Hei insisted.

"Sohmeng *yes*," Sohmeng insisted back, but harder. "You stay past the treeline where you can see me, stick with the sãoni. If anyone tries anything—which I'm pretty sure they *won't*, seeing as Ahn said we're friends—then you come in with your claws out."

"Ahnschen is not here," Hei snapped. "They listen to his sister. "

"They listen to him too! They're both generals! Just because sãoni only have one alpha—"

Their bickering was broken up by a snarl from one of the creatures in question. Ahn's preferred riding sãoni, Sølshend, was scratching at the earth with a menacing look. It was directed at the Qiao Sidhur soldier with the tattoo of Chehangma on her head, who was approaching cautiously with a steaming plate of food.

"Excuse me, guests," the soldier said. "I do not know how long the generals will be speaking. Are you hungry?"

Sohmeng was taken aback; the soldier's Dulpongpa was better than she expected. It was certainly better than Ahn's when they'd first met. "Oh! Um, sure! Food would be great, actually."

The woman passed over the plate, which was piled with a couple rounds of dense flatbread, clearly straight off the grill if the char lines were any indicator. It was spiced with something Sohmeng didn't recognize—whatever it was, it smelled amazing. She passed a piece over to Hei, who scowled, but took it anyway.

"I'm Noula," the soldier said. "And you are Hei, and Sohmeng Minhal?"

"Yeah, that's us." Sohmeng was surprised again that the woman had retained their names so quickly. She eyed her, leaning into curiosity. "Your name—what's the full thing?"

"Hidhrolo Noula Qøngemtsou, Idhrenqang."

Sohmeng furrowed her brow as she thought through each sound. She and Ahn had been practicing this for ages now; it would be embarrassing not to be able to pick up something this simple. "That'll be . . . fourth in Conquest, fifth in Discernment?"

"But who's counting?" Noula smiled.

Behind her, Hei made an appreciative sound. They had torn into the bread with their teeth and were now staring at the remaining piece, wide-eyed.

"We can get you more," Noula said, and that's how she ended up sitting in the sand by the treeline with Hei and Sohmeng, chatting.

It turned out that Noula had begun studying Dulpongpa before ever landing in Gãepongwei, having learned it from her Discernment Master, who had been part of the first expedition five years ago—the very expedition that had disrupted the sãoni migration route. Ahn had mentioned before that this wasn't Qiao Sidh's first time on the continent, but he hadn't offered specifics about the when or where. From Noula, the history came clear and succinct: they had landed near the bluffs of the northeastern coast, and made first contact with Hosaisi, who showed them hospitality for almost a year and a half before the Qiao Sidhur returned home.

It was eerie for Sohmeng, knowing how long the Empire had been at her door.

Now, she wanted to learn everything she could. Noula indulged her questions, answering in between bites of bread. How far was the journey to the lower continent? What part of the Empire did Noula live in? How did she end up on the campaign? How well did she know Ahn? As she listened, Sohmeng shared some fruit from her traveling pack, which Hei only sulked about a little bit.

"My second cousin is Óla's Wen," Noula said, tapping her ear. Unpierced. "We got to know one another more after Wen crossed realms. Discernment was always my speciality, Conquest secondary. Óla convinced me to raise my rank enough to join her as an advisor."

"She does seem . . . convincing," Sohmeng said. What she meant was *intimidating*, but she didn't want to sound afraid.

"A leader has to be, don't you think?" Noula countered. With Hei standing by, a tooth-lined hood slack on their shoulders, Sohmeng didn't have much ground to disagree.

The sãoni hadn't quite relaxed around Noula, but, without Hei giving any orders to attack, weren't displaying any aggression either. This was a huge victory as far as Sohmeng was concerned; even with those big freaky bird creatures so close by, they managed to keep themselves settled.

Noula was curious about the dynamic at play with Hei as alpha, but Hei was firm on protecting the colony's privacy. Sohmeng didn't have to be told twice—this connection was exactly what she had been hoping for, but she also knew that the sãoni were a huge advantage. There was a major risk of them being exploited if the Qiao Sidhur learned how they had been trained.

"Based on everything Ahn's told me, I think I would have picked Discernment too," Sohmeng said, uncrossing her legs to stretch them out. "Ahn said so a while ago, and the more I learn, the more I think he's right. I like solving problems and learning stuff. I'm an ideas guy!"

"Minhal Sohmeng Idhrensammi?" Noula offered, and Sohmeng smirked.

"*Actually*, Ahn said he'd start me at Idhrenhvøs," she said smugly.

"Who am I to argue with Eløndham? Idhrenhvøs it is," Noula said, wiping oil from her hands with a damp cloth. She rinsed the fabric once more before passing it to Sohmeng. "It's not out of the question, you know."

"What do you mean?"

"Everyone in the Empire has the right to walk one of the Paths."

As they shared this meal, Sohmeng had been getting to know Noula as an individual, separate from the Empire as a whole. Noula asked thoughtful questions; Noula was a great listener. Sohmeng liked Noula, found it easy to share with her.

Maybe that's why her blood suddenly ran cold.

"Oh," she said, uncomfortable. A Qiao Sidhur name didn't feel so fun anymore. "That's ..."

She struggled with her words. She didn't want to be confrontational and cause a problem, but she wasn't about to act like she was eager to join up with the Empire. The silence extended, but Noula didn't seem bothered by it. She tossed her orange rind to the sãoni. Qøngem jumped forward, chomping it down happily.

"There's no rush," Noula said, rolling out her wrists. "But it is worth your consideration. The Discernment Path gave me the opportunity to travel, to connect with new people. We're talking right now, aren't we?"

Sohmeng couldn't deny it was true. But despite the shared language, she wasn't so sure they were having the same conversation.

"It's important to understand one another," Sohmeng tried after a moment. "Especially when we have different needs to communicate."

Noula hummed. "That's very true."

As she searched for what to say, what to *ask*, a burst of noise sounded from across the clearing.

At the center of the camp, the flaps of an elaborate tent flung open. Ahn walked out, Óla trailing behind him. Her voice was raised, and Sohmeng didn't need to know Qiao Sidhur to know that she was angry.

Noula rose, and Sohmeng took her arm. "Would you tell me what they're saying?"

The soldier looked unsure, but after a brief moment, she nodded. Her translation was clear and efficient, but she could not suppress the unease in her voice.

"You will not do this," Ólawen snarled at Ahn. "You will not shame yourself this way."

"I'm not ashamed, Óla."

"You will not shame *me* this way. You will not shame your family, your Empire—do they mean nothing to you?"

The Qiao Sidhur soldiers didn't seem to know what to do with themselves. Sohmeng watched them struggle, some moving forward, some stepping back. Some watched closely and others averted their gaze. From what Sohmeng had heard about the rigidity of rank in Qiao Sidh, she wondered if any of them were allowed to interfere.

Behind Sohmeng, Hei whistled. They were securing their supplies, readying the sãoni for a quick exit. Sohmeng watched helplessly.

Noula's translation cut out as Óla shoved Ahn, her voice getting louder. Ahn was a tall guy, but it was like he was shrinking before Sohmeng's eyes. Grand Ones bickered all the time at Chehangma's Gate, but it never looked anything like this.

Sohmeng shook Noula's arm again. "Noula, *please*. Ahn would want us to know!"

She hesitated briefly, running a hand over the shaved side of her head. "Ólawen is insulting him, that's what this is."

"Why?" Sohmeng insisted. "What's she *saying*?"

Noula sucked in air through her teeth, watching the royal siblings. To Sohmeng's alarm and relief, they were coming closer. "I won't repeat it out of respect for them both, but it isn't—"

Ólawen drew her blade.

In an instant, Hei leapt from Green Bites, hood down

and claws out. They snarled a call for the sãoni to stay, claiming ownership of this fight.

"Hei, *no!*" Sohmeng yelled. To her horror, it didn't just catch Ahn's attention—it caught Ólawen's.

She sneered, walking towards Hei with her sword out. Ahn moved so quickly that Sohmeng barely saw it happen. His blade clashed with his sister's, the clang of metal on metal ringing across the beach. Ólawen wasted no time parrying him. Her expression was goading.

"You will not *touch them*," Ahn said in Dulpongpa. Sohmeng had never heard his voice so fierce before. There was fury there, and no word of a lie.

"Duel me then, you coward—oh *gods,* what are you doing Eløndhol?" Noula's own alarm tore through her neat translation, and Sohmeng felt that anxiety ripple out through the camp.

"No," Ahn said firmly in Qiao Sidhur. Their blades clashed again and again at an unrelenting pace. Each strike seemed to test his resolve. Ólawen bore down, and Ahn's voice became weaker, more distraught. "Óla, *no!*"

Sohmeng knew this word from Ahn's panic attacks, from his nightmares. However badly she thought this confrontation could go, she had never imagined this.

The two generals moved with a speed Sohmeng had never seen before, sand kicked up in glittering arcs at each lightning step. Even through her horror, she could see why Ahn had described combat as an art form. The sãoni were ferocious, but they weren't organized. They did not train, and for all that their unpredictability made them dangerous, there was something differently frightening about watching the practiced choreography of war.

All across Gãepongwei, humans trained to defend themselves from predators. From the elements. But there had been no need to defend themselves from other humans since the time of legend.

They were in over their heads. They had to get out, and fast.

Sohmeng ran to Singing Violet and jumped on her back. She cried out to Hei in Sãonipa: *Alpha, go!*

Hei hissed, but took the cue. They made fast for the colony and swung up onto Green Bites, wasting no time as they charged back towards Ahn. The rush of a full-grown sãoni startled Óla into stumbling backwards, and Hei used that moment to yank Ahn up behind them.

Go! they yelled to their colony, and the sãoni took off at full speed, leaving the Great River behind.

As they fled, she heard General Eløndhol yell something to her brother. Sohmeng couldn't make out the words, but as they disappeared into the jungle, she knew they had been issued a warning.

Eleven

THE COLONY RODE STRAIGHT through to nightfall, putting as much distance between them and Ólawen as possible. Lacking Hei and Ahn's years of riding experience, the relentless pace made Sohmeng's entire body ache, but she wasn't about to ask to slow down. Ólawen's voice was still echoing in her mind, punctuated by the clash of steel. The further they got from her, the better.

"How much longer, Hei?" Sohmeng called over the sounds of the sãoni. She had to shout to be heard over the huffing and snarling and claws hitting the earth.

"Until they must stop," Hei said. Their jaw was set, their expression dark.

Sohmeng watched Ahn's arms tighten around their waist. After getting onto Green Bites' back, he'd pressed his face against Hei's shoulder and gone silent. Sohmeng hadn't heard a word out of him since.

All the stubborn Par optimism in the world couldn't hide the facts: things were not looking good. The Qiao Sidhur camp was Sohmeng's first real exposure to the

Empire's culture beyond what she'd heard from Ahn. She had seen the good, the bad, and the very, very complicated.

This was Ahn's home; this was the threat to Gãepongwei. Looking at these facts side by side made her eyes want to cross.

Sohmeng couldn't have counted how many swords she saw this morning, lying around casually as the laundry lines. With one word from Ólawen, from *General* Ólawen, they would have all been pointed in her direction. And that was without even bringing the fire-sand into it.

Then there was Hidhrolo Noula. Sohmeng had enjoyed talking with her at first. She'd been excited for the opportunity to get some actual cultural exchange in—that is, right up until she recognized the woman's calm conviction that her home would successfully conquer Sohmeng's. The most frightening part was that it didn't seem like Noula was trying to intimidate her; she just believed it that strongly.

It was never going to be as simple as a single conversation. Sohmeng knew that now, and the reality sat heavy. This was an issue of worldview—even if she explained the damage that was being done, some people might not care. They might not believe her, even when the truth was right in front of them. A sense of helplessness rose up in her, a wordless dread at the idea that no one would listen.

Par, Go, Hiwei, Fua, Tang, Sol, Jão, Pel, Dongi, Se, Won, Nor, Chisong, Heng, Li, Ginhãe, Mi, Ker, Hiun, Ãofe, Soon, Nai, Tos, Jeji, Minhal.

Sohmeng grit her teeth, forcing her old doubts back. Imagining that *no one* would listen was as naïve as thinking *everyone* would. Defeatism would get her nowhere.

Sohmeng had seen weapons at the Qiao Sidhur camp, yes, but she had also seen embroidery on the tents. She watched a soldier getting her hair braided, and another losing a card game. She had eaten warm bread and peered at Noula's tattoo, and seen circles of footsteps where someone must have been pacing. She saw *people*, all living their lives in the way they knew how. Ólawen was a general, but she was also only one human. The empire that made her had also made Ahn, and he could not be the only person among them willing to change.

But when Ahn finally found his voice, a new challenge emerged.

"You will come back and duel me as a warrior does," Ahn translated that evening, slumped against a tree. He looked completely exhausted, like he had spent the past hours running on the ground instead of riding sãoniback. "That's what she said as I ran from her. By custom, I have a maximum of ten days to answer the call."

"What is the purpose of this?" Hei asked.

"Resolution. When a problem cannot be talked through, it is solved by the blade. The winner of the duel is the winner of the dispute, and there is no further talk on the matter."

"Like sãoni," Hei said, but Sohmeng saw that they were frowning.

For her part, Sohmeng was busy biting back more anger. How was this any useful way to solve a problem? She took Ahn's hand, wanting to encourage him, but it was limp in her palm. "So that sort of fight, a duel, is it like ...?"

The words couldn't make it out of her mouth, even as

her gaze drifted to Schenn's fingerbone. Still, Ahn took her meaning.

"Typically, it ends at either a yield or first blood. But each day that passes marks the severity of the offense. If I arrive on the tenth day, we duel to the death."

Sohmeng's heart jolted. "You don't think—"

"I do not think she would kill me, no." Ahn closed his eyes, his mouth a tight line. "But she also didn't think I would abandon Qiao Sidh. So perhaps we'll both surprise one another."

Sohmeng didn't know what to say to that; any placations would have sounded hollow even to her. She looked to Hei for guidance, but they said nothing, their unhappy expression only deepening. The three of them went to bed uneasy, and woke up the next morning in a similar state.

Ahn was trying hard to act like he was fine, which only highlighted how obviously *not fine* he was. All of the brightness had drained out of him; he moved like he was sleepwalking as he helped prepare the sãoni to ride. Watching him spiked Sohmeng's anxiety, and she knew she had to do something to improve the situation.

"We should make it to Sorwei Chapal tonight, right Hei?" she asked.

"If we move quickly," Hei said. They were also quiet this morning, and Sohmeng didn't know how to pull them aside for a private talk without making things even weirder with Ahn. "They will need breaks, but we can manage one more day at this pace."

"Great! That's plenty of time to make a plan." Sohmeng looked over at Ahn, but he didn't respond. As he climbed onto Sølshend, securing his belongings, she wasn't sure if he was even listening. "How about we start moving the colony at a pace that doesn't make our teeth clang together? Then we can talk about how to manage this whole duel situation. The way I see it, you don't actually *need* to go through with it."

"I'm not sure what you think I'd do instead," Ahn said. "Her terms were clear."

"Well, it's not just about what Óla wants. You've gotta have at least some allies there, right? Noula seems like she could be a lot of help."

"She works for my sister."

"But she also works for you, right?" Sohmeng pressed. "The campaign was supposed to be a collaboration!"

"That collaboration depended on me doing my job," Ahn said, not looking at her. "So I'm fairly certain that that angle is off the table. Are we ready to go, Hei?"

To Sohmeng's frustration, Hei clicked in agreement. She climbed onto Singing Violet, taking a deep breath as she rubbed between the sãoni's head spines. Being cut off like that stung. It felt like she was talking to a different person, which was worrying, and also kind of hurtful. The three of them had been working together every step of the way. How would they manage what came next if they couldn't be a team?

It had been bad enough not knowing how to talk to Ahn after the playfight went wrong. Now he was intentionally *creating* distance, and Sohmeng was stuck behind a wall that she was afraid she couldn't break through. He was her partner, wasn't he? Shouldn't she know how to make him feel better?

For the rest of the day, she kept trying. Up until now,

she and Ahn would spend hours throwing ideas around, waiting for something to stick. There was always a solution waiting somewhere, it was only a matter of finding it. Even if they couldn't figure out how to manage Óla's call for a duel, Sohmeng was determined to at least find a way to get Ahn back to being himself.

She might as well have been talking to a rock. If anything, the more she tried, the worse he started to look, like a plant that had gotten waterlogged in a big storm. He got visibly more upset, but even less communicative.

"So that's something!" Sohmeng attempted, barely able to articulate what her latest plan even was. "What do you think, Hei?

"I think we need to get to Sorwei Chapal," Hei said, "and I cannot think of anything else until then."

The rest of the journey was made in tense silence. The riding pace was brutal all the way through, but Sohmeng was grateful that it shortened the journey. She couldn't take any more time stuck in her own head.

That evening, they arrived in Sorwei Chapal. Sohmeng's whole body was fiercely sore and her brain was fried. The sãoni more or less collapsed snoring outside the hmun, throats glowing green and purple in the dark. Part of Sohmeng wished that she could join them, but the plan was the same as last time: Sohmeng and Ahn would manage the humans, and Hei would stay with the sãoni.

"I won't be gone long this time," Sohmeng said, kissing Hei, trying to convince her own body that it would be true. "Promise, promise, promise."

Hei's lips lingered at hers, and Sohmeng found herself all the more determined to come back to them as soon as possible. Despite the two days they'd spent in proximity, she felt like she'd been completely alone. When Hei pulled back, they extended a hand to Ahn.

"This time," they said, "no pygmy hog pens."

Sohmeng had no idea if this was a joke or not. Either way, it gave her a flash of warmth—and on top of that, it even got a smile out of Ahn. He took Hei's hand, holding it briefly to his heart.

Now *this* was an update. Sohmeng had noticed Ahn and Hei getting closer over the past few phases. She couldn't remember the last time the two of them got in a real fight, and they had all gotten comfortable sleeping in a pile like the sãoni. But this casual display of physical affection between them was something different. She was happy for them.

But also . . . she wasn't. As much as it made her uncomfortable, she was jealous. Why couldn't she help Ahn like Hei could? Did he not like her as much as he liked Hei?

She tried to shake the thought, turning her attention to Sorwei Chapal. After all, it wasn't every day she got to see a new hmun, and this one was remarkable. While Nona Fahang and Ateng had their differences, they did have one thing in common: between banyan walls and mountaintops, it was hard for outsiders to gain entry. In contrast, Sorwei Chapal stretched out like an ocelot in the sun. The hmun spanned a tributary of the Ãotul, with houses situated on small islands and floating platforms, all strung together with bridges large and small. If her father was correct, those little suspension bridges were made from the same type of rope as what they'd used to fix the Sky Bridge.

Arriving at nightfall revealed another piece of Sorwei Chapal's beauty: lanterns carved out of gourds hung along the bridges and illuminated the threshold of peoples' homes. When Sohmeng saw a light steadily moving across the river, she realized it was someone paddling a boat to the other side. Making a crossing.

Sorwei Chapal was not the place she'd grown up in, but it still felt familiar. As she compared it to the other two hmun she knew, something began to emerge: a sense of what *Gãepongwei* was, what it meant. There were threads beyond Dulpongpa that connected everyone as neighbours, hints of the ancient civilization their ancestors had all shared. As Sohmeng learned to recognize these ties, her idea of what "home" meant expanded, and she felt all the more determined to protect it.

As she and Ahn crossed one of the bridges, trying to get deeper into the hmun, another unexpected piece of home showed up.

"Sohmeng! Ahnschen!" Eakang ran to meet them. On instinct they lurched forward for a hug, but then managed to contain themself. "You made it! I'm so glad you're here."

This time, Sohmeng found that she didn't need to brace herself for Eakang's enthusiasm. Honestly, after what they'd all been through, an overexcited fourteen-year-old was the least of her worries. Compared to the past couple of days, it was nice to be with someone who was open with their feelings.

"It's good to be here," she said. "Have the sãoni been okay?"

"Honestly? They've been *great*." Eakang beamed. "They listened really well to me and Polha, and they've been super curious about Sorwei Chapal. Apparently the migration route brings sãoni close to the riverbanks now and then, so the Sorchapa plant silvertongue to keep them from getting too close. A lot of people have honestly been happy to get a closer look, and the sãoni don't mind as long as they have a river to splash in. I think it's going better than any of us could have guessed!"

"Huh." That was a pleasant surprise. She wondered what Hei would have to say about it, or how it might shift the arrangements for the colony while they stayed here.

"I'm rambling though—how about you guys?" Eakang asked, looking at Ahn hopefully. "Did the talk with your sister go okay? Is everything alright?"

Ahn tensed beside her. Ignoring the uncomfortable churning in her own stomach, Sohmeng stepped in. He was already going to have to explain the situation to a group of strangers tonight; it didn't feel kind to make him do it twice.

"It's complicated," Sohmeng said. "Can you bring us to the Grand Ones, or whoever is in charge? The sooner we start working on a plan the better."

Eakang's face fell. They took Ahn's hand. "I'm sorry."

Ahn smiled tiredly. "Me too."

"The Grand Ones aren't far," Eakang said, guiding them through the bridges' path. A closer look at the lanterns revealed that countless tiny holes had been punched out, resulting in an even, muted glow without the risk of a fully exposed flame. "They'll be able to help. They're actually really nice? Things are ... pretty different here." Eakang glanced at Sohmeng as they said this, with a knowing look that Sohmeng was all out of brain power to interpret. She was just glad to be walking in the direction of help.

Eakang brought them to one of Sorwei Chapal's largest islands. It was home to two roundhouses connected by an open walkway with a trellis roof. Vibrant blue bulbed flowers dangled over the sides like strings of jewelry; the roof itself was a garden, lined with rows of flowers, fruits, and vegetables. A young adult in a long white skirt balanced on a ladder, examining a couple of peppers that hung close to the edge.

It took Sohmeng a moment to look past the foliage and notice the colour of the buildings: the larger one was painted white, the smaller one red. Ateng's Grand Ones spoke beneath a skylight, and Nona Fahang's from a public gazebo, but Sorwei Chapal had something completely different. It made Sohmeng imagine making decisions from deep inside the moons themselves.

"We're in Ama House tonight," Eakang said, nodding upwards at the moons. Par had begun the night before. "They alternate."

"What do they do if it's one of the neutral phases?" Sohmeng asked.

"Grand One's choice. From what I've heard, Chehang House has more comfortable seats, but Ama House has better acoustics."

As they stepped into the red moon's house, Sohmeng was met with double the amount of people she'd expected. Next to each of the Grand Ones' seats was a cushion, many of which were occupied by people young and old, each wearing the colour of their respective phase. In Sorwei Chapal, Eakang explained, Grand Ones were shadowed by apprentices, specially selected to take over the role when the Grand One either died or willingly stepped down. This was another difference between Nona Fahang and Ateng both, and one that made sense to Sohmeng. The oldest person in the room wasn't always the wisest.

"Have you noticed?" Eakang asked Sohmeng quietly as the last of the apprentices filed in.

"Noticed what?"

"The seats."

Aside from the nearby cushions, the Grand Ones' chairs all looked like regular chairs to Sohmeng—but then she realized what was off. There were only twenty-four. A phase was missing. At first she tensed, trying to figure out how she would name herself to avoid any danger, but Eakang didn't seem afraid.

A recent memory of her father rose to the surface. As they ascended Sodão Dangde together, he'd told her about the hmun beyond Ateng, how they viewed Minhal and the children born to it. There were some places where it wasn't *Minhal* at all. Could it be—?

"Parminhal," Sohmeng said, quiet awe in her voice.

"Yeah." Eakang sounded equally reverent. She expected them to be jumping around about their discovery, but they were as contained as she had ever seen. They exhaled softly, nodding. "We're under Parminhal tonight."

Tonão had said the phase was used in a hmun far west. Sohmeng wondered if he simply hadn't known it was used here too, or if something had changed since he last visited. What ideas had spread without them knowing? What new possibilities existed that Sohmeng simply did not yet have the imagination to think of?

Once the Grand Ones and their apprentices were settled in, the doors to the house closed to the public. Similar to Ateng, meeting with Sorwei Chapal's Grand Ones was a private event. Before falling from the mountain, Sohmeng was critical of the need for such secrecy. But after being repeatedly shut down in front of a crowd in Nona Fahang, she was relieved by the chance to have this conversation in a container fit to hold it.

During this meeting, Ahn, Sohmeng, Eakang, and Polha Hiwei—who gave Sohmeng a warm hello—were allowed in as representatives of Nona Fahang and Ateng. Sorwei Chapal also had an additional representative of their own: Nepar Ãofe.

Nepar was the most Ãofe-looking man Sohmeng had ever seen in her life. He was *huge*, with a stern face and deep voice that was unexpectedly kind. He looked like he could toss Ahn in the air and catch him. Gods, he looked like he could toss *Green Bites* in the air and catch him.

Which was important, seeing as he was also the leader of Sorwei Chapal's faction of warriors, which was over a hundred strong.

"You have a *military*?" Ahn asked, unable to hide his surprise. One of the Grand Ones huffed out a laugh, but Sohmeng was just as shocked. They hadn't seen anything like that so far in southern Gãepongwei.

"We do," said Grand One Ãofe. "There has been a martial practice for as long as we've existed as Sorwei Chapal. We train new students every year and have them perform."

"Are they prepared to work as an army?" There was an intensity in Ahn's voice that Sohmeng hadn't heard before. "Are they organized?"

"Come by and watch us tomorrow," Nepar offered with a wink. His confidence felt infectious to Sohmeng, and she nudged Ahn with a smile that he didn't quite return. "Though, about a fifth of them are students nearing graduation. It would be my preference to keep them out of this if at all possible."

That was the other thing that had Sohmeng reeling: before Polha and Eakang had even arrived, Sorwei Chapal had been preparing to deal with the Qiao Sidhur invasion. Their relative proximity to both Kongkempei and Hosaisi had made them aware of the Empire's assault, and landed them with some refugees of their own. Shortly after, they'd set up a network of scouts to keep track of the situation. All the while, Nepar Ãofe had been training up his warriors for the first real battle they'd seen in centuries.

"When Polha Hiwei and Eakang Pa—excuse me, Eakang Minhal—arrived, it was a gift from the gods," said Grandmother Parminhal. Sohmeng could not stop looking at her. Her austere posture, her long hair, the bob of the ridge in her throat as she spoke. "As you understand, we need all the support we could get—and the sãoni? *That* we never could have expected. We are grateful to have you as our allies."

Yet again, Sohmeng was speechless. She had spent so much of this past cycle trying to convince people to listen to her. In her determination to be an adult, she'd found herself saddled with responsibilities that she honestly wasn't ready for. Deep down, she had been bracing herself for another struggle to get people on her side.

But here was a group of people who needed no convincing, who'd been on her side before she even walked through the door. Here was a community that was open to working together, ready to exchange ideas and collaborate. A weight lifted from her, and only then did she realize how heavy it had been, the burden of thinking that she had to do everything alone.

"The feeling is *really* mutual," Sohmeng said, and hoped they could feel her gratitude.

"We are also very interested in hearing more from Prince Ahnschen," said Grandmother Parminhal. The entire room's gaze seemed to land on Ahn, and Sohmeng was reminded again of Nona Fahang's trial. This time, there was no blindfold. He would get to—would have to—face them eye-to-eye. "Your friends from Nona Fahang spoke very highly of you and all you have done for Gãepongwei. They told us you went to negotiate with the General, your sister. What news do you bring?"

Sohmeng watched Ahn move to kneel in the Qiao Sidhur way before he caught himself, clenching his fists. "As her fellow General, I urged her to cease the campaign and return to Qiao Sidh. I was unsuccessful, and she issued a challenge against me for shaming her and the Empire. If I win, the campaign ends. If she wins, it continues."

"A challenge," said Grandmother Parminhal slowly. Her apprentice passed her a fresh cup of tea as she considered. "Of what sort, exactly?"

Ahn's voice was flat as he described the terms of a duel. It sounded to Sohmeng like he was telling a story about someone else. It was palpable, the dissonance between his words and the emotions she knew he was carrying. She'd never considered herself to be an especially sensitive person, but standing beside him made her whole body uneasy.

"I promised I would do all I can to make this right," Ahn said, his face unreadable, "and I do not intend to go back on that promise. My blade is yours."

"There may be other ways that you could help," Grandmother Parminhal mused.

"With respect," Ahn said with finality, "there aren't."

"It's only been two days," Sohmeng tried once more. "I'm sure there are other options, Ahn."

She reached for his hand, but he yanked it out of her reach. As Ahn faced her for the first time, she saw something she hadn't expected: he was angry. More than that, he was angry at *her*. "My sister issued a challenge. Where I'm from, there would be no greater insult than disregarding it, and each day we wait raises the stakes."

"Well we're not in Qiao Sidh right now, we're in Gãepongwei." Sohmeng could hear the edge in her own voice. "And I don't really care how insulted your sister feels right now. This whole thing is barbaric and I'm just trying to help—"

"*You aren't helping!*" Ahn shouted, pressing his palms to his forehead. "How many times do I need to explain that she won't listen to you?"

"You're the one who isn't listening! You're not listening and you won't talk to me and you're going to get yourself killed!"

A sharp whistle from Nepar Ãofe snapped Sohmeng back to reality, and she felt heavy with dread as she faced the circle of Grand Ones. For all the mistakes she had made with her elders, she was fairly confident that she'd never made a worse first impression than this.

"I'm sorry," she said, bowing her head. Next to her, Ahn

was kneeling; this close, she could see him shaking. "Truly, I apologize, that was . . . that was inappropriate."

Polha Hiwei came up to her, resting a hand on her back, and Sohmeng found herself trying not to cry. She forced herself to meet Grandmother Parminhal's eye, but the woman didn't look displeased. Baffled, sure, but not mad. On the cushion beside her, her apprentice was looking at Sohmeng worriedly, as though she was a kid who had scraped her knee.

"Well," said Grandmother Parminhal, draining her teacup in one long gulp, "it seems like tensions are a bit high right now. You've traveled far—perhaps a good night's sleep is in order."

"We don't have *time* for this," Ahn said, his voice pained. In Ateng and Nona Fahang, he had been a model of respect. It was a testament to how exhausted he was that he was speaking like this to his elders. "I am sorry, I am sorry that I failed you. Please let me try to fix it, I can't make a mistake like that and just *walk away*. I can't do that again."

Sohmeng glanced at Schenn's fingerbone, hanging heavy in Ahn's earlobe. She wished desperately that Hei were here. Even if they showed it like a sãoni, they were so much better at holding people's feelings.

"Prince Ahnschen, I thank you for your desire to help," Grandmother Parminhal said sincerely. "But we do not make these sorts of decisions when someone is wounded."

Ahn looked up at her sharply, his brow furrowed. "But I'm—I am well. I can fight. I'm not woun—"

"My boy, but you are," Grandmother Parminhal interrupted. She took a deep breath, addressing another Grand One in the circle. "I don't care if it's my phase.

Make a choice here, Jão. This is your domain, not mine."

Grand One Jão's chair was painted with images of their birth phase: Chehang halfway to darkness and Ama halfway to light. Jão children were inclined towards harmony, open to holding peoples' joy and pain alike. The Grand One conferred quietly with their apprentice, a lithe person who had their green eyes lined in black makeup and their curly hair elegantly pinned back from their face. They looked to be in their mid-twenties, and smiled at Sohmeng when they made eye contact.

The elder Jão sighed heavily. "Prince Ahnschen is right about one thing: there never is enough time. It's a cruelty. But we will work with what we have. Lula, I leave this with you."

The apprentice stood, clasping their hands behind their back. "I would suggest beginning with two days and two nights, at absolute minimum."

"Two days and nights of what?" Sohmeng asked suspiciously. No one in the room seemed to have bad intentions, but she was protective. Ahn clearly needed help beyond what she could give, but she wasn't about to abandon him to a group of strangers.

"Healing," Lula Jão said warmly, as if anything was that simple. "It's my specialty."

"I do not *need* healing." Once again, Ahn's voice took Sohmeng aback. He wasn't shouting this time, but there was a roughness to the way he spoke, like when Hei felt backed into a corner or Sohmeng felt like she was being talked down to. She hadn't heard this tone from Ahn, not even the night he had screamed at the sky with her and Hei. That had been the sound of him letting go—*this* was self-destructive. Wounded, like Grandmother Parminhal was saying.

That wound had been festering ever since that stupid playfight she'd set up between him and Hei, and he never acknowledged it. Part of her wondered if he genuinely didn't realize how badly he was hurting. The idea scared her, but she had no idea how to fix it.

"Éongrir Anschen," Grandmother Parminhal said, "do you wish to help us face your empire's army? Answer me truly."

"I do," Ahn responded, pain ringing in his voice. "More than anything, I do."

"Then you will need a clear head and a rested body." Grandmother Parminhal made the statement so plainly that it was difficult to argue. If Ahn had any more protest, he kept it to himself. "Two days and two nights, Prince Ahnschen. We will reconvene then. For now, I'm adjourning this meeting. Let's all get some rest. It's a beautiful night, and we have our work cut out for us."

Twelve

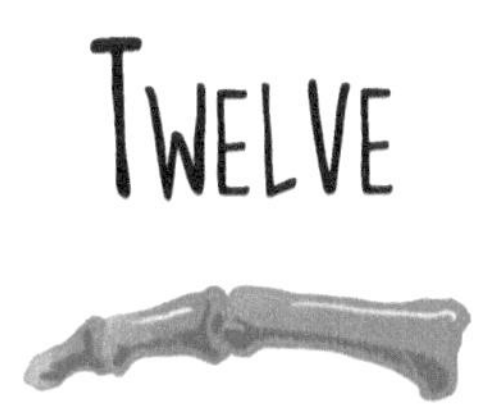

THE ONLY PERSON IN QIAO SIDHUR history to have mastered all nine Paths of Mastery was Shengdhru Allateinn. Historians said he had been real, but nearly a thousand years later, the man had transformed into myth. There were folktales about him, larger than life, recreated again and again to suit the times they were told in.

No matter the story, no matter the time, Allateinn was remembered as a man of quality. In conquest, he was discerning. In discernment, he accounted always for health. In healing, he was beautiful. In aesthetic, he reimagined the possibilities of art. In art, he worked from a deep personal philosophy. In philosophy, he discovered the tools of advancement. In his devotion to advancement, the land was made fertile and rich. And in family and fruitful earth, he found his ties to spirit, which carried him to the realm beyond.

Shengdhru Allateinn, Qøngemhol, Idhrenhol, Hvundparhol, Søngjudhol, Sølshendhol, Siengunghol, Zhøllonghol, Alléndhol, Ødselhol.

It was said that Allateinn was so good and just that all nine of his tenth rankings were awarded at the same time, a mere hour following his death. His name grew long enough to fill its own verse in the ballad of his life.

Like every other Qiao Sidhur child, Ahn wanted to be exactly like him. Legends and academic texts alike taught Ahn about Allateinn's virtues: patience, honour, sacrifice. It was hard to choose a favourite story—the one where Allateinn spoke for three days and nights with an ancient bear, or the one where he avenged his uncle with a bow fashioned from the man's own ribs, or the one where he was visited by the anguished ghost of a lover and appeased her with a song.

In one story, Allateinn came across a man who had murdered his friends in anger over a land dispute. Rage and greed had taken him over, and only after the terrible deed was done did he truly realize the extent of his crimes. The man's heart returned to itself, and he was lost in horror and guilt.

Allateinn had been traveling through town at the time, and was known for his integrity. The murderer approached him and begged for help. He asked what he should do to make it right. His community would never accept him again, he understood this. But how could he earn the forgiveness of his dead friends, whom he had wronged in the worst possible way? What could be done about that which was unforgivable?

Allateinn told him none could answer that question but the dead themselves. *You will join them one day and find your peace together,* he said. *But their spirits will be restless all these years. Do you wish to resolve this conflict now?*

The man said yes. And so, just and gentle and kind, Allateinn offered to do the work himself. He held the grieving murderer with all the tenderness of a brother, and assured him he did not have to be afraid. He sent him to the bilateral realm quickly and painlessly.

There, it is said, the man found his salvation.

Back in Nona Fahang, there had been many times where Ahn had wished for Shengdhru Allateinn to come to him and free him of his mistakes. Not the broken sugar bowl or the careless comment, but the mistakes made on the edge of a blade. The ones that were unforgivable. There were some choices, Ahn learned, that only death could cleanse.

And yet, Nona Fahang's Grand Ones had shown him mercy. He *had* been forgiven, and offered tangible ways to do right by the community he had harmed. It was the sort of second chance that never would have existed in Qiao Sidh.

And then he'd failed.

Speaking with his sister should have been a simple task. They had grown up together. She *loved* him. No one else in Gãepongwei had the same chance of getting through to Ólawen as a prince of the realm, even one eleventh born. But the moment he saw her, the moment he heard her voice, he became weak. This had been the greatest responsibility of his entire life, and it had slipped through his clumsy fingers and shattered on the floor.

When Ahn was brought to the river by Lula Jão, he could not shake the certainty that he was going to be punished. Part of him even yearned for it. Guilt covered his body like a creeping rash, choked him like he'd swallowed hot embers. But no one in Sorwei Chapal addressed it. People knew how he'd failed, and yet no one uttered a word of condemnation. The confusion was agonizing.

"The water connects us," Lula began, holding out their hands for Ahn as they stood in the river. They had brought him to a secluded area; Ahn could hardly hear the bustle of the hmun. "It's valuable to pay it a visit from time to time."

Ahn took Lula's hands, following them into the water. It was cool without being cold, wound around his shins at a pace that steadied him instead of sweeping him away.

"Do you have a body of water that you love, back in your home?" they asked.

Ahn stepped up to his knees, then to his hips. Both he and Lula wore tunics that were beaded with hundreds of shells, and as a shiver ran through him, they clacked lightly beneath the water. "There is a lake, in a place called Hvallánzhou. It reflects the mountains that surround it. I played near it for hours as a child. It's where I learned to boat."

The memory felt numb in his mouth, surreal to be saying here. But Lula simply listened, holding his forearms delicately in their hands. They were willowy, an inch or two shorter than him. Even though they knew this river better than he ever would, he had to resist the instinct to take their waist in case the current picked up.

"Is there another?" Lula asked.

Ahn thought of a different lake, more recently. Floating in its stillness with Hei by his side, listening to Sohmeng play with the sãoni by the shore. How the vivid sky had so quickly been scrubbed down by rainclouds, blue giving way to misty grey. The rain was so cool that the water felt warm. Despite her modesty, that was enough to get Sohmeng to join Ahn and Hei in the water.

Lula smiled, as though he had shared the memory aloud. They took another step back, and the water rose to his ribs. "And another?"

There was. Ahn could feel it. There was another body of water that had held him, but it was hard to remember. It was hazy in his mind, like he was half asleep.

Really? Am I that unmemorable?

A throb in his ear brought the memory rushing in. Him and Schenn, alone in the ocean. They had snuck out that night to watch a meteor shower on a moonless night. Instead of splashing around, they had bobbed in the waves together. Schenn's hand had found the small of Ahn's back, Ahn's lips had found Schenn's cheek. With the darkness blanketing them, the intimacy of these small touches was bearable. They didn't say much as they crept back to their room, but that night they slept in each other's arms. It was the best sleep Ahn had ever had.

Ahn crunched forward, grasping at his chest. It felt like something had cracked along the scar, like he had forced a clam shell open with his thumbs. He only noticed he was crying when Lula's cool knuckles wiped the tears from his eyes, rinsing away the salt.

"We're mostly made of water," they said. "Did you know that?"

Ahn nodded, thinking of his poor marks in his Health courses. He only knew this because of his nannies' and Masters' insistence on fruit juice and water throughout the day, interrupting his playtime to press a cup into his hands. He had been scolded that wine didn't work the same way, which he only started believing thanks to his hangovers in university.

Lula guided him to where a massive tree had fallen in the river. It looked like the people of Sorwei Chapal had bolstered it with large rocks rather than let it be dragged downstream. It was sturdy as a beaver dam, and much more beautiful, with swirled carvings at the thickest point.

"It's essential to consume water, but we also need to just *be* with it sometimes. To remember what we're made of. Like getting a hug from a parent, or a baby." They brought him to a thick branch and placed his hands on it. "Hold on and lie back in the water. I'll be here to spot you. I promise you won't be carried away."

Ahn wasn't sure how much he believed that, but his body made the choice to listen before he could overthink it. He held the branch and lifted his legs until he was float-ing on his back. The tug of the river sent a jolt through him, but the branch was sturdy.

It took a long moment for him to go lax. He could feel the shells on his clothing clinking, but the water muffled the sound. He felt hyperaware of his body, but also like its edges were being blurred by the rush of the river around him.

Lula's hands rested beneath his back, their fingertips the suggestion of security. "You stay here as long as you like, Ahnschen. As long as you need."

It was difficult at first, to turn himself over to the feel-ing. There were so many thoughts competing in his head, so much urgency. He had to talk to Sohmeng, he had to stop his sister, he had to fix the crimes of his entire nation, he had to do all of this, and as soon as possible. It made his fingers curl tight around the branch, made tears of helpless frustration rise.

Lula Jão stayed with him through this, making slight adjustments to his body, keeping his hair out of his face. He asked what to do with all of his thoughts, and they told him to imagine them as leaves, and to send them downriver.

The tears slowed, eventually. Rose again, slowed once more. Lula began humming softly, a tune without words. Enveloped in the sound of music and the flow of the river, quietness finally opened up inside him.

For a while, Ahn was water.

Next came a massage, the likes of which he had not received since leaving Qiao Sidh. He fell asleep somewhere around the time warm stones were pressed into his back, and he woke to small plates of food. A steaming bowl of water was placed in front of him, and he was leaned over it to breathe in the herbs that had been steeping there.

It was restful, but it wasn't easy. Every time he tried to clear his mind, he was met with a thousand racing thoughts. Would his soldiers listen to him? How long until Óla lost patience? Where had he put his sword? Was Hei mad at him? Was *everyone* mad at him?

"I don't know how to fix it all at once," Ahn said, feeling an invisible weight pressing down on him. "I don't know what to do, I don't know where to *start*."

"It can't all be fixed at once," Lula said sympathetically. "And I don't think now is the time to try."

"Then what do I do? I can't live like this, it feels like I'm suffocating. What if I forget something important and it all falls apart?"

"How about I write everything down?" the healer offered. "Then we can have everything in one place for you to return to after you've gotten some rest. It's easier to make choices with a clear head, but then you don't need to worry about forgetting anything."

Part of Ahn worried that seeing everything in one place would make it more overwhelming, but he couldn't take having it all trapped in his head anymore. So he agreed, and Lula Jão sat in front of him with their legs crossed, taking notes by the light of a fragrant beeswax candle.

"I need to do my drills," he said. "I've been slacking on them, and I'm afraid I've lost the basics. And Sølshend, my sãoni—that, that is, the sãoni I ride most often—her left eye has been bothering her. I need to look at it when I'm back. I don't want her to get sick."

"What else?"

"I wrote a letter to my harp instructor, Master Hvu, before I came, but I can't remember if I sent it. I mean, I *think* I sent it? But what if I didn't? I need to send another so she doesn't think I forgot her, but that means I have to get back to the ships. But then first I have to deal with Óla, so I—I don't know what to do, what do I do about that?"

"I've written down *send a letter*," Lula said. "We can figure out the details when the time comes. Are there other things I should write down?"

"I'm not taking good care of my sword. I need to find oil, but I don't want to. I'm afraid I'm dangerous. But also I'm afraid I'm weak—no, I *know* I'm weak. I need to stop being weak."

On and on, it poured out of him. His list ranged from tasks that would take two minutes to difficult exchanges he didn't yet know how to begin. But slowly, Ahn ran out of worries. The list was long, but it was finite. And as he reviewed it, the thing that weighed heaviest on him became clear.

"I'm afraid," Ahn admitted, his face tucked in his knees. Ever since that day with Hei, he couldn't escape the image of Schenn's eyes going dull. "I'm afraid to fight. I am good at it, and bladecraft used to feel very beautiful. But now I'm—I'm afraid. I don't want to hurt anyone else."

"Have you talked to other warriors about this before?" Lula asked.

Ahn shook his head. "I don't think I realized how bad it was until now. And I'm a Éongrir. Who would I talk to?"

"If you're interested, I'm sure Nepar Ãofe would be willing."

It was an unexpected suggestion. At first, it embarrassed Ahn to imagine sharing this problem with another person on the Path of Conquest. But then he remembered that wasn't the case; Nepar Ãofe was a man who understood the martial arts, but he was divorced from the context of Qiao Sidh. Hesitantly, Ahn agreed to try.

That night he sat with the man by the river, speaking for many hours about the art of combat and the horror of war. Nepar told him that long ago, Sorwei Chapal had been two separate hmun, at odds from each side of the river. The conflict was resolved, and the web of bridges constructed; the buildings came after, for the ease and joy of being near neighbours. Now, no one alive remembered the feuding; no one even remembered where the problem had begun in the first place. To honour the dead, they practiced the artform, but vowed never to turn it against their own.

"Family doesn't hurt family," Nepar said, his voice a baritone prelude to Lula's alto translation. "And in this rainforest, all the hmun are cousins. If we lived closer, maybe we would argue more, but we don't hurt each other."

"I'm sorry my family has hurt you," Ahn said. "I truly—I truly am."

"I know, Ahn." The man patted his back in acknowledgment, and Ahn didn't know what to make of it. How could this stranger be more patient than his own blood? "But thank you for saying so."

"I hope," Ahn began, hearing his voice break, "I hope that one day Conquest can have a different meaning in Qiao Sidh. I'd like a dull blade."

They spoke long into the night about the fear in Ahn's body, about the pride and shame of being so skilled in violence. Though he never would have guessed it possible, he slept well. The sun rose, and he returned to the river. Come afternoon, they found a jeibu for him to play; he talked more with Lula Jão as he strummed. Later, he was given a baby to hold, and he felt himself laugh despite everything when she pulled his hair.

With every passing hour, he saw that he could survive sharing the feelings that were too large for his body to contain. It was hard work, but it also eased the pressure that had been expanding inside of him. As the sun prepared to set, he found the courage to ask for one more day, and he was given it without hesitation. It helped.

That night, under the twin slivers of the moons, Ahn found that his rush of panicked thoughts had slowed. In their place was a stillness, and in that held breath was a conversation he had feared and needed for four years.

"Sometimes I'm afraid you aren't there." Ahn rolled the bone earpiece between his fingers, trying to remember the warmth of Schenn's hands. "I'm afraid that when I hear you, all I'm hearing is myself. That your voice is only my imagination of what you would say if you were here. I don't want that to be true—not just because it's blasphemous, but because . . . because I want you to be happy. Wherever you are, I want you to be well."

Silence. Ahn bit his lip. There was so much he wanted to say; in theory, Schenn could hear it all regardless of whether it was said aloud. But it felt important to shape the words on his tongue. To release them into this realm.

"Are you?" he asked softly. "Are you well, I mean?"

The silence endured, and he longed for the flood of warmth that assured him he wasn't alone. In the chill of the night, it was harder to believe it was real.

Did it matter, though? Even if the worst was true, even if he was alone, he needed to be in integrity with himself:

"If I could go back, I wouldn't do it again." His voice broke on the admission, but it wasn't as painful to cry this time. He'd been doing it on and off for two days. Now, it was less like losing blood and more like draining poison from a wound.

"That's terrible to say, I know. And unfair because—" Ahn shut his eyes tight as he visualized Schenn, covered in hay at a harvest festival as he played hide-and-seek with his sisters. Schenn, dressed in the ostentatious imperial fashion, fidgeting with his sleeves. Schenn, watching him so closely as they rehearsed for their Six-ing. "Because what else could we have *done*? We were so far down the Path by then, it would have been the scandal of the decade if we'd backed out. Even me being prince to the Empire wouldn't have saved us from the repercussions—or, no, it wouldn't have saved *you*. I could get away with it, but you'd wear the stain on your reputation forever. I don't know if you'd ever forgive me for that."

The image was awful; Schenn's fierce pride aside, the social implications were undeniable. His options would have been to return home with his head hanging low, or to be kept in court by Ahn and treated as a spectacle, mocked behind his back if not to his face. Qiao Sidh could forgive violence, but it could not forgive cowardice. And yet.

"You would still be alive, though. You'd be alive. I wish I'd backed out, I wish we'd even *talked* about it. It was wrong, what we did."

In a soft, dry bed, Ahn heard the sound of water. In his mind, he watched the leaves drift downriver, and let himself be carried.

"It was wrong," Ahnschen said, "what they did to us."

Sensation flowed along his ear, along his jaw. His imagination, maybe. But also real. Impossibly real.

Ahn thought of the first time Schenn broke his skin while sparring. The boy had cursed, cleaning the wound so neatly that Ahn couldn't look away.

He thought of the time they laughed so hard during a lecture that their Master threatened Ahn, and then blanched when he remembered who he was talking to.

The smirk on Schenn's face was wicked beyond propriety, and Ahn loved every moment.

He thought of the time they stole a bottle of wine, and Schenn kissed him on the mouth, got his hands under Ahn's clothes. He broke off midway, apologizing profusely, explaining that he loved Ahn but he didn't want to have sex with him, but he loved him so much and he didn't know what to do. And Ahn had only grinned like a fool, because for all it felt nice, he always forgot that sex was a thing people wanted to do at all, and wasn't it silly that this was even a problem?

He thought of the day Schenn told him that siblings were meant to love one another, to stand by each other. Ahn told him the only time he had ever been struck was by his brother, who was fifteen years older than him. It left a welt on his face, and Ahn's mother threatened exile. He had been six. Schenn held him so tightly he could barely breathe, and back then, he couldn't fathom why.

He thought of the night in the ocean. Salt and skin, the meteors coming down like rain. Sleeping with their bodies entwined, peaceful as if they had passed into the other realm without noticing. As if day would not break with a practice blade in hand and blood in the weeks to come.

In the years since his Six-ing, Ahn had adjusted to the ever-present weight of Schenn's fingerbone in his earlobe. It was essential that the piece remained, his Masters said, in order to keep the connection strong. It is what kept them as one, instead of two. Ahn would sooner lose his sword hand in battle than he would his ear.

It was an honor to be Ahnschen—but Ahn missed *Schenn.*

He missed being two bodies in contact, two hands held with fingers intertwined. He yearned to be two hearts pressed against one another.

The piercing was sturdy in his ear, but he found a way to loosen the ring that kept it in place, to slip the bone free and hold it in his palm. He examined each ridge properly for the first time in his life. Bleached white, curved gently. All he had left of his closest friend, whom he had killed.

"I have always loved you," Ahn said, pressing a sorry kiss to the bone. "I cannot come to you now, no matter how much I miss you. This can't be resolved by joining you in death. But when the time comes, when I can hold you once more, I'd like to try again. To start over. I'd like for us to have it better than this. Think on it, would you?"

Ahn fell asleep on his side, leaving room on the bed for Schenn to curl up with him. His hand was tucked against his chest, bone to scar. A loved one and the mark he left, a wound learning how to heal.

Thirteen

ALL HEI'S LIFE, there had been a barrier between them and other humans. Sometimes it was physical: a cave system to hide in, a fortress wall to stalk outside of. Other times it was less so: a gap in language, bad timing at birth, the dread of responding incorrectly to any given question. Hei had been born into a human world, but they had never been permitted to exist there in earnest.

Hei told themself they liked it this way, and that was mostly true. It made them uneasy to imagine changing themself for people they did not relate to or care for. They didn't have to wrap their mouth around unpracticed human words. Living in the rainforest let them control the pace and shape of their life. If anyone came to bother them, the sãoni kept them safe.

When Hei left the batengmun in Ateng, they had resolved to wash their hands of the human world for good. Sohmeng's arrival had complicated things—and then Ahnschen, and then everything else.

And now, Sorwei Chapal.

Hei had previously passed this hmun while following the migration route with Mama's colony. They never got close enough to the river to be noticed, but Hei had glimpsed this cluster of humans before, stretched over the water like a bridge of fire ants. They had watched cautiously from the trees then, clenching their hands tightly while they waited for Mama to let them leave.

Now, they were out in the open. When one of the Sorchapa caught sight of them, there was technically no need to hide. It was unusual; it was uncomfortable. But Sorwei Chapal was a place with no bad memories, and so Hei tried to give it a fair chance.

The river was long and wide enough that Hei could splash with the sãoni without coming into contact with anyone else. The rope bridges reminded them of spider-webs, but no one was ever stuck, and Hei's hands itched to know if the texture was soft or scratchy. The residents sailed rafts back and forth throughout the day, some of which were painted bright orange and pink and reflected like small sunrises in the water. The people made a whole lot of noise, speaking and yelling and laughing—but they sang often, too, which Hei liked.

Best of all, because the hmun was used to seeing sãoni nearby during migration, the Sorchapa didn't panic in their presence. This calmed the colony in turn, and both species lived amicably at a distance. In fact, Hei found they needed to urge a few young sãoni to *keep* their distance. They had always been curious, but now they had grown trusting.

This surprised Hei. Even if the sãoni didn't actively hunt humans, they hadn't expected for the two species to integrate this smoothly. Maybe that had been foolish of them. After all, Hei had been adopted by an alpha, hadn't they? That was all it took to be accepted by the colony.

Sohmeng was surprised too, though her surprise was more sour. "It's too simple, Hei," she said as the first day passed without incident. She was pacing, the hatchlings following her and leaving a circle of footprints. "It's not like I want anyone to get eaten or stabbed or set on fire—" Hei clicked with alarm, but Sohmeng didn't seem to hear. "—but is it seriously, *genuinely* going this well? All those phases panicking about the sãoni, training them until we were close to tears, the colony included, and now it's *fine*?"

"We worked hard," Hei said. They had Singing Violet's leg in front of them, and were massaging off some stuck shed with a damp cloth. "We made rules the sãoni are content to follow."

"Yeah," Sohmeng said, but her voice didn't match the words. "It's like, okay, we're lucky, I guess? But Hei, we're *really* lucky. It's not just the sãoni. Sorwei Chapal is helping us, like actual help. They're grateful we're here. They're treating us as equals and I didn't even have to ask!"

Hei frowned. "You are saying this as though it is bad."

Sohmeng tugged on her bangs, groaning at the sky. One of the hatchlings squawked emphatically, and the rest followed suit.

"Sohmeng, would you like to sit with me?" Hei asked. They held out the cloth. "Help Violet."

Sohmeng sighed, but did as Hei requested. Hei watched her hands, imagining the restless energy working out of her joints with every movement. Sohmeng and Singing Violet, shedding what itched and grated together.

"I just feel so *weird*, Hei. We've never been in a better position, we've never had this many allies! We're in the best possible situation we can be considering that the Empire's at our door. So why is it *now* that I'm so stressed that I want to pull my hair out? What's wrong with me?"

Hei hummed, taking her hands. They imagined turning the problem over in their palms like a smooth stone, passing it between them and Sohmeng until they learned something new. "You have been made responsible for many things."

"That's what I wanted, wasn't it?"

Hei considered this. "Leading is a gift, and a burden."

As the colony's new alpha, they understood. There was pride, and there was fear. It was empowering to be able to make decisions, to lead the colony in the way they believed was best. But if anything went wrong, they bore the blame.

That should have made them *more* protective of the sãoni, more wary than ever of allowing their family onto humanity's shores. But the consequences were failing to reveal themselves. In fact, the more they watched, the more they were forced to admit the beneficial aspects of this bond.

Like with Eakang Minhal and Polha Hiwei. Hei hadn't expected the two of them to visit the sãoni they had ridden up to Sorwei Chapal, but they did. There was affection between them now, which Hei observed with tentative appreciation.

Polha Hiwei was a quiet woman; she mostly left Hei to their own devices. They liked that. As for Eakang, Sohmeng's half-sibling was the most natural sãoni rider Hei had ever seen besides themself. They were intuitive, patient and unafraid. They were careful not to bombard Hei with questions, but the ones they *did* ask were always very interesting.

Hei knew Sohmeng was still adjusting to having a new family member. But they liked Eakang. So while Sohmeng was off pacing fretfully around Sorwei Chapal, Hei let Eakang linger with the sãoni as much as they liked, listening to them chatter with a happily chirping colony.

"What a strong swimmer!" Eakang giggled, watching one of the hatchlings flail a few feet into the water. It squawked, clumsily attempting to snatch a fish. "Ohh, so close!"

Hei peeled a banana, eating the inner fruit and tossing the skin to Sølshend. Far into the water, a raft was on its eighth crossing of the day. The sun was preparing to set, spilling deep orange and purple all along the river.

Some of the rafts only passed once or twice. But in the two days since Hei arrived, they had watched this one go back and forth often. It was entirely unpainted, and carried only one or two passengers at a time. Many people were boisterous along the islands of the hmun, but they were always quiet on this raft. When there was no one to cross, the captain would go out on their own, rest the raft against a large boulder, and sit for a while.

Hei swished their fingers in the water, the tips brushing stones long tumbled smooth. A little tug revealed one to be a snail; they put it back down, giving it some extra peace before it likely became someone's dinner.

"Okay, okay, you're almost bigger than me buddy!" Eakang said. The sãoni was leaping at them. For a moment Hei worried, but Eakang let out a sharp Sãonipa sound and it settled. "Good job, thank you."

Hei watched the raft move, slow as an old manatee, searching for the ripples the captain's oar made in the water.

"Eakang?" they asked.

Stroking the sãoni's cheeks, Eakang looked over at Hei. "Mhm?"

"Who is this?" They gestured to the raft. "Who moves the raft."

"Oh!" Eakang waded back to shore, wringing out one of their braids. "That's Baang. She's out there all the time, huh?"

Hei hummed.

"I've crossed with her before. She's very nice." They paused, wiggling their nose in that way they did when they were thinking. "Well, she's quiet. All she asks to help you cross is a good stone, or a shell. She likes the purple ones most, and the black ones, too. But those are harder to find."

That night, Hei gathered six different pebbles. Three were purple, of different shapes and sizes. Two were black. One was grey, but it had a fossil in the corner.

Early the next morning, when the sãoni had not yet woken, they found Baang. They cleared their throat as they approached, and she looked in their direction. Hei opened their palm, revealing an array of treasures for her to choose from.

Baang seemed pleased. She swayed, looking the options over. Hei pointed out the fossil to be sure she'd seen it. She nodded, and settled on a black stone that was perfectly oval in shape. Hei decided to save the fossil for themself.

They were nervous to get on the raft, at first; they had never done anything like it before. But Baang simply waited while they stood there, and offered them a pole to steady themself with. Once they were on the platform, she sailed out.

Hei couldn't have expected how soothing the ride would be. The resistance of the oar against the pressure of the water made them relax behind their eyes, made them want to lie down on the warm wood and sleep. Few people were stirring yet in the hmun, and so human voices hadn't yet joined the murmur of the riverside.

When they realized they were nearly halfway to the far bank, Hei's chest suddenly went tight with anxiety. They tapped the raft, pointed to the boulder. Offered another stone. This time, Baang took a purple one, and then parked them in the middle of the river, looking impassively out across the current while Hei hugged themself and tried to figure out what they were afraid of.

It wasn't the water. It wasn't Baang. It wasn't the distance from the sãoni, or the relative proximity to the humans of Sorwei Chapal. They curled their toes against the coarse rope that bound the logs of the raft together, trying to find clarity.

It only was when Baang started humming that Hei realized it: they were having *fun*. They were enjoying their time with this new human, and they didn't want it to be over yet.

When had this happened? When had human desires stolen back into their heart? How had they not noticed it until now?

It felt like a betrayal of who they were, to seek the company of humans. It felt as though they were coaxing their young self out of the caves and into certain danger.

How could they do such a thing to themself, to *Heipua Minhal* who had no one but their grandmother, and then no one at all?

And what about the colony? The sãoni were their family, but that relationship was hard-earned. Would it be a betrayal of them as well, to remove their own claws from time to time? Would Hei lose their scales if they looked too closely at their skin? As the alpha, it felt irresponsible to even imagine such a thing.

But simply by becoming alpha, Hei already marked a disruption in the previous structure of the ecosystem. And they hadn't taken it by force; it was the sãoni that had given them this title. The sãoni who recognized them as equal.

They could not be the alpha that Mama had been. The world as Hei knew it was changing, and it could never go back to the way it was; change only moved in a forward direction. They needed to be a leader for a different purpose, a different circumstance, a different time.

Hei was grateful to see it was possible. Hei wished it had never come to this.

Trust was the hard part. Humans had hurt Hei, and so Hei imagined humans hurting the sãoni. And it was true, there had been feuds between the two species—but when given the opportunity to live in peace, the hmun had taken it three out of three times. Humanity was offering a treaty of symbiosis after all, and Hei had the power to respond on behalf of their colony of sãoni. They alone had the richness of a shared language.

Still, Hei feared humanity. They did, even now. They feared exile and rejection and cruelty.

But there was also Sohmeng and Ahnschen. Tonão's tears and Eakang's careful questions and Baang, silent on a raft on the river, admiring her collection of stones. There were people who gave Baang stones and did not demand she share her thoughts.

Hei wanted to see the rainforest protected. They wanted the migration routes restored, and to see species living together in harmony. They wanted to tend to the rhythm of that perfect system, where everything eats and is eaten, and from death comes life again. They wanted to see more eggs every year.

And they also wanted this raft, and the quiet water beneath it. They wanted to sit nearer to the communal fire at dinner time, and listen more closely to people sharing stories.

One day, maybe, they wanted to try approaching someone new and say: *My name is Hei. I am eighteen years old. My favourite thing in the world is riding with the sãoni, and maybe you would enjoy it too. Would you like to be my friend?*

They took a shaky breath, wiping their nose. Tapped the raft again to get Baang's attention, and pointed back towards shore. Before the woman took up her oar, she reached into her bag and pulled out a ridged brown shell. She flipped it over to reveal its lustrous green interior, and placed it in Hei's hands.

All the way back to shore, and back to the sãoni, they held this treasure close. They placed it in their moon bag for safekeeping, then decided to wear the bag for a while, just to know it was near. It was the first gift Hei had ever received from a stranger.

That night, they decided they would speak to Sohmeng.

"Ahn asked for one more day to rest," Sohmeng was saying as the two of them cuddled beneath a tent she had set up. She ran a hand over their chest, and they appreciated every inch of contact between her palm and their skin. "It's good, I think. Tomorrow we'll figure out what to do about Qiao Sidh."

"I would like to help."

"Of course," Sohmeng said, yawning into their neck. "Just let me know what you want me to bring to the Grand Ones."

"No," Hei said. "I would like to go to the moonhouses."

Sohmeng sat up, her hair falling into her face. She hardly seemed to notice, busy as she was staring at Hei; they tucked it behind her ear.

"Are you sure?" she asked. Hei had expected her to be doubtful, or eager, perhaps. But she was neither of these things—she was simply looking for a plain answer. In that moment, she looked like Ahnschen.

Hei considered it for a moment longer, just in case.

"I am sure."

Sohmeng leaned down to rub cheeks. She was already smeared with their makeup, and they could feel her smiling against their face. A big smile, one that showed off the lovely gap between her teeth.

"Then yeah, duh! Of *course* you can come." She kissed them once, twice, a third time. Pressed their foreheads together. Hei closed their eyes to hear her better, to keep the sound of her voice close in their mind. "We would all be lucky to have you."

And there, beneath the trees and moons and seeking stars, Hei found that they believed her.

Fourteen

SOHMENG HAD ALWAYS CONSIDERED herself a relatively selfish person. Despite what people like her brother might say, in her mind, it wasn't actually a bad thing. She knew who she was and what she wanted, and she never lost focus when it came to achieving her goals. Sure, it could make her a little sharp, and sometimes she hurt people's feelings, but who didn't? As far as Sohmeng was concerned, focusing mostly on herself had gotten her pretty far in life.

But ever since they'd arrived in Sorwei Chapal, she couldn't take her mind off of how she had hurt Ahn. They'd never fought like that before, and it felt awful to have things unresolved. She needed him to know that she didn't hate him or anything—and honestly, she needed to hear that he didn't hate her back.

The morning after their arrival, she had decided to go to Grand One Jão and see if she could talk to him. "It would be best if we gave Ahnschen some space," Grand One Jão had said. "I promise you he is in good hands. Lula is very thoughtful."

Obviously, Sohmeng had bristled. "I'm not trying to tell you how to do your job, but shouldn't he be able to see the people who love him? Who *know* him?"

"If he asks, then yes."

"Does he *know* he can ask for us?"

Grand One Jão had laughed, but not unkindly. "Sweet girl, we do not keep hostages in Sorwei Chapal. Ahnschen knows you're here, and he cares deeply for you. But he has asked for this time to be private."

Sohmeng didn't like that one bit. In fact, she had sat down beside Polha Hiwei to complain over lunch later that day. She'd gotten to know the woman pretty well back in Nona Fahang, and found it was nice to have an adult who got the situation.

The woman had let Sohmeng talk until she was out of things to say, which took a while. Only then did Polha ask: "Do you want my opinion, Sohmeng Minhal?"

"Yeah," Sohmeng mumbled. "I—yeah, I do."

"That boy loves you," she'd said matter-of-factly. Sohmeng had stared hard into her bowl of rice to avoid meeting Polha's eye. "He is completely enamoured with you, and he is *constantly* worrying about it: if you like him, if he's making you proud, if he's doing enough to make you happy. The boy's a people-pleaser, and you're currently one of the people whose opinion he values most."

Sohmeng had squinted at her. She knew Ahn cared about her, and that he could get goofy about it. But this had never crossed her mind as a consequence of that care.

"This might be news to you, seeing as you ..."

"Don't work like that."

"Mhm. And your other partner is . . ." Polha gestured vaguely in Hei's direction.

"A lizard."

"A lizard," Polha had conceded. "Ahn is sensitive, and worries about what people think. If you're by his side during this, he's going to try and push himself to heal faster than his body is capable of, because he doesn't want to upset you. He needs privacy, Sohmeng. Let him have it, and trust he'll come back to you when he's ready."

When Sohmeng had recounted the exchange to Hei, they'd agreed with what Polha had said. That confirmation was enough for Sohmeng to try and shift her perspective. If Hei could manage to wait outside of Nona Fahang for eight whole phases, she could handle this. Every time she thought about finding Lula Jão and shaking them down for information about how Ahn was doing, she forced herself to take a breath and go for a walk instead.

When the morning came to reconnect at the moon-houses, Sohmeng was pretty sure her feet knew every ridge of those bridges. Honestly, it was a wonder she hadn't paced a hole in them.

Sohmeng stood outside Chehang House with Hei, keeping back from the main door. Hei was examining some hot peppers that were hanging from the roof; they'd been interested in the trellis between the moon-houses, but decided to wait to get closer until fewer people were around.

Sohmeng was still shocked that Hei was here at all. Despite her reminders that they could always change their mind and go back to the sãoni, they'd already made it up. She was grateful, but she was also nervous; humans hadn't been kind to Hei over the years. It was intolerable to imagine that happening again.

She intertwined her fingers with theirs. "It's a lot of people, but they're not actually that loud. Everyone's gotta take turns talking, and the echoes are kind of nice. I think so, at least."

"I will stay by the door," Hei said, scanning the procession that was coming over the graceful curve of the island's main bridge.

One by one, the Grand Ones crossed the threshold, some of their apprentices holding their arms, others trailing in at their own pace. There wasn't much consistency in how these relationships worked: a few of the apprentices were fully grown adults, older than Sohmeng's father; the youngest had just turned eleven, and was incredibly pleased with himself.

Sohmeng quietly put faces to phases for Hei. She doubted they would remember any of them, or even really care, but it was grounding for her, and Hei didn't argue.

And then Ahn was crossing the bridge, his silvertongue hair distinct among the crowd. Lula Jão was by his side, their arm looped in his.

Worry shot through Sohmeng. Despite how badly she'd wanted to talk to Ahn for the past three days, finally seeing him brought all her worries back to the surface. Was he still angry with her? Was he *okay*?

When he met her eye, Sohmeng saw that he—well, he looked *good*. He was in fresh clothing and his hair was neatly braided. Crucially, he looked like he'd managed to get some sleep. Sohmeng had gotten so used to seeing him exhausted that she'd almost forgotten what it looked like when he was rested. There was some embarrassment in his posture, but he didn't look wounded. Not like before.

He parted from Lula Jão at the door to the moonhouses, and walked over to her and Hei. For a moment he stood there, rubbing his arm.

"Hello," he finally said, looking at the two of them like he had no idea what to do next. Sohmeng didn't know either, but she had to do something.

"*Hello*, he says," she scoffed. She wrapped her arms around him, squeezing so tightly that he squeaked like a baby bird. She thought of what Polha had said, about how he wanted her to like him. How could he not know that was already true? "I missed you." She bonked her head against his chest. "I was worried. Hi. How are you? Did they treat you well?"

"Very well," Ahn said, and to Sohmeng's relief, he sounded like he meant it. Tentatively, he kissed her forehead, speaking against her hair. "I am better than I was. I'm sorry for the delay. And for . . . for yelling. I wish I hadn't done that."

"I'm sorry, too." Sohmeng bonked him again. "I was pushy. I mean, I was *worried*, but I get pushy when I'm worried. I didn't mean to make things harder for you, Ahn."

"We've been managing a lot. A fight was bound to happen at some point." He winced. "Though I wish it hadn't happened in front of all of the Grand Ones."

"Yeah, we goofed that one," Sohmeng agreed. She was less bent out of shape about it than he was, probably because she had a pretty substantial history of making important old people mad. "Are we done fighting? I'm not angry or anything, but before we go in there . . . I want to make sure we're good."

"We're good," Ahn said. "I want to talk more after the meeting is done, but not to argue with you. I want to make sure we've heard each other. And I . . . I'd like to be more open with you."

Forehead to his collarbone, Sohmeng felt herself properly relax for the first time in days. Patience had paid off, like Polha had said. "I'd really like that."

A few clicks came from behind her, and Ahn reached out a hand to Hei. They took it, briefly biting the meat of his forearm. Sohmeng knew from experience how sharp their teeth could be, but the gesture made Ahn seem calmer. It was special, watching him learn Hei's language.

"Hei's coming with us," Sohmeng said. "To the moonhouses."

"I heard from Grand One Jão," Ahn said, looking at them warmly. "Thank you. Your perspective will be invaluable."

Hei ignored the compliment, squinting at Ahn. When they reached for Ahn's ear, his and Sohmeng's breath seemed to catch at the same time. But Hei wasn't bothered as they twisted his earpiece, adjusting it until they were satisfied.

"Crooked," they said simply. "Helping Schenn."

Ahn swallowed. "Schenn appreciates it. As do I."

Sohmeng still had no idea how Hei could treat Ahn and Schenn's situation so casually. It wasn't just about culture clash. Losing Schenn—having to *kill* Schenn—had obviously traumatized Ahn; she didn't want to screw up and hurt him even more.

But compared to the other times that Schenn had been addressed, Ahn looked steadier. He was obviously taken off guard (having his dead friend's fingerbone jostled around in his ear would do that) but he didn't look distressed. Something had changed.

As the three of them entered Chehang House together, Sohmeng let herself be hopeful.

They opened with a prayer of gratitude from Grandmother Go, whose phase this meeting was happening under. Sohmeng learned that the daily agenda typically consisted of going through a list of announcements, concerns from community members, project updates, and a period for questions and answers. With the current state of affairs, these items were touched on only briefly before Ahn was given the floor.

"Firstly, I apologize for my outburst. It's not the way I wish to behave, and I hope I can make a better impression this time. Thank you for the second chance—and I thank you once more," he said, holding his hand to his heart, "for your compassion, and for your care. It was not something I ever expected in times such as these. I would not have even known to ask for it. I don't think I have the words to express my gratitude, either in Dulpongpa or in Qiao Sidhur, but ... please know you have it."

"It is our way here," said Grandmother Go. She was an elderly woman, with a friendliness to her that reminded Sohmeng of her own grandmother. "But we recognize your gratitude. What have you found during your convalescence?"

"Clarity," Ahn said. "I have looked within myself and discovered that I do not want to duel my sister—"

Sohmeng was halfway through a sigh of relief when he continued speaking. "—but I also accept that it is my responsibility."

"Sorry, what?" The words were out before Sohmeng could stop them. She looked from Ahn to the Grand Ones and back. "Ahn, you *just* said you don't want to."

Ahn didn't look like he was trying to be self-destructive, which was worrying in its own way. "As prince of the Empire, it is my duty to organize the retreat. As of now, a confrontation seems to be the only way for me to fulfill that duty."

Sohmeng was about to list all of the reasons that didn't make sense, but Nepar Ãofe got there first. He raised a hand, stepping forward to address Ahn. "Your integrity is admirable, Ahnschen. But this is not your burden to bear."

"Certainly not alone," Grand One Jão chimed in. "And you *are* still healing."

Sohmeng caught Lula nodding beside them, and felt a little better about having left Ahn in their care for three days.

"I want to take accountability for what my people have done," Ahn said, a hint of desperation in his voice. "Someone has to make things right, and it's not going to be Ólawen."

A crooked smile spread on Nepar's face. He placed one of his large hands on Ahn's shoulder. "I know you've got good intentions. But there is no world in which I will allow any one person to place the fate of our entire land in their hands."

"You are a strong warrior," Grandmother Go added.

"We have all heard of your skill. But this is *our* fight. We welcome your aid, but Qiao Sidh will not have the final word on how this conflict is managed."

Ahn's cheeks flushed as the message landed. "I understand. Forgive me for overstepping, and thank you for your grace."

With the option of Ahn settling things over a duel off the table, the real work began.

It started with a map more beautiful than any Sohmeng had ever seen. With traders for parents, Sohmeng had encountered maps as a child, but this was something entirely different, large enough for several people to comfortably gather around. Illustrations of each region were lovingly detailed, from Ateng's distinct mountain range to Nona Fahang's banyan fortress to Sorwei Chapal's cluster of bridges. Looking at the map, Sohmeng got a clearer image of Kongkempei's lush pocket of riverland and Hosaisi's coastal cliffside on the northeast tip of the continent. There was another hmun west of Sorwei Chapal, and another two even further south than Ateng, all of which, as far as Sohmeng knew, were still untouched by the Qiao Sidhur invasion.

The illustrations brought Gãepongwei to life. Each hmun to itself, but all in harmony, marking the unique beauty of each region of the rainforest. Even though Sohmeng knew that the location of Polhmun Ão was lost to history, she found herself searching for it. She traced mental circles around the sãoni migration route that Hei had once scratched in the dirt.

Ateng was the place Sohmeng had been born, but *this*, the expanse of land that sustained her and all who came before—this was home. A feeling glowed in her, deep as wovenstone: love, and loyalty. It wasn't a matter of possessing Gãepongwei, but protecting it. Tending to it like a child, and honouring it like a grandparent. Letting it begin and begin again.

"The first Imperial landing occurred about five years ago, not too far from Hosaisi," Ahn recounted. He had roughly sketched his own map on a dried banana leaf, giving everyone a better look at southern Qiao Sidh and the islands that connected it to Gãepongwei. "That expedition was hit by a difficult storm on the way down, and the unfamiliar terrain almost did them in. It was by luck alone that they stumbled into Hosaisi, and began to learn more about the people who lived in the region."

"But they weren't trying to expand back then?" Grandmother Go asked.

"They were," Ahn replied, "but not in the same way. The point was to gather information. It's how we learned the language I'm speaking with you now. These initial occupations are meant to be nonviolent—establishing communication is the first step. But as the presence of soldiers suggests, they are always ready to use force." He grimaced, tugging at his earpiece. "I believe they were here for around a year and a half, placing their own camp nearby Hosaisi—and, unfortunately, disrupting the sãoni migration route. I can't confirm this, but I wouldn't be surprised if they were being hunted. That would be ... quite a prize to bring home."

Sohmeng squeezed Hei's hand as she translated quietly into Atengpa. They said nothing.

"When we returned this past year," Ahn continued,

"we landed on the northwestern coast, which was much more forgiving."

"And found your way to Kongkempei," Nepar Ãofe said, drawing a line with his finger across the map. "And then back to Hosaisi. Both hmun are occupied now, with Hosaisi under harsher rule. We believe they retaliated after violence broke out in Kongkempei."

Sohmeng's stomach turned. She could only imagine how betrayed the people of Hosaisi must have felt to see another hmun attacked by the strangers they had shown hospitality to. *Kejangar*—the Dulpongpa word she had taught Hei when they were first getting to know Ahn. Another core tenet of Gãepongwei that Qiao Sidh had brushed aside.

"I predict that Nona Fahang is next in line for invasion," Nepar continued, "and with the enemy's fire-sand, the banyan walls won't hold for long."

"How do you know the army won't move to Sorwei Chapal instead?" Sohmeng asked. "It's closer to Kongkempei, and right on the river."

Nepar pointed out a portion of the map that was coloured more deeply around the Ãotul, pockmarked with many small lakes. "The wetlands on the western side of the Ãotul are treacherous for those who don't have experience navigating them. It's one reason so many refugees went to Nona Fahang instead of coming our way. If I were Ólawen and I had two options laid out, I would take the path of least resistance."

"They got close to Nona Fahang last time, so we know she already has a route mapped out." Ahn tucked his hair behind his ear; since he'd cut it, his braid didn't hold together as well anymore. "I imagine that's been her project for the last while."

Sohmeng's heart sank as she looked at the map. Not only was that bad news for Nona Fahang, but it was one more disruption to the sãoni migration path.

"Right now, Ólawen is on the coast and Ahn is by our side, which gives us an opportunity to strike hard against the Empire," Nepar continued. "According to Qiao Sidhur dueling custom, we have five days left before Ahn is considered to have forfeited. After that, Ólawen will likely move on Nona Fahang—and I don't doubt she'll be in a sour mood. But before that timer's up, she's out of our way. Now, we've got two choices ahead of us during this window: either free occupied Kongkempei, or preemptively march south to defend Nona Fahang. I'm not writing off Hosaisi, especially when it's in bad shape, but it's a whole lot further and harder to reach. I'm personally in favour of starting with Kongkempei." Sohmeng saw Polha and Eakang react at the same time, Polha's expression dark and Eakang's afraid. "We have the advantage of knowing the terrain. If we take the short route through the wetlands, we can band together with the hmun and overthrow the occupation."

"Plus, the Qiao Sidhur in Kongkempei will be our least martially competent," Ahn added. "Ólawen needs the highly skilled soldiers either marching alongside her, or else stationed in Hosaisi to prevent a second uprising. Those left in Kongkempei will mostly be *saro dhral*—bringers of culture, we call them. Carpenters, cooks, diplomats." He looked at Polha apologetically.

"It would be an easier fight."

"Or not a fight at all," suggested Grandmother Go, "if their prince was issuing the orders."

"And so we let the army walk right into Nona Fahang?" Polha asked with uncharacteristic impatience. "That'll be needless bloodshed, and we know that Kongkempei is stable right now. Why undo an occupation when we can prevent a new one from beginning?"

"We *could* do that," Ahn said. "And I'd be willing to, I would. But if we take that approach, if I deny my sister the duel and then show up ready to defend Nona Fahang ... it's a different tone." Sohmeng remembered what it was like watching the Éongrir siblings draw blades. She could only imagine how horrible it would be if that played out with armies behind them. "And I won't have any Qiao Sidhur allies going in."

"Kongkempei would gather those allies," Nepar said, more gently this time.

"And all the while, Nona Fahang burns?" Polha snapped. Sohmeng couldn't blame her. If it was Ateng being targeted, Sohmeng would be on edge, too. Eakang took her hand, and the woman seemed to gather herself.

"Could we split the forces?" Sohmeng asked. "Ahn goes to Kongkempei with a smaller group of people, and then the rest of us go to Nona Fahang and brace for when Ólawen arrives?"

"I wouldn't feel good about those numbers against Óla," Ahn said quietly. "I mean no disrespect, but ... the odds here are already dubious. This will be challenging enough with your entire army working together. Dividing them would only invite more trouble."

There weren't any good choices. Going to Nona Fahang meant preparing for a battle they might not win, going to Kongkempei would abandon Nona Fahang to a furious Ólawen, and splitting everyone up would be even worse. Sohmeng prided herself on having creative solutions, on coming up with ways to wiggle out of difficult moments. But this was a *lot*.

"I hate to ask it, Ahnschen," Grandmother Go said, "but are you *certain* your sister will still be on the coast? How do you know she isn't on her way to Nona Fahang right now?"

"Because she respects me," Ahn said, and Sohmeng heard the way his breath shook on the words. "Calling for a duel is a serious thing, especially among family. The fact that I'm refusing her is unspeakably insulting. It would be more honourable to grievously wound her—to, to *kill* her even, than to miss this." Sohmeng took his hand, and he held it tightly. "So ... so yes. She'll be waiting for me."

"Then fight her."

Sohmeng did a double-take to confirm that those words had actually come from Hei. Since entering Chehang House, they had done nothing but stare hard at the map in silence, so still that Sohmeng had almost forgotten they were there. She knew Hei preferred to think in private, and sometimes it took them a long time to decide what was worth saying. But she hadn't expected *that* to be their opening statement.

She also hadn't expected the rest of the room to understand Hei—but apparently the simple sentence was mutually intelligible between Atengpa and Sorchapa, because within moments, *everyone* had something to say about it.

Sohmeng tried to hush the rising cacophony, and when it didn't work, Hei snapped a sãoni sound that had everyone just about jump out of their skin. Elegant.

"So," Sohmeng said, her voice strained. Hei stood there scowling, shoulders hunched. "Hei, I think we're going to need an explanation for this one."

"Ólawen is an arrogant alpha. She can only be defeated if she's killed or if she's *appeased*, and you are not going to kill your family, no?"

"I'd really rather not," Ahn said weakly.

"Then appease her. You need to face her eventually, why delay if it will only make her more aggressive? Your soldiers will lose confidence in you, too, if they do not see you return. They will assume you have given up your power. You cannot slink around in submission this way, you must face her wrath head-on. It is where you would be most useful."

The words felt harsh in Sohmeng's mouth even as she translated them. She almost paused to ask Hei if they were sure they wanted to say this, but Hei never said anything they didn't mean.

Ahnschen looked as unsure as Sohmeng felt. He cast a nervous glance about the room. "We … but we agreed that I shouldn't represent Gãepongwei in combat."

"It is not about *representing Gãepongwei*," Hei said impatiently, "it is about distracting Ólawen from her tantrum. She called for a duel, but the outcome of that duel does not have to decide anything for us. You do not even have to win."

"You mean the point isn't for him to beat her," Sohmeng asked, trying to wrap her head around it, "just for him to show up?"

"Confronting Ólawen keeps your colony's respect," Hei said to Ahn. "Whether you win or lose, you are strong, and you find out who your followers are."

Sohmeng thought, of all things, of the feud between Mama and Blacktooth. It was the closest point of reference she had. When it was done, one sãoni had claimed Blacktooth's place as alpha and taken off with the others—but some sãoni had also stayed behind with Mama. They were a part of Hei's colony even now. She was beginning to see what Hei was talking about.

"With us, you are one soldier," Hei asserted. "With them, you are much more. Gãepongwei does not care that you are a prince, but Qiao Sidh does. Use that power on someone who will listen."

Sohmeng was confident that the soldiers would listen to Ahn, but she wasn't so sure about Ólawen. Ahn claimed that she loved him, but love and respect were different things. Ahnschen might be a prince and a general to everyone else, but to Ólawen, he was just—

"—her *brother*." Sohmeng heard herself finish the thought aloud as the final piece clicked in her mind. She grabbed Ahn's arm and shook it. "Ahn, you're her little brother! *That* you can use to your advantage. Okay, okay, we've got something to work with here!"

With the whole group staring at her like she had six legs, Sohmeng did her best to expand on the idea that Hei had begun. They would play into what Ólawen was expecting to see: Ahn would return within the ten days that was standard for a duel, not as a blazing rival, like Hei had suggested, but as a contrite younger sibling. However, he would still ask to complete the duel as a matter of principle, both to resolve their conflict and—

"To act honourably, or whatever," Sohmeng said. "That sounds pretty Qiao Sidhur, right?"

Ahn blinked a couple times, looking dazed. "I suppose it does, yes."

And so the options opened up: if Ahn won the duel, he would see if Ólawen would honor the terms of a full retreat. If she wouldn't, he would use the leverage he won in the duel to take control of the invasion strategy instead. Then, he could guide the Qiao Sidhur soldiers into the perfect location for Gãepongwei's army to win a battle—and from there, he could negotiate a surrender. Whether it was a matter of days or weeks, the Qiao Sidhur invasion would end.

"And what if I lose?" Ahn asked, a thoughtful crease in his brow. "I don't know if I can guarantee a win against Ólawen. Her training began before I was even born."

"Like Hei said, it's more about the distraction than the duel," Sohmeng answered. "If you lose, you lose. But you'd be back in Ólawen's good graces, and that'll stop her from like, burning down the rainforest."

"I don't think I could stop her from invading Nona Fahang, though."

"Even if you couldn't," Nepar Ãofe said, his expression beginning to look less grim, "repositioning you as a leader of the Qiao Sidhur army would also have its advantages. If you kept up the ruse, your influence could mitigate the damage done in an occupation scenario. After we liberate Kongkempei, we'll move south to Nona Fahang, and you can join us when the fighting starts. Take them by surprise."

"I could advocate for bringing fewer Qiao Sidhur soldiers on the march. Claim that the hmun is an easy win." Ahn chewed on his lip as he began strategizing. "It could tip the odds in your favour."

Around the room, the Grand Ones and their apprentices were beginning to lean forward in their seats, as one by one people came around to the idea of this failsafe. With Ahn in this role, even the worst outcomes would be softened. But it was a tricky role for him to play: there was a difference between asking Ahn to beat Ólawen, and asking him to betray her. If he won the duel, their victory would be simple, but if he lost, he would be spending weeks at her side, leading his sister and their army into a trap with a straight face.

Sohmeng caught Lula Jão's eye. It would undoubtedly be useful for Gãepongwei, this multi-pronged plan of theirs, but she wasn't so sure it would be good for Ahn's healing. She was trying to figure out how to subtly ask how he felt about that—when she noticed that Hei had beat her to it.

Hei had not looked at anyone since entering Chehang House, not even as they'd delivered their speech. They had not taken a single step from their spot by the exit. But now they broke their stance, walking up to Ahnschen and taking him by the arm, leveling him with a look that was earnest and kind and deadly serious.

"Okay, Ahnschen?" they asked quietly.

Ahn's gaze lingered on the room, then fell to Sohmeng, to Hei. To Sohmeng's immense gratitude, it seemed like he was genuinely considering his answer. Like with Hei and the sãoni, she knew it would make things worlds easier if he said yes. Right now, it was the only real plan they had. But she wanted it to be a choice he made, not a corner he was backed into.

Time slowed as Ahn pressed his fingers to his lips, then to his earpiece. To Schenn, holding his hand from far, far away.

"Okay," Ahnschen said, either to Hei or himself or to everyone, to all of Gãepongwei. "Okay. Let's do it."

FIFTEEN

SINCE ENTERING THE TRAINING SCHOOL at Kørno Wan, Ahn's life had been measured in a series of countdowns. To his Six-ing, to his school year, to the campaign, to his trial in Nona Fahang, to reaching Ólawen—and now, to dueling her. His mind had been kept in a perpetual state of motion, railing against his helplessness all the while. More nights than not, his thoughts would race until he passed out, only to pick right back up the next morning.

With two days until he left for the duel, the countdown hadn't stopped—but its rhythm had changed. In the waters of Sorwei Chapal, Ahn had finally gotten out of his head long enough to return to the rest of his body. Until that moment, he hadn't realized how far away from himself he had strayed.

"Would you spar with me, Ahnschen?" Nepar Ãofe asked him the morning after the plan was made. He held out a wooden staff in one of his large hands, and Ahn steadied himself to say yes.

Ahn was as strong as he'd ever been, but his instincts

were shaky. Not just from thinking about his Six-ing, but from thinking about the day where he had nearly killed Hei. There was a part of him that remained reluctant to pick up a weapon at all, but he knew that, at least until the invasion was stopped, it was a necessity.

"There are some ways that I would prefer not to be touched," Ahn said carefully, tugging at his earpiece. It warmed between his fingers, encouraging. "I know it is unavoidable in battle, but here ... "

"Here is not battle," Nepar agreed. "We go at your pace. On that note—you should know I have a bad shoulder. Don't take me out of the fight before it's started, alright?"

They fought on a wide platform that was encircled with reeds and lilypads, teaching from one another's traditions. When the big man was out of breath, he whistled over his students, who took turns with Ahn as well. One on one, one on three—he got to one on five before he was overpowered. It was good practice for him. Honestly, it was even *fun*. Even more importantly, it was an opportunity for the budding martial force of Sorwei Chapal to learn more about Qiao Sidhur combat.

He taught them the foundations: classic postures, defensive stances, weaknesses in technique, gaps in armour. He thought of every mistake he had ever made as a student of Conquest, and transformed it into a learning opportunity for the Sorchapa. As the hours passed, Ahn discovered he was an effective teacher when it came to betraying his own people.

Not a betrayal, Ahn. We're trying to change something, yeah?

It was true. It was complicated. While Ahn never strayed from his dedication to Gãepongwei's plight, his emotions were in constant flux. Feeling closer to Schenn made him twice as capable, but also twice as likely to stumble when he was distracted. More than once he needed to pause and breathe until he stopped shaking. Nepar paused with him, and sat patiently by his side. Ahn tried to cultivate that same patience with himself.

Two days, he had. Only two days until he left Hei and Sohmeng behind for Ólawen and the flash of her sword. He took full advantage of those days, welcoming any opportunity for joy, whether it was in hours or in five-minute gaps between responsibilities.

After all, none of them knew how long he would be away for, or what would come when it was done. They deserved more time than there was—they had more than earned it—but being angry about that would only waste the moments they had.

So Ahn took the good as it came, and held each experience as fuel for the road ahead.

By day, he explored Sorwei Chapal with Sohmeng, sampling different types of food and persuading her to try new dances with him. He found a piece of twine and used it to teach her a Qiao Sidhur children's game called Winter Palace, which vexed her endlessly, but she kept insisting on trying again. He could only aspire to such boundless persistence, to such unselfconscious learning.

As the first evening fell, they found a private place to talk. Ahn worried that he would be too awkward to find his conversational footing, but Sohmeng made it easy, telling ridiculous stories about the people she'd grown up with. Despite his attempts to be respectful, an embarrassing tale from Viunwei's childhood left him in stitches.

"He's not even here to defend himself!" he exclaimed, trying to get himself under control.

"The Go phase is the *perfect* time for gossip," Sohmeng claimed, gesticulating at the moons which had risen in twin slivers of red and white. "Go children are warned all the time not to do it, because they're pretty susceptible, but I figure since I wasn't born under that phase, it's probably fine. Also the whole *point* of siblings is to make fun of them."

"And if they take it poorly," Ahn added, "they can always suggest a fight to the death!"

Ahn wasn't sure who was more startled that he had made the joke. After an extended silence, Sohmeng asked, "…do I have permission to laugh? Because that was a pretty good one, but I also don't want to send you back to Lula Jão. Especially when I was planning on kissing you later, or whatever."

Ahn let out a helpless breath. He was going to reassure her that it was alright, but instead surprised himself once more by saying, "You remind me so much of Schenn, sometimes."

Sohmeng's smile faltered. "You … said that before. In Nona Fahang. I didn't know what it meant back then." She chewed on her lip. "Maybe I still don't. I haven't exactly asked."

"To be fair, there hasn't been much time."

"But also—" Sohmeng grimaced, pulling at her bangs. Ahn took her hands, wanting to give them something else to do. "Ugh, Ahn, this feels bad to say, but I've sort of been struggling to talk about this. About Schenn. Hei's been so good at being there for you, but I've screwed it up at every turn. I don't feel like I've been a very good partner. Or friend."

Ahn didn't realize she'd been carrying this. It was true that he had felt rushed through his feelings, and disheartened by the false optimism she was trying to create. But for the most part, he'd been too deeply entrenched in his own sorrow to look closely at anyone else.

"Does it make you uncomfortable?" Ahn asked worriedly. "My relationship with Schenn?"

"What?" Sohmeng shook his hands a little. "No, that's not it at all! I'm not upset that Schenn is *with* you, I'm just … I'm upset about what you were both made to do. It makes me *mad*, but it's also your culture, but it also hurt you so badly, and I have no idea how to talk about it without being a jerk by accident. I don't want to make things worse."

When Ahn spoke, it felt as though Schenn's wry humour was speaking through him: "I'm not sure you can make it much worse, Sohmeng."

She groaned, pressing her forehead into his shoulder. "Look, I have this bad habit of trying to make people I love not be sad. I want to fix their feelings for them, even though it probably doesn't work like that."

"No," Ahn said apologetically. "It doesn't."

"Was Schenn also this way?" she mumbled into his shirt. "If so, does he have any tips or tricks to share from the other side on how to be *less* this way? Also was that okay to ask, because I'm really sorry if I've immediately been an insensitive tool. This is exactly what I've been worrying about."

Despite himself, Ahn laughed. He could hear Sohmeng's

worry, but the truth was that he was feeling more and more relieved as they spoke openly about Schenn. It was painful to face the violent circumstances of his loss, but there was no denying that it had happened—only the question of if Ahn would be facing it alone. What a gift it was, to see that wasn't the case.

"I like that you're asking about him," Ahn said, holding her close. "I *want* you to get to know him as I knew him. Not simply his death, but who he was in life. That's the version of him that I'm trying to hear more clearly, not—" An image came: Schenn sprawled on his back in the arena, struggling through his final breaths. Ahn closed his eyes, breathing deeply, and called forth another memory: Schenn snoozing in the fields of his home in Haojost, the sun on his face, as Ahn sat beside him and read. "I'm angry about the way his time in this realm came to an end. I'm devastated. But I don't want that to be the way he's remembered."

Sohmeng was quiet as he explained, and took some time to think after he was done. When she spoke again, she almost sounded shy. "...would you tell me more about Schenn, Ahn? I really would like to get to know him. Tell him I say sorry for being weird."

Warmth curled around Ahn's ear, rushing down towards where Sohmeng's head was rested. He squeezed her closer. "It would be my pleasure. And don't worry about it—to answer your question, Schenn also tended to get uncomfortable with other people's sadness. I'm sure he won't hold it against you."

"Good to know," she said. "So—what else you got for me, Ahnschen? Tell me some stories."

And so he did. Cautiously at first, and then with the rushing relief of an old dam bursting, he brought his memories of Schenn back into this world. Jokes they had shared ("He made fun of my hair relentlessly—did I ever tell you that it's seen as *unroyal* for not being fully silver?"), spats they'd had ("We were both eleven, but I'm still kind of mad about it?"), what it was like meeting each others' families ("He was mortified, but I really do like his great aunt."), on and on and on. They stayed up late, using the fullness of the Go phase to tell the small stories that made up the larger story of a life.

The first time Sohmeng really cackled at something Schenn had said, Ahn was so overwhelmed that all he could do was hold her. She touched his earpiece, whether in reassurance or curiosity he couldn't tell, and Sohmeng's wish to kiss him came true. They made the most of their privacy, and ended up having sex for the first time. It was easier to let himself know her in this new way when he didn't feel like he was hiding something.

"And this—this seriously isn't your *thing*?" Sohmeng asked afterwards, sounding breathless. "This is what it's like when you do something you don't even care about?"

"I care about being close to you," Ahn said, pressing a cool towel to the back of her neck. "And I've definitely had some practice. I think you can tell that I enjoyed myself. But I'm happy with every other way we spend our time. Going for walks, telling jokes."

"You're better at this than you are at jokes. Even the super dark ones you're working on."

"That—!"

"Don't argue, it's true. I'm easily the funniest person in

this whole relationship, if not the whole rainforest." She rolled on top of him, pressing her cheek against his chest, ear to his scar. "Your legs are longer than mine though. So you've got that going for you."

He had so much *fun* with Sohmeng, and felt the weight of expectation slide off of him. He had hoped that Asgørindad would give him this experience, but it had never happened. As it turned out, being the eleventh-born prince of an empire was still being the prince of an empire—on Qiao Sidhur soil, obscurity was never an option. Despite access to all the power and resources he could ever need, the right to simply *be* had never been his. Here, he was finally being given the opportunity to learn what that felt like, and try to do it gracefully.

Hei was a master of being. Early in their relationship, they'd had no tolerance for Ahn's thoughtlessness and clumsiness, no matter how well-intentioned he was. Now, with trust between them, Hei seemed to have all the patience in the world. They brought him onto one of the rafts, steered by a woman named Baang, and watched the river in silence together. They whistled for his help wrangling a rowdy hatchling—not because they needed it, but because they wanted to improve his technique. In the past he would have thought their frowning silences were a sign of judgement, but he had gotten better at reading them. Even if they weren't speaking aloud, they were always communicating, and he wanted to know what they had to say.

Sometimes, the two of them would sit back to back, and Hei would say a word. Ahn would respond with one of his own that felt connected, and back and forth they would go.

River. Water. Schenn. Bone. Flesh. Blood. Sorry.

"Sorry," Hei repeated, sighing. They took his hand, shaking it gently. "Sorry, sorry."

"Sorry, sorry."

And he was. But he was a lot of other things, too, and he was trying hard not to let himself be swallowed by regret.

Éongrir Ahnschen wanted to be proud of who he was. He wanted to be at peace with his choices. The judgment of Nona Fahang had been difficult to take, but it also had never felt like *enough*. Ahn had wanted to be punished; sometimes, he thought he wanted to be killed, for the spirit of Shengdrhu Allateinn to release him from his mistakes. He longed for forgiveness, but it also terrified him, because he thought himself so utterly unworthy.

The guilt still cut him up, but he had learned something essential: he was no good to anyone hunched over in defeat. Beating himself up wasn't the same as making amends. It certainly wouldn't get them to the other side of this battle, nor get him through whatever came next. Though what that would look like, he couldn't begin to say.

"Do you still want to go home, Ahn?"

The question came when he was on a walk with Sohmeng and Hei. It was late afternoon; by this time tomorrow, he would be far from this place. The three of them were exploring the riverbank, up to their knees in water, searching for snails. He rubbed cool water over his arms, frowning. He'd been asking himself this for a while, but it was different to hear it from Sohmeng's mouth.

"I don't know," he admitted. "Even a few weeks ago, the answer was obvious. I miss the familiarity. My university friends. The food. I miss speaking in a language I'm confident with, even if I was never all that confident in what I was saying." Vaguely, Ahn wondered if this was a thing other people ever noticed. Was the Éongrir at the start of his name enough that his words were given authority, even as he doubted them? "…but I wonder if it'll be the same. I don't know if the Qiao Sidh I knew is real anymore."

A recent memory hit him like a punch to the gut. Óla's hands on his shoulders, the tension in her voice: *they're calling you the People's Emperor.*

The safety of home wasn't a given anymore, now that his siblings had labeled him a threat. It was still surreal; being Emperor had never crossed his mind as a possibility, and it alarmed him to learn that he had become a perceived candidate completely by accident.

In theory, the appointment would make him the most powerful person in Qiao Sidh—but in reality, he would be more trapped than ever. Above all, the Emperor was a symbol of tradition. Ahn would be able to bring radical ideas to the table, but if he moved too quickly, he was likely to be killed before any change could actually happen.

Assuming he survived long enough to ascend the throne at all.

"There's something I need to tell you both," Ahnschen said.

He spread his fingers, feeling the river move through them, and explained the reason his sister had brought him to Gãepongwei. He did his best to capture the nuance of Qiao Sidh's monarchic meritocracy and explain how he had accidentally earned his father's recognition and his siblings' disdain. Even though it was hard to share, he was honest about the danger that came with returning home.

"It was intended as . . . as an act of love." Ahn felt himself wince as the words came out. "That sounds horrible, I know."

Hei clicked an affirmative, but Sohmeng looked thoughtful. "I dunno," she said. "Maybe this is weird, but it makes me feel a little less bad? Obviously I think it's an awful thing to do, but I can understand making a bad choice to protect someone I love."

"Ólawen does not think the choice is bad," Hei countered.

Sohmeng frowned, but she didn't argue. Ahn could see the way she was still trying to connect to Ólawen, despite everything. It worried him, but he knew he couldn't stop her; that stubborn commitment to empathy was one of the things he cherished about her.

"I wish she hadn't done this for me," Ahn said, trying to soothe the shame that threatened to rise. "I know it's larger than me—she would have come down here at some point, trying to attain her eighth rank. But it feels awful."

Sohmeng waded through the river to be closer to him. "If she would have done it anyway, then I'm glad you're here, Ahn."

"Very glad, Ahnschen," Hei agreed.

His throat went tight at this reframing. He never could have stopped the invasion from beginning, but he could play a part in having it end. He felt the pressure to get it right, but there was also comfort in knowing his presence meant Gãepongwei had a better chance.

Ahn thought of Schenn's voice, echoing inside of him for the first time, sending him deep into the rainforest, far from the burning of Kongkempei. Maybe he hadn't been running away from his old life; maybe he had been running *toward* something new, even before he knew what it was.

"I'm not sure what comes next," he admitted aloud.

"You can stay with us," Sohmeng said abruptly.

Ahn froze, feeling his heart flip. Even though he'd worried about returning to Qiao Sidh, he had never earnestly considered that staying in Gãepongwei could be an option. Would that even be appropriate?

Sohmeng took his hand, undeterred. "Seriously. You could stay here."

"Sohmeng..." he began, but she waved off whatever argument his mind was trying to form.

"I know it's not your home, and it would suck not going back. I *get* that. But if it doesn't feel safe, or even if you decide you need a break from Qiao Sidh, there could be a place for you here?" The way she stared at Ahn told him she was completely serious. He had no idea what to make of it. He was grateful beyond words. "You could stick with us, or you could settle down in a hmun. Sorwei Chapal seems cool with you, and Ateng is kind of stuffy, but my grandmother would probably pinch your cheeks forever."

Hei clicked, frowning deeply. "Ahnschen stays with the colony."

"Yeah I mean I'd like that too, but we can't *kidnap* him."

A laugh burst out of Ahn. Having this option open up— seeing Soh and Hei *argue* over where he might go—was overwhelming, was wonderful. Part of him wanted to accept without a second thought. But, again, all of this was bigger than him. He had to remember that.

"I appreciate this," he said, kissing the back of Sohmeng's hand. "But even if Ólawen retreats, I don't trust her to tell the story correctly to our parents. It's not only about stopping this invasion, it's about ensuring nothing like it happens again in the future. So I might have to personally explain it to them, even if I need a couple extra guards by my side for a while."

Sohmeng's face fell, but she quickly tried to mask it. "I guess that makes sense."

"We just don't know yet," Ahn followed up, and even though it was true, the words were clumsy on his tongue. He could feel Hei looking closely at him, but he couldn't meet their eye.

He wanted to tell them both the truth: that the invitation to stay in Gãepongwei was one of the most magnificent gifts he'd ever received. He wanted time to explore the fantasy, to consider the logistics and imagine the possibilities, to discuss it in the day and dream about it at night. But he was leaving tomorrow at sunrise.

Ahn wanted to say yes, or even to say maybe, but he was afraid his heart would break if the answer ended up having to be *no*.

"You'll say goodbye, right? If you decide to go back to Qiao Sidh?" Sohmeng suddenly asked, her voice firm. "You won't just jump back on your big goofy boat or whatever once we kick you all out?"

Ahn rubbed whatever expression he was wearing off his face, and tried to ignore the way his stomach sank. "Sohmeng, of course I'd say goodbye."

"I mean it. I have a whole *thing* about people disappearing forever without a word. Once you win this thing, you need to make sure there's time to see us first."

Sohmeng's attitude never failed to amaze him. Despite the multiple plans in place, she hadn't stopped speaking as though it was a given that he would win the duel. He was trying to absorb some of that confidence while also mentally preparing for what it would mean to return to Nona Fahang under the guise of invading once more.

It would be a performance, but that wouldn't make his actions any less real. His role would be to lessen the chance of violence—but it was *all* violence, with or without blood spilled. He imagined Tonão's family watching him ride in with fresh armour, imagined the betrayal on Lita Soon's face. Imagined the Grand Ones, the elders who had shown him such grace, just to be tricked into thinking he'd used it against them. Could he even perform such a ruse? He would have to, if he failed.

Hei whistled, bringing Ahn back to himself.

"I promise," he said, searching for courage. "I won't disappear."

The next morning, after one final goodbye to Sohmeng and Hei, Ahnschen left as the sun was rising, holding tight to the version of himself that he was trying to become. As he rode through the forest on Sølshend's back, he was confronted by the strange sense of having a second chance. He had first entered the rainforest choking back tears, Schenn's echo in his ear, clinging to Lilin and feeling utterly out of control of his next steps; now, with steady breaths and the guidance of Sorwei Chapal's scouts, he wondered what else could change. What was possible.

He adjusted his body with the sãoni's movements, focusing on creating the smoothest ride possible. There was no river, but he did his best to become water, and when the scouts finally left him to make the rest of the journey alone, his mind was as clear as it would ever get.

So he listened, warmth flooding from his ear down his throat, following a path to the inner compass that guided him.

I didn't think you'd win our Six-ing, you know.

Ahn's fingers curled in Sølshend's harness. "You didn't?"

No. I know I said it could go either way, but that morning, I was sure I had you. Thought I was stronger.

"I think that's true," Ahn said, frowning to himself. He'd spent years adjusting to Schenn's sturdiness, the utter impossibility of getting him to the ground. "I was just faster when it counted, that day. Instinct took over."

We'd never really fought like that, huh?

"No. We hadn't."

The rainforest passed around them in a blur, in a crescendo of colour and light. The sun was pushing through the leaves, illuminating his path. Sohmeng said her people considered the sun to be the combined spiritual power of both moons. He thought of Schenn in the bilateral realm, looking at a large red moon and a small white. Imagined all the possibilities of their lives, shifting and fracturing and re-merging into the truths they were living today.

"Did you know I'd hesitate in the ring?" he asked.

I'd hoped you wouldn't.

"You suspected, though."

You're not subtle, Ahn.

"I'd been dreading it for weeks. I couldn't figure out how you seemed so confident."

One of us had to be. Otherwise we'd back out.

"I wish we'd backed out, Schenn."

Yeah. I know.

Sølshend leapt over a fallen log, and Ahn felt momentarily weightless before the crash of claws hit the ground again. There was still a part of him that wondered how much of this was in his head, how much of it was wishful thinking. Like any other Qiao Sidhur child, he was raised devoted to the teachings of the bilateral realms, but with the weight of such an impossible gap between him and Schenn, it had been easy for doubt to come in. For him to fear he'd severed a bond he was meant to be nurturing.

You with me, Ahn?

He exhaled a breath he'd been holding close as a secret. Tried not to let his voice waver as he asked, "Are you, Schenn?"

Don't ask questions that'll make you crazy. Not right now.

"But you're here?"

Ahnschen.

The name was a chastisement and a confirmation, and Ahn cradled the sound of it in Schenn's voice. Layered it on top of Soh's and Hei's, discovering all of the ways he was learning how to be loved, and forgiven.

You can't hesitate this time. Tell me you know that.

"I don't think I will," Ahn said, and was surprised to find that he meant it.

Why not?

"In our Six-ing, I doubted it was right for the match to happen. This time I know it *has* to. I know it's the right thing to do, even if I don't like it. My only doubt is in my own abilities, I suppose."

Then don't think about your abilities. Borrow mine. What's the point of me being in your ear if I can't tell you how to win? You know I'm not here for harp practice.

Ahn felt himself crack a grin. "No, you're not. But it's good to hear you anyway."

The terrain was looking familiar now; he was nearing the coast. He passed freshly cauterized tree stumps and saw the familiar footprints of the madøng. He could smell the smoky remnants of cooking fires against the brine of the sea. He flexed his fingers in Sølshend's harness, urging the sãoni to slow as he braced himself for the sounds of camp. For his sister's sun-bright fury.

"Ólawen always liked you," he said softly. "She thought you were a gifted warrior."

Then let's go ahead and show her she's right.

And they might have done just that, if Óla had honoured her half of the bargain.

The camp was all wrong. Ahn could tell within seconds of clearing the treeline. The base structures were still in place, tents still raised, but at least half of the infra-structure had been disassembled, the sandy soil turned with the signs of a clean-up project. Last time he was here there had been well over one hundred people present; now there were maybe fifty. And for the most part, they didn't quite seem able to look at him.

Ahn abruptly called the sãoni to a halt, looking around in disbelief.

"What is this?" he barked at one of the nearest soldiers. "Where's Ólawen?"

"Gone south, Eløndham," Hidhrolo Noula Qøngemtsou Idhrenqang said as she emerged from one of the tents. She was dressed in her shirtsleeves; a squire approached with her plate armour, and she calmly refused. Her sun tattoo shone on the freshly shorn side of her scalp.

"Sit with me and talk," she said. "We're in no rush."

Sixteen

WAR WAS PART OF GÃEPONGWEI'S ancient history. The old stories made reference to mythic battles, which had been Sohmeng's touchpoint as she tried to reckon with Qiao Sidhur culture. But it was mostly conceptual. The places Polhmun Ão had been at odds with were long forgotten, and the details of these periods of violence were largely lost to history. War was a habit that had died with its era, and all that remained was the language to prove it had happened at all.

In Ateng, some of Sohmeng's age-mates had latched onto the word *warrior*. They were dazzled by the idea of mighty protectors, with bodies built strong enough to hold their convictions. Sohmeng hadn't been as interested. She admired both integrity and muscles, but didn't know how she felt about the power fantasy.

As fantasy shifted into reality, her opinion solidified fast: it sucked. It was stupid and pointless and a sign of a complete failure to communicate. And now she had to participate in it.

It was obvious that she wouldn't be on the front lines. She had zero martial ability. And even if she tried to leap in and be a hero, she'd mostly be a distraction to Hei, who would be right in the thick of it directing the sãoni. But even though she couldn't fight, she was determined to be useful.

"Look, I'm not just going to sit in Sorwei Chapal and panic," she had said to Nepar and Polha, who were taking the lead in the attack. "No offense to Lula Jão, but being vulnerable with strangers makes me itchy and I'm not a strong swimmer."

Sohmeng and Eakang had shown up as a united front, each ready to prove they had something to offer. Sohmeng had been pleased to discover Polha and Nepar had already been thinking along the same lines.

"I'll be first in command, with Polha as my second. We'll need someone to communicate the big picture," Nepar had said, and handed them each a carved horn to blow. "Sohmeng, you can observe from a distance on sãoni-back and give us the signals we need to decide our next moves. Eakang, you're Soh's second. When it's done, you head right back to Sorwei Chapal to inform them of the outcome, whether it's a win or a loss. Do you think you can both do that?"

"Definitely," Eakang had said confidently. "I've done some similar stuff back home."

Polha nodded along, but Sohmeng saw her frown. The journey to Ateng had been Eakang's Tengmunji, but this situation was going far beyond what was expected, and maybe even what was appropriate. But if the worst came to pass and Nona Fahang was invaded, there would be far bigger problems ahead.

"So my job is to make sure everyone knows how things are looking?" Sohmeng had asked. "Like where soldiers are coming from, or if they have fire-sand?"

"Exactly. And to spread the word if Polha or I call a retreat with our own horns." Nepar had brandished his for emphasis. "Things will be overwhelming on the ground. We want to reduce confusion wherever possible."

"That mind of yours moves fast," Polha had added, "and you're as decisive as they come. We could use your direction, if you're up to the challenge."

After years of being given roles she couldn't thrive in, it was nice to have her skills be properly considered. Sohmeng had never wanted to use them like this, but it was what the situation demanded. So she'd steeled herself and said, "I'd never pass up the opportunity to be bossy."

Now, with Ahn on route to Ólawen, Sohmeng caught herself thinking about her talk with Viunwei back in Ateng. The genuine worry on his face as he asked if she'd be careful. Annoyingly, she understood why he'd had reason to doubt—historically, she'd been pretty reckless. But through this whole thing, she *had* been careful. She'd advocated for earnest communication; she'd fought to see the best in everyone while also planning for the worst. She had tried and tried to be careful, and yet it was more impossible than ever to promise Viunwei she would be safe.

Carpenters, cooks, diplomats. That's who Ahn had said would be waiting for them in Kongkempei. But they wouldn't be sitting under a roof together, talking out their differences over a meal. Fighting for peace still felt ridiculous, but right now, Sohmeng had to participate in the world as it was, not how she wanted it to be.

That would come later, when the battle was done. When they had won.

She held close to that thought, and used it to ward off the waves of anxiety that came and went as they journeyed north. There were not nearly enough trained sãoni to carry the entire force—and the force itself was not trained to ride sãoni anyway—so they advanced at a human pace. It was oddly anticlimactic to go so slowly. All in all, it would take three days to arrive.

Compared to Sohmeng, Hei didn't seem overly worried during those days. Maybe irritable or tense at times, but for the most part they were quiet, focused.

"Is it a lot of pressure?" Sohmeng asked them. "Being the alpha and all?"

"The colony does not pressure me."

"But like—do you *feel* the pressure from the inside? Are you scared?"

Hei's brow creased as they considered this. "I don't know. I think right now I am angry. Maybe I'll be more scared later."

"Or maybe instead we'll be celebrating. Because you'll come in all scary and Ólawen will be like *whoa, nope, I'm out of here!* and then everything will be fine forever."

"Nothing is fine forever," Hei said, and Sohmeng had no idea how they managed to make that sentiment sound comforting. "But we can put a stop to how things are right now."

The days passed. Colourful birds fluttered high in the canopy, occasionally dropping bright magenta feathers, though Sohmeng didn't recognize the species this far north. Marsupials made a racket into the night, perking the sãoni's interest and grating on everyone else's ears. Old trees creaked and groaned, and young sprouts shot up through the ground with silky green enthusiasm. The sun rose and set like it did any other day, and if Eiji knew that it was being threatened, it didn't show it.

Eventually, the terrain began to transform as the wetlands overcame them. Sohmeng noticed it when Singing Violet let out an annoyed growl at the mud sucking on her claws. They trudged along, and the line between land and water became harder to gauge. Bugs buzzed around Sohmeng's ears; she swatted at them, wondering how anyone could tell where was safe to step and where would send them tumbling into the marsh.

But it was no problem for Nepar Ãofe and several of his Sorchapa warriors. The territory was unfamiliar to Sohmeng, but to them, it was nothing more than the inconvenient walk to their neighbours' house. It reminded her of when she first watched Hei navigating the rainforest. Their ease took the fear out of the unknown.

Eventually, the land felt more solid beneath their feet. Hills emerged, fog curling around them like steam from a teacup. Sohmeng, mountain-raised as she was, was comforted to see the land reaching for the sky. The bugs, praise Chehangma, also laid off.

"The mist is thick today," Nepar observed. "We won't have as much visibility as I'd like, but the cover is an advantage, too. Sohmeng, Eakang, this is where we part—you get to higher ground, and we'll hone in on Kongkempei. We should be able to take what soldiers remain unawares, and then we'll press further into the hmun."

Sohmeng was eyeing one of the hills in search of an

ideal spot when Hei hissed out a sound that caught the attention of humans and sãoni alike. Polha raised her hand, and everyone froze. The only sounds Sohmeng heard were the low growls of the sãoni and her blood pounding in her ears.

Mist clouded everything around them, obscuring the source of Hei's warning. The wind itself died down, suspending them in the unknown. And then, through the dense grey haze, Sohmeng caught sight of a glimmer, like the ring she had found in a yellowbill nest moons and moons ago. The silver of a blade.

Qiao Sidh had been waiting for them.

"Minhals, *go!*" Polha shouted, rearing up her sãoni to block them from the sudden surge of soldiers. Eakang took off toward a hill in the west, but Sohmeng found herself cut off by a living wall of armour.

The skirmish began like a crack of thunder, shaking the earth and rippling outwards. Nepar was already in close combat against a Qiao Sidhur soldier, using his size to his advantage to beat them down. Sohmeng had to get out before she was completely surrounded, or she would be trapped without any means to protect herself.

Singing Violet released her claws from the muck to swipe at a soldier, and they met the attack with a clang of their shield. As they raised up their sword, a spear pierced through their neck. For one surreal and endless moment, Sohmeng locked eyes with them, their expressions mirrored in shock and pain.

Hei tore the spear from the soldier's neck as they snarled out an order in Sãonipa:

Move. I love you. Move.

With this brief window afforded to her, helpless to do anything else, Sohmeng screeched a cry to Singing Violet. The sãoni tore through the fight, knocking aside the line of Qiao Sidhur in her path. Nauseous, Sohmeng directed Violet to the perimeter, trying to find a way to distance her heart from her mind.

She assessed the situation as the sãoni brought her high. It was hard to see through the fog, but one thing was clear to Sohmeng: the numbers were all wrong. Based on what Ahn had seen of the expedition, he had estimated there would be one hundred people stationed in Kongkempei. Only a fraction, he said, would be soldiers. This was far more than a fraction.

She raised her horn. First, one loud tone—from the other side of the skirmish, Eakang returned it. Together, in some strange and horrible distortion of music, they painted an image of the battle before them.

Incoming from the north. Holding strong in the west. Sãoni down. Fire-sand, fire-sand.

The heat burned through the mist, revealing the scene in full. As far as Sohmeng could see, the soldiers of Sorwei Chapal were holding their own admirably, particularly with the sãoni on their side. When several madøng were introduced, things got chaotic fast. A swarm of sãoni tore into the raptors, forcing the Qiao Sidhur riders into melee range. The soft ground was no help with their armour, but rather than getting discouraged, it seemed to redouble their ferocity.

Exit blocked east, more soldiers incoming. Three of ours down. One of theirs.

Hei moved with Green Bites like their bodies were one;

their brother's teeth sprayed gore across their face. A flaming sword ate through a tree that had been alive as long as Sohmeng's father, sending it crashing towards a sãoni.

Every death marked a victory, either for the Qiao Sidhur or the Sorchapa. But as Sohmeng watched the violence unfold, thick blood spattering the vibrant foliage of Eiji, she felt vehemently that no one ever really won a war. Angry tears flooded her vision, and she blinked them back in time to see yet another wave of Qiao Sidhur coming.

She toned a warning, which Eakang echoed across the battlefield. The horns bellowed through the cacophony, competing with the clash of metal, the cries of pain, the roars of the sãoni. Nepar's sãoni fell, and Sohmeng felt a jab of panic. He stood to take up the fight on his own, mountain of a man that he was. He shouted something to one of his students—

—when the sword went through his back.

At once, all that noise disappeared from Sohmeng's ears. As Eakang signaled another burst of flame from the north, Sohmeng tried to pass Nepar's command over to Polha Hiwei, but Polha was backed into a vicious brawl of her own, and Sohmeng had no idea if her signal had even been heard. An arrow whizzed past Hei as they drove something sharp into the gap in someone's armour, and it was all too easy to imagine the next one hitting. Eakang was moving higher up their hillside, their sãoni struggling through tangled root systems. Qiao Sidhur soldiers were beginning to surround them on madøng.

It had barely been fifteen minutes. She wasn't sure they'd last fifteen more.

Sohmeng was trying to find Polha in the crowd when General Ólawen emerged. With her chestplate twinned to Ahn's in meticulous detail, she was unmistakable. In the chaos she moved measuredly, ducking away from a Sorchapa warrior before cleanly cutting them down. She stalked towards Nepar, who was on his knees, guarded by a Sorchapa warrior who was barely Ahn's age.

Sohmeng didn't wait for Polha or Nepar's approval. She made the call herself, blowing the horn four long times to signal retreat. But a quick look at the numbers told her that the time for retreat had come and gone.

Weaponless and terrified and determined as she had ever been, Sohmeng rode straight into the center of battle, Singing Violet snarling all the way. She yanked hard on the sãoni's reins, trying to get herself between Ólawen and Nepar before any more damage could be done.

"We surrender!" Sohmeng shouted. "Do you hear me? We surrender, call them off!"

Ólawen's brow cocked in recognition, but she didn't move. Sohmeng had Qiao Sidhur soldiers all around her, but none of them approached. The realization was chilling: she was Ólawen's to kill.

"Éongrir Ólawen-Eløndhol," Sohmeng appealed, hardly recognizing the desperation in her own voice. "Please, I am begging you, call them *off*. Make it stop, we surrender, I surrender."

The general didn't need a translation to hear Sohmeng. She whistled, and with remarkable efficiency, the order went down the line of soldiers. Within seconds, they had paused, with the exception of those who were still defending against the sãoni.

"Hei!" Sohmeng shouted, following up with their Sãonipa name. "Hei, it's done—"

Their eyes burned with fury, but they hesitated for only a beat before ordering the colony to stop. It took a few moments, but the clash of violence slowly died down. All that remained was the aftermath, the sounds of pain all around her. Another bridge falling.

A translator came to Ólawen's side, and Sohmeng scrambled for the right thing to say. She felt like a child caught misbehaving, trapped at the mercy of an indifferent grownup. They had been trying to ambush occupied Kongkempei, and there was no way to deny it.

"Please," Sohmeng said again, though she didn't know what she was pleading for. "Please, I never wanted a fight. I just—I want to negotiate with you."

"I'll bet you do." Ólawen's gaze fell on Nepar Ãofe, who was somehow managing to look dignified despite the amount of blood he was losing. His student had their hands pressed to the wound in his back. "Where's Prince Ahnschen?"

Sohmeng stared at her, baffled. "What? He went to meet you for the duel. You challenged him—"

"I know what I did." Her expression was unreadable. Sohmeng wondered if there was any way to convince her that Ahn didn't know about this plan. But Ólawen wasn't a fool, and she had already proven to be merciless in the face of perceived betrayal. The corner of the general's mouth twitched, and she tugged at her earpiece, looking at her soldiers. "Keep the beasts surrounded, and bring out the fire-starter in case they try anything cute. It keeps them in line. Then round up as many of the humans as you can, we still have detention set up by Køngkanna, don't we?"

A sharp look from Ólawen and the translator paused, leaving Sohmeng in the dark about what would come next. In so little time, the force that had come to liberate Kongkempei had joined the ranks of its prisoners.

Seeing Nepar Ãofe struggle to pull himself to standing, Sohmeng quickly said, "Our wounded. Will you help them, General Ólawen? Please?"

"That's a funny thing to ask," the woman said with a tilt of her head. "Why do you think I would say yes?"

Sohmeng struggled for an answer, but nothing felt sufficient. All she had left was the truth, wrapped in an appeal to an authority she didn't believe in. "I don't know, Eløndhol. I really don't know, but I'm asking anyway. I'm asking for your mercy."

Again, the woman paused to assess her. Her hair was silver all the way through, her jaw more square than Ahn's, but the resemblance was undeniably there. It was uncanny.

"Hidhrolo Noula would say you're all citizens of the Empire, and she's been right about everything else, so. I suppose so." The woman looked deeply unhappy as she spoke, looking around at the destruction. Fallen soldiers, Sorchapa and Qiao Sidhur both. "What a waste."

Oddly, this was something Sohmeng could get behind. Were she not so shaken, she might have even had something to say about it.

"Well," said Qiao Sidh's conquering general, "Ahnschen will be here soon enough." She spat on the ground. "Until then, I suppose you're my guest."

SEVENTEEN

ÉONGRIR AHNSCHEN DID NOT SIT. His feet fell heavy as he paced, a temper he did not know he had lashing out like a solar flare. The remaining soldiers watched in obvious discomfort, and he didn't even care. Every moment he was here was a moment his sister was getting closer to Kongkempei—to Sohmeng and Hei and the sãoni, to the unprepared martial force of Sorwei Chapal. He had learned many of their names, shared meals with them. When a sparring session with three of Nepar's students had landed him face-first in the lily pond, he'd come up laughing. They'd abandoned their weapons and jumped in with him.

Those people were facing off against Ólawen. Ólawen in her full power, in her hurt and her betrayal. No one in the world was more loyal than his sister, and so no one took a perceived slight more seriously. Loving and inflexible, caring and cruel—and that was just to him, her favourite sibling. What would she do to the strangers who she thought had misled him?

"Why didn't she stay?" Ahn demanded. "She challenged me for shaming Qiao Sidh and then wouldn't even stay to honour our—"

"I told her to go," said Noula.

"*Why?*" Ahn asked desperately. "Why would you do that?"

"I had a feeling. General Ólawen told me what you said, about wanting to stop the campaign. This was a good shot for you to take either Køngkanna or Hosaisi while she was waiting. The only question was if you'd join the attack, or come here to face her in the meantime. And, I suppose, which hmun you'd direct your attention to." She paused, and when she spoke, her voice was nearly gentle. "It was a good plan, Eløndham."

It had felt like one. Everyone at Sorwei Chapal had worked hard ironing out the logistics, preparing and preparing. And now it was crumbling before him.

"Why did you assume Kongkempei?" he asked numbly.

"Because you feel responsible. You'd want to make it right before continuing." Noula's voice was lowered as she spoke, as though she was trying to keep the information private. He could see the soldiers nearby trying to pretend they weren't listening. "It's the move I would have made, too. Køngkanna's in better shape to organize, and it's nearer to the ships if you wanted to cut us off from the strait."

The distance between him and Kongkempei suddenly felt impossible to bridge. In his mind, he saw hundreds of weapons pointed at good people. He saw the jungle burning under his sister's disinterest and disdain.

He couldn't breathe. "She's going to kill them."

Noula placed a hand on his shoulder, speaking steadily. "No. She isn't."

Ahn jerked away, his voice rising as he shook with anger. "And am I to thank you for making that choice, too? For telling Óla to—"

"I don't tell Óla what to do," Noula cut in. There was an edge to her voice, an impatience he hadn't heard before. "I could barely do that with Wen, and she was the reasonable half of the two." Ahn hardly knew what to say to that. Hearing herself, Noula grimaced, bowing her head and restructuring her expression to its usual unreadability. "I apologize, Eløndham. I forget myself."

It occurred to Ahn that he could use that against her, throw his status at her and make her grovel. Noula stood by his sister's side, but he could make things incredibly difficult for her, and there was nothing she could do in turn. It would be a public humiliation, with all these soldiers bearing witness. It might even make some of them turn to his side in fear.

You actually think you can pull that one off, Ahn?

His stomach turned, ear pulsing. Of course he couldn't. But he had to do *something*. "No. I'd like you to be honest with me, Noula. Talk to me like I'm a person. I don't have patience for posturing, not now."

Noula assessed him for a moment before speaking. Unexpectedly, she shifted into Dulpongpa. "... come with me to the command tent, Eløndham. Please."

"Why?"

"If we're to speak candidly, I think privacy would serve you in the long run as a leader of this nation. I see that you're upset, and I'd like to approach this in good faith."

It was a smart move, and Noula did not seem to be lying. She felt more like a cousin than a tactician, trying to pull him away from a party after he'd had too much to drink. It distressed him to accept any sort of counsel from her right now, but if he wanted an explanation, there was no choice but to concede.

Noula held herself ready. She was waiting for him to lead her to the tent. To be the Prince, the General, as everyone expected of him.

"Privacy," he commanded through a clenched jaw, and everyone obeyed.

Once they entered the tent, Noula closed the thick flaps behind them, brought over a pitcher of water, and began speaking. "Your sister won't kill your friends because she loves you. And also, she's not a monster."

"She's talked about past campaigns, Noula. I know she's killed people, and she doesn't seem all that sorry. She's proven that here, too."

"Ólawen has a heavy hand," Noula agreed, "but she doesn't crave violence. There have been far bloodier generals in our nation's history. Even in your own family. Ólawen mostly craves the satisfaction of simple answers, carrying a plan through its execution. Seeing results. There's a reason Philosophy never appealed to her. And that's why she's so upset—she doesn't understand you, Ahnschen."

"She's barely *listened* to me enough to understand! She dismisses half of what I say before the words even make it off my tongue."

"I imagine that's been going on long before the campaign began," Noula said carefully. "Forgive me if I overstep."

The comment took Ahn aback. Truthfully, this was something he'd only started to recognize when he last saw Ólawen. When she put the harp in his hands, the harp she'd hidden for months and months, outwardly teasing him about studying music. The gift should have been beautiful, but her delivery revealed a painful truth about their relationship. His sister loved him, but she didn't know him for who he was.

"No," Ahn said quietly. "You'd be right."

"I'm sorry to hear that. Family matters can be difficult for anyone—I can only imagine the pressure of carrying the Empire, as well. I don't envy your position, Ahnschen."

It was a peculiar dynamic to find himself in. Where Ahn's talk with Óla had been overwhelming, Noula spoke without urgency. She was calm, and she listened. In fact, she had listened to him enough to destroy his and Sorwei Chapal's entire plan. Mostly, she had just watched and asked questions of the people who seemed to make him happiest.

Ahn had probably never stood a chance convincing Óla. She was a forceful personality, and their history made it hard for him to stand up for himself. No matter what, a discussion that challenged Ólawen's core beliefs would have eventually become a fight, one that he didn't have the experience or confidence to win.

But maybe he didn't have to fight with Noula. Maybe he could do what Sohmeng had always insisted was possible, and simply have an honest exchange. At this point, it would be foolish not to try.

Ahn took a deep breath. "Would you tell me what happened in Kongkempei?"

Confusion passed briefly over Noula's face, but she responded. "A disagreement escalated—and was mismanaged, if you still seek my candour."

"I do," Ahn confirmed. "What was the disagreement?"

"There was a dispute between a local and a soldier. An insult which the soldier retaliated against with what I would call undue force. The elders were displeased. They raised deep concerns about our presence. There was room for a gentler approach, but Óla put her foot down about this land being under Imperial rule."

"But it isn't."

"Not yet." Ahn didn't like the inevitability in Noula's voice, but it was an important reminder. No matter how reasonable Noula was being, she was still aligned with his sister for now. "The violence flared quickly and changed the tone of the occupation overnight. Securing Køngkanna was supposed to be peaceful."

"And Hosaisi?" Ahn asked. "From what I've heard, our soldiers came in with blades drawn."

The corner of Noula's mouth twitched; her voice was flat with displeasure. "Ólawen was angry, and so was Hosaisi, on behalf of their neighbours. There wasn't much room for negotiation. As I said, the campaign began taking a very different tone than it needed to."

The more they spoke, the more Ahn noticed the contradictions in Noula's words. He could hear her frustration about the direction of the campaign, but he also heard her speaking about the work of the Empire as a good thing. She disapproved of the bloodshed, but still took the value of conquering as a given.

Ahn understood. There was a time not too long ago where

he also believed that empire could be benevolent, that invasion could be nonviolent. Each and every day he was working to unlearn all the ways that had been embedded into his body—and it was hard work, to transform a worldview. He was grieving the harm he had unknowingly done, but he was also grieving the time when things were uncomplicated. When he could be a sheltered prince who viewed war as an artform, divorced from the real and obvious brutality. When he could be naïve.

Noula wasn't naïve. He wondered what it was that kept her attached to Conquest when she also seemed disinclined towards violence.

"How would you have done it?" Ahn asked. "Managed the campaign."

Noula looked at him warily. "That's not my place."

"Indulge me," Ahn encouraged, taking the pitcher of water and filling Noula's cup. "Your primary Path is Discernment. I'd like to know what you think the biggest weakness in this campaign was, and how you'd have changed it."

He couldn't blame Noula for taking a moment to think. This query was the type of trap his older sibling Elønding might've pulled. Asking for your opinion, then twisting your words. She'd gotten a competitor in her schooling executed for that once. Ahn had been eight, and he never quite stopped being afraid of her after that.

"I would have slowed down," Noula eventually settled on, taking the cup from Ahn. "Brought fewer soldiers, focused more on resource management. The occupation was too much too fast, and we didn't know the terrain well enough. If we had treated it as more of an exploration than a campaign, similar to the first landing in Hosaisi, we could have forged better relationships with the different hmun, framed annexation as a deal as opposed to an invasion. Similar to the taking of the Inner Island, or Gurinn."

Another road, huh?

Ahn swallowed. "And if they refused?"

"I specialize in conflict resolution. I'd have done my best to manage tempers and expectations. It's the work I expected to be doing anyway."

Ahn's interest was piqued. "Oh?"

Noula took a long drink of water, like she was testing out the shape of the words in her mouth. As long as Ahn had known her, she'd never been the type to overshare about her personal life. "I could have been an adjudicator back home, but I'm impatient with petty squabbles, and I've always wanted to travel. I gained low-level Conquest ranking to impress my favourite grandfather, and your sister suggested I work my way higher to secure my position beside her. It was the best opportunity to make use of my abilities and interests."

"What interests you?" Ahn asked. "Besides languages."

This was something he had learned early about Noula, and benefited from when they first landed. Her Dulpongpa had been strong coming in—apparently she'd spent the better part of a year practicing with one of the saro dhral from the first expedition. She didn't just speak the Imperial tongue and Dulpongpa, she also knew a few of the less common Qiao Sidhur provincial languages. Once, she'd quoted a proverb he'd only ever heard from Schenn, and it startled him out of his skin.

"I'm curious about other people," Noula said, crossing

her arms. For all her face looked relaxed, the gesture was oddly self-conscious. "I like getting to know them. And obviously I like a puzzle. Your sister has told me I'm sullen when I'm bored, so she keeps me busy. *There's always a problem to solve on the road*, she said."

Language. Connection. Solving problems. Ahn had seen all of these skills at work in Kongkempei. Noula picking up words in Kempeipa and listening in on stories from locals. Reporting complaints, calmly resolving disputes. This was what Noula's skills and interests looked like in the context of Conquest. But outside of an invasion? There were countless ways she could thrive, ways that weren't so harmful—and, Ahn imagined, that might actually be more aligned with her interests. The culture of domination wasn't empowering her; it was holding her back.

"My parents are traditional," she continued. "They expected me to use my Discernment training to manage our estate and dukedom. Get married, sooner rather than later. But court life doesn't suit me, and Ólawen's invitation seemed like a more enriching way to serve Qiao Sidh."

"Do you—" A question rose from Ahnschen's throat, nearly burning with the potential it held. "Do you love Qiao Sidh, Noula?"

"Of course, Eløndham." There was no hesitation in Noula's voice, but neither was there any passion. It was a trained answer, an instinctive response to a member of the royal family.

"No, pretend that—if you can, pretend that I am not who I am. Do you love your Empire?"

"I live here. It raised me."

"But do you love it as you love your family? As you love your dear friends?"

"…no," she said cautiously, "but I am proud to be a part of it."

"Why?" Ahn asked, unable to hide the eagerness in his voice. It was silly, but he'd never had this conversation before with someone else who was Qiao Sidhur. It wasn't until right now that he realized how badly he needed it, to examine this with someone who shared his culture. To know that this great possibility for change could reach beyond him.

Noula, on the other hand, looked exasperated. "Because it's my home, Ahnschen? Why does anyone love where they're from?"

Ahn imagined being posed this question by one of his Philosophy professors. It felt like one of their trials, to ask a question as large as the horizon and ask him to run the length. More often than not, there was no right answer. The point of the activity was to learn new approaches, to open up perspectives, to remove the notion of simplicity and get comfortable with the discomfort of it all. To choose your own values, and act in accordance with them.

No one could make sense of why, at age nineteen and on the sixth tier of Conquest, Ahn had chosen to attend university and chase a new Path from scratch. In truth, Ahn hadn't known either. He'd enjoyed his schooling by day, and privately cursed himself each night for being a coward. Why was he so ungrateful? Why had he fled what he was meant to do, *trained* to do?

All at once it became clear—Ahn had never been running away. Not really. He'd been following a different journey, desperately seeking answers that a blade could not give him:

Why are we doing this? Why did this happen to us? Why does it have to be like this?

Does it have to be like this, Ahnschen?

With a sword, Ahn had learned how tradition felt in his body. With a harp, Ahn had learned how to express himself without words. With a pen and books and a lecture hall, with the patience of friends and professors, with the courage to do something he was scorned for, Ahn learned how to harness his curiosity. How to open himself to new ways of thinking, and connect with different people, and challenge his own knowledge for pleasure rather than fear.

Ahnschen was not throwing away everything he had ever known. He wasn't writing off the entirety of Qiao Sidh. He wasn't salting the earth—he was remineralizing it. A symbol of the Empire and a farm boy, joined by tragedy, determined to watch their home *grow.*

"I love our culture," Ahnschen said vehemently. Despite the shame and the anguish, it was true. The Dulpongpa they had been speaking fell away, tumbling into the language of his youth: "I grew up mostly in Hvallánzhou, and to this day I think it has the best food in the world. I dream of the clear water of Qiao Sidhur lakes, and the way the mountains watch over the caldera. The folksy, earnest ballads? They're my favourite, and I'm not even sorry to say so. I used to hide in the room in the Winter Palace with the tapestries from across the provinces. I love how many cultures we hold—and I am ashamed of how we came to hold them. I *love* Qiao Sidh, Noula, but I do not love the Empire."

Ahn was out of breath, impassioned and afraid of being misunderstood. But Noula was looking at him intently, a crease in her brow. And once more, like a Master or a professor, speaking to him as a boy and not a prince, she said: "Differentiate them for me."

Ahn's hands opened and closed again, trying to grasp the key distinctions. The feeling was so obvious in his body, but verbalizing it was raw and new. He thought about the things he was proud of, and an image came to mind—hours translating the Paths of Mastery to Sohmeng and Hei. The joy of watching Soh light up and ask questions, of digging through his education and experience to answer as best as he could.

A name found its way to his lips, a name that every Qiao Sidhur child learned in their early education.

"Tseir Jin Zhadh," Ahn nearly recited, pacing the room once more, "established the Paths of Mastery nearly five centuries ago as the essentials of a culture, the pillars that held it up. This was back when Qiao Sidh was still its own region, reaching no further than the quiet caldera. He drew on inspiration from other regions of the upper continent, places that would eventually become our provinces. His teachings highlighted how we were all connected. The Paths were only reimagined into tools of advancing the Empire when the expansions began in the Silver Age four hundred years later. But I think, in their original form, the Paths demonstrate what Qiao Sidhur culture can look like *outside* the context of Imperial expansion. I think we're more than that; I think we know how to connect without exerting control." As he felt his heart swell with pride, a complicating thought came to mind. "Though I don't . . . I don't know why Conquest was a Path, before the Empire. Maybe my logic isn't perfect, but—"

"It was a mistranslation."

Ahn paused, not sure what to make of that. "What?"

"A mistranslation," Noula repeated. Her cup was empty; she rolled it between her palms. "In archaic Qiao Sidhur, Conquest could be read as *sacrifice* or *devotion through action*. Challenging unjust rulers, defending the land in times of war. Being willing to die for the wellbeing of future generations. When the Western Island was taken, the meaning was condensed, and then amplified in a surge of nationalism."

This was a footnote Ahn had never encountered in his studies, a key piece of history that he had somehow missed. The language Noula was using was also peculiar, tinged with academia. "Where did you learn that . . . ?"

"My older brother was studious," she said, "and seditious. He spent his time in coffeehouses with political radicals, and spoke about the systemic injustices of Qiao Sidh often before he was disowned by my family. My parents feared he would compromise our standing."

With my family, Ahn didn't say, but felt the weight of it press down from all sides.

"I'm sorry," he said. "Were you . . . close?"

"I wouldn't say we shared all the same political opinions, if that's what you're asking. I was barely twelve when he went west on a ship to ka-Khasta," Noula said wryly. "But . . . yes. I'd say we were close."

For a moment, Ahn didn't know what to say. There were layers and layers of complexity here, of loss on a personal and systemic scale. But Noula was looking at him again, and he realized she was waiting for him to continue.

"I believe," Ahnschen said, "that expanding the Empire leads us in the direction of ruin. It stamps out the unique identities of our neighbours, homogenizes the brilliance that comes from different experiences and perspectives. In Gãepongwei, the differences are what bring people together."

"Many people would be unhappy to hear you say you want to be like Gãepongwei."

"No, I want to be like *Qiao Sidh*. And I believe we are more than an empire. The Paths outdate the Empire, and teach us that Imperial expansion is extraneous from our culture—or, no, no it isn't anymore. It's entwined in a way that is messy and painful, and will not make sense to many people." Ahn wanted this to be simpler than it was, but he wouldn't let the complexity make him shy away from the truth. He grasped his chest, seeking the sureness of his heart. "But Noula—I dream of my culture beyond empire. I dream of the work *and* the pain of doing the work, and the future I hope for but likely will not live to see. I dream of the day where I can be proud of my home again, and understand what it is I'm even proud of. I want the best of Qiao Sidh to be freed from the prison of its own violence, its destructive arrogance. We didn't start like this, and that means we can *stop*." The feeling was too big for one body, too big even for two souls across two realms. He reached for Noula's hand, clasping it in his own, determined to make contact. To let this gentle and dangerous idea take flight. "Would you try something new with me, and use all the skills you love in a way that doesn't have to hurt people? Would you like to stop fighting?"

For a moment she looked at him with those assessing eyes, her steady hand in his firm grip. He wondered if she could feel his pulse in his fingertips, wondered if it would scare her away. Ahn hadn't realized the fullness of his feelings until right now, when they'd come tumbling out of his mouth. He felt certain of what he meant, but uncertain if she followed his meaning.

But her answer was simple: "I would."

Ahn's free hand came to her arm, mostly trying to hold himself up. "You—you would?"

"I would."

There was no hesitation in her voice, just the thoughtful tone of someone adjusting course. Perhaps for Noula, the change was as simple as being given the option to choose differently. Ahn knew this would not be true of everyone, but he was grateful to start here. Grateful not to be alone.

"*Thank you*," Ahn said. He released her and all but collapsed into a chair, draining his cup of water.

Noula sighed heavily, a hand on her hip. "Óla will be livid."

"She will," Ahn agreed. He was tired just thinking of it.

"Do you want my advice?"

"Desperately."

Noula unrolled one of the maps on the war table. She tapped a point with her finger. "We march first to Hosaisi. It's a wrong to be righted, and frankly we'll need the numbers to manage your sister in Kongkempei." Ahn heard it immediately, the switch over from *Køngkanna*. It built his courage. "And you're a new face, which will be valuable, as I doubt your sister would ever earn back trust with that hmun."

"Or any hmun," Ahn added quietly.

"Mm." Noula looked at the maps a while longer before refilling Ahn's empty cup. Her voice took on the same quality as before, more like a cousin than an inferior. Like a person talking to a person. " . . . you should know that she might not talk this through the same way I did. It could very well be war between the two of you."

Ahn had been afraid of this possibility for months now, had been sick with worry over it. Many of his hours in the river with Lula Jão had been talking this through, trying to determine what was anxiety versus fear, trying to separate dread from the threat. But if Noula was giving him this warning as a tactician, then it meant that dark reality could take shape outside his own exhausted mind.

He could not control what Óla did next; he could only choose how he would respond.

"If it goes that way," Ahnschen said, as an ocean breeze whisked through the tent, salting the air with potential, "let it be the last time I ever have to fight anyone I love."

"Here's to a new path, Eløndham," Noula said. "I'll get the camp started packing up."

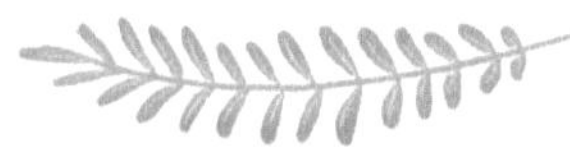

Part Three: Gãepongwei

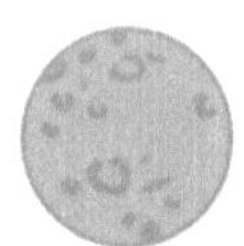

Eighteen

THE SUN ROSE, piercing through the canopy in hazy rays as birds called their full-throated greetings. The hours passed, and the mist of the wetlands transformed into rain showers, cooling the air. Moss took on its evening glow, twin to the sãoni's green and purple stripes. And then morning came again, same as it always did.

Despite the human carnage, despite the taste of smoke and iron in the air, despite all of the bravado and imposition, the rainforest kept to its rhythms.

And Hei kept watch.

Ólawen had herded the Sorchapa prisoners, for they were now prisoners, into a crudely fenced-off plot of land outside Kongkempei. Just like with the sharp-beaked madøng, the boundary lines were clearly marked; unlike the madøng, they were surrounded with beacons of fire, and soldiers standing guard with nearby fire-sand as a threat. Ólawen had segmented her army into smaller groups, which took turns watching over them.

Hei sat in the corner that was furthest from the rest of

the humans, the sãoni growling miserably around them. They could feel the human part of them quavering somewhere deep inside, and soothed it with a rumbling sãoni hum. They imagined the world through Mama's eyes, her prowling investigation, and tried to emulate it in mind if not in body.

There wasn't much room for physical prowling. There was barely room to stretch their legs. The only thing that kept the sãoni from turning on the soldiers was Hei's say-so, as well as Sohmeng's insistence that the colony be regularly fed. Presumably, Ólawen had decided she'd rather have the colony where she could see them, and so for now, they were all stuck.

It was peculiar, acquiescing to the guise that the sãoni couldn't break through these shoddy wooden pikes. But with the fire-sand to contend with, not all of the sãoni would make it, and the colony had taken enough losses as it was. It would also abandon the people of Sorwei Chapal, and to Hei's surprise, that was something they no longer found tolerable.

They had no interest in living in a hmun; that much hadn't changed. But it was no longer so easy to dismiss humans entirely. They were a part of the ecosystem, same as any other creature—and the Sorchapa in particular were interested in keeping that ecosystem in balance, same as Hei. At some point, Hei had begun conceptualizing the members of this hmun as *us* instead of *them*. The connection wasn't just about symbiosis—it was an alliance. And an essential one, if the health of the rainforest was going to be restored. Though their allies had seen better days.

Seventeen of the seventy-five Sorchapa had been killed, and most everyone else had sustained at least minor injuries. True to her word, Ólawen had permitted medical care, allowing the Sorchapa to tend to one another's wounds, occasionally with help from a nervous-looking Qiao Sidhur doctor. They wondered why Ólawen was extending this mercy when she clearly had neither love nor respect for the inhabitants of the rainforest. It was puzzling. Hei wasn't about to say thank you, but they felt fortunate that the conditions weren't worse.

Nepar Ãofe certainly wouldn't be holding on this long without that care. While he might have been more comfortable in a real bed, Ólawen wasn't letting any of the Sorchapa into Kongkempei, nor the Kempeipa into this open-air prison. Hei supposed that was wise. Humans were strongest in large numbers, and the closer they were together, the easier it would be to push back against their captors.

Hei wanted very badly to push back, but they forced themself to stay calm and avoid riling up the colony, who were already on edge. Mama likely would have torn her way out, just like Hei wanted to, but this was not a sãoni problem—it was a human one, in need of a human sãoni. So they worked on the sãoni's injured scales and tails, made sure they were well-fed, and did what they could to help the humans around them.

Well, one human, mostly. Their human.

"How could she have known we were coming?" The battle had badly shaken Sohmeng, and she hadn't slept much since. It wasn't the first time she'd asked this, and Hei was learning there wasn't an answer they could give that would soothe her. They were thankful that Sohmeng had convinced Ólawen that the two of them needed to stay together to keep the sãoni from attacking; they didn't like the idea of her being alone in this state. "Hei, I never could have guessed she'd show up."

"None of us could," Hei said. "It was very unexpected."

"We didn't plan for it at all—I don't know what to do, Hei, I keep thinking but I can't figure anything out."

They took her hand in theirs, pressing into her palm with their thumbs. "It is not your job to fix this on your own."

It was true, Hei thought, but it wasn't very helpful. Nepar and Polha had been separated from them both, so there was no chance to regroup with the adults who had helped shape this plan in the first place. This problem was beyond what any one person could manage, but Sohmeng couldn't be dissuaded from trying.

"Maybe I shouldn't have surrendered," Sohmeng said helplessly. "Maybe I called it too soon? I panicked, I didn't know what else to do."

"You made the right choice."

"How do you know?"

Hei's brow furrowed. "Do you want me to tell you it was the wrong choice? More people would have died, and for nothing. More sãoni would have died. And Ólawen still would have won."

With the surge of fury and the clash of metal clanging in their ears, Hei wasn't so sure they could have made that choice. Adrenaline had kept them in an animal state of focus, might have even made them fight until they died. Or else they might have slowed long enough to assess the damage, and decided to call the sãoni away entirely, which would have spelled defeat for their human allies.

Simply surrendering hadn't been an option in their mind. But it was the choice that had kept them alive and given them time to figure out what came next.

"It was a good choice, Sohmeng Minhal," Hei repeated quietly, pressing their cheek to hers. "It was responsible."

Sohmeng breathed out slowly, scanning the open-air prison. Hei saw them land on Eakang, huddled far away with a few of the younger Sorchapa. They were applying some antiseptic sãoni saliva to one of their wounds. "I wish at least one of us could've gotten back to Sorwei Chapal, so the Grand Ones could know what happened." Her jaw twitched, and Hei saw that she was trying very hard not to cry. "My dad would freak out if he knew what was happening right now. He'd be a mess."

Hei didn't know what to say to that. They did their best to soothe her with sãoni sounds, and were pleased when the colony began echoing them. A small chorus of comfort rose around them, and some of the Sorchapa prisoners even looked glad to hear it.

The Qiao Sidhur soldiers, on the other hand, looked nervous—which brought Hei no small amount of satisfaction.

For all the invading force had been victorious, the mood among the Qiao Sidhur was far from triumphant. Many of the soldiers looked worse for wear, and some of them had even fallen ill. Hei watched the way they gripped their weapons with haggard determination. It was true that they were better armed and organized, and they had fire-sand on their side. But with each passing day, it became clearer that they were exhausted.

If Ólawen herself was getting worn down, she didn't show it. Over the next few days, she came in and out of her tent, frowning and giving orders for one thing or another. Hei couldn't comprehend her words, but they could see the woman was getting restless.

Multiple times, Sohmeng tried talking to her. Hei warned her it would be fruitless, but of course she tried nonetheless, because that was her way—and of course she was disappointed each time.

"She keeps saying we can all talk when Ahn comes back," Sohmeng said with exasperation.

The corner of Hei's mouth twitched as they thought about Ahnschen. His sister had abandoned their duel in exchange for some fresh unknown, and Hei didn't like it one bit. "Talk about what?"

Sohmeng poked uncomfortably at the bread they'd been brought for lunch, a scowl spreading. "How Gãepongwei will be managed." Hei clicked in displeasure, and Sohmeng continued, "It's so weird Hei—she says this, and then she also says that she *cares*, that she's trying to improve our lives. But she doesn't know how anything works here! I'm trying to understand where she's coming from, but it feels like my brain's going to pop out."

Hei was not trying to understand where Éongrir Ólawen was coming from. They weren't interested. Her intentions meant little to them when her actions told them everything they needed to know.

So they kept themself steady, conserving their energy until the moment came to act. Eventually, something would break. They knew that, and so did the sãoni, whose reptilian eyes tracked the soldiers like they were wild boar bumbling through the underbrush.

The hatchlings were having the most trouble staying put. Hei routinely had to call them back to their corner of the clearing, or make up games to keep them occupied. It wasn't fair to the young ones, to have their development interfered with this way, but all Hei could do was try to prevent conflict. The fewer distractions, the easier this would be: with Sohmeng as an intermediary, they made it clear that all human food should be kept at a significant distance from the colony. But apparently even that simple instruction was too much for the soldiers to listen to.

It happened on the sixth day of their imprisonment: one of the guards had left a half-eaten lunch by the fence, and before Hei noticed, two of the more willful hatchlings snuck over to try a bite. Hei and Sohmeng were used to this—everyone who traveled with the sãoni was used to this. But the Qiao Sidhur soldiers weren't.

Hei was up the moment they heard the sword unsheathed. They shoved the soldier hard, snarling for the hatchlings to get back, and was rewarded with a hard smack across the face. With blood in their mouth and an ache in their legs from six days of being stagnant, Hei decided to return the favour.

They weren't sure what staggered the soldier more— that Hei hadn't hesitated to retaliate, or that they'd hooked their claws over their fingers.

"No, Hei, *no!*" shouted Sohmeng, and Hei took a step back. The soldier had four bloody lines across their jaw, down their throat. Not deep enough to kill, but Hei felt their point was made.

There wasn't much time to sit with their satisfaction; very quickly, more soldiers were incoming. One was helping her friend, but the others advanced on Hei, who flexed their fingers and stared them down.

"They didn't mean it," Sohmeng was saying in Dulpongpa, looking for a translator. "Really, it was a misunderstanding—"

"I did mean it," Hei responded calmly in Atengpa. "Their soldier behaved without integrity and I'm glad he's bleeding."

They could hear the sãoni readying themselves to attack, and hushed them with a series of clicks, raising a hand in the way Ahn had taught them. It was almost funny, how that made the soldiers look so unnerved. With patience, Sãonipa was not all that difficult to interpret, but the soldiers weren't interested, and so they chose instead to be agitated.

Sohmeng was speaking rapidly with a translator, working hard as always to resolve things. Seeing how upset she looked made Hei feel bad, and they tried to chime in in Dulpongpa.

"No more problems," they said, and meant it. Their quarrel with the soldier had been solved. Unless anyone else gave them trouble, they were willing to be patient until Ahn got here. Had they not conceded to every other demand so far?

"Hei this isn't good," Sohmeng said, grabbing their arm. "They're going to get—"

Quiet fell around them, and it didn't take much deduction to know who had entered the conflict. General Ólawen strolled over with an aura of calm to match

Hei's own. She tossed a glance at the bleeding soldier, narrowing her eyes as the others presumably filled her in. Hei couldn't deny she was a strong alpha in her own right; her very presence made her soldiers fall in line.

Blacktooth had been a strong alpha, too.

As Ólawen approached Hei, she only broke eye contact to glance at the sãoni, her expression dispassionate. It was only by her stiff back that Hei could see her caution. Her voice was mild as her words were passed through a translator into Dulpongpa: "I hear your sãoni are stepping out of line."

"I hear the same about your soldiers," Hei responded in Atengpa.

Sohmeng was presumably coming up with a lie to translate when the interpreter said a few words in halting Qiao Sidhur. Apparently the words were close enough to their Dulpongpa counterparts to be comprehended. Sohmeng's hand tightened around their wrist, but they did not take it back. They wouldn't have spoken if they did not want to be heard.

Ólawen sucked her teeth, then nodded to herself as she asked, "Will the beasts kill everyone if you come with me?"

"Only if I tell them to," Hei said, which they were fairly confident was true. Sohmeng's voice sounded strained as she translated.

"Are you planning on telling them to?"

"Not today, I think." This time, Hei used Dulpongpa.

Ólawen tapped her fingers against her leg. Her expression was difficult to parse, but she didn't seem to be looking for trouble. "Fine. Come with me."

Sohmeng dropped to her knees, something Hei had seen the other Qiao Sidhur soldiers do several times before. Ahn himself had done it at Hei's feet when they claimed their title as alpha. It was a display of submission, and they immediately disliked seeing Sohmeng perform it.

"Please don't hurt them," she said, "Éongrir Ólawen-Eløndhol, please, it was a mistake. The sãoni didn't mean it, Hei didn't mean it."

"I'm fairly confident Hei meant it. But no, I'm not going to kill them. Not today, I think," she echoed, something like a smile on her face. Even with Sohmeng kneeling, she didn't take her eyes off Hei. "Will you come to my tent or not?"

Hei didn't have much interest in going into Ólawen's stuffy, over-decorated tent. But they had even less interest in seeing what she would do if they didn't. Or what they would do when she decided to push. Her presence was unpleasant and her words were hollow, but playing along seemed the most likely way to get back to Sohmeng and the sãoni with the least amount of trouble.

"Fine," Hei said. They pulled Sohmeng to her feet, kissing her with as much reassurance as they could offer. With a final rub of cheeks, they let her go, following Ólawen to the tent.

It was as humid as they had expected inside, the material all wrong for the rainforest. It retained moisture, thick and heavy; Hei could smell the old water making its mark.

Two soldiers accompanied Ólawen, one of them being the translator. They sat Hei in a chair while Ólawen stood, watching them with her arms crossed. Up close, Hei saw how young she was. They might not have noticed it before, but after being on the road with the other sãoni riders, and spending those weeks in Sorwei Chapal, Hei was getting a better idea of human age.

Ólawen was older than them, sure. But she was younger than Polha Hiwei, younger than Nepar Ãofe. Younger than Sohmeng's father, and Baang on the river. Much younger than Grandmother Nor. Younger, perhaps, than Mama too.

She might try to stand like a mountain, but Éongrir Ólawen was just another human.

"Well," said the human Éongrir Ólawen, "you're the nut I haven't cracked yet. Frankly, I should have come to you sooner. Sohmeng's the talker, but you? You're the person I should be collaborating with. The alpha, right?"

Hei said nothing, watching her.

After a beat of silence, Ólawen asked, "How do you command them?"

Hei scoffed.

"It's obvious that you're in charge of things. The animals respond to your calls. You've kept them tame for six days now—I don't need to have ridden with them to know that's a feat. I also know it's an asset." She opened her arms, and Hei wondered what it was she thought she would possibly receive from them. "So once more, I ask: how do you do it? How do you command your sãoni?"

"Not mine," Hei said, same as they had told her brother.

Ólawen squinted, her disbelief a harsh cousin to Ahn's confusion. "I said this to your friend, and I'm saying it to you: I'm not trying to destroy your home. Qiao Sidh is a nation that seeks beauty, and offers beauty of its own.

There's great potential in this place, and I'd like to help it be the best it can. If you'd offer an ounce of trust, you might find there's plenty to appreciate."

Hei didn't feel that was worth a response.

"There could easily be a role for you in this. We saw how you've taught others to ride the sãoni. I'd like for you to pass that knowledge to us. You could even lead your own force—we'd be more than happy to work together."

Hei laughed. "I don't work with *people*."

"You're working with Sorwei Chapal, aren't you?" Ólawen countered. "And you were working with Ahnschen."

Hei had to concede that their belief about themself was outdated. "This is true. But different."

"How?"

"I do not work with people like you."

"And what am I like?" Ólawen asked, and Hei did not hear any real curiosity in the question.

A bully, they thought. *Big teeth, clumsy feet. Proud of yourself, and for no reason I can see.*

But what came out was a single word: "Incompetent."

Hei watched it land like a slap, Ólawen's lips parting briefly in shock. It flared quickly into anger, a hot edge to her voice. "Watch your tone."

"No."

"No?"

"No," Hei repeated. "I will not watch my tone."

"That is very bold," Ólawen said, approaching them slowly, "for someone who is currently a prisoner under my care."

Hei thought that the words *prisoner* and *care* were inherently at odds, but doubted that discussion was likely to go anywhere. "Is this a threat?"

"It could be. You are here in my camp. As are your friends, as are your sãoni—"

"Not mine—"

"*Interrupting* me," Ólawen said, raising her voice. "Disregarding my generosity. Speaking with the sort of disrespect that would have you dead by countless other generals' blades—"

"Then kill me," Hei interrupted once more, because they had a temper of their own and they were sick of her voice. And, in truth, they were curious if this would provoke her to violence. They were still learning what sort of person Ólawen was. "If it makes you feel so big."

Ólawen's expression twisted into a scowl. "And what would everyone do then? With their sãoni commander dead and me still standing? Are you so naïve to think this would end in anything but more bloodshed?"

Hei stopped to consider what it would look like if they died here. What would the world be without them? The sun would rise and the moons would spin, and the midday rainstorms would roll in as expected. Their brother would take the role of alpha, and the colony would survive, or it wouldn't. Sohmeng and Ahn would grieve, and maybe some others would too, but life was long, and Hei trusted in their capacity to heal. Or they would die, too.

That idea made their sternum feel like it could snap in two—partially because this future was, in the end, inevitable. Their loved ones would die one day. They would die. And the seasons would turn, the cycles would continue. One hundred years from now, no one around them would exist at all.

Hei was a part of the larger system, but a small part. Everyone was small in the end. The thought was freeing.

"Do you hear me?" Ólawen asked sharply, snapping her fingers in front of their face. "I'm telling you to end this your way before I have to end it for you. *Yield.*"

Hei slapped her hand away, ignoring the sharp gasp from the translator. When they spoke, they did it in Atengpa. Whether or not the translator could keep up wasn't their problem.

"Kill me, then. Go ahead and kill all of us. This place will eat you either way." Often, being with humans made them hold their tongue; people could take honesty personally, and Hei wasn't so good at figuring out how not to offend anyone. But here? They could say exactly what they meant. "Look at your warriors. Sick. Weak. You have walked them half to death in a land that will not take pity on them. The rainforest is not a thing you command. It does not listen when you shout. It doesn't grovel. It is a place that demands respect, and you do not know how to respect anything. You'll choke on its good fruit because you don't even know how to *peel* it."

The translator worked slowly, gingerly. Her voice got quieter with every sentence, and Hei trusted their meaning was coming through, because Ólawen had become very still. The echo of their message hung heavy in the tent. Hei let them get good and uncomfortable with it.

"You could have asked, you know," they finally said. "You could have humbled yourself and asked for help. People are welcoming here."

"You sure seem like it." Ólawen's voice was cold.

Hei smiled with all their teeth, imagining two more rows behind. "I'm not *most people.*"

Ólawen watched them for a beat longer, unable to hide the fact that she was unsettled. Hei was glad of it. She should be. Every word they had said was true, and no intimidation tactics could take the truth away.

She turned her back to them, speaking to the guard that wasn't translating. "Bring them back out with the others. We're done here."

Hei left without another word, their chin high. They kept pace with the guard, who moved quite slowly, in fact. They passed people they knew, including Eakang and Polha, other riders who had learned the language of the sãoni. They clicked and chirped, ignoring the way some of the soldiers snickered or whispered.

Okay, they said. *Okay. Safe. Wait. Okay.*

When they made it to Sohmeng, they wrapped an arm around her, accepting the scolding that came. They kissed her head, and they did not argue. They held the hatchlings as they climbed over, and thought about Mama's smooth scales, and were very glad to be alive.

Everything they had said to Ólawen, they believed; no matter the outcome of this invasion, the rainforest would endure. But Hei also believed that *Gãepongwei* would endure as well. They couldn't explain it, but they felt it like the pressure change before a storm. And if Hei trusted anything, it was their instincts.

Nineteen

AT FIRST, SOHMENG DIDN'T THINK she would ever stop being afraid. The Sorchapa were cooped up in a pen by swordpoint; the sãoni were on edge, their throats glowing ominously next to the pyres at night. People were injured, and Sohmeng had no idea if they were going to make it through. And Ahn was far away, most likely crumbling under the terror of how everything had gone wrong.

But as the days passed into weeks, Fua into Tang into Sol, she began to adjust to the rhythm of the prison. The soldiers traded shifts around the same time, and meals were delivered twice a day. She could tell when Ólawen was near, because the soldiers' backs would all straighten at once. The regularity of it eased some of her jumpiness, but something worse came in its place: boredom.

Sohmeng was so freaking bored. Her knee was bouncing constantly, her bangs greasy from messing with them. She could only stare forlornly into the distance for so long before her whole brain itched, so she tried finding ways to occupy her time: she taught the hatchlings to spin around, made houses out of sticks, tossed rocks into the pyres until a guard made her stop. The highlight of her days tended to be when Eakang helped bring food to the sãoni; being fourteen, nobody viewed them as a serious threat.

Occasionally the guards would snap a command or two, but otherwise they didn't have much to say to the prisoners. The few times that Sohmeng tried to talk to Ólawen were completely brushed off, which felt patronizing and stressful—and, after the general's private talk with Hei, downright tense.

Sohmeng had tried asking Hei what happened, but they mostly shrugged it off. "I chose not to be afraid of her," they said, picking a scrap of food from their teeth. "She didn't know how to respond."

As much as Sohmeng truly loved that approach, she couldn't figure out how to crack it herself. She *was* scared of Ólawen, and not knowing what the woman was going to do next was driving her up the wall. She didn't know how much longer she could deal with this dreadful tedium.

But one day, Ólawen didn't come out of her tent. From sunrise to sunset, there wasn't any sight of her. It was a break in routine, and it caught Sohmeng's interest. The following afternoon, when she saw Ólawen outside, the general looked worn thin, like all her self-confidence had been pulled right out of her. Hei was very pleased with this, but Sohmeng was apprehensive. It was a significant change in energy, and had a ripple of repercussions.

First, the prisoners were given more leeway to speak. No one had ever stayed completely silent—Sohmeng might have actually died if that had been the case—but conversations that got too loud or went too long had usually been hushed. Now, the guards didn't seem as invested in bossing them around.

Then, some of the Kempeipa were brought in to assist with the prisoners' medical care. They were still heavily supervised, but after weeks of intentionally separating the hmun, this new loosening of restrictions was noteworthy.

Strangest of all, the Qiao Sidhur themselves were acting more friendly. Now that they weren't in the thick of battle, Sohmeng finally saw the carpenters, cooks, and diplomats Ahnschen had talked about. Regular people. An artist came around with a sketchbook in hand, only ever pausing his craft to help collect dishes. He didn't speak any languages of Gãepongwei, but gestured to the sãoni and his notebook, emphatically requesting to draw them. Hei didn't stop him, and Sohmeng watched the illustrations come to life, peering over his shoulder. His smile was dazzling, and a little bit sorry.

These developments made things objectively easier, but they also unsettled Sohmeng. In Nona Fahang, Ahn had been given explicit instructions while he awaited his trial; the consequences of not following them were clearly laid out. But now, she had no idea how the rules were changing. The pyres stayed lit, but Sohmeng found herself wondering to what end.

"They're worn out," Hei speculated, watching a soldier idly toss a rock into the same pyre Sohmeng had been scolded for tossing rocks in. "We gave them a good fight, and they still have Kongkempei to hold onto."

"I don't know," Sohmeng said, stroking the sãoni whose head was plonked in her lap. Lazily, he rolled over and opened his mouth for Eakang to drop some meat gristle into. "It seems like they've all . . . relaxed? But I can't figure out why."

Quietly, with their back to the nearby guard, Eakang offered: "It was a letter."

"A letter?"

"From the ships. Some people came in on a small boat, and one of them passed a parcel to Ólawen. Those soldiers, um . . . they looked better than these ones. That's how I knew they weren't stationed in Kongkempei."

Sohmeng's stomach dropped. "Qiao Sidh is sending more people."

"Do you think so?"

In that moment, Eakang looked like the kid they were. It made Sohmeng's chest tight, and awkwardly, she took their hand. She and Eakang had both served as witnesses to the violence: it was a different experience from the Sorchapa warriors or Hei, a specific species of pain that she and Eakang now shared. It felt very Minhal, like they were each pockets of darkness, trying to pull perspective from the unknown.

"I don't know," was all she could offer. "I hope not."

That night, feeling disheartened and defeated, Sohmeng tried to imagine what her life might look like if the Empire was successful after all. It wasn't like they were planning on burning the rainforest to the ground; conquering and destroying were different things, according to the Qiao Sidhur. In all likelihood Ahn's protection would ensure her safety, and Hei's too, if they accepted it. It might not be that everyone she knew and loved would have to die. Far from it—Hidrholo Noula had even said that Sohmeng could walk one of the Paths as a citizen of the Empire. Was that where her future was heading?

She couldn't entertain the thought for more than a couple minutes before it made her feel sick. Cultural exchange didn't work when one party was armed, and everything that was being rebuilt was a symbol of what had already been destroyed. You couldn't force something on someone and call it a gift.

But trying to prove that point to Ólawen was futile. The general had already said she wouldn't even speak to Sohmeng without Ahnschen there; discussions about the *management of Gãepongwei*, as she'd called it, would wait until her brother showed up.

Which made it really confusing when Ólawen suddenly invited her for a private walk the next morning.

"Is Ahn here?" Sohmeng asked on reflex, glancing nervously at the translator.

"No," Ólawen said. A corner of her mouth crimped. "Are you coming with me or not?"

Sohmeng wasn't sure she had much choice in the matter, but, as usual, her curiosity outweighed her sense of self-preservation.

They went to the edge of camp together, walking the perimeter; Sohmeng felt the muscles in her legs sigh their relief after weeks of so little movement. She'd gotten used to being constantly active with the sãoni, and learned the hard way that her brain worked best when she was on the move.

For a while they walked in a silence that wasn't companionable, but wasn't menacing either. It felt ridiculous to squander this opportunity to talk, but Sohmeng was honestly kind of scared, and didn't want to start stumbling over her words. Oddly, the charismatic

Ólawen looked pretty subdued, herself. Sohmeng tentatively allowed herself to take in what the region had to offer: the unfamiliar birdsong, the size of the sky, the fog tumbling over the hills, catching light from the sun. She didn't know mud could smell this nice.

Ólawen didn't seem to take in much at all. Whenever Sohmeng stole a glance at the woman, she saw the frown on her face deepening with every step.

When the general broke the silence, she did it abruptly. "Has he been alright?"

"Huh?"

"Ahnschen," Ólawen said. Sohmeng received the words through the translator's mouth, but she could hear the tension in Ólawen's voice. "Has he been well, while he's been here with you?"

Viunwei's face came to mind, the way his tone would get sharp when he was worried. Sohmeng had spent years misreading anxiety as anger. She answered Ólawen carefully, trying to summon a degree of gentleness. "Yeah. He has. We've been looking after him."

"I heard he was imprisoned."

"I mean, we're also imprisoned right now, so?" So much for being gentle. Groveling wasn't going to get her anywhere, and she'd never been any good at it anyway. "Honestly, it was nicer than here. After one night with some pygmy hogs, which are the cutest animals you've ever met, he slept in my dad's house. He had chores and stuff, but they were mostly his choice, because he wanted to be helpful. He was allowed to walk around, as long as he was monitored." She hesitated. "I think we might have different ideas of what *imprisoned* means. We don't really ... do that here."

Ólawen's brow creased, but she didn't say anything. Sohmeng went quiet too, taking a deep breath to steady herself. She paused her walk as a procession of round, peeping pheasants trotted across their path. Ólawen stopped beside her, watching them with faint interest. It did something funny to Sohmeng, to see her do that.

"I wish things had gone differently," Sohmeng said slowly. "People would have been more welcoming if—"

"Your friend told me. If we hadn't come barging in."

"I mean … yeah."

It was uncomfortable. She wished she wasn't scared of Ólawen, but it was a reasonable feeling to have, after everything. She couldn't imagine what Ahn's other siblings were like if *this* was the one he felt safe with.

The final pheasant cooed as it hopped into a bush, and Ólawen began walking again. "I had hoped getting him out of Asgørindad would be good for him. Let him use the skills he'd trained with, so they wouldn't feel like such a waste."

Sohmeng's looked at the bone in Ólawen's ear. When she spoke, it was very carefully. "Did he say it felt like a waste?"

"He was listless," Ólawen said, not answering the question. "Distant. I'd never seen him like that, and no one else was doing anything to help, so I brought him here with me. Seemed like a better birthday gift than another gala. They get dull, eventually."

Sohmeng resisted the urge to say something about how an invasion was a pretty lousy gift in its own right. It was unexpected to see Ólawen making these attempts to connect; insensitive as they were, Sohmeng didn't want to rebuff her. This was the first time she felt like she was being allowed to see Ahn's big sister Óla, not General Eløndhol. Despite herself, she didn't want to scare the moment away.

"Is that what you did after your *Qøngzhir Asten*?" she asked, using the Qiao Sidhur word for Six-ing. "Go on a campaign?"

Ólawen looked at her with genuine surprise. Whether it was surprise at the question or the fact that Sohmeng had actually done a pretty great job with her pronunciation, she wasn't sure.

Ólawen tugged at her earpiece before answering. "I did. Though, it was less *campaign* than it was *management of minor insurrection*. Mostly paperwork in the end. Not my favourite. We spent a week on the rebels, signed a couple treaties, and then I put on a tournament to boost morale. Wen always liked those."

Wen. The girl who lived in a bone in Óla's ear. Another Schenn. Sohmeng had no idea how Óla said her name so calmly, but she also didn't know the woman that well. Maybe time had made it easier.

"Do you always consider what Wen thinks?"

"I do my best."

"Does she ... talk to you?" Sohmeng hazarded. She still wasn't sure how the metaphysics were supposed to work, and it had been a sore subject with Ahn.

Ólawen's mouth quirked. "In her way. And even if she didn't, I'd still have to think it through. It's part of the agreement."

"I'm bad at considering other people sometimes," Sohmeng admitted. "I can't imagine having to make all that compromise."

Ólawen chuckled, a sound that was warm even as it scattered a few low-perching birds. "Sounds like we have that in common, Minhal. I've been known to dig my heels in, criticized and celebrated for it. But someone has to make the hard choices when the time comes. Someone has to tell it like it is."

It was hard to gauge if she sounded proud or tired. If her voice was firm because she believed in her words, or because she had to believe them in order to keep herself upright. Sohmeng slowed her footsteps, looking at Éongrir Ólawen. For a moment, with the sunlight in her silver hair and her armour left behind, she looked like a person. A person who made horrific decisions, but a person nonetheless.

"Hey, um," Sohmeng said, "do you know what phase the moons were in when you were born?"

This earned her another odd look from Ólawen. "I do, actually. White one was dark in this realm, and the red was just peeking out. From the other side, it would have looked like two apples: a whole white one, and a red one someone's started to slice."

"Par!" Sohmeng blurted out. The gods had a strange sense of humour. "You're a Par."

"Oh, is that the, ah . . . ?" Ólawen waved up at the sky.

"Yeah, our lunar system. Par is a great one, it's actually—" *Mine,* she almost said. She hadn't thought of herself as Par in a while; it was odd to feel the warmth of familiarity as she found a touchpoint between them. "My mom was a Par. She was really cool."

"I," Óla said with a smug look, "have *also* been called really cool."

This made Sohmeng laugh, and the feeling made her hurt, because she could see it. She could tell that outside of this context, Ólawen was probably a lot of fun to be around. She was the harbinger of the Qiao Sidhur invasion, *and* she was Ahn's sister. Ahn's sister, who could afford to be nicer to him. Who loved him so much, and showed it all wrong, but was still trying to show it.

In another world, Sohmeng could have shared a meal with her and talked it through. In another circumstance, they probably would have been friends.

"I know what the night sky looked like for Ahn, too, if you're interested."

Sohmeng's grief took a brief pause in favour of her special interest. "*Yes.*"

Ólawen whistled for the translator, who passed her a small notebook and some charcoal. Sohmeng could see some notes written down, and wondered what they said.

"Wen was an astronomer," Óla said, sketching out the night sky. She began with the position of the stars before the moons, which Sohmeng thought was neat. "We'd both just entered Kørno Wan when Ahn was born, and I couldn't stop bragging about him. I never thought I'd get to be an older sister, and I was livid that I couldn't get more time with him. Wen drew me a picture of his birth sky for me to keep. It's how I learned my constellations."

As the moons took shape, Sohmeng couldn't help but grin. "Fua. Knew it. What a people-pleaser."

The translator seemed a bit reluctant to say these words in Qiao Sidhur, but Ólawen got a chuckle in. She tore out the page neatly, passing it to Sohmeng. "He really is. I worry about him, you know."

"He told me."

Óla's expression faltered briefly. "Did he?"

"Yeah. He talked a lot about how much you love each other. He's missed you a lot."

Ólawen went quiet again. It was easier when they'd been walking, but right now, they were both still, silent save for the sounds of the wetlands. Sohmeng didn't know what to do. The Ólawen she had seen before was so tactically minded, so brazenly confident. But this felt personal, like something on the edge of vulnerability.

She wondered if a part of Óla yearned for the softness her brother possessed, for the interest in communication before escalation. Or if Wen did—if in some other realm, everyone was just talking it through, and things never had to be this violent, because Ahn didn't have to kill Schenn, and Óla didn't have to kill Wen, and none of them had to keep trying to make that loss worth it by doubling down.

Sohmeng wanted better for everyone, even the Qiao Sidhur. For once in her life, she wished desperately for two dark moons in the sky, for the gods to look away so everyone could do what they wanted, destroy and rebuild everything that kept them bound to traditions that wounded them. No laws, no expectations. Just the chance to take a big breath in the dark, and then try again as the sun rose.

Mortifyingly, Sohmeng felt that her eyes were wet.

She rubbed at them, and Ólawen passed her a handkerchief, which actually made it much worse. She didn't want to be comforted by the person who was doing the thing she needed comforting about. It was excruciating to find common ground and still know that her humanity wasn't going to be respected.

"Are more soldiers coming?" Sohmeng suddenly asked, her voice wavering with tears. "Is that what the letter said?"

Immediately she cursed her impulsive tongue, groaning as Ólawen raised her eyebrows. "I saw it, okay? I saw a letter delivered, and then you started being weird, and I've been stuck sitting around, and I'm used to being someone who does things because when I think too hard my choices end up *more* stupid, and I do things like use information that I probably should have kept private." She took in a shuddering breath. She had covered for Eakang, but she had also revealed more of herself than she meant to. "But now I've asked, and I need to know, because I'm starting to lose it here. I need to know if more soldiers are coming."

Ólawen paused for only a moment before she spoke. "No. They aren't."

"Are you lying?" Sohmeng demanded.

"I'm not."

She wasn't sure if the calm in Ólawen's voice made her more or less confident that she was telling the truth. All she could do was believe in Par honesty, and try to feel reassured enough to sleep tonight.

Moonless audacity already on a role, Sohmeng continued her train of thought, sniffling all the while like Viunwei. "Ahn thought you'd be there to duel him. He prepared and everything."

"Plans changed," Ólawen said, now frowning. That answer only made Sohmeng angrier, because it meant the challenge had been real.

"That was a nasty thing you did, challenging him like that," Sohmeng said quietly, rubbing her eyes again. "He just *cried*, Óla. He thought you'd kill him, or that he'd have to kill you, and he didn't want to. I know you don't care about me or any of the people here, but you should know that you really hurt your brother. Because I don't know if he'll tell you, because he doesn't want to disappoint you, either. And you should know how he feels, and you should *think* about it, because you can't really love someone right if you don't listen to how they feel." Her words were interrupted by an embarrassing hiccup. She swallowed, trying to gather her dignity. "And if we're actually anything alike, I figure you're the kind of person who wants to be good at everything, so ..."

A strained laugh came out of Ólawen. When Sohmeng looked at her, she had a helpless expression on her face, baffled and speechless.

Sohmeng felt pretty helpless herself. She passed back the damp handkerchief. "Are you going to bring me back to jail now so I don't make things weird between you and your translator? Sorry. Wish we had a shared language."

Ólawen pocketed the handkerchief, letting out a long exhale. "Yeah. Let's get you back."

"Cool," Sohmeng said, trying to shake off the discomfort. "Oh, um, and could you send a healer to do a couple of double checks on the Sorchapa? There's someone whose wound looks like it might have an infection starting."

"I—yeah. I can do that."

"Thanks."

They turned back toward the camp, their silence slinking behind them. Sohmeng found herself wondering what Ólawen had wanted from this talk in the first place, and whether she'd got it. Whether she would listen to Sohmeng about Ahn, even if the woman wouldn't listen to her about Gãepongwei. Whether she would take her answers to heart.

The first smells of breakfast wafted from the cooking fires. Somewhere along the line, their footfalls fell into a rhythm. In another world, they almost would have passed for phase-mates.

Twenty

AHNSCHEN AND NOULA BEGAN in Hosaisi. As much as Ahn wanted to rush to Soh and Hei and everyone in Kongkempei, it was ultimately more urgent to relieve the hmun that had suffered the worst of the invasion. Noula agreed with this plan—and noted the benefit of building the force he was bringing down to Ólawen. If all of his soldiers were in one place, it would be logistically easier to organize a retreat.

The framing of his arrival was easy: one general against another, caught in conflict. There was a reason there weren't many Qiao Sidhur co-generals in history. He wielded his rank to order an immediate withdrawal of their forces, and in front of the Grand Ones, fell to his knees and pressed his forehead to the earth. He apologized as deeply as he knew how, and explained his intention to bring the invading army out of these lands.

Noula and his soldiers weren't quite sure what to do with this display, but no one protested. He knew many of his kinsmen didn't even comprehend why he might be sorry, and so he did not ask them to perform regret, simply to pack and leave as unobtrusively as possible.

"I know I cannot undo what my sister and I have done," Ahnschen said, "but if there is anything you need from me to help repair the harm done to your hmun, I would answer that call."

"First, Kongkempei," said Grandfather Tang. "We will decide later if we want any more business with Qiao Sidh."

"Kongkempei," Ahn agreed, and bowed low to the ground once more. This time, Noula joined him.

In total, about seventy new people were added to their ranks, bringing their force to over one hundred. Ahn had expected more soldiers from Hosaisi, but sickness had swept through in the past month, taking a dozen Qiao Sidhur with it. Still, Ahn did not look dramatically outnumbered compared to the one hundred and fifty or so that Ólawen had in Kongkempei. While he highly doubted that Ólawen would turn their people against one another, the numbers were important. They were a visual display of sway and influence, crucial players in the myth of sixth and seventh-ranking warriors on the Path of Conquest.

In reality, Ahn was well aware that most people probably thought he'd lost his mind, and were following him because there wasn't another option. With days of travel ahead, he tried his best to open up dialogue about his choice to retreat, which almost none of them took him up on except to say "yes, Eløndham" or "very good, Eløndham."

"What do I do?" Ahn asked Noula one night, pacing around with a cup of Qiao Sidhur elderflower wine. "I want to talk to them directly, but I don't want them to think I'm some sort of radical!"

"You are some sort of radical, Eløndham."

"Well, yes, I suppose that's true," Ahn said, exasperated. "But I don't want them to think they can't trust me. I don't want to reach Ólawen and have a hundred people telling her my brain's been replaced with a madøng egg!"

"Mm. It's a risk."

"Noula, please."

"It is," Noula repeated, refilling her own cup. "But I don't think it's a large one."

"Why not?"

"Because you have me," she said matter-of-factly, "and because your behaviour might not surprise as many people as you think. You're notorious for treating your guards like they're your friends to the point where they get lectured on accepting favours. You managed to spend extended time with common people without running any patronizing fundraisers. While the rest of your siblings have been quarreling about producing the next generation of heirs, you became *vice* president of the Zhørmozhør Advocacy Group. Second rank Health courses now include a curriculum on sexual diversity, did you know that?" Ahn felt himself going more and more red as she ticked off each example on her fingers. "If you'd stayed in Qiao Sidh, I'd be willing to bet headlines would be running within the year that would warrant a serious talk with your royal parents."

Ólawen's face came to mind, that guarded concern. *You have a fanbase, baby brother.* "The People's Emperor," he mumbled to himself.

"The very same," Noula said. "A leader for the people is still a leader. They'll follow your orders whether they like them or not. You can be uncomfortable with that, or you can use it to your advantage. I have a feeling you'll end up influencing some beliefs along the way."

For eight days, they marched south towards Kongkempei, struggling with the mountainous terrain all the way. Ahn had the benefit of riding on sãoni-back, but everyone else was on foot or madøng, lugging baggage and supplies along a largely unfamiliar route. Quickly, Ahn could see why the first expedition in this very region had been such a mess; a combination of maps from Noula and instinct from Sølshend was what saved them from taking twice as long. Had Hei been there, they would have laughed right in his face.

When they made camp each evening, Ahn took the opportunity to speak with his people. Precious few wanted to discuss the reasoning behind his exit strategy, but there was one topic that everyone took an avid interest in: home. They all wanted to go home.

"What are you most excited to go back to?" Ahn asked, rubbing Sølshend's glowing throat stripes as she snoozed.

"My bed, Éongrir Ahnschen. My back is killing me."

"The Asgørindad Opera."

"I miss my dog. I thought it would be my boyfriend, but it's absolutely my dog."

"Eløndham, I would *swim* back to Qiao Sidh if I knew my grandmother was sitting on the beach with a bowl of her spicy fish stew. I'm sorry, but I would defect here and now."

He cheerfully commiserated with the soldiers, asking

about their families and sharing restaurant recommendations. Noula smiled mildly as she refilled his wine, and the conversations filled him in turn.

It was an earnest effort to connect. It was also strategic. No matter what happened with Ólawen, Ahn would have one hundred supporters at his back, all of whom were sick of dragging themselves through a campaign they didn't even care about. They missed Qiao Sidh, and no matter what the premise of Conquest dictated, they all knew that this place wasn't their home. Despite everything, he was feeling optimistic.

It got harder when they made it to Kongkempei. Óla had told the truth—the destroyed structures had been rebuilt, and the people seemed to have more freedom than they did in Hosaisi. But he remembered the fire. He remembered the violence and the panic, and the person who had died by his blade. Kongkempei was where this campaign had begun, and it would be where it ended, too.

People, Qiao Sidhur and Kempeipa alike, gawked from a distance as he rode into the hmun on sãoni-back. He stopped in front of the first soldier he saw, and asked, "Where is she?"

"The general is with the—the prisoners," the soldier stammered, glancing at Noula. "I can bring you, Eløndham."

"Please."

It wasn't the soldier's fault, but Ahn could hear how cold his voice had gotten. As they approached the open-air prison that had been constructed, the camaraderie he'd built with Noula over the past couple of weeks took on a sour tinge. She was the one who had suggested this plan to Ólawen. Ahn doubted he would get any satisfaction by snapping at her, but his tension must have been notable, because she left some extra space between them.

He focused on his breathing. Ólawen was the priority. The family he had made in Gãepongwei was the priority. He just needed to make sure they had *survived.*

The prison was bordered by a crude wooden fence interspersed with pyres, which were the real threat, especially once fire-starter was brought into the mix. As he approached, the captive Sorchapa gathered at the edge of the fence; a couple of people even called out to him. The soldiers at the gate looked decidedly uncomfortable.

"Eløndham," they said in unison, dropping each to one knee.

"Stand," Ahn ordered. "Douse the fires."

"Eløndham," one said nervously, "General Ólawen ordered us to keep them lit ... "

"And I am ordering you to put them *out,*" he said, an unfamiliar edge to his voice. "Not just these—all of the pyres." Quickly, they did as they were told, sending word down the line to douse the rest. With a word from Noula, the soldiers behind him fanned out, framing the gate like a crescent moon. "Where's my sister?"

"In her tent, Eløndham."

"Good. And where—"

He heard the sãoni a second before he saw them, a cacophony of clicking and growling that Ahn had somehow come to associate with safety. Sølshend chirped restlessly in response, and Ahn took off on her back around the perimeter, scanning it for the two humans he needed most urgently to see were safe and well.

"Ahn!" Sohmeng yelled, waving her hands.

Ahn all but leapt off Sølshend, catching Sohmeng in a hug the moment they were close enough. He was certain she could feel his heart right through his armour. Hei was within arm's reach, and he forgot himself, grabbing them by the shirt to yank them in for a cheek press. Hei squawked at how quickly he had moved, but returned the gesture firmly, the colony vocalizing behind them.

"Are you hurt?" Ahn demanded. "Did they hurt you?"

"I—I mean it was a battle, so it sucked, yeah?" Sohmeng said, pulling back enough to get a look at his face. He wondered if his expression was twin to her own worry. "But Hei and I are okay, and so are most of the colony. Not *all* of them, but ..."

"I'm sorry," Ahn said. "That was abysmal behavior on Ólawen's part, and I'm *sorry*." He interrupted Sohmeng's alarm with a kiss, overwhelmed both by his relief to see her alive and his rekindled anger.

He took quick stock of the situation, trying to count the prisoners, human and sãoni both. The sight of the colony in a pen was ridiculous; Ahn knew the only reason they hadn't immediately broken free was because Hei had chosen not to unleash that mayhem on everyone.

Now it was his turn to play his part. He kissed Sohmeng again. "I'm finishing this, alright? I'm sorry it took me so long to get back."

Hei let out a series of slow clicks, focused on something behind Ahn. He knew immediately that it was Ólawen. There was a sound to her approach: voices quieting, armour clinking as everyone straightened up and stepped out of her way. The world always seemed to stop for Ólawen, but

Ahn wasn't willing to participate in that pantomime today.

He pulled away from Sohmeng, unsheathing his sword with the slick scrape of steel. This time, he would not waste his breath trying to find the precise words to reach her. He would speak to Ólawen in the only way she understood: with the language of a bared blade.

She seemed to receive the message. The wicked grin she'd met him with last time was gone, and it took her a beat before she spoke.

"Ahn," she said. "You've put out the pyres."

"Éongrir Ólawen-Eløndhol, Qøngemding," he responded, raising his voice so all around them could hear. "I come to honour the terms of our duel, issued by you *twenty-five days past*, which you were not present to meet."

It was a scathing way to make his point. A hush went over the camp, a preternatural stillness that reached soldiers and prisoners and sãoni alike. Ahn could hear the blood pounding in his ears, feel each curve of his sword's hilt tucked in his hand. Ólawen looked at him for what felt like forever; he thought he caught a shadow under her eyes. Ahn knew she'd always been one to cool down as fast as she blew up, but this conflict was well beyond a typical disagreement.

Something was strange about her. Ahn didn't like it.

"Will you honour it, or no?" he demanded.

Ólawen didn't unsheathe her own weapon. Instead she raked a hand through her hair, taking a deep breath. "Come. Speak with me."

"*Speak* with you?"

It was almost funny. Weeks ago, this was all he had wanted: a chance to speak with his sister, and have her take him seriously. He should have been relieved to finally have this outcome, but it made him furious. All of the work he had done to manage his despair, to prepare himself for further grief, and *now* she was ready to talk? He felt like he could scream.

Ólawen must have seen it on his face. "Ahnschen," she said. "Little brother, please."

Where heat usually came to his earpiece, this time there was a brief pulse of coolness. An encouragement to resist lashing out in a moment of wounded pride.

This is an opportunity, Ahn. Use it, yeah?

"Fine." Ahn sheathed his sword and went with her. He wondered if Schenn and Wen were standing together in the bilateral realm. Despite being trained as warriors, despite *dying* for the title, perhaps each was doing their part to hold back their respective Éongrir sibling from violence.

The tent was like a container for everything that had gone wrong since they arrived. A symbol of war, and a source of personal anguish. Last time he was in here, trying to be brave and speak openly, all Ólawen had done was talk over him. She had given him a harp that had been a hostage, confident that it was the kind thing to do. She had drawn her blade, humiliating him in front of the camp.

He had expected a public confrontation today, and was being offered a private discussion instead. He had been confronted with the version of his sister that wasn't so hot-headed. But Ahn still didn't feel safe. She had already shown him that she couldn't handle a difficult conversation. Why should now be any different?

He practiced the breathing he had worked on with Lula Jão, drew strength from the late night talks he'd had with

Noula over the past few weeks. Whether or not he felt safe with his sister, he felt safe with himself. With Schenn. He could do this.

The dense fabric curtains of the tent shut behind them. Even with the cloak of privacy shielding them from their soldiers, the very air between them felt strained. Ólawen sighed and turned away from him, moving to tidy her desk. Ahn watched in silence, burning for an explanation.

Finally, she placed a brass paperweight on a stack of notes and broke the stalemate: "We're going home."

"…What?" Ahn couldn't have heard her correctly.

"I got a letter from Dad," Ólawen said. "We're going home."

Ahn could only stand there, dumbfounded. He'd spent all this time searching for an exit strategy. A missive from the Emperor had not even come close to crossing his mind as a possibility. "Why?"

"Family squabble. War's coming."

To anyone else, these two statements might have looked dissonant side by side. But as a child of the royal family, as the youngest generation of Imperial blood in a long and complex history, Ahn took Ólawen's meaning easily, even as it made his heart fall. "Who's leading the coup?"

"A cousin from up north—rumour has it that he might have a couple of our siblings' ears. I don't think it'll come to anything, but it'll be messy in the meantime. The more of the family that's backing Dad, the less credible his cousin will look, and the faster this whole thing can get shut down. Politics. You know the deal." Óla was quiet for a moment, knuckles rested on her desk. Her map, Ahn now saw, was rolled up and tucked to the side. "It was a small campaign, anyway. Doesn't matter."

He could hear the disappointment in her voice, and a fresh wave of agitation rose hot in his chest. They had hurt people, killed people, made them unsafe in their homes. This *small campaign* had an impact Ólawen either couldn't fully grasp, or just didn't care to.

But they were leaving. Did that make this outcome a victory?

"Let me see the letter," Ahn said, and Ólawen passed it to him.

It bore the torn royal seal, and was written in the tidy looping handwriting of his father's secretary. It confirmed everything Ólawen had said. Distantly, Ahn remembered reading letters like this in his studies, the notes that had become artifacts that would mark the timeline of significant historical events. Love letters; war missives. The manifestos of the dying. As Ahn lingered on his own name, he was struck by an odd sense of his place in history, a curiosity about how his life would be read by his descendants.

Tell Ahnschen we regret these circumstances, and hope he is not disappointed. We are very proud of all he has undoubtedly accomplished by your side.

He read it a second time. A third. The brushstrokes blended together, as muddled and overwhelming as Ahn's own feelings. He should be relieved, he thought. After all of the pain and dread and doubt, the campaign was *done*— and he didn't even have to fight his sister for it. It was the best case scenario that he never even thought to ask for.

And yet he was frozen in place. Disoriented. He felt as though an arrow had gone straight through him, but he couldn't find the wound.

"Óla," he heard himself say, "why didn't you meet me for the duel?"

His sister didn't manage to hide her wince. "Ahn. Don't."

"I know Noula advised you. But why did you *listen* to her?"

"We don't need to have this conversation—"

"Yes we *do*," Ahn said, feeling the edge of the letter crumple in his hand. He put it back on the desk, smoothing it out with a shaky breath. "Why would you ... why would you issue such a serious challenge if you weren't one hundred percent certain that you would follow through?"

"So you *wanted* a duel?" Ólawen asked, sounding baffled.

"No!" Ahn heard his voice rise in volume. He took out his sword, still sheathed, and dropped it heavily on her desk. "No, I didn't. And you *knew* that, you knew that and you forced my hand anyway."

She rubbed her face, groaning. "I got hot-headed, Ahn. Is that a crime?"

"Well, it was enormously irresponsible of you as a leader," he snapped. "And it—"

It hurt me. The words caught in his throat like a fish hook, cutting off anything else he might have wanted to say. It wasn't so difficult anymore, to take a stand for Gãepongwei. But being vulnerable with Ólawen was a different experience; he didn't even know where to start.

She looked at him for a long time, a frown at her brow. He was expecting at least some pushback about challenging her leadership, but nothing came.

"Is there anything else that you want to say to me?" she asked slowly.

Their shared discomfort was palpable, and Ahn waited for her to push through to her point. But she didn't. She simply waited, leaving him to decide if it was worth sharing with her.

In the end, he decided to take the risk.

"You scared me, Óla," Ahn said quietly. "I've never been scared of you until then."

She looked as though he'd slapped her. "You have to know I'd never harm you, Ahn. I already told you, I did all this to protect you!"

"A fight to the death doesn't make me feel *protected*."

Ahn's hand went to his chest, over the long-closed wound Schenn had cleaved into him. He never wanted to go through something like that again. Not with anyone, but especially not with someone he loved. He saw Óla looking at him, her expression pained. She had been by his bedside while that wound healed, telling him stories and trying to make him laugh. Once, when Ahn had woken groggily from a medicated sleep, he'd seen her sitting beside him, hunched over, face in her hands. He had called to her weakly and she straightened right up, grinning as though they were at a party and not in a hospital.

Ólawen exhaled slowly, her knuckles softly rapping against the wood of the desk. Frustration and anxiety warred on her face, which was usually so confident. He barely recognized her. He wanted to hug her, but he couldn't make himself move.

"I'm sorry, kid." Now *that* was bizarre. Ólawen had never been the type to apologize outright, and Ahn was grasping for a response when she continued: "I've been a real ass to you. And yeah, I know, according to you I've been a real ass to *everyone*, but you're the one I care about, so that's what you're getting from me. I brought you here because

I wanted to get you away from everyone who would hurt you, and it turns out I ended up doing the job myself." She paused, trying to gather her words. Her voice was hoarse. "Never wanted that, Ahn. Looking back, I see how I . . . well, I strong-armed you out the door. I was worried about you. You're so *sensitive*, you know?"

"I know." He found that acknowledging his sensitivity didn't make him sad or small. It was what helped him move away from the parts of himself he wasn't proud of.

"You know," Ólawen echoed.

Ahn wondered what Ólawen saw when she looked at him. She had been there through all the years of his life. She had held his hands when he learned to walk, and knocked him to the ground when they sparred with practice weapons. She had wiped drool off his face when he babbled, and held his hair back when he was sick from drinking too much with her. She boasted about his Six-ing, and she couldn't understand the source of his overwhelming sorrow.

Baby brother, she called him, and she'd passed him a sword and pointed toward a place for him to wield it.

There wasn't a soul in his family he loved more than Ólawen, and he was fairly sure she felt the same about him. Nothing could change that. But even love was not enough to bridge the chasm between them. Not all the way.

Ólawen cleared her throat, not quite looking at him. She tugged once on her earpiece, though whether she was looking for or receiving guidance was impossible to say. "I don't think you should go back to school for while. I'm not *against* it or anything, I'm really not. I just don't think it'll be safe, you know?"

"I agree," Ahn said quietly.

"That's—that's good," Ólawen said, and the relief on her face broke Ahn's heart, because he knew then what he had to do. "Yeah, just for now, right? It's not like they'll expel you or anything, from what I've heard your grades are great, which makes sense, you're a smart kid."

Ahn gathered his courage, watching her shuffle papers around on the table as her words tumbled over the rapids of all her pent-up energy. There was a lump in his throat, and he swallowed it, savouring this final moment before he wounded her more deeply than any blade ever could.

"We could send you off somewhere for a while, maybe up north, but honestly, I think that'll be more suspicious. I know you're miffed at me, but the safest thing would probably be for you to stay cl—"

"Óla," Ahnschen said, "I'm not going home."

His older sister froze, looking at him like she hadn't heard right. Her eyes scanned his body as though he was foreign to her, a different creature entirely. Ahn waited. He knew the value of being given a moment to gather your thoughts.

"You're ... staying here," she said slowly. Her voice didn't seem to know whether or not it was a question.

"I am," he said. "Hei and Sohmeng invited me to stay."

"And the rest of them?" Óla nodded towards the doors of the tent, to the world that somehow still existed outside this room. "I mean, they won't *hurt* you, or ...?"

Ahn smiled a little as he shook his head. He didn't say the words out loud, but they both heard them nonetheless: *You and I aren't the same.*

A soft, disbelieving sound escaped from Ólawen. "Look at that. I brought you here to keep you safe, and instead I lose you."

He walked right up and pulled her into a hug. Not as a child clinging for balance, but as an adult who had learned to put his feet on the ground. When he spoke, he could feel Schenn's voice behind his own, certain as the sun. "But I live."

"I want you to live, kid."

"I want to live, too."

She cursed, holding him tighter, and he pretended not to hear the way her breathing had become unsteady. If their roles were reversed, he would have wanted to be comforted while he cried, but Ólawen was not Ahnschen. She couldn't be anyone but herself.

Eventually she composed herself, clearing her throat. She took a bottle of wine from a trunk, pouring them each a cup despite the fact that it was early in the afternoon. "So what am I supposed to tell everyone about what happened to the People's Emperor, huh? You're putting me in a real spot, you know."

"I am," Ahn said, his voice all warmth and apology. "I'm sorry about that. Do you—do you know how you're going to explain? About the campaign?"

Ólawen grimaced. "Don't make me say it."

That was it, then: she would say she had failed. Ahn was too relieved for Gãepongwei to feel any real sympathy for Ólawen's ego, but he recognized what a personal blow this would be to her. She took a long drink of the wine and he followed suit. Distantly, he realized that he might not be tasting anything like it for a very long time.

"Really though," Ólawen said, "we're going to need to figure something out, or Mom and Dad are gonna send me straight back here to drag you home. And then exile me, probably. They like you more and don't even try to deny it."

Ahn laughed. Despite everything, he laughed, and somehow, she laughed too. For a moment they were just two people trying to figure out what to do with their difficult parents.

"I think we need to talk with the others before any real plans are in place," Ahn said. "There's a lot of damage to clean up."

"Ah." Ólawen looked like she had something tart in her mouth. "Well, *that's* not going to be very comfortable."

"I'd assume not, no."

She leaned her head back, groaning in a way that was almost petulant. Ahn wished that she would show some sort of remorse, but by now he knew he wasn't going to get it. He would have to settle for this. Somehow, for him, it would have to be enough.

"I love you, Óla."

"Yeah," she said, "I know."

"You love me too?"

"You know I do."

"Would you say it anyway?"

"I love you, Ahn."

"Okay."

"Okay?"

"Okay."

Twenty-One

WHEN SOHMENG WAS GROWING UP, the Grand Ones often told her change was meant to unfold very slowly. Nothing about a mountain moved quickly, including its inhabitants. And that was *before* the Sky Bridge fell and everything came to a standstill. There were certain Grand Ones who pushed for progress on behalf of their phases, sure, but in Ateng at least, nothing ever happened without an impossibly long wait.

Now? Change was happening. And it was happening *fast*.

It began the moment Ahn exited the tent with his sister. He put out the order to dismantle the prison, and when Ólawen didn't argue, the soldiers got right to work doing as he said. Cautiously, the Sorchapa moved into Kongkempei, and Sohmeng, Hei, Nepar, Polha, and Eakang went with Ahn to Kongkempei's Grand Ones.

They were situated in a gazebo beside a lake that would reflect the moons on the rise. There were lily pads wide enough for Sohmeng to wear as skirts, and massive yellow fish swimming just beneath the surface. Hei brought

Green Bites along, and kept him on the far side so he wouldn't get distracted by the glimmer of their fins.

Once everyone was assembled, Ahn presented the startling new reality they had to contend with.

"So … that's it?" Sohmeng asked. Part of her wondered if she'd actually heard him correctly. "Qiao Sidh is just leaving?"

Nepar made a skeptical sound from the cushion he'd been given. Sohmeng could see the varying degrees of confusion and doubt on everyone's faces. It made sense; between the physical and mental wounds they had suffered, it was hard to immediately start jumping for joy. A few steps back from everyone else, Ólawen stood with her arms crossed, her gaze occasionally darting to Noula, who was standing by Ahn's side.

"The goal is to have us on the ships back north within the week," Ahn said. He hesitated briefly, looking from the Grand Ones to Sohmeng. His voice was quiet. "With … one exception." Sohmeng's heart flipped. "If you'll have me."

Before she could stop herself, she grabbed Ahn's hand, trying not to think about all the people who were looking at them. "Don't be a moron," she whispered, not trusting herself to say anything else until they were alone.

Ahn bit back a smile, returning his attention to the rest of them. "That is, if all of you would find that acceptable. I have personal reasons I want to stay, clearly, but I also think Gãepongwei's troubles with Qiao Sidh aren't over yet. I'd like to help from here, if I can."

"You've been an invaluable ally," Polha said, Nepar nodding beside her. "I know I'd welcome your help."

"I'd also be really happy if you stayed," Eakang chimed in.

They'd refused to leave Polha's side when she was called to this meeting, and Sohmeng didn't feel right leaving them out just because they were the youngest. "But . . . isn't it over? The point was to stop the invasion, and now it's done."

"An exit on Qiao Sidh's terms isn't a victory," Nepar said. "If this is only happening on the Emperor's whim, there's nothing to stop another invasion from happening the next time it's convenient."

"Exactly," Ahn agreed. "This is already the second excursion to Gãepongwei, and I have no reason to believe there won't be a third some time in the future. Do you think that's fair, Noula?"

"Depending on if civil war breaks out, I'd assume the invasion would resume within the next ten years," Noula said. "Most people would see it as an unfinished endeavour."

After giving her answer, she repeated the words in Qiao Sidhur. Her voice had been a constant murmur of translation through the conversation so far. Ahn, on the other hand, had been speaking in Dulpongpa the whole time—which meant the translation was solely for Ólawen's sake.

Sohmeng glanced over at the general, who was saying nothing despite the visible tension in her shoulders. She wondered if Ólawen had ever been in this position during a campaign, having a genuine discussion rather than just announcing a plan. Having to meet people as equals.

"Is there some sort of . . . agreement we could make?" asked Sohmeng, tucking a loose strand of hair behind her ear. "Like formalizing that this can't happen again in the future? We could write it down, in a couple of languages maybe, so people couldn't lie or anything."

"Has Qiao Sidh made those kinds of agreements before?" Polha added.

"We have," Ahn said slowly, but Sohmeng could feel the awkwardness that rippled between him and Noula. There was a beat of silence before an unexpected voice spoke out in Qiao Sidhur.

"Plenty of times," said Ólawen. No one interrupted her, but Sohmeng could feel the way everyone was immediately set on edge. "Some of them hold up. Others get renegotiated a few generations down if continuing expansion seems feasible."

"They get broken," Hei said flatly from their spot just outside the gazebo. They leaned against Green Bites' side, whittling a piece of wood with their claw. Sohmeng couldn't figure out what they were making beyond *pointy stick*.

"If that's how you want to look at it," Óla said tersely.

Sohmeng jumped in before Hei could respond, possibly with the pointy stick to emphasize their opinion. "Yeah, given how all this went down, I think we are gonna look at it that way. Do you think an agreement would hold up here, Óla?"

"It might. It depends."

"I'd be surprised," Noula said, prompting a glare out of Ólawen that she ignored with admirable tranquility. "Gãepongwei is far from the Empire. A violation wouldn't feel real to anyone back home, and so there wouldn't be social consequences. Most people wouldn't think much of it."

"I don't doubt *you'd* return, if you could," Nepar said roughly to Ólawen, a hand resting on his bandages.

Ólawen said nothing, eyes narrowed, and Sohmeng found herself wondering whether that was true.

"If the agreements aren't made to last, then what's the point of making them at all?" asked Kongkempei's Grand One Jão.

"Avoiding bloodshed," Ahn said, wincing slightly at the reactions that earned him. "Trust me, I know that's difficult to believe after everything that's happened here, but nonviolent expansion *is* more ideal for Qiao Sidh."

Sohmeng remembered the look on Ólawen's face as she stood among the carnage of battle. *What a waste*, she had said. But she had said it with her hand around a sword.

"Nonviolent or not," Noula said, "the point is to grow. Expansion is the engine of empire."

"Then how are we supposed to hold it back?" Eakang asked quietly. "If we can't change everyone's minds, what do we do?"

The long silence that followed proved that Eakang had voiced the fear no one else wanted to name. It was pure luck that the Qiao Sidhur force was being pulled out, that a real fight between Óla and Ahn hadn't been given the chance to unfold. This battle was over for now, but a world of unknowns had opened up, too, vast as a moonless sky. Sohmeng bit her lip, trying to imagine this darkness as a place of possibility rather than an absence of hope. That was the point of Minhal, wasn't it?

Ólawen broke the silence, Noula's reluctant translation not far behind: "There's nothing you can do."

"Óla, don't—" Ahn began, but the damage was done. Anger spread through the gazebo until even Green Bites was growling. Polha had a hand on Nepar's shoulder, keeping him from getting up and hurting himself.

"I'm not *threatening* you people," Ólawen snapped. "I'm being realistic. The invasions won't stop until someone's claimed the land for themself. For Qiao Sidh."

Ahnschen yanked on his ear, agitated, while Noula rubbed along her tattoo. Both of them were looking grim—and in a way, so was Ólawen. At the very least, she wasn't gloating.

Sohmeng took a deep breath, assessing the situation. These three people were serving as representatives of Qiao Sidh; theoretically, two of them were some of the most powerful voices in the Empire. If they were saying the invasions wouldn't stop until Qiao Sidh had staked its claim, then there weren't grounds to argue. The people of Gãepongwei knew the rainforest, and Ahn, Noula, and Ólawen knew the Empire.

The terrain was an advantage for Gãepongwei; it had nearly killed everyone on the first Qiao Sidhur excursion, and had exhausted most of the soldiers on this one. But they had learned from their failures. Last time, they had relied on Hosaisi just to survive, but *this* time, their tactics helped them take two hmun in under a year. Who was to say what a third invasion would bring? Any campaign would have significant losses for Qiao Sidh, but there were always more soldiers to send and more glory to be gained. Even if they failed again, they could always sail back home with the story that they had made progress.

"How much do people back in Qiao Sidh know about what's going on here?" Sohmeng asked, feeling the stars of an idea beginning to align in her head.

"What do you mean?" Ahn asked.

"When we're this far away," Sohmeng continued, "how much of the truth actually makes it back?"

It was Noula who caught on first. Noula Idhrenqang. When the woman met Sohmeng's eye, there was something Sohmeng recognized there: the thrill of beginning to untangle a problem that felt impossible. "Only as much as we care to tell them. The soldiers themselves will share their personal stories, but unless it's an abject failure, the facts can easily be manipulated—we weren't unprepared for the terrain, we *gained new insight.* We didn't attack two villages, we *began forming strategic relationships.*" The examples didn't earn her much warmth from the Grand Ones, but Sohmeng felt they landed. "It's not about the truth. It's about the spin."

"And when we're all the way across the sea, there's no one to really deny it." Sohmeng felt herself getting excited. "It's not really about *winning*, right? It's about people thinking they've won. We could make that happen."

Qiao Sidh had already invested resources into establishing a colony in Gãepongwei, and when the civil war was over, it was likely this venture would start right back up. But if people were under the impression that the land was already claimed, not so *untilled* anymore, there would be no incentive to try again with full force.

"What are you suggesting, Sohmeng Parminhal?" asked Grandmother Mi. She was younger than Ateng's Euna Mi by a couple of decades, but had that same curious glint in her eye.

Sohmeng took a deep breath, smiling despite the circumstances. Parminhal, indeed. "I think we might have some opportunities to get creative."

The idea found its way to fruition: with the supervision of Gãepongwei, a small group of Qiao Sidhur people would form their own hmun. No military force would be allowed, and all fire-sand would be removed before they so much as dug a ditch. A group of Grand Ones would be brought in to guide them, and people from across Gãepongwei could choose if they wanted to participate in the experiment. It would be a Qiao Sidhur colony in name, but without any true power. A victory on paper for the Empire.

"We would place it somewhere that wouldn't disrupt the sãoni migration route," Sohmeng said, glancing at Hei. "I think that would be better for the whole ecosystem, honestly."

Hei was frowning, but Sohmeng could see that they were genuinely considering it. They crouched down and began using their claw to map things out in the dirt before someone stepped in with charcoal and paper. They also brought a couple of sweet buns for Hei and Green Bites, who was behaving really well on the condition that he was given a snack twice an hour.

Grandfather Heng watched them warily. "I'm still not sure I like the idea of keeping a group of invaders nearby—and I don't think Hosaisi's representatives will either. How do we know this won't escalate sooner or later?"

"Alpha," Hei said, echoing the word in Sãonipa. Green Bites nudged their side with his nose.

"What?" asked Grandfather Heng.

"They follow the alpha."

"It's about leadership," Sohmeng translated, and the final piece locked into place. She grabbed Ahn's hand, looking at him seriously. "Ahn, you could do this. It would be perfect!" He looked immediately appalled by the idea, and she quickly followed up: "You were one of the generals in this campaign, and Qiao Sidh wants you to have done well. If you say that you were victorious and set up a colony here, why wouldn't they listen?"

"Sohmeng, I do not want to claim ownership of any part of Gãepongwei."

"And you wouldn't be!" She looked around at the Grand Ones, who were displaying varying degrees of caution and curiosity. "Bear with me: if we did this, Ahn wouldn't actually *own* anything. He'd be responsible for the Qiao Sidhur people in this new hmun, and act as an . . . I don't know, an *intermediary* between the Empire and Gãepongwei. Our ally. He's already here, he's already planning on staying, and we already know he's on our side."

"If a Qiao Sidhur presence has to be here, I wouldn't be comfortable with anyone leading it who I didn't know personally," Polha Hiwei said. That earned a round of nods from most of the Grand Ones.

"Do you think it would work?" Sohmeng asked Ahn, who was wincing at the question. She realized then that she was asking the wrong person, and took a deep breath. "Ólawen, do you think it would work?" An echo of Noula's voice, and Ólawen raised her gaze to Sohmeng. "Would saying that Ahn's in charge stop other invaders from coming in? I figure no one would want to step on the Éongrir family's toes."

"They wouldn't, no," Ólawen said, drumming her fingers on her thighs. She didn't acknowledge the implication of Sohmeng's statement: it was expected that Ólawen herself would never lead another army on these lands.

"Ahnschen's already known for being something of a radical back home," Noula added, first quietly in Qiao

Sidhur and then a bit louder in Dulpongpa. "It wouldn't be hard to sell the story that the People's Emperor has taken on a new project, Eløndhol. It would help answer questions about why the campaign isn't progressing traditionally—and why he isn't coming home with you."

"I *really* don't know how I feel about this," Ahn said, rubbing his face.

"Be smart, Ahn," said Ólawen, to Sohmeng's surprise. "It would put things on your terms."

"Which means they would be on *our* terms," emphasized Sohmeng. The energy around the circle was changing as the conversation progressed, and she began to feel her optimism rising.

"This is all assuming," Grandfather Heng said, pointing in Ólawen's direction, "that *this one* stays out of it."

The corner of Ólawen's mouth twitched. For the first time in this meeting, Ahnschen approached his sister. He took her hand as he spoke, his voice quiet. "Assuming that you had our back. You would be the one framing this to our parents, Óla. Could you do this as we asked?"

Sohmeng didn't know how to interpret the look that passed between them. Despite it playing out in plain sight, it felt private, like Sohmeng should be averting her eyes.

Ólawen took a deep breath, breaking to the other side of the moment. "Yeah. I could do that."

"I'm not sure why we should believe you," Nepar Ãofe deadpanned. He clearly wasn't the only one who shared this concern.

"Because I'd be leaving my little brother with you, soldier," Ólawen said, the sharp edge to her voice returning in full force.

Sohmeng bit back the urge to assure her that no one here was going to hurt him. But Ahn said nothing, and so she kept her mouth shut, too. If Ólawen was going to view Ahn's safety as collateral, it could only benefit Gãepongwei, even if Sohmeng didn't like it.

"Could you do this, Ahnschen?" Grand One Jão asked. The moons were still passing through their phase, and Sohmeng couldn't help but send some gratitude in the direction of Lula, back in Sorwei Chapal. This conversation probably wouldn't even be possible without them. "Is this a role you would be willing to take on?"

Sohmeng saw the conflict on Ahn's face, the way he looked around the circle, thinking and overthinking his way to an answer. His fingers came to Schenn's bone in his ear; after a moment, he nodded. "If this is where I'm wanted, if it would *help*, then yes. I would."

"A vote?" Grandmother Mi suggested.

And just like that, it was done. A decision had been made, a radical experiment for an unprecedented situation. The new hmun would be built. Sohmeng heard Viunwei's voice in her head: *these aren't traditional times.* Sohmeng had never been great at upholding tradition. With the horrors of the invasion behind them, she dared to let herself look to the future with hope.

The meeting adjourned for the evening, with many more to come in the days and weeks ahead. This was only the beginning. For now, the Kempeipa took in the Sorchapa, ensuring that everyone was fed, cleaned, and cared for. Everyone moved through the hmun in a quiet state of gratitude and disbelief, and celebrated their first night of freedom in many, many months.

Even from outside Kongkempei, Sohmeng could hear the music and smell the food. But she didn't feel the need to join in. With her hand in Ahn's, she found her way to the sãoni, who had claimed a spot away from the humans and made a camp of their own. The glow of their throat stripes, a perfect match for the bioluminescent moss that climbed the trees, was so comforting that she thought she could collapse right there. Ahn held her steady, but she could feel the tremor in his hands.

Hei turned from the shelter they had been building to face them, and Sohmeng could see their exhaustion. For fifteen days, they had both been Ólawen's prisoners. Fifteen days, waiting for her anger to rise or abate. Fifteen days, with no way of knowing where Ahn was or when he would arrive. It had been harrowing.

Sohmeng took a shaky breath, but before she could figure out if she was about to cry, Ahn and Hei had wrapped her in a hug. They all clung to each other, unable to say anything for a while. It was *over*. A new future was opening up, but the threat they had been facing down for months had finally passed. There weren't words that could express how big that felt.

The wind swept in around them, like the rainforest itself was trying to free them of the brave faces they'd been forced to wear. Soon, they found their way beneath the shelter, curled up like melomys in a burrow.

Eventually, Sohmeng heard herself say, "You're staying."

"I am." Ahnschen held her and Hei closer. Hei's head was leaned on his shoulder, their arm draped across him so they could hold Sohmeng's hand.

As always, something in her mind felt called to ask

questions, to start planning for the future. But she was tired, so she quieted it. "I'm glad."

"Me too."

Hei clicked quietly, long since done with human words for the day.

Above them, a night bird was singing. Sohmeng didn't know which bird it was, but the call was familiar, and lulled her closer towards sleep. Tomorrow, the work began again. Good work, promising work, but work nonetheless. Gãepongwei could have the three of them back tomorrow, but tonight was for themselves.

They slept, and slept peacefully.

The next morning, the sun rose on a new beginning for Gãepongwei. Sorwei Chapal, Kongkempei, and Hosaisi were beginning the process of reconnecting to help one another heal from their shared suffering. But Sohmeng wouldn't be there for that work; her job was to help escort the remaining Qiao Sidhur back to the coast.

Sohmeng was there when Ahn and Noula explained what came next. The Qiao Sidhur were told that, with the possibility of civil war emerging, the Emperor had chosen to call them home, but Ahn would be staying behind to continue building a relationship with the people of Gãepongwei. Very few people actually seemed disappointed about this; most of them looked as exhausted as Ólawen. It hit Sohmeng strangely that many of the people who had worked to destroy her home hadn't even really wanted to be there.

But when Ahn opened up the opportunity to join him for this project, there was some interest. Not so much from the soldiers, but from the *saro dhral*. A cook from the coastal camp was quick to start asking questions, and the artist from Kongkempei smiled at Sohmeng shyly. This warmth was what she had always wanted and expected of visitors; she wanted very much for a relationship to still be possible after all that had happened.

Ahn planned on personally interviewing everyone who wanted to participate. Those that the people of Kongkempei expressed concern about were barred from the opportunity, as well as anyone at all who had been stationed in Hosaisi.

It didn't take long for Ólawen to have the ships prepared. Once Ahn had chosen his participants, all that was left to do was for the Qiao Sidhur to set sail. By the time Sohmeng made it to the beach on that final morning, there were hardly any people left on the shore.

That was probably for the best. Even she had to admit that it was a little weird that she'd come to say goodbye.

Still, as she stood before Ahn's sister, she knew it was the right choice for herself. Up close, she could see the subtle similarities between the youngest Éongrir siblings. They had different hair, but the same eyes. Different smiles, but the same frown. Sohmeng looked closely at Ólawen, knowing that she would very likely never see the woman again. "I just wanted to say that I hope you have a safe trip."

"That's . . . kind of you," Ólawen said, her interpreter matching her uncertain tone. She looked back at the rainforest. Sohmeng couldn't tell whether or not she was sorry to be leaving. "I hope all of this—I don't know. Does what it needs to."

Sohmeng had given up on the dream that Ólawen would suddenly realize the error of her ways and commit herself to repair. Honestly, even a straightforward apology currently seemed out of reach. But her hope sounded sincere, and that was something. "Thanks. Me too."

"He—" Ólawen cut herself off, clearing her throat. Sohmeng watched her try to compose herself, but she could hear the question in her voice. "He'll be safer here."

"…yeah," Sohmeng said softly. "I think so."

"Good."

The air was different on the coastline. Sohmeng could taste the salt, could feel the tiny crystals gathering behind her ears. When the wind blew without any trees to interrupt, it felt like it enveloped Sohmeng's whole body, like it would carry her away. But her feet remained firm in the sand, grounding her to the long stretch of land that she had fallen in love with in more ways than she ever could have expected.

She was certain that there was more she wanted to say to Ólawen. But the words were slow to come today, and the translator was looking strained, and Ahn still needed to see Óla before the ships set sail for good.

"Goodbye, Ólawen," Sohmeng said in Qiao Sidhur.

"…Goodbye," Ólawen replied in clumsy Dulpongpa. Discomfort immediately twisted her expression. Sohmeng wanted to tell her that her pronunciation wasn't half bad, but Ólawen was already walking away, tugging at the bone in her ear.

Twenty-Two

AHNSCHEN WATCHED THE SHIPS fade into the horizon, their sails open like birds in flight. His hand was stained with ink, an inevitability after the hours he'd spent writing letters for Ólawen to bring back to Qiao Sidh. His parents would be receiving an entire essay, providing something to support his sister's explanation for why he had stayed behind. But he also had warm words for his school friends, and a long letter of thanks for Master Hvu.

And, of course, he had messages for Schenn's family, too. This was partially logistical, notes on how they would be allocated half his royal stipend, how they could send word to Ólawen should they ever need something. But it was also deeply emotional: Schenn's family was his family. He felt more warmly towards them than he did most of his blood siblings. Ahn wrote letters for both Schenn's parents, and one for each sibling and close cousin. He even tucked in a note for the local florist, who had hosted one of the loveliest tea dates that Ahn had ever enjoyed.

By staying in Gãepongwei, Ahn was taking the last piece of Schenn away from his family. That loss wasn't easily discounted.

"What will you tell them?" Ólawen had asked. Better than anyone, Óla knew the obligations that came with being bound to another half.

"The truth." Out of respect for her role as messenger, Ahn shared that truth with her, too: "Schenn was the one who brought me here."

Ólawen hadn't known what to make of that, but she promised she would deliver each letter personally, and Ahn believed her. She left one of the longships in his care, a way to take his leave if it became necessary. She said she would send a small delegation south once the coup simmered down, "just to check on you, okay?". The Gãepongweipa council consented cautiously to this, and Ahn found himself hoping that ship would come bearing return letters. He looked forward to the adventure ahead, but already found himself aching for the parts of Qiao Sidh he loved, and that he would have to leave behind.

This change meant he would not watch the sunset from his bedroom in Hvallánzhou. He would not stay out too late at a jazz club, ignoring everyone's protests when he footed the bill. He would not feel the bite of a northern winter as the seasons turned. Not for a long, long time, at least.

It was a hard goodbye.

The next goodbye was also difficult, but at least he knew it wouldn't be so extended. Hei and Sohmeng were heading south in the coming weeks to tell Ateng about their victory over the Empire, and about the experimental hmun that would be built in its place. A new hmun had never been added to the network before, and the Grand Ones felt it was important to inform the others about their new neighbours—as well as offer the chance to move in.

"I have a hard time believing anyone from those stuffy mountains will take us up on it," Sohmeng said, wrinkling her nose. Ahn was strolling along the beach with her and Hei, pointing out clouds and picking up nice pieces of driftwood.

"Really?" Ahn asked, watching her dip her fingers into the long stretch of the waves. "I have to imagine at least some people would be as adventurous as you. Especially after having been trapped for so long."

"Um, first of all, *no one* in Ateng is as adventurous as me." She lifted a stick of driftwood, gave it a little frown, then tossed it back into the surf. "Second, even I've still got to figure out what I want."

"What do you mean?" Ahn asked. He realized abruptly that he might have been making some considerable assumptions. "Do you not want ... ?"

Sohmeng gave his arm a light whack. "Look, I *know* I want to be a part of the new hmun in some way, but I also want to be with Hei and the colony. But I *also* want to be able to see my family. The problem is I want *everything*, and I haven't figured out how to make it happen."

Hei made a quiet sound in Sãonipa. He recognized it as similar to a human hush. They made it often when Ahn was feeling overwhelmed, and even though it wasn't directed at him, it made his shoulders relax.

"I know, I know," Sohmeng sighed. "I don't need to start planning yet. We visit the hmun first."

"We have time," Ahn agreed, but he understood how

hard it was to slow down after weeks of rushing towards safety. The three of them were still figuring it out.

Hei had been managing much better than him or Sohmeng, which made sense to him; they had always seemed more comfortable working at a slower pace. They gazed now at the ocean, their green eyes bright in the direct sunlight. He almost never saw them this way.

"What about you, Hei?" Ahnschen asked. "Do you know what you want, now that the invasion is behind us?"

Hei scoffed, but they did the courtesy of answering him anyway. "I will be with the sãoni. I need to learn how to be alpha."

"You've been doing a really good job so far," Sohmeng encouraged.

Hei shook their head, eyes on the horizon. "I have barely started. Everything has been for humans. We do not know our—" Looking for the word, they pivoted to Atengpa, and Sohmeng took on the role of verbal shadow. "Our rhythms, or our seasons. The colony and I need to learn about our new relationship, especially after I have tested them so much."

"Are you going to keep them involved with humans?" Ahn asked. He couldn't imagine Hei allowing the sãoni to become fully domesticated, but the interspecies relationship they had built was remarkable.

"If *I* want to be with humans sometimes, then the relationship must be there," Hei said plainly. "But right now, I want my problems to have six legs. First, we'll do a full loop of the migration route. It will give me a look at how the colonies are doing. And other wildlife." They paused, brow furrowing. "I am happy for the humans'

Gãepongwei. But I will always love the rainforest more."

"Well, humans are part of the rainforest," Sohmeng said, and gave them a big kiss on the cheek. "So I guess that means you love *everything*, huh? You big softie." Hei went in for a bite, but Sohmeng refused to be dissuaded. "It's true! You love everything in the world, no matter how much you show your teeth about it!"

Despite the silliness of their roughhousing, the words landed tenderly in Ahn. A wave came up, and a stretch of seawater rushed to his ankles, refreshing and cool. For a moment, it felt like he was watching himself from outside of his own body, suspended in a moment of significance.

It came out before he'd even decided to speak: "Does it still make sense?"

"Huh?" Sohmeng stopped wrestling with Hei.

"To be together," Ahnschen clarified. "In partnership. We said we would do this *for as long as it makes sense*, and I'm not leaving anymore so I wanted to ask if . . . " Hei and Sohmeng were both looking at him, patient as he found his words. Found his courage to ask a question he was fairly certain he had the answer to, but needed to ask anyway. "Does it still make sense to you? Because I love you. And you don't—you don't have to say it back, or feel exactly the way I do about it, but both of you have my heart in one way or another. And so I wanted to ask."

Sohmeng walked over to him with a sigh. "You're a real romantic, huh?"

"I am," Ahn said helplessly. "And I know you aren't—"

"I'm not," Sohmeng said, and stood on her toes to kiss him. "But that doesn't mean I don't love you, you beautiful meathead."

Hei snorted, but Ahn saw that they were smiling.

"I do!" Sohmeng insisted, looking at both of them. "I love both of you, in my way. I love the … the world we're making together, or whatever."

"Or *whatever*," Hei repeated.

"Please, keep ruining the moment, Hei."

A larger wave crashed, and Sohmeng squealed as the foamy water caught her calves. Ahn held her steady, looking over the top of her head. "And you, Hei? What do you think?"

Hei took a moment before they answered. "It makes sense. I like the three of us."

"Honestly, it makes *more* sense," Sohmeng chimed in. "If you were in Qiao Sidh, I have no idea how letters would even work. Hei can't write, and I can't write in Qiao Sidhur. We'd have to like, draw what we were thinking or something. Or get help from Noula with translation, which would be so embarrassing, honestly. Yuck."

Hei was smiling as Sohmeng rambled, but they didn't move to speak again, and Ahn realized he'd been hoping for more. Maybe that was foolish of him; after all, Hei was often a person of few words. But he couldn't help wanting to hear their assessment, not just of the *three* of them, but the *two* of them as well. Hei and Ahnschen. He wanted to know where they stood.

Hei caught him watching them and narrowed their eyes. That intense look of theirs had scared Ahn when they first met. He hadn't been able to read it, and it had made him afraid.

He could still rarely guess what was on their mind. But it didn't unsettle him anymore. It just made him curious.

Later that evening, when Sohmeng was practicing Qiao Sidhur with Noula, Ahn asked Hei to join him for a private conversation. They walked back into the rainforest, out of view of both the humans and the sãoni. Hei ran their hand along a low tree branch; Ahn followed suit, enjoying the rippled texture of the bark beneath his palm. A dragonfly buzzed by Hei, and they ducked their head with a little *tsk*, like it was a younger sibling insisting on getting underfoot.

Ahn had never known anyone else who participated so fully in the natural world, who inserted themself into it so seamlessly. Or maybe it wasn't *inserting* at all—maybe they had always been certain of their place in everything, in their sense of belonging. Maybe that's what led them to roam the rainforest how they did. Knowledge was power, but despite Hei's unparalleled knowledge of Eiji, they did not demonstrate an ounce of entitlement. They took what they needed without trying to own a thing.

For all they said very little, it still seemed to Ahn that Hei knew how to talk to everything. How to listen when it talked back.

"You are looking at me again, Ahnschen."

Their back was turned to him, but Ahn supposed he had never been good at being subtle. Not with Hei. "I am."

"Why?" they asked, rubbing a leaf between their fingers to catch the dew.

"Because I like . . . " Ahn paused, looking for an explanation. As always, Hei didn't interrupt. "I like the way you look at things. I want to learn from you. And keep getting to know you."

"Know what about me?"

"Whatever you would share."

Now, Hei did turn to face him. Unexpectedly, they looked nervous, like they were searching for something. This time, it was Ahn's turn to be quiet; perhaps that would help them find what they were looking for.

"We," Hei began, averting their eyes, "are not here for only Sohmeng."

Ahn knew it was a question, even if it sounded like a statement. "Maybe not," he agreed.

Hei's fingers were back on the branch, investigating the texture. Cautiously, Ahn approached them, resting his hand on top of theirs. They made no move to pull it away.

"You are good, Ahnschen."

Ahn's stomach flipped. "Am I?"

"You keep being good," Hei continued. Was it praise or a command? Ahn couldn't tell, but their hand had moved to his wrist, fingers rested over his pulse. "I like this."

Tentatively, he touched the scar on their arm, the line he had burned into their skin upon their first meeting, haloed by dots from Green Bites' sharp teeth. "I like you."

"I know." Hei exhaled through their nose, and though it was a quiet sound, it reminded him of the sãoni. He missed Mama's heavy sighs. "You may ride with sãoni, Ahnschen. With me. If Sohmeng is there or somewhere else. Okay?"

When Sohmeng first told him he could have a place in Gãepongwei, Hei had said that Ahn would stay with the colony. But it was different to receive this invitation. It was unspeakably special to be trusted not just as a member of the colony, but as a human companion to Hei. It was hard-earned.

Words failed him, but he didn't think Hei minded. Instead, he tried his best to produce an affirmative in Sãonipa. Their smirk told him two things: he hadn't done a very good job, and they had understood him anyway.

Hei's expression transformed into a thoughtful frown, and that was the only warning Ahn had before they were kissing him. It was different from how Sohmeng kissed; there was a sharp edge to it, a scrape of teeth that made him grip tighter to their hand.

After a moment they pulled back. It looked like they were still deciding how they felt about it. "Hm."

"Hm," Ahn repeated, grinning. It reminded him of being with Schenn—the experience of not quite knowing what they wanted from each other, but knowing they wanted *something*.

As they walked back to the beach, he savoured every minute of the silence they shared. There was no wordless company quite like Hei's. With all the work ahead of him, Ahn knew that he would feel its absence in the weeks to come.

After a week or so to stabilize, Kongkempei and Hosaisi sent representatives to where the Qiao Sidhur remained at the coast, awaiting their next steps. Sorwei Chapal and Nona Fahang sent people too, including a few of the younger Grand Ones. Nepar Ãofe and Polha Hiwei both volunteered to participate, and even though Eakang went home to be with their family, they insisted that they would come back the moment they'd convinced their mothers it was safe. It felt good to be working with allies again—friends, even—especially when they were being guided by hope rather than fear.

During these meetings, Ahnschen's job was to sit as a representative of the Qiao Sidhur who had stayed behind.

Ultimately, he was in a consultation role rather than a decision-making one. He found it liberating.

First came the matter of where this hmun would be located. It needed to be accessible and practical to trade with, but it wasn't permitted to be in close proximity to Kongkempei or Hosaisi. Following notes left by Hei about the sãoni migration route, they chose a location that still clung to the coast, but was slightly further south; Sorwei Chapal would be the nearest neighbour and point of contact.

"We've bridged two hmun before," Nepar Ãofe said, his voice carrying nearly all of its old strength after some time to recover. "Who says we can't do it again?"

Ahnschen found those words to be encouraging and daunting both. Sorwei Chapal might have successfully alloyed cultures before, but it was entirely new for Qiao Sidh, even if the thirty people who had stayed behind were civilians. While about half the remaining Qiao Sidhur had never left the coastal base camp, the other half had been situated in Kongkempei. Save for Ahn and Noula, not a one of them was a soldier—but even bladeless, even under orders they might have personally disagreed with, they had come in uninvited. They had been present during the first attack on Kongkempei; Ahn himself had killed a member of the hmun.

And so it was obvious that before any hmun-building could begin, some sort of relationship-building had to happen first. Repair. The problem was, now that the soldiers were gone, Ahn had no idea what that would look like. This was even more challenging for Noula, who, after months by Ólawen's side, had not earned much trust. The Grand Ones had gone through several private interviews with her before agreeing that she could stay behind. In the end, her proficiency with Dulpongpa had been her saving grace.

But despite the shared language, she and Ahn were struggling with how to make amends. They had asked the Grand Ones what they could do to make things right for this new beginning, and had been given a decisive answer: it wasn't possible.

Noula presented one idea after the other: several months of labour; aid building roads between the hmun to improve travel; a donation of some sort from the Empire. None of these suggestions were well-received. When a Grand One asked why the Qiao Sidhur thought loss of life could be paid off, Ahn began worrying that they were in over their heads.

"Do they not *want* us to try and fix things?" Noula asked, sounding uncharacteristically defeated. "It's normal for there to be tension after an invasion, but they aren't really giving us much to work with, Eløndham."

"Ahnschen," Ahn corrected, which she acknowledged with an exasperated wave of her hand. He had a massive headache. "And I don't know. I've never done this before, Noula."

"I have, though. I've organized three different pacifying projects in the outer provinces, and they always go well." He could hear her frustration as she grasped for solutions. "I built a theater last time, a theater *specifically* for their local shows. Do you think something like that would work?"

Ahn got the abrupt sensation of receiving a hard flick

to the ear, and he suddenly felt very foolish. "We aren't in Qiao Sidh."

"That is, indeed, the point, Eløn—Ahnschen."

"Then why are we relying on Qiao Sidhur ideas?" He stood up, trying to pace away his old instincts. "We need to stop thinking about *fixing* things. They already said this isn't fixable. I think we're coming at this wrong."

It was impossible to undo the invasion. This experimental hmun was only happening *because* of Qiao Sidh's attempted conquest; trying to erase that or smooth it over went against its very foundation.

So the next morning, Ahn came to Gãepongwei's representatives with a question instead of a solution.

"What do you need from us to start building trust? Besides time, that is." The words felt clumsy on Ahnschen's tongue. He was glad to be asking in Dulpongpa; they would have felt even more stilted in Qiao Sidhur. "We feel great remorse, but how do we ... show that?"

It almost felt embarrassing to be asking. Like something he should know already, despite having no cultural precedent. But as it turned out, that feeling of *needing to know already* was precisely what had been blocking their way forward. The council took his fumbling, earnest inquiry better than any proposal he or Noula had brought forth before.

"At last," Kongkempei's Grandmother Ginhãe said, eyeing him with an expression that was nearly a smile, "a discussion worth having."

There wasn't one simple answer. The hmuns' representatives took time to privately confer, and came back with their answers: Sorwei Chapal was satisfied with the part

Ahn and Noula had played in ending the invasion; Nona Fahang felt similarly, requesting only that the remaining Qiao Sidhur find ways to be of service to others, just as Ahn had done while awaiting his trial; Kongkempei asked for an oath significant to Qiao Sidhur custom, performed and repeated under each lunar phase for a full cycle; and Hosaisi asked for birds.

"This is a sunshower bird," said Hosaisi's young Grandmother Ker. She held a carved wooden bird in her hand, painted with elaborate colours. "They sing most loudly after storms have passed, and fly in magnificent murmurations. In Hosaisi, we carve these birds when we've greatly hurt someone, and offer them as gifts."

"There are one thousand, two hundred and thirty-six people in Hosaisi," said the hmun's Grandfather Li. "To the invasion, we lost forty-eight. Before this project begins, we ask for one thousand, two hundred and eighty-four sunshower birds."

It came out to about forty birds per person. Looking at the wooden figurine in the Grandmother's hand brought tears to Ahn's eyes, though he didn't quite understand why. Beside him, Noula looked puzzled, but said nothing.

"It will be done," Ahnschen vowed, in two languages.

Grandmother Ker herself volunteered to teach them. She brought her young daughter along, who was carving her first bird for an age-mate she had hit. With steady, nimble hands, Grandmother Ker showed them how to carefully wield the carver's tools. She painted a guide to the symbolism behind the different colours and patterns, and encouraged them to think of meaningful ways to use each one.

When she was satisfied with their skillset, she left the Qiao Sidhur to their work, and the time that would be remembered as the Days of Murmurations began.

These were some of the most purposeful weeks Ahn ever experienced. Together, he and the new members of this infant hmun grew a flock of birds from their hands, and talked about what it meant to be sorry. To hurt, and to be hurt; to forgive, and to want to be able to forgive. It was cathartic. It was the most intimate way Ahn had ever gotten to know a group of near-strangers.

With their hands duly occupied, the conversation flowed like a great river. Together, thirty-two Qiao Sidhur people shared the details of their lives, from the mundane to the extraordinary; they opened each other up to new ideas, gently challenged each other's beliefs, compared recipes for baking bread. It didn't take long for people to begin calling him Ahnschen, just like back when he was in school. He learned that he had a mutual friend with one of them, and when it hit them both that they would not see her again, they shared a very long and emotional hug.

The birds were meant for Hosaisi, but they healed something in Ahn—in everyone, it seemed. They took turns cooking, cleaning, comforting, weeping. And they laughed, too. There was a symbol for laughter, for *I would like to be joyful with you*, and there came a day where everyone agreed they would paint a bird with that pattern.

One night, a young Qiao Sidhur woman came to Ahn privately. She told him about the nightmares her grandfather used to have about the day the Éongrir family invaded his province and destroyed the home that had been in his family for generations.

"I don't know why I'm telling you this," she said, wiping her eyes. "I just needed you to know."

"Thank you for sharing that with me," Ahn said through tears of his own. "And I'm sorry. On behalf of my family, I'm sorry."

He carved her a bird, too.

The Days of Murmurations gave people from different hmun time to arrive on the coast. Quite suddenly, it seemed, they had amassed surprising numbers of curious would-be participants. When the last bird spread its wings, Hosaisi formally accepted the gift, and asked that the figurines be divided between Hosaisi, Kongkempei, and the new hmun. A way to remember how this had all begun; a promise that nothing like it would ever happen again.

So the building began. Gãepongweipa and Qiao Sidhur architects collaborated on designing the magnificent buildings that would be raised. A book of history was begun, along with a census. It was agreed that Dulpongpa would be the official language of the hmun, but Qiao Sidhur lessons were offered to all to open another avenue of communication. Ahn knew Sohmeng would be furious that these classes had begun without her. A list of interested Grand Ones from across Gãepongwei was compiled, and gazebo-style moonhouses were built. Nearby, they made room too for a small Qiao Sidhur shrine.

Ahnschen had never seen anything like this. He hadn't known it was possible. The story he had been raised on in Qiao Sidh was one of *improvement*—arriving in a new place and making it more than it already was. Better, more beautiful. And yet the Empire could never have produced something so beautiful as this. It was only in the *absence* of empire that it blossomed, a creativity unencumbered by the weight of domination.

As travellers continued to arrive at the site of the new hmun, passing under the fresh-painted arch, he saw his awe reflected in them. He also saw a few familiar faces.

"Ahn, this looks *amazing!*" Eakang exclaimed, rushing to him for a hug. He lifted them off the ground, earning a squeal of glee. They had just arrived with their parents, Pimchuang Ker and Jaea Won, and their little brother Kuei.

"Eakang!" He looked them over with the affection of an older sibling. "Did you travel alright? Your, your family—"

"They agreed, they're doing it," Eakang said, the words gushing out of them. "We're going to see if Damdão will come here too! And maybe his family? I don't know, maybe it won't work, but I'm so—*Polha!*" They wiggled out of his arms, full of energy. "I'll be right back, wait just a minute!"

Ahn watched them bound away, overwhelmed with gratitude. His mind was already spinning with what this could mean for Sohmeng's family. She had talked about wanting to have it all; was this changing world really so kind that it would allow that? It would feel right. It would feel more than fair, after all she had done for it.

"Hey, tsongkar."

Ahn turned abruptly to face Lita Soon, who stood with his arms crossed. Ahn tried to greet him, but the words got trapped; this wasn't someone he had expected to see.

"Probably can't call you that anymore, huh?" Lita said. "Seeing as you're invited now."

"Your choice," Ahn said. "For old time's sake, if you want."

Lita let out a breath of a laugh. A long moment stretched before he said, "Your Dulpongpa's better."

"Thank you. I've had a lot of practice."

Lita hummed, looking around at the recently completed homes, each with little wooden birds at their threshold. Someone was working on a rooftop garden in the style of Sorwei Chapal. Where Ahn had been immersed in enthusiasm for the past few weeks, he recognized wariness on the man's face; while building this hmun had become part of Ahn's daily life, it was still a new idea for Lita Soon, and many others like him. He would have to remember that.

"How's your leg?" Last time Ahn had seen Lita, he'd been recovering from a nasty wound from the attempted Qiao Sidhur attack on Nona Fahang. "It's a long journey here from Nona Fahang."

Lita shrugged. "Healed up fine. You all chose a good spot for this thing—the path isn't too bad. It'll make it easier on the Grand Ones who join your circle."

Ahn nodded to himself, and another awkward pause found its way into the conversation. During Ahn's trial in Nona Fahang, Lita had skirted him like a furious shadow, hurt and rage spilling out of him at every opportunity. It made sense, it was justified—but Ahn wondered whether it had felt good for Lita, to burn that way. When Ahn's own despair had threatened to overtake him, Grand One Jão had called him *wounded*. He hoped some of Lita Soon's wounds had been given the attention they needed to heal, too.

Tentatively, Ahn asked, "Are you thinking of joining us? I could show you around, if you'd like to know more about the project."

Lita snorted. "No. Now that I've escorted everyone up from Nona Fahang, I'm going back to Kongkempei for good. My family's there. We're ready to be done with this nightmare."

"I'm sorry, Lita," Ahnschen said, the same as he had said to the Qiao Sidhur woman who approached him. But different, too. That apology had been for an old hurt; this one was young, and personal. "I know it doesn't make the loss go away, but I wanted to say it. I apologize for what I did to you, your family, your home. I was a coward, and you all deserved better."

"We did," Lita agreed. He met Ahn's eye, considering. "I don't think I forgive you, Éongrir Ahnschen. Not now. Not yet. I don't know. But I appreciate the apology."

Ahn bowed his head in acknowledgment; it was unexpected to find that he didn't need Lita's forgiveness. "If there's ever anything I can do for you and yours, you know where to find me."

"I guess I do." The man took a deep breath. "Don't screw this up, alright?"

"If I do," Ahn said, attempting a smile, "like I said, you know where to find me."

Despite himself, Lita Soon smiled back. He shook his head and wandered over to the Fahangpa who were chatting with their new neighbours. Ahnschen watched him go, and silently wished him well.

That night, he went to the ocean. Ahnschen was there most nights, either sitting with his fingers curled in the silken sand, or wading up to his waist to stare at the stars. Somewhere in time, far across the sea, Ahn and Schenn were doing much the same, watching the meteors fall.

There were no meteors tonight, and the sky was illuminated by the double full moons of Chisong; in Schenn's realm, there was the perfect darkness of Minhal, better for stargazing.

"The water connects us," Ahn murmured, an echo of Lula Jão. The tide rushed around his knees, its rhythm calling him closer to shore and deeper to sea, back and forth.

And it's warmer on this side of the equator.

Ahn smiled as heat swirled through the shell of his ear. "Is that why you brought me here?"

Must have been.

"Must have."

When Ahn closed his eyes, he saw Schenn's face as clearly as if it were reflected back in a mirror. That careless grin as he sprawled beneath a tent, allowing himself the luxury of a lazy afternoon. The relief that overcame him when he caught sight of Ahn at a busy party. The way he, at age eleven, had cocked his eyebrow as he sized Ahn up, not caring a bit that he was the prince of anything.

"I miss you," Ahnschen said. "I'm glad you're here with me."

Far beyond, on the obsidian edge of the waves, the moons cast two shimmering lines of light. Like a road, like the soul of a road—the spirit of connection without any pavement in sight. Like a new path, promising, mysterious, ready to welcome the first step.

Twenty-Three

"COME ON, GREEN BITES, you know better than that!"

Sohmeng indulged the sãoni in a brief game of tug-of-war before yanking her cooking pot back from between his teeth. After weeks stuck outside of Kongkempei, getting back on the move kept the sãoni in high spirits. They were a handful when they got playful, but it was also a relief to watch. It reminded her of the early days of walking Eiji, except now she wasn't afraid. What was there to be scared of when she was family to the biggest predators in the rainforest?

Green Bites growled happily as he butted his head into her side. She rubbed his back with an exasperated sigh. "Sure happy you didn't eat me now, huh?"

Noticing the special attention Green Bites was getting, a few other sãoni lumbered over for pets. Much as she wanted to get started on dinner, they could afford a cuddle break. There weren't any deadlines to meet; they were moving at Hei's discretion now. Ateng was their next human destination, but Hei had set the colony back on the migration route for this journey south. That way they could audit the current health of the rainforest as they went.

Gãepongwei had fundamentally changed after the Qiao Sidhur invasion, but the rainforest was resilient. Adaptable. Sohmeng was coming to understand that, short of a world-ending catastrophe like that which had befallen Polhmun Ão, the land could endure all sorts of changes. That was the point of the perfect system.

Sohmeng was enjoying the opportunity to engage with this system up close, just like her mother had done. She was living the life she had been promised as a kid—even if there were more lizards than she'd anticipated. Everywhere she looked, there was something new to discover, and with Hei as a guide, those discoveries were put into a greater context.

"Lots of catfish," came Hei's voice. They were soaking wet up to their hips, and carrying a huge fish on a line to highlight their point.

"What do we mean by lots?" Sohmeng replied, keeping a protective hold on her pot.

"More than I would have expected from a good spawning season alone." Hei growled at an encroaching sãoni, and it shuffled back from their fish. "We should keep an eye on how murky the water is looking. If they're thinning out the mussel population, we'll notice."

"So I'm hearing that catfish is going to be on the menu for a while?" Sohmeng asked. "Not that I'm complaining, but you're gonna be filleting them unless you want to be eating bones."

"Eventually, you will need to learn to do it, as well."

"But I'm the best and most beautiful mate in the *world*. Don't you want to provide for me?"

Hei rolled their eyes, but they were smiling as they hooked a freshly cleaned claw over their finger and got to work deboning the fish. Ever since they began moving south, Hei had carried an air of calm that Sohmeng hadn't really gotten to see before. Despite the fact that this was their first time leading the migration route as alpha, they were completely in their element.

To Sohmeng, this journey was a major milestone, a hard-won victory. But it had also been Hei's daily life before Sohmeng had come barging in. She hadn't even spent a full lunar cycle with them before they met Ahn and the invasion took precedence.

In some ways, it felt like they were meeting all over again. Sohmeng Minhal, with nothing left to hide; Hei, with no pressure to be anything but themself. They introduced her to flora and fauna like they were old friends, each species given a special name that Hei had made up. Sohmeng didn't mind when Hei had their quiet hours or days, but she never got sick of listening to them talk. When their ideas started flowing, she was riveted. She was pretty sure they were the smartest person she knew.

She wondered what these plants and animals were called in the other hmun, what wisdom had been gleaned long before Hei was born. She could only imagine the possibilities if they were to collaborate, the hmuns' established knowledge paired with Hei's firsthand experience.

But it was a stretch. Sohmeng knew Hei, and knew that their first priority would always be the sãoni, not humanity. Especially now that they were alpha. Hei would spend their life migrating, dictated by nothing but the natural rhythms of the sãoni; that was the role they wanted to play in the system. That was where they would find happiness.

Was that what would make Sohmeng happiest? What was it that *she* wanted? Could she be content here, journeying along just the two of them, occasionally persuading Hei to pause so she could visit a hmun for a couple of phases?

In her heart, she already knew the answer. But it was hard.

Sohmeng loved being with Hei, but she loved being with humans, too. All her life, she had fought for the right to be herself with other people, to make friends who recognized how much she had to offer. To be creative. To be curious. Ateng had never let her shine the way she wanted to, but there were other hmun that would take her in—and a new one on the horizon that she could play a part in actively shaping. It was the perfect opportunity for her, and it was entirely at odds with the life Hei wanted to live.

Part of Sohmeng wanted to avoid talking about it. Hei had been there for her from the very beginning of her journey, and she didn't want to hurt them or make them feel abandoned. But they were perceptive, and she was bad at being subtle, and she knew it would come out eventually. Might as well be on her terms.

So as they sat together at the foot of Sodão Dangde, with her return to Ateng set for the morning, Sohmeng gathered her courage for yet another difficult conversation. She and Hei were spoiling Singing Violet by polishing her claws. It was a special occasion; she had just laid her first clutch of eggs, along with several other female sãoni, and her cheek pockets were chubby from storing them.

"Alright. So the last time I dropped some big revelation on you near Sodão Dangde, it went pretty bad," Sohmeng said, wrinkling her nose. "Granted, I just sort of screamed *Minhal!* in your face because I was overwhelmed, so I've been trying to be calm about this one. But I'm nervous, and it might come out all wrong, and please don't hate me if it does."

"I will not hate you," Hei said with calm certainty, examining Violet's midfoot. "But yes, please do not scream."

"I want to live in the new hmun," Sohmeng said abruptly. She braced herself for a negative knee-jerk reaction, for Hei to be hurt or upset or confused, but nothing came. And so she readied the speech she had been practicing. She took a deep breath—

"I think that's a good choice for you."

"Please know this doesn't mean I don't w—" Sohmeng cut herself off as Hei's words reached her ears. "Wait. You do?"

"I do," Hei repeated. Gently, they rested Singing Violet's foot back on the ground. "It is the choice I assumed you would make. I was planning on encouraging it, if you were uncertain."

"But—but why? I figured you thought I was staying with you and the sãoni."

"You said you hadn't decided yet. Only that you wanted many things."

"Don't you *want* me to be with the colony?" She immediately felt childish for saying so. Here she had been the one worrying that Hei would feel rejected, and now *she* was feeling stung.

"Of course I do," Hei said. "But you like people, Sohmeng. You like sãoni too, but you would get bored here eventually." Sohmeng frowned, feeling a defensive instinct to deny it, but it didn't seem like Hei was judging her. "You would want to adventure, not to roam. And then I would feel rushed. Neither of us would like it."

Sohmeng was stumped. Hei was completely on the same page as her—she didn't even get to use her speech!—but she didn't feel any better. On the contrary, new frustration seemed to rise up.

"Well that isn't *fair*," Sohmeng said.

"That I would feel rushed?"

"No! Yes? I don't know!" Sohmeng lay flat on the ground, looking up at the canopy. Hei adjusted her head so it could rest on their thigh. "It's unfair that I would get bored. It's unfair that we like different things. It's unfair that the migration route is so big. I'm so excited about the new hmun, burning godseye, it was half *my idea*. But I hate that it means I'll have to give up being with you and the sãoni."

Hei tilted their head. "But you don't have to do that. It is very possible to have both."

"As much as I'd like to be in several places at once, I don't think the world is prepared for more than one Sohmeng."

"You must have thought this through," Hei said, frowning. "You could split your time, Sohmeng. It's perfectly possible."

"But I'd *miss* you."

The words came out without even having to think about them. Sohmeng was lucky enough to have friends and family all over Gãepongwei, but at some point in the journey, traveling with Hei had become her idea of home. With Hei, she wasn't restricted or judged. She didn't have to accommodate so many rules that she didn't agree with, because communicating with Hei was easy in a way she'd never experienced before. Who'd have thought that a spontaneous bite to the neck would eventually make so much sense?

She flicked her gaze to Hei's face. Their sharp eyes made sharper from a smear of dark makeup, their mess of hair that Sohmeng worked so hard to keep tidy, the freckle on their upper lip. "Hei, I'll miss you so much."

"I'll miss you too," Hei said, their expression softening. They took her hand, tracing lines on her palm with their claw. "And then I will see you. And you can talk my ear off, and join me on a loop of the sãoni cycle. We can pause at other hmun along the way, just for a little while, and you can say hello to your humans. And then I bring you back to your new home, where you and Ahnschen and all of your friends can be loud together, and make and solve new problems." They leaned down to kiss her, and when they smiled there was a shimmer in their eyes. The colour was somewhere between wovenstone and monstera leaves; their expression held a little bit of everything. "You cannot have everything. But you can have this."

"It's not a bad deal," Sohmeng said, pushing Hei's hair out of their face. It was the understatement of the century. "Guess I better say yes, huh?"

"You do not need to do anything except what you want to do."

Sohmeng grinned, poking them in the nose. "You always know just what to say."

The next morning, Sohmeng walked the traders' stairs up Sodão Dangde. This was her third ascent, now: the first with Hei to find the batengmun, the second with her father to repair the Sky Bridge, and now this one, alone. Sohmeng's legs were already aching when she thought about the fact that she'd be going right back *down* the mountain in a few short days, but it was special to have that time with herself.

The stairway had become familiar, both the well-worn route and Hei's secret passage. Sohmeng let her eyes adjust to the dark as she breathed in the mineral smell, and then was startled by something new.

Voices. *People.*

She had seen the rebuilt Sky Bridge high above them. She'd known logically that the crossing had been made while she was still up north. But this was proof. Sodão Dangde wasn't a tomb anymore—it was *home*. The home she had been born in.

Sohmeng ran the rest of the way, as fast as she could, which resulted in some seriously undignified wheezing as she collapsed into Sodão Dangde's main chamber. But it couldn't take away from the sheer excitement of seeing it: houses occupied once more, sunbeams shining down on the people she'd grown up with, lichen lush on the walls from overgrowth. Or maybe the walls had always been this mossy, and she'd just forgotten as resources in Fochão Dangde grew scarce.

"Sohmeng?" came a child's voice, and she saw it belonged to one of Jinho's younger sisters.

"I lived!" she croaked from the ground. "Go tell my family. And get me some water. Doesn't anyone respect their elders around here?"

Sohmeng felt supremely cool in her childhood home as she recounted a rough (and maybe slightly embellished) version of Gãepongwei's victory over Qiao Sidh. She tried to tone down the scarier parts, not wanting to worry Tonão or Viunwei more than she needed to, but it was a lost cause, and she was glad that she was alive to deal with their fussing.

In exchange for her adventure, Sohmeng's family shared all of the updates they had about Ateng. The Sky Bridge had been repaired, obviously, and was staying completely open for a cycle so Chehangma could get a good look at their work. The Grand Ones had elected to skip one more round of Tengmunji, not wanting to leave anyone behind after this long tragedy. A memorial was being made for the batengmun who had died in Sodão Dangde. A family of enterprising yellowbills had made a home *inside* the cave, and everyone was trying to figure out what to do with them.

"The Grand Ones have been asking when we'd be interested in finding a damwei," Jinho said, ladling food into Viunwei's bowl. "But we told them we need more time."

"Yeah, you literally *just* got married," Sohmeng said. "They could afford to lay off. Especially considering the fact that our half-brother is still a toddler. Sorry but like . . . *Uncle Baby*? Weird. No thanks."

Tonão's laughter made Sohmeng's heart soar; he looked happy, healthy. His time in Ateng had been serving him well. "Give me just a while longer before I become a grandfather."

"Oh!" Sohmeng exclaimed. "You should know that you *are* gonna have grandlizards soon—the sãoni finally laid their eggs!"

"*Grandlizards?*" Viunwei repeated, judgmental as always.

"Viunwei, don't talk about your family like that," Sohmeng scolded. "What kind of community member are you?"

Once Sohmeng's belly was full and her family had endured all they could of her antics, she went down to Chehangma's Gate to tell the Grand Ones how the world had changed.

As she presented the concept of the experimental hmun, they took an unexpectedly active interest. It was a far cry from the days where she was shut down just for asking for a change of job. Back then, she'd thought they were being aggressive and belittling for no reason. She had taken it personally. But now, between Ateng and Nona Fahang, Sohmeng had become familiar with what it looked like when the people in charge were scared. She was curious to see how this council of Grand Ones would behave in more abundant times.

"And *all* of the hmun have the opportunity to send up new members?" Grandmother Nai asked.

"Anyone who wants to join can come," Sohmeng confirmed. "That includes Grand Ones—we're hoping to gather wisdom from all across Gãepongwei."

Reactions around the room gave Sohmeng an immediate

read on how everyone felt about that. While that old frog Grandfather Se wrinkled his nose, Grand One Chisong looked intrigued, and Grandmother Mi gave her a wink.

"Well, we ought to let people know, then," Grand One Chisong said. "Let's gather a list of potential participants for you to bring north."

They gave Sohmeng permission to share the news with Ateng during announcements the next morning. She described the project with enthusiasm, fielding questions as they came. A lot of her answers amounted to "we don't know yet!", but it didn't feel demoralizing. It was an opportunity to gather feedback, alongside a whole whack of good ideas.

It turned out that Ahn was right: there were more Atengpa than Sohmeng would have thought who were hankering for adventure. Her list of names grew long, then longer. And, wonderfully, several of them belonged to her own family members.

"Well I'm sure you all know my answer already," Grandmother Mi said exuberantly. Sohmeng had to keep her from packing up to try and ride up with her and Hei immediately. "I'm old but I'm not *that* old, and there's no Mi quite like me, so good luck to any of the other ladies in my path!"

"Take it easy, Mom," Tonão said, but he hadn't stopped grinning since he wrote his name down. The last time Sohmeng had seen him, he'd been quietly agonizing about how to balance the two families he cherished when they were so far apart. Now, it looked like there might be a way for him to be with both at once. "Do we know how long it'll be before they're ready?"

"No idea," Sohmeng said. "Hei and I will need a few phases to get back to the coast and see whether they're ready to receive people, and then we'll need to organize getting everyone up."

"It's a long journey," Jinho said. He was sitting by Viunwei, who hadn't spoken very much. "I think it sounds exciting, but is the travel practical? Some of the Grand Ones are frail."

"*I'm* not frail," Grandmother Mi insisted. She gave Tonão a gentle whack on the thigh. "And he can grow this back. He just needs to eat his vegetables."

Tonão took her hand, giving it a kiss. "Thank you, Mother."

Sohmeng laughed as she watched them. "We can get a cart or something! We'll need to get everyone's things up anyway. If our ancestors could make a big journey after the end of the world, we can definitely do it now."

After years of feeling like her home was too small to contain her, Sohmeng was amazed to be dreaming aloud with her family. Her father looked as young as he had when she was a child, and her grandmother was clearly ready to take the world by storm. She recognized the same wonder on Jinho's face that she had noticed when he looked out over the vibrant lushness of Eiji.

But one person was still quiet.

Viunwei had kept to himself during this discussion, his hand in Jinho's. It had been years since she and Viunwei had played rainforest together; was this idea something he even wanted to participate in? She knew he would come along if his whole family did, especially since Jinho seemed interested too, but she didn't want it to feel like he was being forced.

"What about you, Viunwei?" she asked carefully. "What do you want?"

Everyone waited for his answer. After a long moment to think, Viunwei took a deep breath, wiped his eyes, and spoke his mind: "It sounds like something Mom would like."

With Lahni Par's spirit invoked, everyone knew the choice had been made. The new hmun would have a place for Sohmeng's family; she would get to see her past and her present weave together into a new and spectacular future. The very best of Ateng would be right beside her.

It made another sort of victory possible. One Sohmeng had been pondering on and off since entering the caves at the base of the mountain. It was inherently risky, but now that her entire family was set on coming north with her, it became possible. She just had to clear it with them first.

She brought it up quietly, this final and necessary conversation. It was carried out in the very room she'd been born in. Then, bolstered by their response, Sohmeng went one last time to Chehangma's Gate.

This time, she faced the Grand Ones alone. She looked around this circle of elders, with their moon-tattooed cheeks and their cups of mountain marrow, their designated spots beneath the skylight. Their feet were covered with blankets, their backs cushioned by thick moss. They were the most important people in the hmun. They had been kids once, just like her.

Twenty-four people, twenty-five seats.

Par, Go, Hiwei, Fua, Tang, Sol, Jão, Pel, Dongi, Se, Won, Nor, Chisong, Heng, Li, Ginhãe, Mi, Ker, Hiun, Ãofe, Soon, Nai, Tos, Jeji—

"I'm a lucky person, you know?" said Sohmeng Minhal. "I've always been lucky. I was born to the best parents I could ask for, with a damwei who loved me, and a brother who protected me, and a grandmother who showed me that I belonged. I'm funny, and I'm smart, and honestly, even my bad ideas are a whole lot better than most peoples' good ones. I'm *lucky*, Grand Ones. So you're probably going to be pretty confused when I tell you that my name is Sohmeng Minhal."

The shocked silence told her that she was right. It stretched long enough that Sohmeng could hear water dripping in the cave, and she let it sit until Grandmother Par found it in herself to say what was on everyone's mind: "…What?"

"I'm so glad you asked, Grandmother Par." Despite years of nightmares about being discovered, she found she was finally ready to say her piece. "I was born under two dark moons, only three hours before Ama got her eye on me. My family and I hid it from you for sixteen years, and you can be as mad as you want, but it won't make it any less true."

"Mi," Grandfather Heng asked, his eyes darting between the two of them, "would you like to explain what your granddaughter is talking about?"

"Is there something you're not understanding?" was Grandmother Mi's answer. Her hands were crossed calmly in her lap; Sohmeng wondered if this felt like a burden being lifted for her, too. "It's a barbaric tradition, and I'm not sorry I defied it. If you'd like to exile me and my family, we've all agreed to accept it."

"You can't just defy traditions because you don't like them," Grandfather Se snapped.

"Well she *did*," Sohmeng snapped back. Her voice was stern to her own ears. "We all did, and that's why I got to be alive in this time where you all needed me. I'm a child of Minhal, *and* I fixed the Sky Bridge. I faced off with the Qiao Sidhur Empire. I saved Ateng." She looked boldly around the room, daring anyone to contradict her. "I did that, and I did it with the help of people who aren't afraid of who and *what* I am."

Sohmeng did see fear in some of the Grand Ones' faces, but she saw other things too. Awe at this fresh display of audacity. Admiration, even.

"This is absurd," said Grandfather Se. "Where do you—"

"Let them finish, Se," said Grand One Chisong, and that's when Sohmeng knew her decision had been the right one. She met the eyes of her polarity, the speaker for illumination as she was speaker for the unrevealed. Without one, Sohmeng realized, the other had no meaning. They completed each others' story.

"In our new hmun, there *will* be others like me," Sohmeng said ardently, feeling deep solidarity with the phase-mates she hadn't yet met. "Other Minhals. And I can see in your faces that it scares a whole bunch of you, that you actually think the world will come crashing down about it. But most other hmun don't do this. This is *your problem*, not the gods', and on behalf of every Minhal child that Ateng has ever left to die, I'm telling you to find somewhere else to put that self-righteousness, because this is shameful and embarrassing and cruel." Sohmeng was shaking. Not with fear, but with triumph. This time, no one interrupted her. "If anyone from Ateng is choosing to join our new hmun, they're going to need to get real comfortable with Minhal. This whole thing is a dark sky of an idea—there isn't room to be scared of the unknown. And if you can't handle that, well . . . that's really unlucky for you."

Her gaze moved across the room, letting each of them get a good long look at the person she had become. At long last, she faced that empty Minhal chair, and she bowed low.

"Their watchful eye upon you. Thank you for everything."

When Sohmeng met Hei at the foot of the mountain, she threw her arms around them. For a long time, she didn't say a word, and Hei met her kindly in that silence. Time seemed to stretch as the paths of their lives aligned. Hei, exposed and rejected; Sohmeng, hidden and alone. Each a different aspect of injustice, holding a unique kind of grief.

Sohmeng took Hei's hands in her own, feeling the human lines, the human callouses. Their hands had probably never had a chance to be soft, climbing and scrambling over the rough caves through their entire childhood. For the sake of the kid that Hei had been, she told them about what had happened in Ateng. What she had done. They listened, and they held her. They held it all.

"Were you afraid?" Hei asked softly.

"No," Sohmeng said, laughing shakily. "I wasn't. Or, or maybe the fear had just changed. Maybe I was more afraid of being hidden forever than being exiled. I was tired of exiling *myself.*"

She imagined another realm, like what Qiao Sidh had. A place where the generations of hãokar Minhals were thriving and growing instead. Hundreds of children, told they were unlucky and left to die—she imagined a world where they were safe, protected, happy. She hoped, with all the ferocity of the bright morning sun, that that world could become this one.

The light sieved through the canopy in soft rays, giving a dreamy quality to the air around them. Nearby, the sãoni were mellow, content with their place in the family of things. When Hei wiped Sohmeng's eyes, she realized she was crying. Hei was too, and they pressed their forehead into hers, breathing together.

"They don't deserve us," Sohmeng said, her voice wavering, "but I hope they come around. I hope they give us a chance. The more Minhals they meet, that they have to acknowledge, the harder it'll be to say we're all bad. If the gods didn't want us here, we wouldn't be. They have to see that."

Hei sighed, but their voice was warm. "You're always trying to fix the world, Sohmeng Parminhal."

"I am," Sohmeng insisted. "That's the only way it happens. If people *try*."

The two of them held each other close: alive against the odds, family to the creatures who were supposed to have eaten them, auspicious despite everyone who said otherwise. Resilient, committed to watching over one another whether the sky was dark or shining bright. Perfect as the day they were born.

"It's a good world," Hei said, nudging her nose with theirs. They looked at Sohmeng with the kind of affection that slipped through all her feist and made her shy. "I'd like to show you more of it."

"I'd like to see it." Sohmeng filled her lungs with fresh breath. She felt lighter than she had in a very long time. "So, where's our next stop?"

"Have you forgotten? Last time we were here, I promised you a waterfall."

Sohmeng perked up as the memory came to her. Far below Sodão Dangde, she had seen it: the rush of rippling mist, powerful and enticing, a new piece of rainforest for her to fall in love with. Her adventure in Eiji had really only just begun. There was so much to look forward to.

How could she express how grateful she was for all that Hei had brought into her life? Talkative though she was, Sohmeng knew that words would never be enough—and so she nuzzled into their neck and showed it with her teeth.

"You bit me!" Hei said with a laugh.

"Uh-huh." Sohmeng grinned. "And I'd do it *again.*"

Nearby, a sãoni chirped inquisitively; they would be ready to get back on the road soon. Hei stood, offering a hand to help Sohmeng up. Their eyes were bright. "Me too."

Twenty-Four

IN THE TIME THAT HEI and Sohmeng had been traveling, the coastal hmun had sprouted from seed to sapling. The bones of soon-to-be homes had been constructed with all the efficiency of an ant colony, and no one showed any sign of slowing their happy work. Hei understood their satisfaction; they had become quite proud of building their own rain shelters these past few phases. It was nice to create things.

When word spread that the sãoni colony had arrived, Ahnschen had come running through the hmun to greet them. Hei saw that his skin was tanned a deep bronze, his hair pulled messily back from his face; he was dressed in clothing that looked like it came from Sorwei Chapal.

"You're back!" he exclaimed, pulling Hei and Sohmeng into a tight hug. He was out of breath from running, sweaty from whatever labour they had interrupted. "You're, you're just in time. We've *just* finished putting up the trellises, you have to come see!"

Hei didn't think they had ever seen Ahnschen so

enthusiastic. Just as Hei's time on the migration route had made their world feel more sense-making, it looked like Ahn's time here had been good to him, too.

"Ahn, if you've finished everything without me, I'm going to *freak* out." Sohmeng tried to give him a playful pout, but she couldn't hide her eagerness to start exploring.

"Trust me," Ahnschen said gleefully, "we aren't even close."

The sãoni he had named Sølshend lumbered over to him, headbutting him in the side. He stroked her head, cooing to her in Qiao Sidhur.

Hei had wondered if the colony's old wariness of humans would return during their time back on the route, but it hadn't. They prowled around nearby, flicking their tongues and bumping their noses against everything that caught their interest. Hei saw a few humans looking nervous, but their fears were soothed by several Sorchapa that Hei recognized.

Hei rested a hand on Green Bites' back. He rumbled, and Hei replied with a few low clicks.

"Where do you think's a good spot for the colony?" Sohmeng asked Hei. "I know they're a little overdue for a rest, so they shouldn't wander too far, right?"

"They will stay near me," Hei answered. "I'll make sure they don't break anything very important. But we should hang silvertongue around the foodstores."

"Can I give you both a tour?" Ahnschen looked between them. "I know you've only just arrived, so please don't let me rush you, but whenever you're ready . . ."

Hei wanted a moment to settle, but they weren't sure that Sohmeng was physically capable of waiting. They waved their hand at the two of them. "You both go. I can see after."

"Thankyouthankyouthankyou!" Sohmeng gave Hei a big kiss on the cheek, and then tore off with Ahnschen, both of them talking happily over each other as he showed her the home he'd been making with his new community.

For their part, Hei sat down on a large, flat boulder and took some time to get their bearings. They had been preparing for this moment over the past few days, when they would be immersed again in the human world. It had made their throat tight—after all, their most recent experience had been the weeks trapped in Ólawen's prison—so they tried to soothe themself by recalling how things had felt in Sorwei Chapal. But this was already different from the river hmun. For one, there weren't nearly as many people. This hmun was young, still making its way out of the egg.

Hei had always liked watching hatchlings scratch their way into the world, chipping off one piece of shell at a time. They had a similar feeling as their eyes followed the glide of a handsaw through logs, the skilled precision of a mason's hammer strike, the long arcing movement of a painter's brush across a facade. The sounds of Dulpongpa and Qiao Sidhur buzzed like a pair of dragonflies around their ears. The energy was animated and contagious—but nobody bothered them. They suspected they had Ahnschen to thank for that. The inhabitants of the new hmun paid Hei little mind, and perhaps those people might have found it strange, but that space was exactly what Hei needed to let their curiosity grow.

The next day, they went to the sea and washed off their makeup, trying their best not to let the salt sting their eyes. As they applied a fresh coat, a young sãoni came over to investigate. Hei dabbed some of the charcoal paste on its nose, and its eyes crossed trying to get a look at what they had done. This made Hei laugh. They decided if they were relaxed enough to laugh, then they were ready for Ahnschen's tour.

Predictably, he was a magnanimous guide. Hei didn't have many questions yet, but when they stopped to take a closer look at something, like a Qiao Sidhur-style oven or the moon carvings on the Grand Ones' gazebo, he didn't rush them. In fact, they had to hiss once or twice to keep him from hovering. He obeyed the order cheerfully.

Hei stayed close to him as they wandered through the hmun. Ahnschen felt like a safe barrier between them and the other people, even though everyone seemed to have something to say to him as they passed by. Instead of dragging Hei into conversation, he politely told each one that he would get back to them later. Hei appreciated this; it made it easier to focus on the seemingly endless flow of his words.

"I think our next most important project is mapping out safe trails between the different hmun," Ahnschen was saying. "This experiment won't get far in isolation. There's little point asking people to join us if they can't make the trip."

"You will find a way," Hei said, taking a closer look at the gardens that were being built. Insect-repelling herbs had been clustered wisely around the borders. Hei pinched a leaf gently between their fingers, borrowing some of the bright-smelling oil for themself.

"I would love your opinion, if you'd offer it," Ahnschen said, resting his hand on their arm. Hei glanced at it, but didn't move away. "Of course, there's no pressure. You've already done so much for us already—*oh no*."

Hei saw it at the same time as Ahnschen: a sãoni, wandering around with its nose stuck in a basket. A basket that had, presumably, once had some sort of food in it.

Hei sighed heavily, clicking in displeasure. "Silvertongue, Ahnschen."

"I thought we used enough," he said weakly.

"You did *not* use enough."

And that was how Hei ended up helping sãoni-proof the new hmun. They pointed out the best posts to weave silvertongue around, but they also knew that the leaves would dry out sooner rather than later. It was impractical to reapply fresh ones every day, and so Hei decided instead to seek out the plant, dig it up from the roots, and rehome it around the food stores and kitchens. Ideally, that would keep the sãoni from digging around peoples' houses in search of snacks.

This was a job that required multiple hands—and Hei didn't really want to be stinking of silvertongue anyway—so, with Sohmeng's help, they guided a small group of people to seek out the plant. Again, the hmun-builders respected Hei's desire for personal space. But there was one quirk that all of them, Gãepongweipa and Qiao Sidhur alike, seemed to share: they could not escape the instinct to greet one another.

Whether it was a warm smile, a nod, or a quick wave, it was rare that Hei walked by anyone without at least a brief acknowledgment. It was a part of humanity that Hei had never seen before. Even if no one spoke to them directly, it was impossible for Hei to hide in the shadows how they were used to. Bizarrely, it reminded them of the sãoni, who compulsively chirped when they were near one another.

Hei would be returning to the migration route in a couple of phases, and gone for a long time as they looped around the rainforest. By the time they returned to this hmun, it would be full of many new faces. They were thankful to be dealing with this gentle attention when there were still less than a hundred people present. It made it easier for them to practice nodding back now and then, their eyes on the ground.

It was new, and a little uncomfortable. But they must have been doing something right, because one day Sohmeng came to Hei with an unexpected request.

"So, please don't feel like you have to say yes—"

"I don't."

"Healthy boundaries as always, love that about you." Sohmeng pinched their ear; Hei swatted her hand away with a click. "But as I was *trying* to say, there's someone who wants to know if you'd be willing to work on a project together."

Hei curled their sãoni claws, looking at her warily. "More silvertongue?"

"No, actually! I think we've got a whole farm going at this point. This is something a bit . . . bigger." She gestured toward one of the Grand Ones' gazebos, where someone was peering up at the beginnings of a wasp nest. Hei had wondered what they were going to do about that. "That's Sahi Ker. She's from Kongkempei, and she's been studying the rainforest for *ages*, and her whole thing is river ecosystems. Honestly, I feel bad that she wasn't born with gills. Seems unfair."

"Gills would be convenient for everyone," Hei agreed. "What does this have to do with me?"

"Well, we got talking and hit it off, and I told her about what you were saying about the thing with the catfish and the mussels. Sahi was wondering if you'd update her on how that's looking after your next journey down the route. And just like, if there's anything interesting going on with the Ãotul in general?" Sohmeng smiled sheepishly, blowing her bangs out of her face. "Look, if you say yes, I can get you some more specific questions. You wouldn't have to talk to her or anything—we can just pass messages through me, and I'll try not to mess them up too badly."

Hei considered this as they watched Sahi Ker, who had waved over someone else to get a look at the nest. Hei recognized him as the Qiao Sidhur artist who had drawn the sãoni in Kongkempei. His sketchbook was tucked under his arm even now, and he took it out when he saw the nest.

Sohmeng noticed Hei's interest. "Oh, that's Lannol Tang—he came here as Midhril Lannol Sølshendtsou, but he's trying on Lannol Tang Sølshendtsou. He's sweet. Him and Sahi are actually trying to make a book together about the local wildlife. It's going to have sketches and everything, which sounds like a pretty smart way to teach people about local plants no matter which language they're better with." Sohmeng nudged Hei slyly. "Help them avoid your saka fruit sabotage."

Hei squawked at Sohmeng, feeling their face warm. They had a feeling she would never be letting that go, even though they and Ahnschen were long past it.

"Anyway," Sohmeng asked, "how does that sound? It's obviously fine if you want time to think about it."

Strangely, Hei found they didn't need it. Their answer came up to meet them like the flash of a fin in clear water. "Tell her I say yes."

Sohmeng blinked. "Really?"

"I say yes," Hei repeated. "You can bring me her questions about the Ãotul."

As the next couple of days passed, Hei found that they were looking forward to this project. Before now, they hadn't known anyone else who paid attention to the fish—besides the sãoni, who were only interested in eating them.

Sohmeng brought Hei a list of Sahi's questions, which Hei regularly ran through their mind so they wouldn't forget any of them. But the more they thought about the questions, they realized that they had questions of their own. Was that allowed, they wondered, to pass questions back to Sahi Ker?

From a distance, they observed her, trying to figure out what kind of a person she was. She was tall and slim, and even though Sohmeng said she was most interested in river ecosystems, she seemed to pause and investigate anything that caught her eye. Lichen, sand, birds' nests—once she was so focused on a rock in her palm that she forgot she had lunch on the fire. The meal ended up horribly burned, but she took other peoples' teasing in stride as she nibbled on a scorched piece of meat.

Sahi Ker spent lots of time with Lannol Tang, and was quick to whistle him over if she found something she wanted drawn, and just as quick to give him a boost if it was too high to get a look at from the ground. Hei was alarmed the first time Lannol leapt down from a tree, but he landed gracefully, and Sahi applauded like he was putting on a special show just for her.

Hei realized quickly that neither of them were very fluent in the others' language, but they compensated with a wide array of gestures. And with patience, too.

Maybe that meant Sahi would be patient with their questions. Maybe she would even like some of them. But there was no way to know unless they asked. And so they practiced asking, wanting the words to be just right before they were given to Sohmeng to pass along.

"How much rainfall is normal for the wet season?" Hei murmured as they brought some food scraps over to the sãoni. "Can you tell when there is going to be a flood? Why do crabs turn a different colour when you boil them?"

Green Bites huffed at Hei by way of an answer. Hei huffed back, and went for a walk by themself. They wandered deep into the rainforest, where the canopy gave them greater privacy. They weaved between trees, brushing their fingers through ferns.

"Why is the silt so dark in the southern part of the Ãotul? How can I tell where water snakes make their nests? Do you have a favourite fish?"

Hei walked Eiji like a maze, finding a new curiosity in every footfall. By the time they were returning back to the hmun, they knew that this was far too much to ask all at once, but the practice had helped settle their nerves.

And it gave them the courage not to hide when they stumbled across Sahi Ker and Lannol Tang sitting with their backs against a giant, ancient tree.

Sahi had a large beetle on the back of her hand, which Lannol was rapidly sketching. Hei knew that species of beetle had wings, and so they stayed very still, not wanting to scare it off. Lannol caught Hei's eye briefly, offering a grateful smile before continuing to draw.

Do you know this tree is hundreds of years old? Have you seen the mushrooms that are growing on the other side? Did the beetle land on you or did you catch it?

With a rattling sound, the beetle spread its wings and flew away. The two friends slumped against the tree trunk with twin sighs of relief; presumably, they had gotten what they needed. It was only then that Sahi Ker noticed Hei was there, and she straightened right up, her eyes bright and hopeful.

Hei had spent days wondering which question they should tell Sohmeng to share first, and hadn't settled on a satisfactory answer. But now that they were face-to-face with Sahi, they knew exactly what they wanted to say. They just needed to be brave enough to say it. To give themself, and others, a chance.

"Hello," Hei said, their voice hardly shaking at all. "My name is Hei. Would you like to be my friend?"

Epilogue

SOHMENG HAD ALWAYS LOVED to sleep in, but on the morning of her seventeenth birthday, she woke with the sun. Far south, in a mountain range shaped like a hand reaching for the gods, the people of Ateng were preparing for the crossing. But in coastal Minhdão, Sohmeng would be welcoming the new year with both feet on the ground.

"Minhdão," she said to herself, covering her face as she smiled. "This is Minhdão. Welcome to Minhdão, it's really good to have you here."

Minhdão: *Family born of Minhal.*

The name had been chosen during the last Chisong phase, and Sohmeng had been repeating it to herself ever since, scarcely able to believe it. What she had once needed to hide for the sake of survival was now being celebrated by people from all across Gãepongwei. Together they were embracing the darkness of Minhal—not as the dark of the void, but the dark of rich soil, ready to grow something spectacular.

Especially today. It was the pivot point of First Parminhal, the transformative moment where, mid-phase, the red moon Ama gave her first mischievous wink. The perfect time to mark the hmun's official inauguration.

A yellow gecko scuttled along Sohmeng's doorway. In a bizarre burst of sympathetic energy, it prompted her out of bed, where she got dressed and proceeded to pace circles around her room. It would probably be nicer to go for a walk on the beach, but she wasn't ready to see people just yet.

Viunwei must have sensed this wish for privacy because, busybody that he was, it didn't take long for him to knock on her door. She almost regretted letting him stay over the night before, but he had asked to be the one to celebrate her birthday before anyone else, which was sweet, so she'd let him hang out. She'd also kicked his butt at two games of dice, which helped.

"Sohmeng? Are you up yet?" he asked through the door.

"You know I am."

"Well, can I come in?"

Sohmeng rolled her eyes and swung the door open. "What is it?"

"I was wondering if you wanted…?" Viunwei was holding a comb and a few pins in his hand. He held them up to her by way of an offering. Sohmeng's brother hadn't helped with her hair since she was maybe ten years old. Standing on the precipice of this next stage of adulthood, she decided to take him up on it. Why not take one more moment to be young?

Following tradition, he still tugged her hair when he combed, and she still whined about it the whole time.

She tried not to squirm too much as he pinned an ornament into her hair. It was a birthday gift from Ahn, carved from pearlescent shell, and she was absolutely in love with it.

When it was done, Viunwei pressed on her shoulders, like he could anchor her to the ground. "Are you ready, Soh?" he asked.

"I'm terrified," Sohmeng admitted. "But also, I don't think I'd really want to do anything else."

"That sounds about right."

"What's *that* supposed to mean?"

"Exactly what it sounds like! Do you really want to pick a fight right now?"

Viunwei's aggrieved sigh made her burst into laughter, but she couldn't stop herself from throwing her arms around him. Despite neither of them being big huggers, Viunwei caught her and held her tight. By the time she walked out the door, she felt more ready than she had when she woke up, the love of her family warm like a mantle around her.

Minhdão stretched before her in a splash of magnificent colour. Many of the recently-built homes—Sohmeng's included—were brightly painted in the Qiao Sidhur style, and others were lined with rows of silvertongue and flowers. Here and there, on a fencepost or a lintel or perched beside a door, sunshower birds roosted, a reminder of everyone's promise to be good to one another. They culminated in a swirling sculpture at the center of the hmun, where Hei's friend Lannol Tang often sat and doodled.

Sohmeng exchanged hellos with a group of early risers tending to the flourishing community gardens. In a nearby copse of trees, she saw a fishing vessel upturned on a boulder, halfway through construction. Just past that was the silvertongue-free space where the sãoni lounged whenever Hei paid a visit.

There was a shelter for Hei there too, which Sohmeng had been helping them decorate when they were last here. One stormy night, they had begrudgingly admitted that the sound of raindrops on the roof lulled them into the best sleep of their life. A few of the hatchlings had apparently agreed, and climbed in alongside them until the shelter was full to bursting with happily wiggling lizards. The memory made Sohmeng smile, even though it was bittersweet; she'd spent the last few days hoping for any sign of Hei, but they hadn't made it on time.

She told herself it was okay. The two of them had different priorities, and she couldn't expect—

A low growl came from behind her. Sohmeng whipped around, all prey instinct long trained out of her, and looked Green Bites right in his smug, many-toothed face.

"Green Bites!" she yelled, nearly headbutting the sãoni in her excitement. "You're here! What, *when*, when did you get here? Where's Hei—burning godseye, I'm talking to a lizard."

With a quick scratch behind the sãoni's head spines, Sohmeng's leisurely walk promptly picked up into a run. She weaved through Minhdão, calling for Hei and undoubtedly waking up everyone who had dared to sleep in. She found her father hanging laundry with little Kuei on his hip. He had one pant leg rolled up, proudly displaying the wooden leg that had been re-carved to depict Sohmeng's birth phase as Minhal.

"Dad, have you seen Hei?" Sohmeng demanded, grinning like a fool.

Tonão gave a dramatic shrug. "Who could say?"

Sohmeng groaned, planting a kiss on his cheek before taking off again. Some of her neighbours looked suspiciously nonchalant—Sohmeng wondered how many of them were in on this game. Polha Hiwei and Nepar Ãofe made a whole show of examining one of their pygmy hogs rather than point her in the right direction.

When Sohmeng finally came across Eakang with a tiny hatchling in their arms, they took pity on her, laughing. "The moonhouses, Sohmeng!"

"You're the only person I like in this whole hmun, Eakang, did you know that?"

And with that, she made her way to the last place she would have expected Hei to be: by the moonhouses, red and white, all prepared for their inaugural meeting. Instead of having twenty-four separate initiations, today the new Grand Ones would do a ceremony together—the first of its kind in recorded history.

Sure enough, there Hei was, smirking next to Ahnschen, who looked beyond pleased with himself.

Sohmeng grabbed Hei by the cheeks and pulled, prompting a shout out of them. "When did you get here? How did *everyone* know but me?"

Hei answered with a bite while Ahn took a more verbal approach: "Yesterday morning. They hid deeper in the rainforest with the colony so we could keep it a secret. Are you surprised?"

"Yeah, Ahn, I'd say I'm a little surprised!" Sohmeng exclaimed, and kissed him and Hei one after the other.

"I can't believe you. This is incredible."

"Well, it's a big day," Ahn said, and then she realized that he was holding a flower crown.

"Did you make those for everyone?" Sohmeng asked, arching one eyebrow. The gazebos were filling in as the incoming Grand Ones got themselves settled. The sound of Grandmother Mi's laugh was impossible to miss. "I can't go making everyone jealous on day one."

"They'll manage," Ahn said, carefully placing the crown on her head. "Let us celebrate you, Sohmeng. You deserve it."

Hei clicked in agreement, and barely stopped themself from rubbing cheeks and covering her with their makeup. It looked like it had been freshly reapplied that morning.

"I could get used to it," Sohmeng said, beaming bright. The wind blew through the hanging jade vines trailing from the gazebos, and she gave a little twirl, feeling her dress billow around her. "All this celebrating me and stuff."

"You will have to," said Hei matter-of-factly, "because we aren't going to stop."

Ahnschen pressed a kiss against her forehead. "No we're not, Grand One Parminhal."

At age seventeen, Sohmeng Parminhal had become the youngest Grand One in Gãepongwei.

When her name had come up in the list of proposed elders, she'd almost called the other Pars and Minhals out on their prank. She was glad she hadn't, because they'd been serious. Now, after a couple months to let it sink in, she felt both deeply humbled and oddly self-assured.

Terrified, like she'd told Viunwei, but also confident. It was the greatest honour her community could bestow on her, the greatest thanks they could give her for what she had done for them all.

"Say that again?" Sohmeng asked, feeling her neck go warm.

"Grand One Parminhal," Ahnschen repeated, his Dulpongpa elegant as a thrumming jeibu. She tugged fondly at his earpiece in response. Beside them, Hei opened a pot of their makeup, and Sohmeng realized that they would be the one to paint the Minhal phase on her cheeks.

For all the energy buzzing inside her, Sohmeng stayed perfectly still to receive this blessing. A cloud rolled over the sun, bathing them both in shade. She closed her eyes, feeling the rough catch of Hei's practiced fingertips, the tenderness they laid in pigment on her skin.

"Go," Hei said, close to her ear, when they were done. "Make and solve your problems."

The sun broke free, and Sohmeng felt the return of the warmth reach right down to her bones, seeping through the hollow spaces where her shame used to hide. She could feel herself growing, right alongside Gãepongwei. It didn't scare her. She had chosen this life for herself. The moons had shaped her for potential, and her parents had named her for transformation.

Who was Sohmeng becoming today? She didn't know. But as she stepped across the threshold of the moonhouse, she couldn't wait to meet her.

Acknowledgements

To everyone who has listened to me cry, complain, and scream over the past few years: it's done! The book is done! The time has come for gratitude and celebration!

If you have one of the original copies of *Three Seeking Stars*, you might notice that this book was originally due to come out in 2023. Thank you, dear readers, for your patience as these two extra years transformed me into the person I needed to be to finish this story. I spent a lot of time working through the grief that accumulated since I first began writing the Sãoni Cycle in 2018. I wondered (loudly and often) how I could finish a hopeful story when I felt so hopeless—but that's the nature of the hopepunk genre, isn't it? To choose hope precisely when it's hardest to do.

So: thank you Soh, Hei, and Ahnschen. Every draft, every edit, and every big cry guided me back to the radical need to resist despair. I'm ready for this chapter to close, and I am so grateful to have had this time with you.

On Earth, there are many people, creatures, and places that held my hand through this work:

Sonia Urlando, who has been a kind and steadfast friend; Brandon Crilly, who championed this series from the start; Claudie Arseneault, who is an advocate for queer, kind, indie books—and aromantic representation in particular! Maya Baumann, who hosted me on Manitoulin Island where I could breathe clean air and find my way towards the sunshower birds. Haley Rose once again created a stunning, stunning cover for this series. Terese Mason Pierre and Amy Wang sat patiently through many tearful phone calls. My therapist, Ruby, should get royalties for the work they did helping me ground through these very intense years.

My dad has held Shale's chubby little fingers as it's grown from infancy into childhood. My mom has made me laugh as she asked for spoilers, only to quickly follow up with "no, no, wait, don't tell me, I want to read it!" I am so lucky to have parents who have supported my artistic career, regularly checking in, encouraging me, and occasionally talking me off the ledge. The same goes for all of my siblings (how are you all so good when there are *so many* of you?), but I have special shoutouts for Ryan, who has logged the most hours listening to me complain, and Emma, who has all the bright Minhal compassion of Eakang. Thank you for the second chance to be close even though I was mean to you when we were kids.

My cousins (there are also a million of you so I'm shouting out the superstars here and you're going to have to work with that): Cass is the artistically superior Meehan to me, despite my insistence otherwise in the year 2002. Sara was my very first reader of the completed manuscript, and is a delight in every way. Corrie made me weep when I learned they were reading *Two Dark Moons* aloud to friends. Becca made me *Sãoni Cycle*-themed vivarium decorations for Christmas; you are correct that the mountains *did* look kind of like turds, but what beautiful and heartfelt turds they were!

Thank you to all of the Grand Ones who urged me to keep reading, and keep writing. My Grammy sang the praises of the first two books in this series; I wish very much that I could have put the final book in her hands. And Grandma Ronnie, your spirit of adventure guides my own.

Two of my three bash'mates, Brendan and Carisa May. Carisa has supported Shale from day one, and is someone I would scream in the rain with any day of the week. Brendan's Curse of Strahd campaign has somehow brought families together since 2023, and reminded me why art matters to me at all. You're both my family. I love you so much.

It must also be noted that the final scenes of *One Morning Sun* were finished over the course of two weeks with the help of five cats: Meiko, Simon, Raz, Honey, and Bunny (who screamed at me the entire time). The ghost of Jevick, our diabolical little bearded dragon, haunts these pages with Green Bites levels of cheerful menace.

The places and spaces that gave *One Morning Sun* shape: in Hamilton, The Cannon, Coffee Culture, and William's; in St. Thomas, Zesty, Streamliners, the STPL, and the Atrium, owned by the wonderfully supportive Elle Crevits. The final words of this book were written in the Atrium, in the encouraging shadow of the plant wall. The Can*Con team and community, as well as Bakka-Phoenix Books, have been host to the people and events that make "author stuff" so much fun.

Kevin Penkin composed the soundtracks that carried me through the entirety of the writing process. Certain songs will always sound like Eiji to me. Thank you.

To my sweetest shadow, you know exactly who you are. Have I given you the story you asked for? I hope so. You deserve all that and more. Really truly really truly really truly.

And Sienna—we did it. *We did it.* This book would not be finished (literally, in the case of several passages) without your keen eye, deft hand, and dear heart. Thank you for the tussling, biting, and companionable silences. Thank you for typesetting. Thank you for your grace. Thank you for falling back in love with this story with me. I cannot wait for what comes next.

Finally, thank you to everyone who has read, reviewed, and shared these books! Thank you for staying with me through this long journey. Stay weird. Take courage. Together, we can make a kinder world.

With love and a bite *(and another for the road!)*,
Avi Silver
June 2025
St. Thomas

Glossary

GÃEPONGWEI

Ama—the small red moon, feminine; ruler of reason and material matters

Ateng—a southern hmun situated high in a mountain range; the birthplace of Sohmeng and Hei

batengmun—initiates; singular form is "tengmun"

Chehang—the big white moon, masculine; ruler of emotion and spiritual matters

Chehangma—the sun, conceptualized as the combined eyes of the moons Ama and Chehang

damwei—the third party required to make a baby, either a surrogate or sperm donor; affectionately referred to as "damdão"

Dulpongpa—the language used by traders in Gãepongwei to communicate between hmun

Fochão Dangde—the mountain Ateng has recently departed from; "Brother Mountain"

Gãepongwei—a name for the interconnected hmun network; recently coined

hãokar—the exiled; literally "without family"

hmun—term for a village/community in Gãepongwei

Hosaisi—a northern hmun, the first to have made contact with Qiao Sidh in their initial campaign; under Qiao Sidhur occupation

kejangar—Dulpongpa for "hospitality"; an important organizing principle for the hmun

jeibu—a lap harp with twenty five strings, played in certain hmun

Kongkempei—a northern hmun, under Qiao Sidhur occupation

Nona Fahang—a central hmun surrounded by walls formed of living banyan trees

-pa—denotes a language or the people who speak it, e.g. Sorchapa (Sorwei Chapal), Kempeipa (Kongkempei), etc.

Sodão Dangde—the mountain Ateng's people have recently returned to; "Sister Mountain"

Sorwei Chapal—a large, central hmun spanning a tributary of the Ãotul river; used to be two separate hmun, long ago

Tengmunji—initiation into adulthood

tsongkar—a Fahangpa word for intruder, invader; "one who did not ask"

QIAO SIDH

Asgørindad—the university where Ahnschen studied Philosophy

elønd—the word for "beloved", used in formal titles to denote children of the royal line

Gurinn—the last region of the upper continent to fall to the Qiao Sidhur Empire

Haojost—the small town Schenn grew up in before attending Kørno Wan

Hvallánzhou—one of Qiao Sidh's capitals, where the Winter Palace resides

Kørno Wan—the academy where young and privileged Qiao Sidhur train in the Path of Conquest

madøng—large flightless birds, used by the Qiao Sidhur as mounts and beasts of burden

saro dhral—"bringers of culture", the non-military recruits that accompany Qiao Sidhur generals on their expansion campaigns

Qøngzhir Asten—the "Six-ing", a necessary requirement to achieve sixth ranking in the Path of Conquest; a fight to the death

zhørmozhør—asexual; rarely used outside of a lecture hall (but used more often now, according to Noula)

THE NINE PATHS OF MASTERY

Alléndou—Fertility

Hvundpar—Health

Idhren—Discernment

Ødselo—Spirit

Siengung—Philosophy

Søngjudh—Aesthetic

Sølshend—Arts

Qøngem—Conquest

Zhøllong—Advancement

HOW TO COUNT TO ELEVEN
(IN QIAO SIDHUR)

one—sammi

two—hvøs

three—asá

four—tsou

five—qang

six—zhir

seven—ding

eight—tot

nine—tøn

ten—hol

eleven—dham

PATREON | THE SHALE PROJECT

A massive thank you to everybody who supported us on Patreon!
You made this work possible; we love you to the moons and back.

Charlotte Ashley

Nick Calow

Carisa Catherine

Spenser Chicoine

Emily Colgan

Laurence Dion

Maria Dominguez

Stephanie Elnomany

Cheryl Hamilton

Minh

Natalie Lythe

Nicholas Mackenzie

Cass Meehan

Susan Meehan

Amy Raboin

David Senft

Joy Silvey

WWW.PATREON.COM/WELCOMETOSHALE

About the Author

Avi Silver is a speculative author, poet, editor, and co-founder of The Shale Project. Along with the *Sãoni Cycle*, they are author of the Aurora Award-nominated novella *Pluralities*. Their poetry has been published in *Strange Horizons* and *Uncanny Magazine*, and received an honourable mention in the Rhysling Awards. Find their short fiction in *Common Bonds: An Aromantic Speculative Anthology* and *Nothing Without Us Too*. Avi currently lives in St. Thomas with creative and life partner Sienna Tristen. Read on at www.mxavisilver.com

About the Project

The Shale Project is a multimedia storytelling initiative roughly in the shape of a planet. It's about three things: top-notch worldbuilding, daring and exploratory fiction, and the philosophy that art is medicine. You can discover what else it has to offer at www.welcometoshale.com

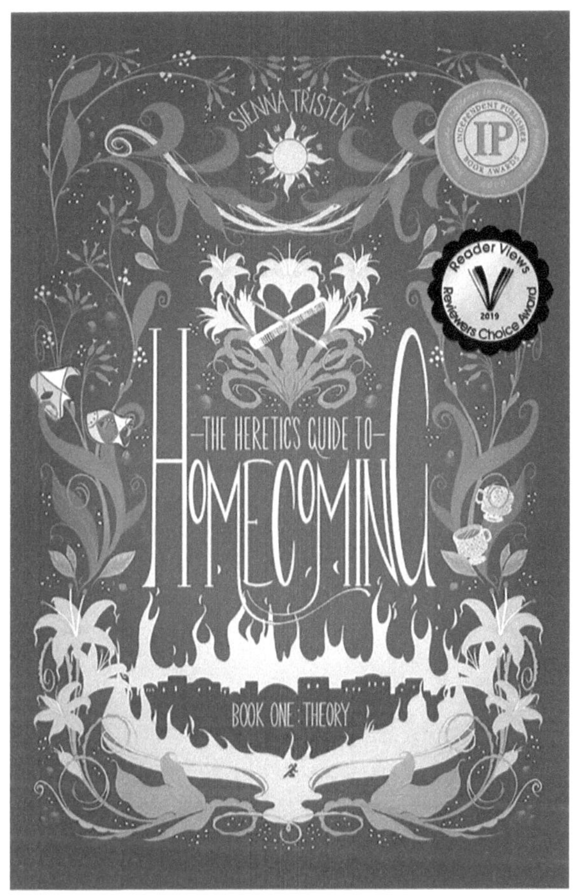

The Heretic's Guide to Homecoming
Book One: Theory

Sienna Tristen

"Compelling and complicated in all the right ways."
—Reader Views

". . . fans of detailed fantasy worldbuilding will revel in this voluminous story."
—Publisher's Weekly

MORE FROM THE WORLD OF SHALE

The Heretic's Guide to Homecoming
Book Two: Practice

Sienna Tristen

"Tristen wields language like they invented it, effortlessly imbuing the smallest of details with beauty and meaning that transforms them into something mythic."

—Every Book A Doorway

www.ingramcontent.com/pod-product-compliance
Lightning Source LLC
Chambersburg PA
CBHW031743180726
48283CB00005B/1640